Praise for *The Traitor Baru Cormorant*

"Baru Cormorant as a character is magnificent. I found it impossible not to root for her even amid horrors of her making, to grieve with her and for her at various points, to clench my fists in her defense and in desperate need for her to stay whole. There is so much to admire and so much to mourn throughout the building tragedy of this novel. . . . A crucial, necessary book—a book that looks unflinchingly into the self-replicating virus of empire, asks the hardest questions, and dares to answer them."

—NPR

"Assured and impressive. . . . Dickinson's world-building is ambitious and his language deviously subtle; both are seductive in their complexity. He combines social engineering, economic trickery, and coldhearted pseudoscientific theories to weave a compelling, utterly surprising narrative that keeps readers guessing until the end."

—*Publishers Weekly* (starred review)

"Smart. Brutal. Gut-wrenching . . . Highly recommended."

—Kameron Hurley, Hugo Award–winning author of *The Geek Feminist Revolution*

"A beautiful, perfectly formed crystal of a novel borne out of a tight plot mated with elegant language."

—John Chu, Hugo Award–winning author of "The Water That Falls on You from Nowhere"

"A brutal tale of empire, rebellion, fealty, and high finance that moves like a rocket and burns twice as hot. *The Traitor Baru Cormorant* is a mic drop for epic fantasy."

—Max Gladstone, author of the Craft Sequence

"Brutal, relentless, and with the heartbreaking beauty of the best tragedies . . . A haunting book that asks hard questions about revolution, change, and what it means to keep faith."

—Aliette de Bodard, Nebula Award–winning author of *The House of Shattered Wings*

THE TRAITOR
BARU CORMORANT

SETH DICKINSON

A TOM DOHERTY ASSOCIATES BOOK
NEW YORK

This is a work of fiction. All of the characters, organizations, and events portrayed in this novel are either products of the author's imagination or are used fictitiously.

THE TRAITOR BARU CORMORANT

Map by Jon Lansberg

A Tor Book
Published by Tom Doherty Associates
175 Fifth Avenue
New York, NY 10010

www.tor-forge.com

Tor® is a registered trademark of Macmillan Publishing Group, LLC.

The Library of Congress has cataloged the hardcover edition as follows:

Dickinson, Seth.
    The traitor Baru Cormorant / Seth Dickinson.—1st ed.
        p. cm.
    ISBN 978-0-7653-8072-2 (hardback)
    ISBN 978-1-4668-7512-8 (e-book)
1. Imaginary wars and battles—Fiction. I. Title.
    PS3604.I293 T84 2015
    813'.6—dc23

                                                                    2015019187

ISBN 978-0-7653-8073-9 (trade paperback)

Our books may be purchased in bulk for promotional, educational, or business use. Please contact your local bookseller or the Macmillan Corporate and Premium Sales Department at 1-800-221-7945, extension 5442, or by e-mail at MacmillanSpecialMarkets@macmillan.com.

First Edition: September 2015
First Trade Paperback Edition: November 2016

Printed in the United States of America

0 9 8 7 6 5 4 3 2 1

For Gillian

ACKNOWLEDGMENTS

Sine qua non: Rachel Sobel. Jennifer Jackson. Marco Palmieri.

Sophia and colleagues. Jackals, Blue Planet, my brother, and a loon.

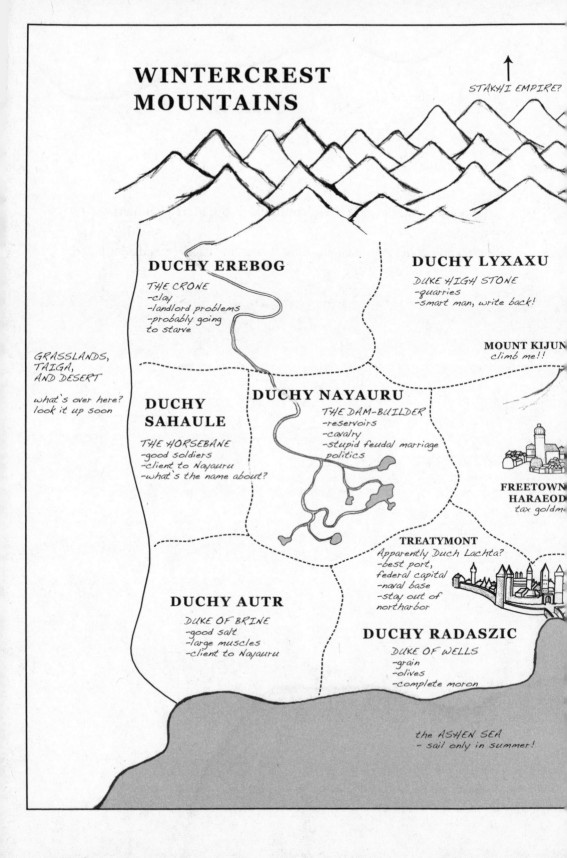

WINTERCREST MOUNTAINS

STAKHI EMPIRE?

DUCHY EREBOG

THE CRONE
-clay
-landlord problems
-probably going to starve

DUCHY LYXAXU

DUKE HIGH STONE
-quarries
-smart man, write back!

MOUNT KIJUN
climb me!!

GRASSLANDS, TAIGA, AND DESERT

what's over here? look it up soon

DUCHY SAHAULE

THE HORSEBANE
-good soldiers
-client to Nayauru
-what's the name about?

DUCHY NAYAURU

THE DAM-BUILDER
-reservoirs
-cavalry
-stupid feudal marriage politics

FREETOWN HARAEOD
tax goldme-

TREATYMONT
Apparently Duch Lachta?
-best port, federal capital
-naval base
-stay out of northarbor

DUCHY AUTR

DUKE OF BRINE
-good salt
-large muscles
-client to Nayauru

DUCHY RADASZIC

DUKE OF WELLS
-grain
-olives
-complete moron

the ASHEN SEA
- sail only in summer!

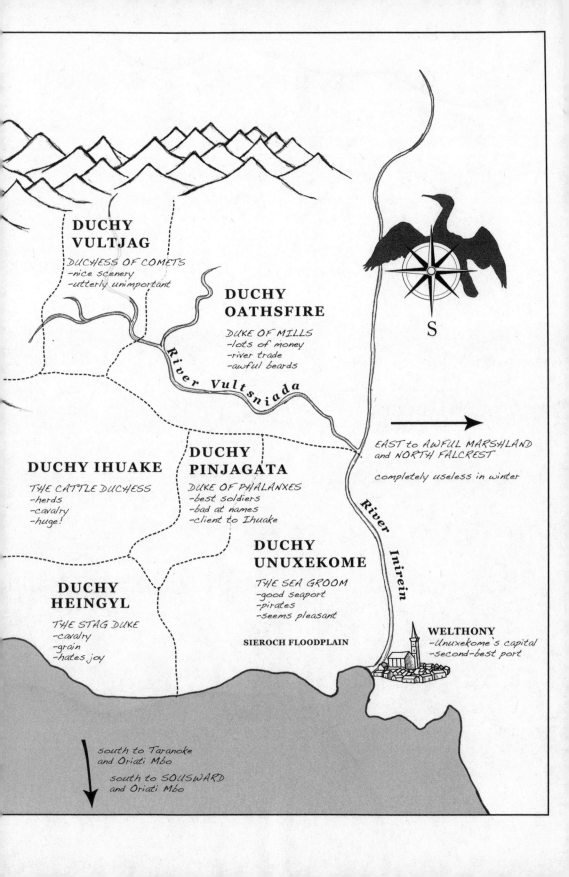

DUCHY VULTJAG

DUCHESS OF COMETS
- *nice scenery*
- *utterly unimportant*

DUCHY OATHSFIRE

DUKE OF MILLS
- *lots of money*
- *river trade*
- *awful beards*

River Vultsniada

DUCHY IHUAKE

THE CATTLE DUCHESS
- *herds*
- *cavalry*
- *huge!*

DUCHY PINJAGATA

DUKE OF PHALANXES
- *best soldiers*
- *bad at names*
- *client to Ihuake*

DUCHY UNUXEKOME

THE SEA GROOM
- *good seaport*
- *pirates*
- *seems pleasant*

DUCHY HEINGYL

THE STAG DUKE
- *cavalry*
- *grain*
- *hates joy*

*EAST to AWFUL MARSHLAND
and NORTH FALCREST*

completely useless in winter

River Inirein

SIEROCH FLOODPLAIN

WELTHONY
- *Unuxekome's capital*
- *second-best port*

S

*south to Taranoke
and Oriati Mbo*

*south to SOUSWARD
and Oriati Mbo*

Interesting economic approach (not about love triangles or dramas)

Morality hard to pin down.

Her character is cold & unemotional, but she lets her guard down occasionally (around women mostly)

What kind of traitor is she? To her people or govt?

suble ways to convince people another way of life is best.
Family structure; caring for children corporeally

Ideology?
Marxist, Confuscianist, French Rev.
Is this how conservatives are viewed by the left?

A PROMISE

This is the truth. You will know because it hurts.

ACCOUNTANT

T RADE season came around again. Baru was still too young to smell the empire wind.

The Masquerade sent its favorite soldiers to conquer Taranoke: sailcloth, dyes, glazed ceramic, sealskin and oils, paper currency printed in their Falcrest tongue. Little Baru, playing castles in the hot black sand, liked to watch their traders come in to harbor. She learned to count by tallying the ships and the seabirds that circled them.

Nearly two decades later, watching firebearer frigates heel in the aurora light, she would remember those sails on the horizon. But at age seven, the girl Baru Cormorant gave them no weight. She cared mostly for arithmetic and birds and her parents, who could show her the stars.

But it was her parents who taught her to be afraid.

In the red autumn evening before the stars rose, her fathers took Baru down to the beach to gather kelp for ash, the ash meant for glass, the glass for telescope lenses ground flat by volcanic stone, the lenses meant for the new trade. When they came to the beach, Baru saw Masquerade merchant ships on the horizon, making a wary circuit around Halae's Reef.

"Look, Das," Baru said. "They're coming in for the Iriad market."

"I see them." Father Salm shaded his eyes and watched the ships, peeling lips pressed thin. He had the shoulders of a mountain and they corded as he moved. "Go fill your bucket."

"Watch." Father Solit, keen-eyed, took his husband's hand and pointed. "There's a third ship. They're sailing in convoys now."

Baru pretended to dig for kelp and listened.

"Pirates make a good excuse for convoy," Salm said. "And the convoy makes a good excuse for escort." He spat into the surf. "Pinion was right. Poison in that treaty."

Watching their reflections, Baru saw Solit take Salm's shoulder, callused hand pressed against his husband's bare strength. Each man wore his hair braided, Solit's burnt short for the smithy, Salm's an elaborate waist-length fall—for glory in the killing circle, against the plainsmen.

"Can you see it, then?" Solit asked.

"No. It's out there, though. Over the horizon."

"What's out there, Da?" Baru asked.

"Fill your bucket, Baru," Salm rumbled.

Baru loved her mother and her fathers dearly, but she loved to know things just a small measure more, and she had recently discovered cunning. "Da," she said, speaking to Solit, who was more often agreeable, "will we go to Iriad market and see the ships tomorrow?"

"Fill your bucket, Baru," Solit said, and because he echoed Salm instead of indulging her, Baru knew he was worried. But after a moment, he added: "Grind your glass tonight, and we'll have enough to sell. You can come along to Iriad and see the ships."

She opened her mother's hand-copied dictionary that night, squinting at the narrow script in the candlelight, and counted through the letters of the Urunoki alphabet until she came to: *convoy—a caravan, or a group of ships, gathered for mutual protection, especially under the escort of a warship.*

A warship. Hm.

It's out there, father Salm had said.

From the courtyard of their ash-concrete home came the shriek of stone on glass and the low worried voices of her mother and fathers, a huntress and a blacksmith and a shield-bearer. Worrying about *the treaty* again.

She looked that word up too, hoping to understand it, as understanding gave her power over things. But she did not see how a treaty could be poison. Perhaps she would learn at the Iriad market.

Baru put her mother's dictionary back and then hesitated, fingers still on the chained stitches of the binding. Mother had a new book in her collection, bound in foreign leather. From the first page—printed in strange regular blocks, impersonal and crisp—she sounded out the title: *A Primer in Aphalone, the Imperial Trade Tongue; Made Available to the People of Taranoke For Their Ease.*

There was a copy number in the bottom corner, almost higher than she could count.

* * *

WHERE the sea curled up in the basalt arms of the Iriad cove, beneath the fields of sugarcane and macadamia and coffee that grew from the volcanic loam, the market preened like a golden youth.

Since a time before Baru could remember how to remember the market had filled the Iriad docks, the most noisy and joyous thing in the world. There were more ships in harbor this year—not just Taranoki fishers and felucca, not just familiar Oriati traders from the south, but tall white-sailed Masquerade merchant ships. With their coming the market had outgrown the boardwalks and drifted out onto bobbing floats of koa and walnut where drummers sounded in the warmth and the light.

Today Baru went to market with a new joy: the joy of plots. She would learn what troubled her parents, this knot of warships and treaties. She would repair it.

Her family went by canoe. Baru rode in the prow while mother Pinion and father Salm paddled and father Solit kept nervous watch over the telescopes. The wind off the sea lifted flocks of scaups and merganser ducks, gangs of bristle-throated alawa giving two-toned calls, egrets and petrels and frigate birds, and high above great black jaegers like wedges of night. She tried determinedly to count them and keep all the varieties straight.

"Baru Cormorant," mother Pinion said, smiling. In Baru's eyes she was a coil of storm surf, a thunderbolt, as slow and powerful as sunlight. Her dark eyes and the teeth in her smile were the shapes that Baru imagined when she read about panthers. She worked her paddle in strokes as smooth and certain as the waves. "It was a good name."

Baru, warm and loved and hungry to impress with accurate birdcount, hugged her mother's thigh.

They found a quay to unload the telescopes and the market swept up around them. Baru navigated the crowd of knees and ankles, trailing behind her parents because the commerce distracted her. Taranoke had always been a trading port, a safe island stop for Oriati dromons and islander canoes, so Baru grew up knowing a little of the structure of trade: arbitrage, currency exchange, import and export. *We sell sugarcane and honey and coffee and citrus fruits*, mother Pinion said, *and buy textiles, sailcloth, kinds of money that other traders want—Baru, pay attention!*

Lately she always paid attention. Something fragile had come into the air, a storm smell, and not understanding made her afraid.

The market smelled of cooked pineapple and fresh ginger, red iron salt and anise. Through the drums and the calls of the dancers and the shouts of the audience in Urunoki and Oriati and the new trade tongue Aphalone came the ring of hard coin and reef pearl changing hands.

"Sol-i-i-i-i-t," Baru called. "I want to see—!"

"I know." Solit spared a smile from his work. He had been a smith, and he was generous to everything he made, including Baru. "Go wander."

Excellent. Now she would pursue the true meaning of *treaty*.

She found a foreign trader's stall painted in Masquerade white. The man who watched over the piled broadcloth—woven from sheep, which she understood were large dull beasts made entirely of hair—could have passed for Taranoki from a distance, though up close the different fold of his eyelids and flat of his nose gave him away. This was the first impression Baru had of the Falcrest people: stubborn jaws, flat noses, deep folded eyes, their skin a paler shade of brown or copper or oat. At the time they hardly seemed so different.

The man looked bored, so Baru felt no qualms about climbing up onto his stall. He had guards, two women with shaved heads and sailors' breeches, but they were busy trying to bridge the language barrier with a young Taranoki fisherman.

"Hello, dear," the man in the stall said. He moved a stack of samples and made a space for her. Baru made curious note of his excellent Urunoki. He must be a very dedicated trader, or very good with tongues—and cultures, too, because traders did not often understand how to be friendly on Taranoke. "Do your parents need cold-weather cloth?"

"Why are they bald?" Baru asked, pointing to the guards. By gesture or linguistic skill, they had made their fisherman friend blush.

"There are lice on ships," the merchant said, looking wearily out into the market. He had heavy brows, like fortresses to guard his eyes. "They live in hair. And I don't suppose your parents need cloth, given the climate. What was I thinking, trying to sell broadcloth here? I'll go home a pauper."

"Oh, no," Baru assured him. "We make things from your cloth, I'm sure, and besides, we can sell it to traders headed north, and make a profit. Do you use the paper money?"

"I prefer coin and gem, though when I buy, I'll pay in paper notes."

He had to his left a stack of sheepskin palimpsest—ink-scratched records that could be scraped clean and used again. "Are those your figures?"

"They are, and they are certainly too important to show to you." The broadcloth merchant blew irritably at a buzzing fly. "Do your parents use paper money, then?"

Baru caught the fly and crushed it. "No one used it at first. But now that your ships come in so often, everyone must have some, because it can buy so many things." Then she asked about something she already knew, because it was useful to hide her wit: "Are you from the Masquerade?"

"The Empire of Masks, dear, or the Imperial Republic. It's rude to abbreviate." The man watched his guards with a paternal frown, as if afraid they might need supervision. "Yes, that's my home. Though I haven't seen Falcrest in some years."

"Are you going to conquer us?"

He looked at her slowly, his eyes narrowed in thought. "We never conquer anyone. Conquest is a bloody business, and causes plagues besides. We're here as friends."

"It's curious, then, that you'd sell goods for coins and gems, but only buy with paper," said Baru. The shape of her words changed here, not entirely by her will: for a few moments she spoke like her mother. "Because if I understand my figures, that means you are taking all the things we use to trade with others, and giving us paper that is only good with you."

The broadcloth merchant watched her with sudden sharpness.

"My parents are scared," Baru added, embarrassed by his regard.

He leaned forward, and abruptly she recognized his expression from markets and traders past. It was avarice. "Are your parents here?"

"I'm fine alone," she said. "Everyone here knows everyone else. I can't get lost. But if you want to buy a telescope—"

"I *crave* telescopes," he said, perhaps thinking she had never heard of sarcasm. "Where are they?"

"Up there," she said, pointing. "My mother is the huntress Pinion, and my fathers are Solit the blacksmith and Salm the shield-bearer."

At that his mouth pursed, as if the idea of fathers troubled him. Perhaps they had no fathers in Falcrest. "And you?"

"My name's Baru," she said, as names were gladly given on Taranoke. "Baru Cormorant, because a cormorant was the only thing that made me stop crying."

"You're a very clever girl, Baru," the merchant said. "You're going to have a brilliant future. Come see me again. Ask for Cairdine Farrier."

When he came to speak to her parents later, he could not seem to stop looking at her fathers, and then her mother, and pursing his lips as if he had swallowed his own snot. But he bought two telescopes and a set of mirrors, and even wary Salm was happy.

THE last Masquerade convoy of the trade season circled Halae's Reef and anchored off Iriad harbor in the company of a sleek red-sailed frigate—the warship that father Salm had expected. Barking sailors swarmed her deck. A child with a spyglass might, if she were too curious for her own good and too poor a daughter to attend to her work, climb the volcano and watch their proceedings all day long. Baru had such a spyglass, and she was just that kind of daughter.

"They have soldiers on board," Baru told her parents, excited to discover such a portentous thing herself. Now she could be included in the courtyard councils and whispers of poison treaties. "With armor and spears!"

But father Salm did not buckle on his shield to fight them. Mother Pinion did not take Baru aside and explain the taxonomy of sergeants and officers and the nature and variety of Masquerade weapons. Father Solit fed her no pineapple and asked for no details. They worked in the courtyard, murmuring about treaties and embassies. "Once they have built it," Salm would say, "they will never leave." And Solit would answer in flat fighting-without-fighting words: "They will build it whether we sign or not. We must make terms."

Feeling neglected and therefore unwilling to attend to her chores and figures, Baru nagged them. "Solit," she said, as he bagged their kelp harvest to carry to the burners, "when can you start smithing again?"

When Baru was young he had made beautiful and dangerous things out of ores that came from the earth and the hot springs. "Once the trading season's over, Baru," he said.

"And will mother go across the mountain, into the plains, and use the boar-killing spear you made for her?"

"I'm sure she will."

Baru looked happily to her mother, whose long strides and broad shoulders were better suited to the hunt than to telescope-making, and then to her other father, who could drum as fiercely as he could fight. "And when the soldiers come, will father Salm use the man-killing spear you made for him?"

"You're covered in filth, child," Solit said. "Go to Lea Pearldiver's home and get some pumice. Take some paper money and buy their olive oil, too."

BARU read at great length about *treaties* and *currency* and *arbitrage*, and when she could read or understand no more, she bothered mother Pinion, or sat in thought. Clearly there had been some mistake: her parents had been happier last year than this.

The trend would have to be reversed. But how?

At Iriad market the merchant Cairdine Farrier sat in his stall with his two guards, who had the satisfied look of gulls. That market fell on a stormy end-of-season day, gray and forbidding, close to the time when the Ashen Sea's circular trade winds would collapse into winter storm. But the Iriad cove sheltered the market from the worst of the chop and the drummers still drummed. Baru made straight for the wool-merchant's stall.

Farrier was speaking to a Taranoki plainsman who had clearly come all the way across the mountain, and Baru had always been taught not to speak to plainsmen, so she went to Farrier's guards instead. The bald women looked down at her, first with perfunctory regard, then irritation, and then, when she stayed, a little smile—from one of them, at least. The other woman looked to her companion for guidance, and thus told Baru that they were probably soldiers, and also which one was in charge.

Her reading and her thought had not been idly spent.

"Hello, little one," the woman in charge said. She had skin the color of good earth, wide lips, and brilliant blue eyes like a jungle crow. She wore a stained white tunic with her breeches. Her Urunoki was as superb as Cairdine Farrier's.

"You've been here all season," Baru said. "You never leave with the trading ships."

"We'll go home with the last convoy."

"I don't think you will," Baru said. The other woman straightened a little. "I don't think you're Cairdine Farrier's personal guards, or even merchants at all, because if you were you would have learned by now that you don't need guards at Iriad market, and he would have sent you to find more business."

The stiff woman said something in Aphalone, the Falcresti language, and from reading the dictionary Baru caught the words *native* and *steal*. But the woman with the blue eyes only knelt. "He said you were a very clever girl."

"You're soldiers, aren't you," Baru said. "From that ship. The warship that stayed here all season, anchored out of sight while the other traders came and went, sending back your reports. That's obvious, too. A trader wouldn't learn a little island's language as well as you have, which makes you spies. And now that the trade winds are dying, your ship's come in to harbor to stay."

The blue-eyed woman took her by the shoulders. "Little lark, I know what it means to see strange sails in the harbor. My name's Shir and I'm from Aurdwynn. When I was a child, the Masquerade harbored in Treaty-mont, our great city. They fought with the Duke Lachta, and I was scared, too. But it all ended well, and my aunt even got to kill the awful duke. Here—take a coin. Go buy a mango and bring it back to me, and I'll cut you a piece."

Baru kept the coin.

At the end of the day the red-sailed frigate in the harbor put down boats. The soldiers began to come ashore, led by officers in salt-stained leather and steel masks. Through her spyglass Baru watched Iriad's elders escort the Masquerade soldiers into their new building: a white embassy made of ash concrete.

Later Baru decided this must have been when the treaty was signed: *An Act of Federation, For the Mutual Benefit of the People of Taranoke and the Imperial Republic of Falcrest.*

At sunset they raised their banner: two open eyes in a mask, circled in clasped hands. And the next morning they began to cut tufa to build the school.

STORM season blew down on Taranoke and everything began to fall. Baru relied on her mother's love of knowing and telling to understand. But Pinion grew distant and temperamental, her loves overshadowed by a terrible brooding anger, and so left Baru to piece together the clues herself.

This was how she explained it to some of the other children, Lea Pearl-diver's and Haea Ashcoke's, her second cousin Lao oldest among them and already growing into a long-limbed stork of a person who had to fold herself up between the salty rocks of their secret seaside bolt-hole to listen to Baru's stories—

"The plainsmen are angry with us," Baru would say, "because of the treaty. They say it's because Taranoke stands alone, and we've betrayed that by letting the Masquerade build an embassy. But we know better." (At this everyone would murmur in agreement, having been raised to know the jealous ways of the soggy people from Taranoke's eastern plains.) "They think we've bought a foreign ally to hold over them. They think we want a monopoly on the new trade."

And events proved her right. Early in the rainy season all the children from around Halae's Reef packed themselves into their briny seaside fortress so Baru could explain the fires. "The plainsmen sent a war party," she told them, relishing the power to make them gasp and lean in, and especially the power to make Lao hug her knees and stare at Baru in terror and admiration. "They came over the mountain and burned some of our sugarcane and coffee. It was a message, you see? So the harborside families took council at Iriad, and sent out a war party of our own. Champions to bear their shields east and answer the challenge."

"What will they do?" Lao asked, to Baru's immense satisfaction.

"Talk if they can," Baru said, playing at nonchalance by tossing a stone to herself. "Fight if they can't."

"How do they fight?"

How extraordinarily satisfying to be the daughter of Salm the shield-bearer and Pinion the huntress, foremost among the harborside champions. "Wars are fought between champions in a circle of drums. The drums beat and the champions trade spear-cast and shield-push until the loser yields or dies." Baru cracked her throwing stone against the stone beneath her, to make them leap. "And then the plainsmen go home to sulk, and we sell them textiles at outrageous prices."

But it didn't happen this way. When the war party set out to cross the mountain and challenge the plainsmen, the Masquerade garrison marched with them. The treaty spoke of *mutual defense.*

This was where Baru lost track of events, because mother Pinion and father Salm marched with them too—the war party with their shields and man-spears and obsidian knives climbing the flank of the mountain in a motley peacock throng, Salm's braids a mark of glory among them, Pinion's spear strapped across her brown back. And the Masquerade garrison masked and columned behind them, banners flying, churning the road to mud.

It had been a long time since war between harborside and plainsmen. Around Iriad there were old vendettas, wives who would not take plainside husbands, men who would not add their seed to a plainside woman's child. But it had been easy to forget that hate as long as times were fat.

Baru and father Solit stayed at home. The glassmakers had stopped burning kelp and so there were no mirrors to grind. Without Masquerade traders in harbor the paper money was worthless, except it wasn't, because everyone wanted to have it when the trade winds picked up again, and bartered outrageously for even a few slips.

The wool-merchant Cairdine Farrier came in person to invite Baru to attend the new school, a great tufa-walled compound above the cove. "Oh," father Solit said, his voice hard. "I don't know. What could you teach her that she couldn't learn from us?"

"Lands around the Ashen Sea," Farrier said, smiling conspiratorially at Baru. "New sorts of arithmetic and algebra. Astronomy—we have an excellent telescope, built by the Stakhieczi in the distant north. Science and the disciplines within it. Various catalogues"—his smile held—"of sin and social failure. The Imperial Republic is determined to help those we meet."

"No," father Solit said, taking her shoulder. "Your help is a fishhook."

"You know best, of course," Farrier said, though the avarice had not gone from his eyes.

But without Salm and Pinion, father Solit was lonely and disconsolate, and Baru insisted that she be allowed to attend this wonderful school, which might be full of answers to questions she had barely begun to form—*what is the world* and *who runs it* and more. Whether because she made Solit furious, or sad, or led him to realize he no longer had any control, her pleas struck home. (She wondered about this often, later, and decided it was none of that. He had seen the fire on the horizon and wanted his daughter safe.)

She went into the school, with her own uniform and her own bed in the crowded dormitory, and there in her first class on Scientific Society and Incrasticism she learned the words *sodomite* and *tribadist* and *social crime* and *sanitary inheritance,* and even the mantra of rule: *order is preferable to disorder.* There were rhymes and syllogisms to learn, the Qualms of revolutionary philosophy, readings from a child's version of the Falcresti *Handbook of Manumission.*

They know so much, Baru thought. I must learn it all. I must name every star and sin, find the secrets of treaty-writing and world-changing. Then I can go home and I will know how to make Solit happy again.

She learned a great many other things as well: astronomy and social heredity and geography. She made a map of the Ashen Sea and its seasonal trade winds, which carried ships in a great easy circle that ran clockwise (another new word) around the ocean, starting at Falcrest in the east and running south near Taranoke and Oriati Mbo, onward past lands with many names, all the way north to Aurdwynn and then back to Falcrest again.

So many lands. Oriati Mbo below, learned and fractious, a quilt of federations. Cold Aurdwynn above, where instead of a storm season they had *winter,* and no decent fruit, and wolves.

And Falcrest. It must be full of secrets to learn.

"You *could* go to Falcrest, Baru Cormorant!" The social hygienist Diline, a gentle man the color of whitefish, aimed his stylus at her. "At the end of your schooling, every child of promise will sit the civil service exam, the Empire's great leveler. Through the methods of Incrastic thought, we will determine your social function. You may become a translator, a scholar, even a technocrat in a distant land."

"Does the Emperor live in Falcrest?" second cousin Lao asked. At night they whispered rumors of the silent Emperor and the Faceless Throne on which he sat.

Diline smiled blandly. "He does. Who can recite the Hierarchic Qualm?"

Baru could.

The civil service exam became Baru's guide-star. It would ask her to recite the secrets of power, she imagined. It would require her to make father Solit smile again.

But that very same day Diline taught them the proof of strict limited inheritance. "One male father," he said, watching the class carefully, as if waiting for a boar to burst out from among them. "One female mother. No less. No more."

The class did not believe him. Cousin Lao began to cry. Baru tried to disprove this idiot *proof,* and had her first shouting match. She was the daughter of a huntress and a blacksmith and a shield-bearer, and now they would tell her she was *not*?

She had to ask mother Pinion.

But Pinion came home alone.

Came home from the war, the blood-soaked catastrophe at Jupora, where Masquerade marines shot dead the plainsmen champions and slaughtered their war party. Cradling father Solit's trembling face in her hands, she rasped her own catastrophe: "Salm vanished on the march home. There were men among the foreign soldiers who hated him. I think they took him."

"For what?" Solit's voice sealed, frozen, desperate to keep things within or without. "What could they find to hate?"

"You. None of these men have husbands. They *hate* husbands." She lowered her forehead to his. "He's gone, Solit. I looked—I looked so long—"

When this happened, it was because of the class on Scientific Society and Incrasticism that Baru could only think to ask: "Was Salm my real father? Or was he only a sodomite?"

It was because of this that father Solit cried out, and told mother Pinion about the school. It was because of this that mother Pinion struck her in rage, and cast Baru out of the courtyard to run sobbing back to the white walls and the masked banner.

Her mother came to apologize, of course, and they cried and were reunited as a family, or at least a grieving part of one. But the hurt was dealt, and the school seemed to know more than even mother Pinion, who taught no more—only whispered with Solit about fire and spear and *resistance.*

"Stay at school," Solit said. "You'll be safest there. The Farrier man"—his nostrils flared in disgust—"will not let you be harmed."

I must learn why this happened to Salm, Baru thought. I must understand it, so I can stop it from ever happening again. I will not cry. I will understand.

This was Baru Cormorant's first lesson in causality. But it was not quite the most important thing she ever learned from her mother.

That came earlier, long before the school or the disappearance of brave father Salm. Watching the red-sailed warship in Iriad harbor, Baru asked: "Mother, why do they come here and make treaties? Why do *we* not go to *them*? Why are they so powerful?"

"I don't know, child," mother Pinion said.

It was the first time Baru could ever remember hearing those words from her.

2

SHE lost her father Salm, and from this she nearly lost her mother, too.

"You cannot believe what they teach you," mother Pinion hissed in her ear. (They smiled together at the chaperones who brought Baru to visit her home, which seemed strangely squalid now.) "You must remember what they did to Salm, and give them nothing. The families are taking secret council. We will find a way to drive them back into the sea."

"They will never go back," Baru whispered, pleading. "You cannot fight them, Mother. You don't understand how huge they are. Please find some way to make peace—please don't die like Salm—"

"He isn't dead," Pinion growled. "Your father lives."

Baru looked at her mother, at Pinion's eyes red with fatigue, her shoulders bunched in anger, and wondered what had happened to the woman who was a thunderbolt, a storm cloud, a panther. Of all things Pinion looked most like a wound.

And Pinion, looking back, must have seen an equal disappointment in Baru's eyes. "He lives," she said again, and turned away.

The argument grew between them like a reef.

By Baru's tenth birthday, she came to expect visits from the wool merchant Cairdine Farrier more often than her mother or father. He always had advice. Dress this way, never that way. Befriend her, or him—but not him. She liked his advice better than Pinion's, because it was full of things to accomplish now rather than things to avoid forever.

The school's Charitable Service instructors came from many foreign places. There were more and stranger people among the Masquerade garrison than Baru had ever seen at Iriad market. "If they can be teachers," Baru asked, "then I can be one, too? I can go to another land and make little girls stop reading at unjustly early hours?"

"You can be anything you want in the Empire of Masks!" Cairdine

Farrier, grown fat these past few years on island life, tugged affectionately on her ear. "Man and woman, rich and poor, Stakhieczi or Oriati or Maia or Falcrest born—in our Imperial Republic you can be what you desire, if you are disciplined in your actions and rigorous in your thoughts. That's why it's an Empire of Masks, dear. When you wear a mask, your *wits* matter."

"You don't wear a mask," Baru said, studying him intently, wondering if there might be flaps behind his ears, fastenings in his hair.

Farrier laughed at her words, or her stare. He was like Pinion or Solit in his love of her sharpest thoughts. But he was like lost Salm in another way, in the way he relished Baru's effrontery, her willingness to reach out and ask or take. "The mask is for acts of service. The soldier wears a mask on his patrol. The mathematician wears a mask defending her proof. In Parliament they are all masked, because they are vessels for the will of the Republic. And on the Faceless Throne the Emperor sits masked forever."

A deflection. How unacceptable. Baru pursued her question. "When do *you* wear a mask? How do you serve?"

"It's too hot on Taranoke for masks. But I am here to sell wool, and help occasionally in matters of charity." He scrubbed Baru's close-shaved scalp with his knuckles. Fat had plumped out his cheeks and weighted his jaw, but when Baru thought of fat men she thought of happy old storytellers at Iriad, pleased to be old, and large with joy. Cairdine Farrier did not seem that way. He carried his weight like a thoughtful provision, stored in preparation.

"What if you could wear a mask?" he asked. "What would you want, Baru?"

It had not occurred to Baru to want anything except stars and letters until the day when the red-sailed frigate moored in Iriad harbor. It had not occurred to her to want the impossible until she lost father Salm, first to that awful *doctrine,* and then to death.

Perhaps the death of fathers could be outlawed.

Perhaps doctrines could be rewritten.

"I want to be powerful," she said.

Cairdine Farrier looked down fondly. "You should study hard for your service exam," he said. "Study very hard."

*   *   *

THE service exam would not come for eight years. Baru worked herself raw for it.

Falcrest, she whispered to herself at night. Empiricism. Incrasticism. The academies of Falcrest. Parliament, and the Metademe, and the Morrow Ministry, and all their secrets. If only I can go to Falcrest—

So much to master, in that distant axis around which the Empire of Masks and the world turned. Secrets her mother had never dreamed of.

The terror did not stop with Salm.

Outside the walls of the Masquerade school, plague swept Taranoke. Quarantine closed the gates. The Taranoki children in the school, unable to get news of their relatives, waited bravely through their inoculations (a Masquerade concept, like a feeble sickness carried on a swab or a needle). But the quarantine did not lift, not that trade season nor the storm season after.

When rumors of the dead crept into the school, the sobs of bereaved students kept Baru from her sleep. Sometimes the rumors were false. Not often.

On lonely nights in the dormitories, surrounded by mourning, Baru would think with cold resentment: at least you know. Better to see the body, and to know how your beloved kin passed—better that than to lose your father in the night, as if he were a misplaced toy, a ship at a fraying moor.

Then the scale of the death outside became clear—the pyramids of corpses burning on the black stone, the weeping sores and lye stink of the quarantine pens. Baru didn't weep at that either, but she desperately wanted to.

"Why is this happening?" She cornered Cairdine Farrier during one of his visits, furious and desperate. "What does this mean?" And when he made a gentle face, a face for blandishments and reassurance, she screamed into the space before the lie: "You brought this with you!"

And he looked at her with open eyes, the bone of his heavy brow a bastion above, the flesh of his face wealthy below, and in those eyes she glimpsed an imperium, a mechanism of rule building itself from the work of so many million hands. Remorseless not out of cruelty or hate but because it was too vast and too set on its destiny to care for the small tragedies of its growth. She saw this not merely in the shape of his eyes and the flatness of his regard, but in what they recalled—things he had said and done suddenly understood. And she knew that Farrier had let her see this, as a warning, as a promise.

"The tide is coming in," he said. "The ocean has reached this little pool. There will be turbulence, and confusion, and ruin. This is what happens when something small joins something vast. But—" Later she would hold to this moment, because it felt that he had offered her something true and grown-up and powerful rather than a lie to shield her. "When the joining is done there will be a sea for you to swim in."

The Masquerade teachers and sailors came and went freely. They were immune. Baru deduced the arrival of a second Masquerade frigate from a whole flock of new faces, including a lanky black-skinned midshipwoman who couldn't have had more than two years on Baru but got to wear a sword. Baru was too embarrassed of her accented Aphalone to say hello, to ask how an Oriati girl had made herself an officer in the service of the Masquerade so soon after the great Armada War between the two powers.

Children began to vanish from the school, sent back out onto the island, into the plague. "Their behavior was not hygienic," the teachers said. *Social conditions,* the students whispered. *He was found playing the game of fathers—*

The teachers watched them coldly as their puberty came, waiting for unhygienic behavior to manifest itself. Baru saw why Cairdine Farrier had advised her on her friendships. Some of the students collaborated in the surveillance.

When Baru turned thirteen, her friend and second cousin Lao, two years older and bitterly unhappy, came to her with twisting hands. "Lao," Baru whispered, in the limited privacy of her curtained bed. "What's wrong?"

"My special tutor," Lao said, eyes downcast, "is a—" She lapsed from Aphalone into their childhood Urunoki. "A pervert."

Lao's special tutor was the social hygienist Diline, from Falcrest—gentle, patronizing, skin exotically pale. He took sessions with rebellious or homesick students. Baru had decided a long time ago that Diline could not help her on the civil service exam. "What has he done?" she hissed. "Lao, look at me—"

"He thinks I have a social condition." Lao covered her eyes in shame, a gesture they'd all learned from their teachers. "He thinks I'm a tribadist."

"Oh," Baru said.

Later she would hate herself for the calculation she made here: *What will it cost me to be associated with her, if she is?* For the science of sanitary inheritance they had learned made it very clear what a horror it was to lie with another woman, and what punishment the tribadist would receive. The Imperial Republic had been born in revolt against a degenerate aristocracy, their bodies and minds twisted, Diline had explained, by centuries of unhygienic mating. From this Falcrest had learned the value of sanitary behavior and carefully planned inheritance. *The diseases of tribadism and sodomy must be eradicated from the body and the bloodline . . .*

But she and Lao were both Taranoki, born of Taranoki families, and that loyalty had come before the Masquerade and its doctrines.

"What will he do?" Baru asked.

Lao drew her knees to her chest and looked out through the curtains around the bed. "There's a treatment. Conducted with the hands. Last time he suggested it, I told him I was on my period."

Baru nodded. "But you have appointments with him every week."

Lao's face folded in the shadows. "I don't think there's anything we can do," she said. "Even you, though you're their favorite. Perhaps it's for the best—it has to be cured young, they say, before it enters the hereditary cells—"

"No. No!" Baru took her hands. "Lao, I know exactly who to talk to. I can fix this."

Lao squeezed her hands gratefully. "I can survive this. You have so much to lose."

But Baru was already planning her movements, drunk on the thrill of it. Later, just as she would hate herself for her calculation, she would remember: *This was my first exercise of power. My first treason.*

B UT she was wrong. She did not know exactly who to talk to. Cairdine Farrier was no help at all.

"Listen to me, Baru," he said, speaking softly, as if afraid they would be overheard here in the empty tufa courtyard in the corner of the school compound. "Young women express numerous hysterias and neuroses. It is a scientific fact, an inevitable consequence of the hereditary pathways that have shaped the sexes, that the young man is given to rage, violence, and promiscuity, while the young lady is given to hysteria, perversion, and disorders of the mind. If you want to be a powerful woman—and there are powerful women in the Empire, a great many of them—you must be a *strong* young woman. Is that clear?"

She took a step away from him, her eyes too wide, her mouth betraying her shock. It was the first time he had ever seemed angry with her. "No," she said, with a naïve directness that she would later regret. "That's not true! And besides, it's Lao who has this problem, and—and why is it about Lao, anyway? It's that tutor Diline who wants to put his hands on her!"

"Quiet!" Cairdine Farrier hissed. "Diline reports on social hygiene to the headmaster, and those reports go into your permanent files. Do you understand what it means for your future if you make an enemy of him?"

A year or two past she would have shouted *I don't care!* but now she knew that sounded like hysteria, and despite her revulsion she focused on practicalities. "If you act," she said, "then *I* won't be making an enemy of him, will I? Just have Lao ejected from the school. She hates it here anyway. The headmaster could judge her unfit for service."

From the near distance came the sound of a dish shattering in the kitchen and a man shouting angrily in Aphalone. Cairdine Farrier steepled his hands, a gesture that he always made when explaining things he thought were complicated. "Men like Diline give up their lives to work for your betterment. You will respect them. You will be agreeable toward their arts, even when they seem unpleasant. If Diline thinks your friend shows unhygienic tendencies, then he will cure her." His eyes were dark beneath the redoubts of his brow. "Child, believe me: the alternatives will bring her much more pain."

He's explaining it to me, Baru thought, which means he thinks I can be convinced, which means he hasn't given up on me. But if I push—

It's not worth losing his patronage over this.

"All right," she said. "Forget I asked."

Cairdine Farrier smiled in pleased relief.

Dᴵᴰ it work?" Lao whispered, while they swept the floor beneath the quarantine seals.

Baru met her eyes and smiled half a smile, a crow smile, a lie. "I'm still exploring the options," she said.

Looking back on this from adulthood she could not deny that she had considered abandoning Lao. Sacrificing her in the name of forward progress.

If she got to Falcrest, if she learned the mechanisms of power, surely she could save more than just one Taranoki girl. No matter how clever and brave Lao was, no matter how dear.

But Baru had another plan.

"Hey," Baru said, as throatily as she could manage. She was thirteen, gawkily tall, intimidated by her target.

"Hey yourself," the lanky Oriati midshipman said. Every other day she brought a package to the headmaster's office and left the school through this back corridor, and that was where Baru had waited to intercept her.

Baru combed her louse-free stubble with one hand. "You're an officer, aren't you?"

"With an officer's duties." The midshipman squared her shoulders and began to push past, toward the outer door. Her Aphalone had its own accent. Perhaps she had been raised in a Masquerade school, just like Baru. "As you were, student."

"Wait." Baru caught her by the elbow. "I need your help."

They stared at each other, almost nose to nose, Baru trying to stay up on her toes just to match the other woman's height. She had very brown eyes and very dark skin and an intelligent brow and her arm worked with muscle.

"You're a curious thing," the midshipman drawled, adopting the easy superiority of Masquerade officers speaking to Taranoki. "Mind your hands."

"That's my problem," Baru muttered, drawing closer, gambling that her impudence was more intriguing than revolting. "Hands. If you know what I mean."

She had done a little thinking and a little reading about the Imperial Navy, a navy that expected its sailors to climb masts and work ropes and rigging, a navy that boasted a cadre of women captains and admirals who were by any account capable and respected. A navy that must, in the course of packing crews of mostly men onto tiny ships for months at a time, have confronted problems of this order.

The midshipman disengaged sharply, a quick step back and a turn that tore her free of Baru's grip. Baru drew a nervous breath, ready to be struck or reprimanded.

"My name's Aminata," the other woman said. She checked the far end of the hallway, a guilty glance so familiar that Baru had to drown a chuckle. "I'm from Oriati Mbo. My family used to trade on Taranoke, and if you tell anyone I spoke to you I'll gut you, you understand?"

Baru lifted her chin. "Not if I gut you first."

Aminata considered her, smiling a little. Baru thought of a king-fisher eyeing a colorful frog. "We can't talk in here," she said. "I could get in real trouble for letting you out of quarantine."

"I didn't ask you to."

"You certainly never did," Aminata said, lifting a small brass key. "Now come on. I'll tell you how to solve your hands' problems."

S HE followed Aminata down the path behind the school to the edge of a bluff that overlooked Iriad harbor, giddy with fresh salt air and dis-obedience, with the rumble of thunder on the horizon, with the conspir-atorial wariness of the older girl's glances. "It won't matter if anyone sees us," Aminata said. "There's a million of you little island rats, and if you're not in the school they assume you're just an orphan looking for errands."

"Orphan?" Baru frowned at that. Taranoke's robust nets of mothers and fathers, aunts and uncles, had never left many children alone.

Aminata hawked and spat off the edge of the bluff. The sea rumbled and crashed below. "The plague's been hard."

"Oh," Baru said, thinking: yes, of course, I knew that. The island of her childhood was gone. It had died in pus and desperation while she took lessons behind white walls.

It was storm season. In the harbor a pair of Masquerade warships roosted with their sails furled.

"C'mon." Aminata sat on the bluff, legs dangling, and patted the rock beside her. "Tell me about your trouble."

"I have a friend—"

"You don't have to pretend it's a friend."

"I have a friend," Baru said, although Aminata snorted, "who has attracted some unwanted attention. From a man."

"And he's done something to your friend already?"

"Not yet." Baru sat beside her, fascinated by her red uniform. The

Masquerade officers wore exquisite wool waistcoats, the broadcloth tight against weather. Aminata, sensible about the heat, wore the coat rakishly loose, and it seemed rather dashing. "Not yet. But he's tried."

"There's a rule here." Aminata squinted out at the horizon, an old-seahand squint, strange on her young face. "No false claims. You can't be doing this because you fucked and now he's bragging. Men like to think that false claims are a woman's weapon, you know. Men close ranks about these things. Even good men."

Baru had never thought about these things, and said the first thing that came to mind: "Bragging? What would he brag about?"

Aminata leaned back on her hands. "I don't know how it is on Taranoke, but in the Masquerade you play by Falcrest rules. And Falcrest rules say the man gets to brag and the woman's got to be silent."

That's not fair was a child's protest, Baru reminded herself. "Okay," she said. "I understand the rules."

"Now what you do," Aminata said, not without a certain relish, "is you get your friends, and you wait until he's asleep, all right? Then you gag him and you tie his hands and feet to the bedframe, and you beat his stomach and feet with stockings full of soap. If he does it again, you beat his balls until he can barely piss. And if he tries to complain, everyone will know what he did. Those are the rules in the navy. They're not written, but they're true."

Baru, who had been expecting some political subtlety, did not try to conceal her disappointment. "We're not in the navy," she said, "and we don't have stockings, and besides, we can't get into his room at night."

"Oh." Aminata's eyes narrowed. She uprooted a hibiscus flower and began to pluck it methodically. "A teacher."

Baru shrugged. "Might be."

"So he's got some excuse to paw your friend. He's got protection from on high. That's difficult."

"There must be a way to stop it," Baru said, staring down into the harbor, at the place where Iriad market had been. The Masquerade had torn down the promenades and boardwalks and built a dockyard that cradled the skeleton of a new ship. Troops drilled in the muddy streets of the village. "What do you do in the navy when it's an officer who comes after you?"

"It used to be there was nothing you could do." Aminata finished plucking the hibiscus and cast it aside. "But now there are enough women—women, and men who've served with them—in the officer corps that all it takes is a quiet word in the right ear. It's all done unofficially. But it's done."

"So you can go to your officers for her, and they'll stop it!"

Aminata pursed her lips and shrugged, and Baru remembered that for all her uniform and stature, she was a midshipman, and probably not more than sixteen. "I don't know. Could be risky, setting the Navy against the Charitable Service just for the sake of one little islander girl. What's in it for me?"

Baru felt her own lips curl, felt her own jaw set, and did not try to hide it. "Nothing, I suppose," she said. "You haven't even asked my name, so I suppose you don't really have to care."

They sat on the edge of the bluff in cold silence for a little while. The wind picked up.

"You should get back," Aminata said. "And so should I, before the watch officer notes I'm overdue."

"You'll have to let me back in," Baru said stiffly.

Aminata shrugged. "Won't. Those doors only lock from the inside."

"Oh." Baru got to her feet and turned back to climb the bluff, wishing sullenly for her mother's boar-killing spear, or just for her mother, who would have had fierce words for Aminata, and fiercer treatment yet for the hygienist Diline.

Maybe she'd been right. Maybe the only way to stop this kind of thing *was* the spear—

"So what is it?" Aminata called. The wind had begun to gust fiercely.

"What's what?"

Aminata made a little *out-with-it* gesture with her hand and, to Baru's perplexingly mingled anger and pleasure, smiled a little.

"Baru Cormorant," Baru said. "And the problem's name is Diline."

DURING the next week, in the middle of the night, her second cousin Lao came to her in the dark and kissed her brow. "Thank you," she whispered. "You're the only good thing left, Baru. Thank you."

They were in an art studio—learning to draw foxes, which they had never seen—when word came around that Diline would be leaving the school for an appointment in Falcrest when the trade winds picked up again. A captain of the Masquerade marines stopped by personally to congratulate him. Baru felt pride, and sick relief, and worry, because she had not done anything at all herself. Aminata had acted for her.

She was powerless without her patrons. Could power be real if someone else gave it to you?

"Hey," Aminata said, when next she passed Baru in the halls.

"Hey yourself." Baru grinned, and was reprimanded by the hall proctor for disrespect to an Imperial officer.

Later that year the school announced a class on swordsmanship, in order to prepare its students for possible service. Aminata was the instructor's assistant, walking through the ranks, barking in students' faces, seizing their elbows to adjust their form. When she came to Baru she was no gentler, but she smiled.

They were friends. They whispered, gossiped, speculated. Aminata had come into Imperial service from the outside, like Baru—daughter of one of the Oriati federations that stood wary to the south, fearful of a second losing war with the Masquerade. Together they invented small rebellions, commandeering food, conspiring against teachers and officers. Of all their insurrections, Baru's favorite was the cipher game—Aminata knew a little of naval codes, and Baru used that knowledge and her own formal figures to make an encryption for their own use. It proved perhaps too ambitious, certainly too ornate (at one point it required three languages and complex trigonometry), but through exasperation and a lot of squabbling in the teachers' larder they whittled it down into something usable.

And Baru came into the habit of slipping out of the quarantine, sometimes with Aminata, sometimes alone with the key Aminata had provided her, to see her mother and father and assure them that she was not yet lost to them.

If Cairdine Farrier knew about this, he showed no displeasure. But when Diline left Taranoke, he visited Baru in a curt mood and said: "We will need to find a replacement of equal diligence."

He looked at her with guarded eyes, and she thought that he knew what had been done to save Lao. But she could not decide if he was pleased, or angry, or waiting to see what she would do next.

More and more of her fellow students began to leave the school. She found herself assigned special duties, puzzles and tasks, riddles of coin and account-books, geometry and calculus. The teachers began to murmur the word *savant,* and behind their glances she saw Cairdine Farrier's eyes.

S HE mastered figures and proofs, demographics and statistics. Struggled with literature and history, geography, and Aphalone, all of which should have been interesting but in practice bored her. All these fallen empires: the husk of ancient Tu Maia glory in the west, their blood and letters scattered everywhere, and the Stakhieczi masons now dwindled away into the north, maybe someday to return. They were yesteryear's methods, the losers of history. Falcrest had surpassed them. Even the Oriati, artisans and traders sprawling away to the south in a quilt of squabbling federations—well, Aminata didn't seem to miss her home so much, and their strength had not been enough to win the Armada War, so what could they offer?

Easy enough, at least, to perform with unremarkable competence in social hygiene and Incrasticism, the Masquerade's philosophy of progress and hereditary regulation. And she excelled in swordsmanship, surpassing even most of the boys, who by seventeen were now, on the mean, bigger and stronger than the girls.

But swordsmanship was not on the civil service exam, and as the proctors and teachers and Cairdine Farrier kept reminding her, as she told her mother on her forbidden nights out, the exam was everything. The key to Falcrest, to the academies and the murmured Metademe where they made special people of clarified purpose; the key—perhaps—to a seat in Parliament.

If the Masquerade could not be stopped by spear or treaty, she would change it from within.

And at the beginning of that trade season the exam came, shipped in from Falcrest in wax-sealed tubes, brought in under armed escort and prepared for the remaining students like a banquet.

Cairdine Farrier slipped her a flask of clear spring water, mixed with some invisible drug which he assured her would help her focus—"All the polymaths in Falcrest use it!" She left it in her bed and sat down to take the exam with her mind clear, all worry and fear pressed into clean geometric lines, everything focused on this day and the day after.

She did not let herself think about the way her whole life from this moment on would pivot around how well she could write on these papers.

Falcrest, she did not let herself think. *I will go to Falcrest and learn to rule, as we have been ruled. I will make it so no Taranoki daughter will lose a father again.*

She was eighteen.

Two days passed, and she turned the exam over to the headmaster knowing she had demolished it. "Did the placebo help?" Cairdine Farrier asked, eyes sparkling.

That night she worked in the training room with Aminata, the brutal naval routine of partnered exercises and dead weights meant to keep a woman ready for ropes and masts and combat. They dueled with blunted longswords, Baru losing but still high on her own future, on the knowledge that she had *won.* Taranoke would not be her cage. (When had Taranoke become a cage?)

"You didn't tell me," now-Lieutenant Aminata said, panting between clashes.

"Tell you what?"

"Why that hygienist was going to treat your 'friend' a few years ago."

Baru lifted her blade and set herself at the wide mensur, two footsteps away, sword at the day guard. "Should I have?"

"One of the merchants told me yesterday," Aminata said, her blade down in the fool guard. "He told my captain, who told me."

Baru breathed in, out, in, trying to center herself.

"Diline didn't want some lewd congress," Aminata said. "He was trying to cure your *friend* of tribadism. Of love for women!"

Baru struck. Aminata struck in counter, fast as reflex where Baru still needed thought. Rode her sword down the length of Baru's into a killing stroke to the neck that threw Baru back and left her gasping and pawing at her throat.

"Surely you've heard of that condition!" Aminata advanced, unrelenting, striking again. Baru missed the counterstrike and suffered a crushing blow to her gloved fingers. Crying out, she disengaged, but Aminata followed still. "It's common on this island, I'm told. A pervasive affliction!"

"He had no right to put his hands on her!" Baru gave ground, in the ox guard, blade at brow and waiting for another stroke. Her heart hammered and it was impossible to tell the battle-rage from the rising sickness of betrayal.

"I had to learn it from my captain!" Aminata's guard was down but Baru sensed a trap and held back. "Do you know what's done to a suspected tribadist, Baru? There's a list somewhere, a list of officers who'll go nowhere. And do you know what's done if the crime can be proven?"

Baru struck, weary, weak. Aminata batted the stroke aside contemptuously.

"They'll take a knife to your cunt," she said, and struck Baru's hands so hard she dropped her blade.

Aminata stepped into the opening, seizing Baru beneath the shoulders, clinching her arms in a hold she remembered from firelight and drums and lost father Salm wrestling some other champion. She struggled, roaring, but could not escape.

They stood locked together, panting, Aminata's proud high-browed face close and ferociously angry.

"It's a crime against law and nature," Aminata hissed. "And you should've told me."

She dropped Baru to the matted floor and left.

A merchant told her captain, Baru thought, her mind awhirl. *A merchant—I know only one merchant—*

And when the results of the placement exam came back from Falcrest, and Cairdine Farrier came to her smiling to say: "Congratulations, Baru. You've excelled beyond all expectation. You'll go to Aurdwynn, to prove yourself as Imperial Accountant in those troubled lands. And perhaps later to Falcrest."

When this happened, she knew she had been punished for going against him.

"Don't be disappointed," Cairdine Farrier said, patting her shoulder. "You've come so far, given where you began."

3

EIGHTEEN and hungry, the memory of father Salm an old scar kept close at hand, Baru made ready to leave Taranoke.

Imperial Accountant for the Federated Province of Aurdwynn. The north. The wolf land. Troubled Aurdwynn and its thirteen treacherous dukes. A test? Or an exile? Had Cairdine Farrier betrayed her?

It felt like he had. "You will have high station," he'd told her. "Dangerously high, for one so young. It will ask everything of you."

But it was not Falcrest. It was not the power she had warned her mother of, in their endless, spiraling war: *You will never change anything with your hut and your little spear! They are too vast, and you understand too little! We cannot fight them from here!*

And her mother's answering disdain: *Go, then. Learn all their secrets. Cover yourself in them. You will return with a steel mask instead of a face.*

Iriad harbor gave birth to a new ship, hulled in Taranoki lumber, flying the red sails of the Imperial Navy. Baru's letter of assignment said it would take her north—two children of Taranoke, cut and worked by the Masquerade, leaving together.

Walking down to the harbor, blunt practice blade on her belt, she found herself looking across Taranoke with Imperial eyes. *Plentiful lumber. Good labor. A fleet base, securing the southwest of the Ashen Sea.* Feed the forests to the shipyards, expand the plantations, tame the plainsmen and use their land for cattle—

All of this would happen. They would marry their bureaucrats and shipwrights into decimated Taranoki families, a gift meant to stop the devastating plagues carried here from Falcrest's pig pens, plagues against which the Taranoki had no immunity. Incrastic eugenics would dictate the shape and color of the island's children.

There would be families who clung to the old ways, both in their marriages and in their trading habits, but the island's economy was a Masquerade economy now. There was no reason to buy or sell anywhere but Iriad.

While she had waited behind the walls of the school, her home had been conquered. The soldiers of the invasion, the paper money and the sailcloth, the pigpen diseases, had won. The old divisions of harborside and plainsmen exploited before she was even old enough to understand them.

Had she been conquered, too?

No. No. She would play their game, learn their secrets. But mother Pinion was wrong. It would only be a mask. She would come home with the answers of rule and find a way to ease the yoke.

She looked up to the slopes of Taranoke, where as a child she had brought her spyglass, where the dead volcano slept. Raised a hand in salute, in promise: *After Falcrest. Once I find the way.*

I N Iriad she spoke and signed an oath to the Emperor, and another oath to the Imperial Republic and all its many organs. She received her papers of citizenship, slick with beeswax for waterproofing: socialized federati (class 1) with a civil service star and a technocrat's mark, inflected with the mathematician's sign. Marriage rights after hereditary review, with further review after first childbearing.

"You can go to the docks now," the clerk said. He was Taranoki and younger than her, but his Aphalone was perfect. Probably an orphan, raised in a Charitable Service school. A whole generation amputated from its past.

Orphan—

They aren't coming, Baru thought, her throat dry. They're too angry with me. I *wrote*—maybe I wrote the letter in Aphalone, and didn't notice, and they couldn't read it—

But there at the harborside she found found mother Pinion and father Solit, dressed in mulberry-cloth skirts and work shirts as a concession to the new modesty. She saw them in the crowd before they saw her, and had time to straighten herself, to blink a few times, to call: "Mother! Father!"

Mother Pinion took her by the shoulders. "You're strong," she said. "Good. Daughter—"

"Mother," Baru warned, breathing raggedly. Her eyes prickled.

"I want you to answer two questions." Her hair had no gray in it and her gaze was very firm, but plague scars pocked her cheeks. "Why are you leaving? So many of your cousins are staying as interpreters or staff. Have you forgotten how I named the birds and the stars?"

"Mother," Baru said, her heart breaking within her (how formal the old Urunoki sounded now, when set next to fluid simple Aphalone), "there are strange new birds where I'm going, and strange new stars."

Her mother considered her in silence for a moment, and nodded. "Well enough. And are you still ours?"

"Yours?"

Pinion lifted her eyes to the dead snow-speckled peak. "You spent more time in that school than you did with us. Are you still ours?"

How much betrayal had Pinion seen? How many of her cousins still fought? How many of them had taken on new jobs, new husbands, saying as her own daughter had said: *We cannot win?*

"Mother," she began, stumbling, trying again: "I'm going to find another way to fight them. Be patient. Be strong. Don't—don't waste yourself on futility. They are vast, and no count of spears can change that."

"You chose one kind of strength, daughter," Pinion said. "I choose another."

Baru took her mother by the shoulders and kissed both her cheeks, unable to answer that. It was father Solit who took her by the shoulders next, and asked his own question: "Do you remember Salm?"

And Baru took him in her own arms, shocked by how frail he felt, by how close they were in height, and whispered in his ear: "I remember my father. I remember my fathers."

She felt his breath go out of him, a slow release that felt like it had waited years. They stepped away from her, their faces dour now, as they had to be. "Go, then," her mother said, and then, with softness: "I hope you return carrying all the things you want."

Baru backed up a few steps, not ready to look away. But it hurt too much to see them receding step by step, so at last she made herself face the sea.

She went down the quay, and found Cairdine Farrier waiting for her by the skiff. He beamed at her.

Baru held his gaze and shook his hand as an equal. "You'll accompany us to Treatymont and then continue on to Falcrest, I presume?"

"I'm going home," he said, "just as you're leaving it. My work on Tara-noke is done, and now you can begin that same work in Aurdwynn. It feels like a design, doesn't it? Like a made thing. Elegant."

"And what work is that?"

"My favorite work," he said, tugging at the breast of his summer jacket. "Finding those who deserve more, and raising them up."

They settled themselves in the skiff. Baru glanced over the crew, as-sessing their ranks and races, and found someone else watching her in return. "Lieutenant Aminata," she said, smiling, her stomach turning with uncertainty and anger. "Congratulations on your new post."

"Likewise," Aminata said, and smiled back. "Congratulations on your service appointment. I understand you performed remarkably."

The new ship was a frigate called *Lapetiare,* and from her deck Baru saw for the first time the whole shape of Taranoke, hazed in birds, black and fertile and oh so tall, falling down past the horizon and into memory.

*L*APETIARE turned north with the trade winds, racing along the Ashen Sea's western coast. Baru kept to the main deck and practiced her navigation. The master's mate took sightings of passing landmarks, logging their course by coastal navigation, but Baru preferred to watch the sun and stars—more beautiful, and more absolute. Computing lon-gitude demanded more than an hour of hand-scratched calculations. Baru resolved to work that time down to twenty minutes by the time they reached Aurdwynn. If she failed as an accountant, at least she could find a ship.

Spray crashed off the bow. The warm trade winds carried dark-winged shearwaters with them and the southern sailors, from Oriati Mbo and its many islands, threw them salted fish and called out wishes in their own tongues.

"Salt and citrus," Cairdine Farrier said, joining her at the stern with half a lemon in each hand. "The chemicals of empire."

"Salt to preserve food for long journeys," Baru recited. "Citrus for scurvy." Farrier had made the trip into an extended service exam (his very first question when aboard was *Do you recognize the name of the ship,* and she had; Lapetiare was a character from the revolutionary classic *The Antler Stone*). It might have annoyed her, but she was restless and appre-ciated the chance to work herself.

She'd grown proud.

"They have a strange red salt on Taranoke." Farrier arranged himself against the stern rail and threw a gnawed bone into the wake. "Iron salt, I believe it's called. I've sent samples home to Falcrest these past few years. Two of my colleagues are greatly interested in exploratory chemistry."

Baru pursed her lips. "I'm sure the work being done in Falcrest is very important."

"Falcrest is the heart and mind of the world."

"So I've been taught."

Farrier offered her one of the lemon halves. She waved him away without a glance. He clucked at her, shaking his head. "You're being petulant. Falcrest isn't lost to you. There are other paths than the service exam. Paths that reward patience, loyalty, and ability."

"One wonders which I've failed to demonstrate."

"You are young. The hereditary strengths of your people are untested, and their degenerate, unhygienic mating practices are a source of great unease. You should be pleased to—"

"And here I thought only wit mattered behind the mask."

Farrier drew a sailor's knife and began to cut the rind free of his lemon. The motion of the ship made him cautious with the blade, and he laughed softly at himself. "Perhaps you're asking the wrong questions," he said. "It could be that you've demonstrated truly *exemplary* capability. That you've been judged fit for additional tests. More rigorous evaluations, in more demanding environments, without the usual slow path of apprenticeship and advancement. The Imperial Republic is, as you justly remind me, a meritocracy through and through. And we will need merit in the years to come. There are wolves to our north, rising from cold dens, and water buffalo in our south, circled and ferocious. Very soon the Masquerade will win or lose a great game."

She lifted her eyes to judge the winds by the course of distant birds, playing for time. She was nervous, unsure of her position. Cairdine Farrier was not a simple merchant—she'd suspected that since the early days of the school on Taranoke, been certain of it since he meddled with her service exam. "I prefer to know who's testing me, given the choice. I prefer to know why I've been given an Imperial province and a high office, instead of an apprenticeship."

"You will have to trust that the Imperial Republic knows how best to permit you to serve it," Farrier said. He lifted his peeled lemon in toast.

Baru went to find her practice blade and a sailor who could test it.

THAT evening Baru summoned her new secretary to her cabin. "Muire Lo."

"Yes," he said, slipping sidelong through the doorway. "Your Excellence. At your service."

He was a slim man, narrow-shouldered, his skin almost invisible to Baru in that it was so very Taranoki (a little pale, perhaps, like someone who shut himself up inside, like father Solit). He wore gentle Falcrest-style makeup over a careful composed face. Instantly and inexplicably Baru wondered if he could sing, and only after a moment did she realize that he reminded her of a finch, curious and abrupt in his movements. She hated to trust these impressions: there seemed no reason for them to be true.

"You're from Aurdwynn," she said, gesturing *sit, sit*. There was barely room in the slot cabin for two and a table. She'd tidied her effects with a nervousness she preferred not to admit. This was her first subordinate.

"Yes, Your Excellence." He had a way of showing deference with his eyes, downcast and polite, but he couldn't quite hold it. Every few moments he glanced at Baru. When he did this his eyes were sharp and probing, frankly curious. "I left at thirteen. After the Fools' Rebellion. A Charitable Service selectee." When she didn't ask for details (somehow it felt dangerous to even discuss rebellions) he took his seat. "Several years in Falcrest at a School of Imperial Service. Then two years on Taranoke, assisting in the census of labor and resources."

Falcrest-educated. She felt a snap of resentment and possessiveness at that. He was four years older, too, but no matter, no matter, it was for the best. In Aurdwynn she would have to command her elders, and the Falcrest-educated. If Muire Lo or anyone else challenged her authority on those grounds, she could always invoke that delightful word *savant*.

"Muire Lo is a Tu Maia name, isn't it?" This said mostly to bait him. She knew how the Maia had risen in the west to rule half the Ashen Sea in centuries past. Legend and linguistics said their children had settled Taranoke long ago.

"Yes, Your Excellence. Aurdwynn's families descend from the Maia and the Stakhieczi, for the most part." He hesitated for an instant, too brief to be an affectation. "If a native eye might be of use, I've prepared a brief survey of the province. At your discretion, of course."

Baru made a small gesture of permission, much more subtle than the relief she felt. How fundamentally satisfying to have a knowledgeable subordinate—like a little auxiliary mind. But she would have to be careful: he had been chosen for her.

They opened a map and tried to remedy Baru's atrocious grasp of geography. "Aurdwynn stretches north to the Wintercrest Mountains," Muire Lo said, tracing the contours of the land with long ink-stained fingers. Bent over the map, some of the self-consciousness had gone out of him. "East to the river Inirein, which can only be bridged here—and—here. West to the old Tu Maia keeps at Unane Naiu, and the desert beyond. And—obviously—"

"The Ashen Sea to the south."

"Quite, Your Excellence."

She traced the facts of stone and water that boxed Aurdwynn, made it small and desirable and impossible to escape—an arena, a cage, a pulpit. Empires had grappled and died here. But whoever ruled Aurdwynn ruled the north of the Ashen Sea, and whoever ruled that piece of sea controlled the seaward approach to Falcrest itself.

The Masquerade ruled from Falcrest and its rule was like an octopus: stealthy, flexible, smart, gripping half the Ashen Sea—but soft, so soft. It had to surround itself in hardness to armor itself against the Oriati and its other rivals. Taranoke in the west, as a fleet base to check the Oriati. And Aurdwynn to the north, as a bastion. . . .

"You were a child when the Masquerade arrived," she said, running her fingers over the landlord-manors of Duchy Erebog, the clay lands that gave Aurdwynn its pottery and its oldest duchess.

Muire Lo kept his eyes on the map. The lamplight shone on the perfumed oil in his dark hair. "Aurdwynn has been a federated province for twenty years. I was two when Xate Yawa—she's the Jurispotence now—killed the old Duke Lachta and arranged our formal surrender."

"But there was a—" If it was foolish to mention rebellion, it was more foolish to shy away from it. "A rebellion. You lived through that."

"The Fools' Rebellion gave up arms when I was twelve. Not even a man. I have always been loyal."

I'm sure you have, Baru thought. I'm sure those early years involved no tumult at all, in Aurdwynn or in your heart.

There was no question Muire Lo had been chosen to watch over her. Everyone was someone else's instrument. But she would have to take him into confidence and use him as a trusted instrument nonetheless. She could afford to make some of her agendas known to Farrier and Farrier's creatures. Far more dangerous to shut him out and deny even the illusion of control.

"They want to hold Aurdwynn because it protects Falcrest and the heartlands." She touched the Wintercrests. "From the Stakhieczi in the north, who could invade by land through Aurdwynn and then east across the river Inirein. And from any rival on the Ashen Sea, who would have to sail clockwise with the trade winds, and follow the coast of Aurdwynn to reach Falcrest."

"*We* want to hold Aurdwynn," Muire Lo said softly. "Your Excellence."

"Thank you." She drummed her fingers on the map, considering both the map and the loyalties of Muire Lo. Exhilaration rose in her: here, before her, a problem of power, a riddle of empire. A chance to show her worth to Cairdine Farrier, whoever he really was, whatever great designs he hinted at. "What a cauldron. What a trap."

Alpine forest and rugged mountain, coastal plain and rich cold fisheries. A land of mineral and animal wealth. An economic dream and a military nightmare: a land of valleys riven by dangerous geography. Cavalry would be king in the lowlands, the key to controlling the Sieroch floodplains and the capital at Treatymont. But in the north, rangers and woodsmen roaming the towering redwood forests would be able to close the roads during summer. In winter there would be no forage to feed an army to chase them.

And the tumult of the geography was nothing next to the politics. "How many times," Baru said, leafing through the parchment, "has your home been invaded?"

"I believe we have lost count."

Five hundred years past, Aurdwynn had been overrun by waves of Stakhieczi and Tu Maia armies, invasion and counterinvasion between two great empires at the peak of their power. The warlords and dukes left behind when the empires collapsed (a mystery Baru's schooling had not touched upon, though one often blamed on unhygienic mating) had settled into uneasy coexistence. A dozen contenders had tried to unify Aurdwynn in the centuries since. A dozen alliances rose to amputate their dreams of a throne.

On the gates of Lachta, the old Stakhieczi outpost that everyone now called Treatymont, the stone bore ancient words—

"Aurdwynn cannot be ruled," Baru murmured.

"*Only the Masquerade can rule Aurdwynn,*" Muire Lo said, eyes still downcast in respect. "The Northgate engraving has been amended."

Why had the civil service exam arranged for her to go *here*? Why had Cairdine Farrier wanted his savant, groomed from childhood, thrown to the wolves?

"Give me the Treaty of Federation." Baru beckoned and Muire Lo searched his folders for his waxed copy of Aurdwynn's treaty with the Empire. She scanned it, lips pursed, chuckling again at the flock of Iolynic signatures that crowded the final page—all the dukes and duchesses of Aurdwynn, Autr through Vultjag, gathered to submit their mutual surrender—until she found the passage rankling at her.

Aurdwynn shall have a Governor, appointed by the Emperor in Falcrest, with power over the legal Imperial military and its garrisons—yes, yes, and so forth—*and who shall serve as liege lord to the dukes and duchesses of Aurdwynn by sworn oath.* Fine.

Aurdwynn shall have a Jurispotence, who shall have power over all the courts, and power to review the law, and who shall oversee the dispersal of cults, the teaching of proper Incrastic thought, and the sanitation of heredity. Falcrest's eye and lash. Not a popular post.

Aurdwynn shall have an Imperial Accountant, who shall have power over foreign and domestic trade, who shall gather the Imperial tax, and disburse Imperial funds as they see fit. And that was her, the purse-watcher. It couldn't be much of a station if they would give it to an exam-fresh stripling technocrat.

Could it?

She steepled her hands and looked up at the ceiling of the tiny slot cabin. "Aurdwynn is a hive of duchies," she said. "We've installed a governor to keep the dukes in line, which is an extraordinary task. So he must either be a despot, who rules with his garrison, or bound up in their politics. Is that fair?"

"Governor Cattlson gives great leeway to the duchies, I am told," Muire

Lo said, "though I am also told this is due to their equally great mutual respect. It is said he rides with Duke Heingyl the Stag Hunter, and that together they hope to find a Falcresti husband for the young lady Heingyl Ri."

"Touching." She traced the borders on the map. "And Aurdwynn must be a barking mutt of bloodlines, full of old faiths and heresies. We have put a Jurispotence on top of all that, who cannot possibly regulate the faiths and marriages of all these valley peasants. So she must have given up on her job, or pursued it zealously. Either she's ineffective and ignored, or effective and despised."

"I could not possibly say whether Her Excellence Xate Yawa is despised—"

"Come now, Muire Lo." She gave him a cross glance. "You're my secretary. I command you to be honest with me. Especially if I'm wrong."

He raised his gaze from the map and the twitch of his lips might have been a very schooled and very subtle smile. "You're not wrong," he said.

Baru leaned back on the creaking oaken bench, staring at the map of Aurdwynn, seeing Taranoke, all the ways they differed, all the ways they were the same. "The dukes have no foreign trading partners," she said, "except the Masquerade, and each other—all the other duchies and valleys. Since they have no central bank or common currency, they use our Imperial fiat notes. The value of those notes depends on foreign trade and the policies of the Fiat Bank."

And she controlled that trade and that bank. She was the Imperial Accountant.

"A cogent assessment, I think," Muire Lo said, quite properly, but she could see in the tightness of his eyes and lips, worried and amused at once, that he had seen just what she had. She controlled not just the purse-strings of the provincial government, but, through the Fiat Bank, the economic prosperity of every duke in Aurdwynn. She could do what the Governor and the Jurispotence could not: keep the dukes in line.

If she played this game as a good Imperial citizen, she would be an effective functionary in an ineffective government.

If she played it well, played for herself, she would be the most powerful person in Aurdwynn.

She made Muire Lo wait while she drummed her fingers on the hardwood and considered her goals.

There had been younger queens. There were younger characters in *The Antler Stone,* in *The Handbook of Manumission,* youth who had played key roles in Falcrest's revolution. Perhaps Cairdine Farrier intended to test his Taranoki find on the grandest scale. Perhaps he had offered her exactly what she wanted.

"Muire Lo," she said, fingers following the web of duchies through the distant forested north, down the tangle of freetowns and landlords that hatcheted the Midlands, out over the grain-rich coast. "Assume that I was sent to Aurdwynn to complete a task—some great difficulty, some problem of rule. What would you expect that problem to be? The economic waste of sharecropping? The ducal debt crisis? What ails your home?"

"Aurdwynn has one great habit, Your Excellence, one constant touchstone, no matter who rules." Her secretary hesitated over the map, his own fingers half-curled, as if of half a mind to draw her hand away from a flame. "Rebellion."

S HE had seven more weeks to prepare as *Lapetiare* leapfrogged up the coast, taking on fresh fruit and meat, exchanging mail and passengers. At sea they ate salted fish and drank beer even in dinners with the captain. The crew submitted to brusque exams from the ship's doctors, a pair of southern Falcresti who kept fanatically to the Incrastic creed of sanitation. Twice a day they all washed in salt water without care for modesty, sailors all hooting and hollering at each other and throwing sponges, as untroubled by each others' nakedness as any Taranoki. What attention Baru got was practical: one woman marine asking after her exercises, a sailor telling her she looked as sleek and mean as a tiger shark, and finally the boatswain, who challenged her to a rope climb (she lost, but loved it).

"Cover your cocks," the men sailors sometimes joked. "They're always hunting sodomites."

"What do they do to sodomites?" Baru asked.

They looked at her with some astonishment. "Hot iron," one said. "Hsssssssssss."

"Thought you would have seen it plenty on your home," another muttered.

Baru shrugged indifferently, to hide the pain of the thought that took her: father Salm dying just that way.

When they harbored, Baru took Muire Lo ashore and dictated diligent notes on everything she could find. In a harbor called Chansee, where the people were astonishingly pale northerners, gregarious and welcoming, they visited a cancer ward. Cairdine Farrier walked the beds, examining melanomas and conditions of the skin, apparently common among the Stakhieczoid racial type in these latitudes. "A troubled line," he said afterward, brow furrowed in concern. "We will have to mate them with themselves, and see if their best traits can be reinforced. Perhaps they can be specialized." He turned on her with sudden enthusiasm. "The Aurdwynni are a mixture of these Stakhi types, Imperial Maia blood, and the fragile Belthyc natives. Perhaps you will have a chance to arrange an experimental marriage. My colleague Hesychast is always looking for new bloodlines to Clarify."

Baru took note of his interest, troubled in her heart. She found his games of heredity and eugenics queasy, invasive, deeply frightening. When he spoke of Incrasticism, she heard Aminata's warning, the terrible fate that awaited the sodomite and the tribadist, and thought: I am a part of this, but I do not have to love it. I only have to play my role. Survive long enough to gather power. Gather enough power to make a difference.

The Masquerade had taught her all the names of sin. But her parents taught her first.

And she knew in her heart, in the habits of her eyes and thoughts, what she was.

The air chilled. Storm petrels paced them as they turned northeast. She went through her notes again and again, committing personalities and legalities and tongue-breaking family lines to memory, dukes and duchesses.

What would it be like to meet these people, stare them down, inflict her will on them? Could she confront the dukes Oathsfire and Lyxaxu, one short and stout as a badger, one tall as redwood, and tell them she would tax their river trade? Would they go whispering to their old northerly rival Erebog, the Crone in Clay, and arrange some revenge? What courage would she need to write to Nayauru Dam-Builder and Ihuake the Cattle Duchess, saying: ah, yes, hello, Nayauru, young and proud and most beloved of your people, and greetings to you, Ihuake, lord of all milk and wool, whose might is a stampede. I see you have worked diligently to divide the rich Midlands of Aurdwynn between you, and to build a great alliance, with three proud dukes as your clients. But no matter that, noble ladies. I have been appointed on grounds of merit, and in the name of distant Falcrest I am here to take your wealth.

She risked the wrath of those *born* to power.

And, too, there were strange gaps in her notes. The Phantom Duke of Lachta, who ruled Treatymont in name alone—nobility without power or presence. Who was he?

Why, too, did she have the names of the previous Imperial Accountants, Su Olonori and Ffare Tanifel before him, but no reason for their dismissal? Why was there no mention of existing staff waiting for her? Surely there would be a staff—the Imperial Republic ran on bureaucracy and a bureaucracy needed *staff*—

"What does the Empire of the Mask fear most in Aurdwynn?" she asked Cairdine Farrier.

He looked pleased. "Parliament, as ever, fears a poor tax season." He leaned in conspiratorially. "But those who see farther remember certain . . . troubles our regime has encountered. Difficulties that may not yet be wholly mastered. Aurdwynn has such a deep and fractious history . . . it is difficult to fit those pieces together into something that will not break again."

"What happened to the prior Accountant, Su Olonori?" she asked. "And Ffare Tanifel?"

He smiled tauntingly. "Nothing a wool merchant would know."

And then, on the scheduled morning, they came to Treatymont harbor. Baru came on deck to see stern stonework and blackened iron, towers set against far white mountains that scraped the bottom of the sky. Caged beauty.

The Horn Harbor waited for them, its two sentinel towers burnt and shattered by the Masquerade navy twenty years past, left to stand like dead men. A pair of great torchships in Masquerade red guarded the harbor mouth and from them came the clamor of bells, welcoming *Lapetiare* to port, congratulating her on making good time, beating out some code spoken only by captains and admirals: *riots ashore,* perhaps, or *pirate waters,* or *all well.*

She stood at the prow of the ship while Muire Lo fussed over her. "They prefer women gowned. You could pass as native, you know. You have good

Maia skin, if not the Maia nose. But if you want to make a statement—well, the trousers will do—"

She let him tug at the cuffs and buttons of her jacket. She'd abandoned her practice blade, thinking it childish, but the symbolic chained purse strapped to her side did not pair well with an empty scabbard.

"Lieutenant Aminata," she called.

They hadn't spoken at any length since embarkation. Baru had avoided her studiously during the riotous bathing-times. Aminata approached with a sailor's rolling, casual gait, her uniform jacket loose in defiance of the cold. "Your Excellence," she said, without apparent sarcasm. "Can I help you?"

"I need a blade. One suitable for—" She gestured to the city spread before them, its narrow stone streets. "Such close conditions."

"The officer's boarding saber, Your Excellence." Aminata drew her own sword and offered it, head inclined, eyes politely downcast. "Single-edged. Falcrest forged. A symbol of Imperial power. Will it do?"

Baru considered the woman and the sword, her expression carefully neutral, mind racing through permutations of etiquette and plot, trying to sense some meaning here: was it a traditional gift between lovers? Some insult in her ancestral Oriati Mbo? A reminder of where her loyalties had to lie—or a question of the same? Had Aminata and Cairdine Farrier spoken since Taranoke? What could it mean if she took the blade, or if she refused it?

Aminata waited, head bowed, legs braced against the slow rock of the ship, the blade balanced between her two open palms.

"It will do," Baru said. "Thank you, Lieutenant." She took the saber and sheathed it. Too short for this scabbard, but no matter. Other scabbards could be had.

"Good luck, Your Excellence," Aminata said. She turned smartly and returned to her duties.

MUIRE Lo went first, to see to the handling of luggage and papers, and then Baru took the second skiff ashore and presented herself. Her stomach bobbed with the harbor chop. She was eighteen, foreign, a woman—and here in Aurdwynn they did not even pretend that this was not a disadvantage to the ambitious. She was alone.

The proper place of a Taranoki, she imagined Cairdine Farrier saying, looking back on the disastrous failure of the Imperial Accountant in Aurdwynn, *is among a large extended family, in a restricted environment, where her natural limitations can be overcome—*

She stood and went to the front of the skiff, defying the spray and the roll of surf, and set one booted foot up on the prow. If she was going to throw up, she decided that she would do it now; and when nothing came she resolved to believe it would not happen at all.

They came to the quay. Baru caught a ladder and lifted herself up before the sailors had even roped the skiff. The waiting party looked at her in surprise as she clambered up like a common sailor, purse and sword banging awkwardly beneath her.

They stared at her for a moment and she felt them measuring her, this savant they must have been warned of: just a tall usefully built islander girl with warm brown skin and dark eyes (intent, Pinion would say, always so *intent*), competent and strong in her motions and yet always, Aminata had complained, so impatient.

"Gentlemen," she said, because she'd given no one a chance to announce her, "and ladies: I am the Imperial Accountant."

The governor of Aurdwynn looked like his portrait in the books: tall, muscular, pale, chin a jutting prow. The kind of man they respected here. "Your Excellence Baru Cormorant," he said, taking her hand, beaming out from beneath an awful or majestic (she wasn't sure) wolf's head cap. "A pleasure. You are certainly vigorous."

"Governor Cattlson, Your Excellence, I am honored." In the Imperial Republic all civil servants got the same honorific, in the spirit of post-revolutionary fraternity. She matched his grip and smiled easily, oh so easily. She would manage this.

"Ah, at last, at last," said the next in the party, standing between Cattlson and the column of Masquerade regulars in their blue and gray tunics. "Please—if I may—"

Jurispotence Xate Yawa took Baru's hand and kissed it delicately. Her silver hair fell over a formidable collared gown. She was an Aurdwynn native, some admixture of Stakhieczi and Maia blood. And she had done such mighty work, work Baru had studied with respect—twenty years ago, as the common-born assassin of the old Duke Lachta, she'd ripped out the heart of the resistance and arranged her nation's surrender to the Masquerade invaders. This station was her reward. Her brother

Xate Olake had been given Duchy Lachta, but he ruled in name alone, a ghost of rumors and supposition. Lachta had been taken by the Masquerade so thoroughly that now even the native-born called it Treatymont.

"That is how we greet a lady here." Xate Yawa straightened to beam at Baru. "Ah, so fresh! So full of promise! Climbing docks in trousers—I remember having that fire."

"Jurispotence Xate, Your Excellency, I am honored," Baru said, and marked the woman an enemy: her greeting had started at *foreign,* gone to *woman,* then *young,* and last of all to a reminder of what Xate had done. It was a subtle strike, maybe only a petty snipe from a petty mind. More likely a probe to test Baru's vigilance.

She held the woman's gaze and let her mind chase a sudden stabbing intuition.

Aurdwynn has one great habit.

Baru met the cold blue jungle-crow eyes of the Jurispotence of Aurdwynn and realized that the phantom crisis might be very, very close at hand. She'd assumed Xate Yawa would be weak, ineffectual, powerless to control a rising insurrection. But there were other alternatives, weren't there? Perhaps she wanted the opposite of control. . . .

"Young, but so qualified!" came a third voice.

Cairdine Farrier beamed out from behind Governor Cattlson's wolf's head. "I thought I'd come ashore with the first skiff," he said, "and make sure everything was ready! And oh, they are excited, Your Excellence— they know about your staggering performance on the civil service exam. So precocious, such a sterling find—you are the youngest Imperial Accountant appointed in several decades! Merit, after all, is our greatest concern in these things!"

He clapped the Jurispotence on her frail shoulder, seized Governor Cattlson's wrist as if to bring them together in some kind of dance, and looked between them with feverish intensity. "She could go so many places, if she succeeds in addressing our—difficulties here," he said, still beaming. "Please do give her every opportunity."

And Baru noted, to her disquiet, that Governor Cattlson barely checked a gesture: a polite, deferential bow, as that of an officer to a superior.

4

THEY had horse-drawn carriages waiting, one in black oak and iron for Xate Yawa, one with wire enamel in white and gold for her. "Horses!" Baru exclaimed, delighted. "They're enormous! Please—excuse me, Governor, Jurispotence, I simply must."

She went to them, marveling at their saddled strength, the atlas of muscle and ligament splayed out beneath their chestnut hides, the shoes *nailed* directly into their hooves. Cairdine Farrier spoke to Governor Cattlson behind her, delighted in his own way: "There is no higher terrestrial life on Taranoke, you see, and she is so curious."

Baru circled the beasts, skittish around their teeth and hindquarters, thinking all the while: they must have been ridden by Tu Maia warriors—Aurdwynn had no native horses, nor the Stakhieczi to the north—and bred down the centuries for the cold and for warfare. Thus their size, their notorious hunger. They were weapons and symbols, ostentatious and huge.

They'd been bred to serve for generations.

She looked toward Cairdine Farrier, drawn by the thought. But there was a stallion between them.

"You must learn to ride," Governor Cattlson called to her across the span of the drive team. "The coastal dukes built their power on cavalry. They respect a good rider. My friend Duke Heingyl conducts all his business on the hunt."

She ducked to eye him beneath the horse's belly. "You must be an expert, then."

He patted the horse's flank and grinned boyishly. "Talented enough to teach. If you can find a minute for leisure, that is! Cairdine Farrier speaks so highly of your dedication. Please, Your Excellence, your carriage. You'll need time to change before the dinner."

She watched him mount his own charger, feigning interest in his technique, trying to play for time so she could study Cairdine Farrier's by-play with Xate Yawa. But Farrier's chatter only seemed to bore the Jurispotence. If she feared or respected Farrier, she could hide it well.

Cattlson knew who Cairdine Farrier really was. But the Jurispotence, Falcrest's spymaster and judge in Aurdwynn, *didn't*. Because of her blood? Or did Falcrest share Baru's suspicions—that their Jurispotence might have her own agenda?

Xate Yawa vanished into her carriage. It closed around her like a gauntlet.

Baru let her doorman help her up into her own ride. She found Muire Lo waiting—"Your Excellence," he said, head bowed—but took a minute to latch the door and check the passenger cabin for vents before she spoke.

"I'm going to make a list of questions. You're going to start answering them while I waste my time at this gala they've set up. Do you have something to write on?"

"I have an excellent memory," he offered. The stagecoach jerked into motion beneath them.

"That makes it seem like I have something to hide, Muire Lo, and if you're keeping watch over me for someone else—which I assume you must be—I want to assure them I am not a woman given to intrigue." She had already begun to cluck (just like her mother) at his hurt, had already prepared some reassuring blandishment, when she saw that his only response was a sage nod. She sat back in the seat and decided that her secretary had to be more competent and more dangerous than she'd assumed.

"Your office is in the Governor's House." Muire Lo splayed a sheaf of marble-cream paper. "The letters that described a separate office for the Imperial Accountant are out of date. All Imperial functions have been centralized in one location. For efficiency, I'm told."

Baru crooked a brow and waited for him to speak past the double-talk.

"I have heard suggestions that there may have been a problem of security at the previous office."

"Well," she said, "put that down as the first question I want answered." It would have been the first anyway, the most pressing threat: *precisely what happened to the last Imperial Accountant?*

"I sense some urgency?"

She would need to bring him a little ways into her confidence. "I have become concerned," she said, rearranging the chained purse, "that we are surrounded by conspiracy."

"But we've only met Imperial functionaries, Your Excellency."

She laughed at that. "If you wanted to seed conspiracy, where else would you be?"

Hooves clattered outside. Baru drew back the curtains, expecting to see Governor Cattlson showing off for her, or a Masquerade armsman moving past. But the charger pacing the carriage was stark white, the color of snow on volcanic stone, cantering alongside at a spear's reach. The woman riding wore a leather tabard, shoulders mailed in stark ornamental iron. Baru marked the spurs, the towering charger, the minimalist display of wealth, and guessed she must be minor nobility—some feudal landlord?

The rider stood in her stirrups, displaying the casual strength of good health and a rich diet, and turned to meet Baru's gaze. Impressions in a flash—fierce, aquiline nose, broken and reset. Skin in Maia tones of copper and fallow soil, so close to the Taranoki phenotype but for the high cheekbones and proud nose. A smile that still had all its teeth.

A duchess, then. Maybe an important one. Ihuake? Nayauru? Would the influential Duchess of Cattle or the fiery young Dam-builder have come down from the Midlands to show the colors for their proud alliance?

The rider considered her through the caged glass of the carriage window, her smile narrow and lopsided, and then spurred her mount ahead.

Baru settled herself on the bench with the uneasy sense she was prey.

THE Governor's House stood not a quarter mile from harborside, an edict in iron and granite, gates guarded by Masquerade marines in red tabards and steel masks and gauntlets sleeved like a surgeon's sterile garb. The stone of the compound wall had been acid-etched clean.

The Imperial Accountant got her own square tower, her quarters at the very peak. "The ball will expect you at the end of the afternoon watch," the steward that escorted her up informed her, and took her leave.

"You'll be painfully late if you arrive then," Muire Lo warned her. "There will be drinking, introduction, and politics beforehand. If you miss it, all they will talk about is your age and the rumors of your homeland. Someone's trying to embarrass you."

"I should think." Baru threw open the doors between the waiting room and the audience hall. "Look at this place."

The tapestries and carpets told stories of embroidered figures doing battle on horseback and in bristling phalanxes. "Get some staff and tear it all down," Baru ordered. "The carpets, too."

"They are likely quite expensive—"

"All the better. I want to look like a common-born provincial with no idea what wealth means. Wrap the whole waiting room in an anchor and chain, I don't care." She flipped through a stack of palimpsest at the secretary's desk. "Get anything with written Iolynic out of here, too—or Urun, or Stakhi, anything I don't speak. I need to look self-conscious about it. Post a sign demanding that all business, verbal and written, be conducted in Aphalone. The whole city will think I can't speak anything but."

"Your Excellence, you *can't* speak anything but."

"I'll learn." Her childhood Urunoki was a descendant of Maia Urun, and the Iolynic creole that the Aurdwynni often spoke would follow from there. She perched on the edge of the redwood desk. "Tell me about this ball. What do I need to do to save myself?"

He pursed his lips, rather like a displeased aunt. "You will need a gown. A woman in Aurdwynn simply cannot attend a formal function in trousers. And unless you wish to make a reputation as a sailor, you should bathe and find a wig, both of which will require some time. As a representative of the Imperial Republic you are expected to have a formal half-mask."

"I can bathe myself. Find me my mask and something modest to wear and have it brought up—no, bring it up yourself, I don't know the staff yet, and you've had chance enough to be improper on the ship. Forget the wig, I'll go ship-headed. Then—" She paused in thought. "Then go to the master-at-arms and find out what happened to the last Imperial Accountant. I'll see if the stories they tell me at dinner align with what you learn."

She scrubbed herself raw with pumice in the bath (from Taranoke? it could be), then made herself modest by Masquerade standards and allowed Muire Lo to guide her through the technicalities of the darted damask gown he'd found. The half-mask they'd made for her, porcelain and as featurelessly white as the fabric, fit awkwardly—the craftsmen had assumed Falcresti features and a smaller brow. But it would do. She was a technocrat now, a gear in the great machine, and when she performed that function she would need a mask.

If it troubled Muire Lo's pride or modesty to dress her, he hid it masterfully. "Good luck, Your Excellence," he offered. She waved him off, too tense to walk the line between confident poise and formal etiquette.

No time to wait in the annex. Straight onto the board. If Aurdwynn *did* teeter on the edge of uprising, if the rebels knew the power the Imperial Accountant wielded—

It would explain what had happened to the last two names to hold the station.

She buckled on her scabbard and the chained purse. They did not match the gown, but her short hair and heavy boots had already ruined that. After a moment's consideration, she laughed at herself and left the scabbard and sword beneath her bed. Then she went down the tower, breathing slowly and easily, working her fingers one by one into the white elbow-length gloves that had come with the gown.

A Falcresti servingman in exquisitely applied makeup greeted her at the ballroom door. "Your Excellence. Shall I announce you?"

"Please," she said, and waited to hear what he would say with her eyes closed behind the mask and her heart clotted shut. Just this one last moment of weakness. Just the one.

"The Imperial Accountant!" he called. "Her Excellence Baru Cormorant!"

SHE went in through the wide door and the crowd pressed in around her, pale Stakhi and Maia like the rider she had seen and every shade in between, a shout of whispers in Iolynic passing among them. Governor Cattlson waited across the room, Xate Yawa unmistakable in a brilliant ice-blue gown by his side, a stern man in deerskin and leather behind them—Duke Heingyl, surely. Safety there, at the Governor's table. But the distance between them was a crater. She could feel eyes on her like sunglare, and at once wanted water.

"Governor," she said, nodding into the hush. "Jurispotence. Dukes and duchesses. Your Excellencies of the Judiciary." The nobility in the crowd were motley, variegated, Masquerade judges clustered among them like rooks. "I look forward to knowing all of you as well as I know your account books."

Nervous laughter broke out. She tried to judge the geography of the crowd, to map alliances and circles—was that Duke Unuxekome the Sea Groom, rumored to be a pirate, watching her with clever eyes? But her throat closed at the sight of so many faces. With slow deliberation, she stepped down to the ballroom floor and turned away from Governor Cattlson and the Jurispotence, saying to herself and the crowd: *I do not need them yet.*

But to her horror she found the crowd withdrawing from her, turning back to its circles and cliques.

She caught the eyes of Xate Yawa across the room, hooded in her own black half-mask, and fixing on her own name heard, quite distinctly, the words: *"Baru? I suspect no one wants to be the one to tell her."*

Someone touched her arm. She leapt only a little. "Welcome to Aurdwynn," murmured the voice in her ear: a woman, her Aphalone accented. Baru turned and found herself face-to-face with the rider with the broken nose, still in her tabard and jodhpurs, her cheeks painted in red slashes and her long black hair bound up. "You should have ridden, not taken the carriage. Men like Heingyl Stag Hunter already expect you to be weak."

Baru set herself across from the woman, giving herself space as curious onlookers began to gather. "I've been offered riding lessons," she said, careful to press any accent from her own tongue.

"By Cattlson himself, I'm sure." The horsewoman smiled faintly. "I'm sure he'd love to ride with you." Someone in the crowd tittered.

Baru didn't understand Aurdwynn well enough to find her footing here. What was scandalous? Proper and improper? There was too much to grasp, too many cultures, too many eyes—but forget all that. Breathe. Focus on the woman in the riding leathers, the woman with the lopsided smile, and on her own strengths.

"Duchess," she said, trusting in her earlier guess to impress the onlookers. "You're a talented rider. Perhaps I'd be better off learning from you."

The crowd murmured. The duchess tapped the back of one gloved finger against her glass and made it ring softly: a salute of sorts. "Tain Hu," she said. "Duchess Vultjag."

Vultjag—Baru couldn't remember the details of that estate, but she recognized the Stakhi word and tried to pry it apart into cognates. Jag? Something about a forest, so her estates must be far north. She had Maia features and a Maia name, a Stakhi title, a sharp tongue—odds were she was not a friend of the Masquerade in Aurdwynn. Probably here to sniff for weakness, like a wolf after the sick.

Answer weakness with strength. Look for her allies.

"Duchess Vultjag. My pleasure." Baru stepped into the little circle between them and—to the crowd's delighted shock—cupped the duchess Tain Hu's chin in one gloved hand. "Your bones speak to Maia blood, but you have Stakhi in your ducal name. And here you are, a forest lord trapped in the city. All the paradoxes of Aurdwynn bound up in one woman. I think I could learn a great deal from your lessons, Tain Hu. And perhaps in exchange I could take you to Falcrest and show you to the polymaths, as an exemplar of your kind."

The crowd hushed. Baru wondered how she must look, in her barren white gown, her bone-white mask, her long gloves the color of snow.

Tain Hu smiled between Baru's thumb and forefinger. "You have never been to Falcrest."

"Not yet."

Tain Hu cocked her head, eyes narrowed, and opened her lips as if to speak; but she said nothing, and left Baru suddenly conscious of those unpainted lips, those fierce dark eyes, the slow surge of her breath. She could see the black silk shapes of Masquerade judges among the crowd, and understood Tain Hu's move. *A foreigner,* they would whisper, *from a land of certain crimes—*

"Show care," the Duchess Vultjag murmured. "The Jurispotence is always watching, and her Cold Cellar is always hungry."

"The Jurispotence is my colleague."

Tain Hu's smile widened between Baru's fingertips

Somewhere behind them a quartet of musicians began to play a piece on oboe and plucked lute. Baru released her grip and turned away, heart pounding. "Governor Cattlson!" she called, preferring the appearance of retreat to disaster at Tain Hu's hands. "You have a challenger on horseback!"

The crowd laughed, delighted and scandalized, and while Cattlson—red-faced and tipsy—roared something about hunting, Baru saw the Jurispotence Xate Yawa, smiling beneath her black half-mask, exchanging glances with Tain Hu. Saw the pirate duke Unuxekome nodding silently to a bearded man at his side.

And there in that glance across the ballroom, in the factions and complicities it implied, Baru heard the old carving: *Aurdwynn cannot be ruled.*

From all the possible configurations of maneuver and intrigue, feeding on the map and the history she'd learned and the hints Farrier had dropped and the menace in Xate Yawa's greeting, on Tain Hu's name and presence and smile, Baru's intuition plucked the most dangerous scenario and offered it up.

The rebellion was not coming. It was here, among the dukes, in the very heart of the provincial government. Rising. She had no proof, no evidence, no axis of action. But *it was here.*

THEY sat for dinner at long hardwood tables heavy with venison and duck and buttered squash, golden breads and dumplings stuffed with veal. Baru fumbled with chopsticks over food her stomach had never met. She ate little, Governor Cattlson to her right, Jurispotence Xate Yawa across from her, pleading caution to each of them—"I'll need a week to settle my palate and digestion with these new spices, it's a scientific fact"—and wondering all the while: *I suspect no one wants to be the one to tell her,* Xate Yawa had said. Tell her *what?* Something to do with the last Accountant, the one she'd replaced?

So when dessert came and Governor Cattlson roared for more wine, she asked.

"What!?" Cattlson bellowed, eyes wide, voice pitched to shout above an absent gale. "You weren't told?"

"How curious." Xate Yawa poured the Governor another glass, her veined hands steady. She had a light voice, untroubled, and she used it without hurry. "One would expect the new Imperial Accountant might be given such important information."

"You're perfectly safe," Cattlson insisted, thumping the table. "Between the marines and the walls of the House, you cannot be reached. Not like that dockside whorehouse where Olonori worked—we should've given up on it after Tanifel, but Olonori insisted he had to be near the ships."

"Excuse me." Baru rubbed the rim of her half-mask where it met the skin. "What happened to Tanifel and Olonori?"

"His Excellency Su Olonori was murdered." Xate Yawa smiled graciously, as if in apology for a matter of decorum. "Cut apart in his bed.

Please don't fear, though, our retaliation was harsh and precise. And he was only here because Her Excellency Ffare Tanifel, who came before him—"

"Was a *traitor*." Cattlson's fist rattled glasses all the way to the far end of the table. "A corrupt and perfidious slattern. Yawa put her on trial and I had her drowned. To think! The Throne's taxes trickling out into those woods, probably all the way north to the Stakhi in their rat dens—"

"Oh," Baru said, understanding. Tanifel, native-born, had gone over to the brewing rebellion, and the Masquerade had killed her for it. And then Olonori (an Oriati name, he would have been a foreigner and harder to corrupt) had refused to go over, and the rebels had killed him in turn.

Where was Cairdine Farrier? Shouldn't he have been at the ball? When he had spoken on the docks—*our difficulties here*—had he known?

She'd never had wine before. "Jurispotence," she said, smiling as well as she could manage. "Just one glass, please."

Ducal representatives came to greet her, their petitions disguised as compliments. *We wish to discuss matters of inheritance law, and the taxation of landlords,* Duchess Nayauru's seneschal murmured, and then some man from Oathsfire, the Duke of Mills, right on her heels asking after *transit taxes along the Inirein.* Then Duke Heingyl in his hunting garb, cold and plainly hostile except when he introduced his daughter, Ri, a tiny woman with sharp fox eyes and elaborate jewelry who made her father's hands tighten with some kind of wary protective love. "Your Excellence," Ri murmured, kissing Baru's hand. "It is a difficult station for a foreigner. I hope no one will regret your appointment. Least of all you."

"You are gracious," Baru said, rather daftly—the wine made her feel like her thoughts echoed, and Ri's eyes were damnably disarming.

"There are worthy young minds in Aurdwynn too. Savants of our own." The Stag Duke's eyes smiled whenever he glanced at his daughter, and froze again when they went to Baru. "We hope the Imperial Republic has not forgotten them."

Baru had to lift her chin to meet his eyes. "I welcome their correspondence."

"I have concerns about the stability of the Midlands. Tensions of infrastructure and inheritance between Nayauru and Ihuake." Ri released Baru's hand, smiling softly. "Doubtless you will swiftly detect and resolve them."

Baru, distracted by Duke Heingyl's unblinking armored stare, made no reply.

She should have been attentive. But she could barely understand their accented Aphalone, barely focus on their words when all she wanted to do was look into their eyes and guess—

Loyalist? Rebel? Or waiting for your chance to choose?

A FTER the ball, Muire Lo returned from the master-at-arms and confirmed what she'd learned. Su Olonori, Baru's immediate predecessor, had been murdered in his bed by parties unknown.

Fine. Mortal danger: an incentive to set everything else in order. Her job in Aurdwynn was to make sure tax and trade money went to Falcrest, where Parliament seemed intent on banking for renewed war with the Oriati federations.

One task at a time.

At dawn the next morning she dressed, washed, rang Muire Lo for breakfast, and sat down in her new office with a caged candle to sort through the Imperial Accounts. Parliament—or Cairdine Farrier and his *colleagues*—had given her this high station even knowing Aurdwynn was unstable. Therefore there would be an extensive staff for her, the kind of support that would cushion her youth and inexperience.

But no—she found disaster.

Su Olonori had been so eager to clear out Ffare Tanifel's corruption that he'd sacked the entire Accountant's staff. Meticulously paranoid, he'd kept his own books, working in incomprehensible shorthand that defied both double-entry protocol and any clear mathematical sense.

There should have been ledgers for every key entity in Aurdwynn: the Imperial Trade Factor and its all-important Fiat Bank, the Judiciary, the provincial government and its suborgans, and most critically, each duke and duchess. These books would record a web of debt and credit, and from this web she could map out the arrangement of power in Aurdwynn. No ship could be hired, no land developed, no army raised without some money changing hands. These books were Baru's spyglass, her map, her sword and edict.

But all that depended on having good books. She could barely sort Su Olonori's ledgers by date, let alone subject or point of origin. Nor was there anyone to ask for help. His staff ledger listed only a personal secretary and a few housekeepers on the payroll. Before his murder, he had managed the Imperial Accounts alone.

A scrap of parchment in Su Olonori's fevered handwriting fell from the records: *V. much land sale?* Then a run of Oriati text; he had lapsed into his home tongue.

Someone knocked on the door. She went and opened it.

"You should just say 'come,' Your Excellence. In Falcrest I mastered the ways of doors." Muire Lo brought the tray of breakfast to her desk. "I'm assembling a cold-weather wardrobe for you—I got a sense of your measurements while dressing you. And the Governor wishes to know if you'll be joining him for lunch."

"I think I will." She clapped Su Olonori's master ledger down on the desk. "Find a literate Oriati speaker and hire her. I need these books carted down to the basement and translated into Aphalone."

"These are the key ledgers, Your Excellence." Muire Lo hopped back a half step in a kind of avian alarm. "You can't conduct business without them."

"I'm going to start new ledgers. This will mean a great deal of travel. Find me a carriage and a driver." She knifed a grapefruit and managed to spray Muire Lo with the juice. "Sorry—and that reminds me, find me Cairdine Farrier and make him an appointment. When that's done, we're going to need to start hiring a staff. I'll need trustworthy people and that means I need the Jurispotence's advice, so make her an appointment as well."

"Your Excellence, perhaps the Governor should approach the Jurispotence—"

"We are the Imperial Accountant's office!" she snapped, angry at the mess she had inherited, at the time and effort it would waste to sort it all out, at the distant technocrati who had looked over her service exam and judged this a useful application of her talents. "We will not sit here like schoolchildren and beg for appointments. We control the payrolls, Muire Lo, and that means *they* work for *me*. Remind them of that."

"That is bluster, Your Excellence," he said softly, "and they will be quick to challenge it."

"All I have is bluster." She swore at the grapefruit and tore a dripping length of meat from it. It came apart into sticky ruin in her hands. "These books say nothing. The Fiat Bank could be printing money and loaning it to the dukes as toiletry and I would be blind to it. I cannot prosecute with that two-faced Jurispotence in control of the courts, and after Olonori's death I cannot even sleep easy in my own bed—"

I don't want this! she almost shouted. I want Falcrest and telescopes, proofs of geometry and the fluorescence of certain sea life! I want to know the world, not these sordid little people in their shattered little land!

I want to save my home!

But she bit down on her own temper and wiped her palms on the hips of her gown. Muire Lo grimaced pointedly at that—a kind of charming little puncture in his deferential composure. "You are, at the very least, an officer of the Imperial Republic, masked and armed with the technocrat's mark. Not a provincial auxiliary."

"So?" She pushed his suggestions around in her head, trying to put them together in some useful way. "I am a ranked officer and can request the aid of Imperial forces. I suppose I could use them to make a show of strength. But Governor Cattlson is the legal commander of Aurdwynn's garrisons. Why would he give his troops to"—she slipped into self-pity here, for one or two brief syllables—"an untested islander girl?"

Muire Lo offered a linen napkin for the grapefruit. He'd folded it into a perfect triangle, like a lateen sail. "Our frigate *Lapetiare* is still in port," he said, "and will not sail for a week."

"Oh," she said, straightening. "*Oh.*"

5

SHE wrote a letter to *Lapetiare*'s captain, and then—impatient now, eager to pursue this new avenue—went to her scheduled lunch with Cattlson.

He had a beautiful dining room, flooded with light through walls of small paned windows set in redwood. With the light she expected warmth, but no: she sat shivering. Aurdwynn was cold. The cold made her want to move. She wanted to get back to her office, or to the harbor, and keep constructing her plan.

It was only when Cattlson had finished his third glass of wine that she realized this, too, could be part of that plan.

"We're here to help them," he said, staring at his hive of windows, at the huddled city beyond. "I write it in every report to Falcrest. I see it in all the statistics from Census and Methods. The wealth we feed the dukes to keep them happy drips down to their peasantry. We're helping them. But we could be helping them more."

She drank politely. "Should we be pressing Parliament for a policy change?"

"Parliament." He snorted. "Parliament is a theater for the mob. The Throne sets these imperatives." He stood abruptly, going to the windows, leaving Baru alone at the wide table.

The Throne. The Masked Emperor. Could Cairdine Farrier be the sovereign, unmasked? No. Absurd.

"It's the burden of empire." He touched the window glass, hand splayed. "We know how to help them best . . . and sometimes we have to help them a little less right now, so that we can help them a little more later. Does that make sense to you, my fellow Excellence?"

"No," she said, trying to bait him into seeing her as a student, a daughter. "Everything the Masquerade brought to Taranoke helped us."

"Taranoke!" He laughed. "I hear all sorts of things from itinerant Cairdine Farrier—boasts of warm winters and easy women." At this he frowned sharply, as if he had just delivered a rebuke, or reined in a bother-some new mount. He had a square face, a strong jaw, skin the color of weathered oak, and Baru quibbled for a moment over the feeling that this man chosen by Parliament had no design to conceal, no machinations to guard—just a plain honesty, too naked to last. That could be a clever camouflage.

He continued. "If you'll forgive me, my lady, I mean no slight. But this is not Taranoke, you see? This is a cold and grudging land. Every valley's got a duke, and a lot of starving muddy serfs rooting in the earth for their shallow livelihoods. Their children die—the polymaths tell me that they're all used to losing one in three, and assure me that as a result they don't love them at all. But I've seen the mothers weeping. One in three! In a good winter!"

She didn't know how to answer this. Child rearing on Taranoke had been safe, communal, full of fathers and warmth. She took another short drink and listened.

Cattlson set his shoulders and raised himself erect. His wolfskin mantle gathered in troubled bunches. "I want to teach them sanitation. I want to extend the roads, give them better crops, send a hygienist to every village. I want everyone in Aurdwynn to have a bar of *soap*. But if the peasants are happy and safe, the duchies will not fear rebellion. If the duchies do not fear rebellion, we cannot rule them. And if we cannot rule the duchies by fear of rebellion, Parliament asks, what shield will we have if the Stakhieczi come south over the mountains again?"

What similar calculus did they make on Taranoke? Had they let the plagues run rampant, saving inoculant only for the children they planned to steal away? Had they—but she could dwell on this later. She'd had time enough to obsess over it in school. "Rule demands harsh arithmetic."

"Arithmetic." He chuckled joylessly. "Do you know what I want from my station? I want to see the children of Heingyl and Radaszic at hunts, not funerals. I want to find a good husband for Heingyl Ri, observe the resulting bloodlines, present a nice report to the Committee on Incras-tic Thought. Instead I hear: *keep them divided and afraid, so they need us.* Do you know how I made a loyal brother of Duke Heingyl? I showed him I could give his children the world. But Parliament says—*let the children rot.*"

He would take bad news poorly with his temper up, but she went ahead anyway, hoping to make him angry about something smaller. "Our master accounts have been poorly kept. I'll have to rebuild them from local statements. With your understanding, I'm going to begin at the Fiat Bank, to be sure the trunk's solid before we move on to the branches."

"Whatever you please." He leaned his brow against the windows. "You'll see to the arithmetic Farrier says you're so talented at. Xate Yawa will chase their little ykari cults and drunken sodomites like a mad dog. And I'll send the letters home: *we are helping them.*"

"I'm concerned about the possibility of revolt."

"You're new." He sounded impossibly weary. "Aurdwynn threatens revolt the way a jealous mistress flirts. You'll grow accustomed to it."

Baru could not permit herself to feel sorry for the man. He was close to her, and weak. "This is dangerous talk," she said. "It could harm you, in the wrong ears."

She'd made a threat, hadn't she?

He stiffened, drew breath to speak, and was silent. "Cairdine Farrier was right," he said, after a time. "You *are* precocious."

"Your Excellence, I must attend to business at the harbor."

"Go, go." He did not turn. "I'm leaving tomorrow to hunt with Duke Heingyl."

"We'll have to ride together when you return," she said, trying to be patient, to offer him a salve for his pride. But his shoulders slumped: shame, or something enough like it that he would not answer.

S HE had already sent word ahead to *Lapetiare,* sealing the missive with her technocrat's mark. When her carriage came harborside she found the marines already ashore, ranked in red like a leash of foxes come up out of a forest of salt and mast, faceless in their enameled steel masks.

Gulls called over the soft whickering of her carriage team as she dismounted. To her limited surprise, it was Lieutenant Aminata who took her hand and helped her down from the carriage. "Your Excellence. We await your command."

Baru took a breath of salty harbor air and put thoughts of home out of her mind. "Is my authority clear?"

"The captain recognizes your authority. Without direct orders from the Province Admiral, we report to the highest-ranking Imperial factor ꞏre."

"Good. Unless we meet the Governor or the Jurispotence, your orders come from me—and if we do, you bring them to me and I make myself clear to them, understood?" She tugged on the wrists of her woolen over-coat, itching at the heavy fabric. Aminata waited in silence as she checked her belt, first the symbolic chained purse, then her sword.

One last breath. "Fall in, then. I'll lead the way."

Every bit of power she wielded in Aurdwynn stemmed from money. Most of that money was now Masquerade fiat paper, backed only by care-ful monetary policy. Any idiot at the provincial Fiat Bank could ruin the value of the fiat note by printing too many or too few, and without her ledgers, she had no way to keep that idiot in check.

"Where to, Your Excellence?" Aminata fell into step beside her, and on her heels the column of marines snapped into easy cadence.

"We're going to the Fiat Bank," she said, "to conduct an audit."

"And you need marines for that?"

She allowed herself a little smile for Lieutenant Aminata's benefit. "I don't need marines for the audit," she said. "I need marines to tell them not to trifle with the auditor."

And to demonstrate to the eyes watching from Treatymont's alleys and stone arcades that the new Accountant had full command of her powers.

BEFORE the Masquerade seized Lachta and made it Treatymont, the Fiat Bank had been a huntsman's hall, full of hardwood rafters and smoky charm. They'd left the stag heads up on the walls, and Baru con-sidered them with a certain fascination, counting the branches of their antlers.

"Pointed horse," she said. "They're pointed horses."

"Excuse me?" the man at her side croaked.

The Treatymont garrison kept a unit of regulars on guard here, their loyalty doubtless gilded by performance bonuses, but where they'd bristled at the column of *Lapetiare* marines gathered in the plaza out-side, one impatient wave of her purse—the technocrat's seal glaring at them from the steel chain—melted their line. Now Aminata and a file of marines stood watch over the exits as Baru wrote out her requests.

All ledgers, general and specific. Make copies for yourself, and
    provide me the originals.

All orders to and receipts from the moneyprinters. Make copies,
    provide me the originals.
All account standings, as above—
A hand count of all physical holdings by my officers—

The Principal Factor for the Aurdwynn Provincial Fiat Bank stood beside her and his makeup ran with his sweat. Bel Latheman was a handsome man by Falcresti eyes, young, by all reports talented, and dressed in such exquisite fashion that she took it as a sign of honesty— no one would advertise corruption so blatantly, would they?

She hadn't asked for his papers and marks. It would give the impression that this was personal.

Save for the quiet sound of her pen, silence took the floor. The clerks and factors sat stiffly under the eyes of the marines. She found it hard, very hard, not to savor their faces, each and individually, like candies in a rack—all united in trepidation, all afraid that she might find *something*, guilty or innocent—

Maybe this was how the teachers had felt. Maybe this was how Diline had felt.

"I admire your animal heads," she answered the Principal Factor, signing the palimpsest in Aphalone letters. "I've never seen the like. Take these orders and execute them at once. I'll wait in your office until you can bring me the records."

He pursed his lips and struggled visibly to keep himself reasonable. He'd been sweating since he saw the chained purse—thinking, perhaps, *the last two died; this Accountant was mad to take the post.* "The records I can, of course, provide, though this is most irregular. But we cannot open the vaults for a hand count. Especially not for these soldiers—Your Excellence, they will be leaving the country within a week and will feel at liberty to steal. It would be criminally irresponsible."

"A salient point." He had the diligent, precise mind his bearing and presentation suggested. She laced her gloves in thought. "Lieutenant Aminata, you will have ample time to search *Lapetiare* during your return to Falcrest, correct? Keelhaul any marine found with contraband."

She had no power to dictate military justice, but Aminata saluted ⌐martly nonetheless. Baru smiled coldly at her, and only had to hide the ⌐th.

The poor assailed Factor went down into the old ice cellars to open the vaults for inspection and left Baru to make a restless pacing home in his office, wondering at the wisdom of acting so viciously so soon. A pale Stakhi-blood woman in a ruffed bearskin coat offered her beer (the Aurdwynni did not, as a rule, seem to trust their water) and quiet words through pursed lips: "Bel Latheman is *very* scrupulous. Things were so confused under His Late Excellence Olonori, however, that I do worry— please be kind to him. He's never bent a rule in his life."

"The numbers will speak to that." She wanted to apologize at once, out of pity for Latheman, and out of respect for the loyalty his staff showed him.

But the woman in the bearskin coat only bowed and extended the heavy mug. Her downcast eyes were dark as thunderheads. "I am Ake Sentiamut, liaison to the moneyprinters. Whatever you find, Your Excellence, I ask this: be good to Bel Latheman. He has been kind to us."

Sentiamut. She remembered that name from tax records—a family from the north. Baru felt a twinge of empathy for Ake, who must have left her home behind to serve in Treatymont. But Baru could not be soft. "He is the Factor of this bank. Responsible for everything and everyone within it."

Ake Sentiamut held the bow. "Of course, Your Excellence. I only fear that Latheman would take on blame better left with others."

She left the mug and went before Baru could reply.

At length the Principal Factor returned with a parade of secretaries carrying waxed records and palimpsests reeking of oat bran. She waited in silence for them to set the records out and begin the copying. After a few minutes she found a pen and joined their sullen ranks.

She had seen rebellion in the eyes of Tain Hu and Xate Yawa. Glimpsed it in the maps and histories. But the stink of it would be here, in the numbers, rotting on some back page.

Aminata's touch on her shoulder snapped her out of her work trance. "The count's proceeding apace, Your Excellence. The vaults are full of metals and jewels gathered for tax season, so it will take time."

How deep would the rot run, how high the rebellion reach? Could Ffare Tanifel's arrangement, the corruption Su Olonori had been so desperate to root out, still be marked in the ledgers here? Was the Imperial Accountant still the key to the plot?

When would the rebellion come for her, to court or kill?

"Thank you, Lieutenant." She tapped Aminata's hand, once then twice, the deliberate rap of a schoolteacher. "Mind your familiarity."

I T took all day and every clerk in the bank to finish copying the ledgers, and another night for the marines, working in shifts, to count the vaults. Late in the evening Muire Lo arrived with coffee and a train of servants, and with their help Baru began shuttling the originals back to her office.

By the letter of the law she'd gone too far. The originals had to remain on the Fiat Bank's premises. But Baru would take the risk. She needed these records, and she needed them untampered with. If the Imperial Accounts could not be kept in order she would be powerless and blind. Without a strong arm and a sharp eye, Aurdwynn would throw her overboard and drown her.

In her tower she found Cairdine Farrier napping behind her desk. He woke at the sound of the door, eyes slitted lazily, and considered her in smug silence for a moment. "You wanted an appointment with me?"

Oh, to snap at him, to say the first and least wise things that occurred: *That's my desk; get out, get out of my tower, get out of my province. Or tell me what you sent me here to do.*

She unbuttoned her greatcoat with slow deliberation, folded it, and set it aside. Wine and goblets stood ready on a side table. She poured something red as if she'd picked it herself. "I'm glad you're here," she said. "Please, find a seat." *A new one.*

He chuckled and stood with a low groan. Dark half-moons hung beneath his eyes. "It's a very nice office. Lovely vaulted ceiling. This was Stakhieczi stonework, built for the new Duke of Lachta—he's vanished, by the way. Even his sister Yawa doesn't know where he's gone, or so she insists. They call him the Phantom Duke, though I suspect he's just very bashful, probably due to excessive childhood exposure to Yawa—where was I? Masonry, yes. The Stakhieczi are unparalleled, they have masonry in their bones. Shame about the previous Accountants, isn't it?"

"Immaterial to me." She circled the desk to claim her own chair. "My job is to perform my duty to the best of my ability. The unhappy fates of Olonori and Tanifel are only history. Knowing the last Imperial Accountant was murdered would only have been a distraction."

This was her rebuke: *why didn't you tell me*? But Cairdine Farrier did not rise to it. Instead he shook his head in reproach. "History is never only a distraction."

She shrugged with affected weariness, studying him, his round face and flat nose, the weight he'd gathered during years on Taranoke. The hair at his temples had silvered. He would probably die before her, and when that day came, what would she think?

"I can't control history," she said, "so it's not part of my job."

"Control. Good." He drummed his fingers at the edge of the desk. "When you speak of control I know you learned the right lessons from Taranoke. But history *must* be part of your job."

"You made me an accountant. Not a scholar."

"We *do* have an emperor, you know." Cairdine Farrier sniffed his wine. "He sits on a throne in Falcrest with nurses to feed him mush and wipe his ass. When he dies, another one's installed, and behind that mask no one can tell the difference. It might be a new man every day. Do you ever wonder why that is?"

"He's a figurehead. Parliament is the real power." Except Cattlson hadn't thought so. *A theater for the mob.*

"That's a schoolchild's answer."

His disappointment looked real and hard, not a pedagogue's theater. Baru remembered things she had seen in his eyes, in years long past, and mastered a shiver. "You chose the school."

"You've always been bored by history. It's your greatest weakness."

"I am the Imperial Accountant of Aurdwynn," she said softly, "and you are a merchant, Cairdine Farrier. No matter what I owe you or what patronage you've provided, now you must show me due respect."

She knew as she said it that it was a stupid and childish posture to assume, because he couldn't be *only* a merchant. But she hoped to bait his pride.

"When the revolution came," he said, "all those years ago, we—I say *we* although I hadn't been born yet—resolved to tear down the aristocracy and build a republic for the people. But no one believed a Parliament could rule with authority. No one believed they could act with unity and decisiveness when the Stakhieczi came down out of the north, or the Maia rose again, or the Oriati federations fell under one lord and found new ambition, or—forbid it—the whispers from east across the Mother of

Storms came true. Parliament would dissolve into corruption, patronage, and graft. So the chemists offered a solution.

"Every five years we would choose a wise and scholarly citizen to be emperor, and he or she would drink a secret potion—a draught of *amnesia*." He leaned forward conspiratorially. "Behind the Emperor's Mask, he would be unrecognizable; and behind the fog of that potion, *he would not recognize himself*. He would retain his knowledge of the world, its history and geography, its policies and pressures. But he would have no idea who he had been before he was Emperor."

Baru watched him, wondering if this was the pride she'd probed for, or the history she should've mastered. He sat back in theatrical satisfaction. "Clever, no? A man who does not know who he is cannot have self-interest. Without family or wealth to lure him from the common good, he would rule fairly. When his term ended and the potion wore off he would return to his station, whether pauper or merchant prince, suffering from or benefiting by his own policies. Behind the Mask, the Emperor could be just."

"But the potion is a lie," Baru guessed. "The chemists never learned how to make it."

"Of course." Cairdine Farrier snorted. "The coronation of the Emperor is simpler than that—it involves a pick through the eye socket and a great deal of drool. But the mob *believes* in the potion. They believe in the Mask. They think the vegetable on the Faceless Throne is one of them."

"You've written your own history." The point was blunt but she fed it back to him anyway, although it was a concession. "And it gives you power."

He might have sighed in exaggerated relief, in another, more playful mood. But he did not. His voice was sharp, empty of ornament. "If you want to excel, if you want to have the station you think you deserve—" He gestured with his wineglass, and his eyes narrowed in the lamplight. "If you want to understand *real* power, the kind of power that made us lord of your little land, you will learn to manage all its forms."

The candles on the desk danced briefly in the draft.

"Who are you?" she whispered, too curious to resist the direct approach. "Really?"

He set down his glass and held up his empty hands. "Parliament," he said, lifting his right palm; and then his left. "And the Emperor on the Faceless Throne."

He left the rest of the exercise to her: filling in the negative space between them, the head behind the empty hands.

"Aurdwynn will rebel," she said. "Rebellions are expensive. That's why you made me Accountant. So I could follow the money to the proof."

Cairdine Farrier took a long drink of wine. "You know," he said, swallowing thoughtfully, "I have a bet with my associate Hesychast. He believes that your race is fundamentally unable to rule. That your easy island life and culture of unhygienic appetites has left you soft and biddable, and that you are all fit primarily for farming, fishing, and pleasure. He maintains that we rule you because it is your hereditary destiny to serve."

She set her glass down with soft precision. "And you?"

"I have wagered that you will stop the rebellion," he said and, smiling, lifted his glass in toast. "And now I take my leave. You have work to do. I'll see you in Falcrest, if you make it."

"Who killed Su Olonori?"

"I don't know. I've made no effort to find out." He paused by the door. "The same people who'll try to kill you when you get close to stopping them, I presume."

WHEN Cairdine Farrier had gone, she found herself sick with the awful need to know. She had learned what she could about the Throne and Farrier's colleagues, about their tests. But there were other secrets, closer and more terrible, and she could not delay the confrontation forever. She was part of this now, the apparatus of rule.

She had to confront the beast that had eaten father Salm.

She went to the Cold Cellar unannounced, white-masked, gloved, flashing the technocrat's sign to the gate guard, printing her mark in the logbooks. Passed through layers of vigilance and examination into white acid-washed walls, concrete, clean, buttered in lamplight.

The heart of Jurispotence Xate Yawa's power.

From the conditioning cells came soft bell chimes. Near the surgical theaters a quartet of musicians played oboe and lute. A sign by them: PLEASE DO NOT DISRUPT THE SOOTHING MUSIC.

Baru walked the transient wing. "For minor corrections," the functionary at her side explained, a plump Falcresti woman, plainly brilliant, precise and brisk. "This woman, for instance."

A gaunt Stakhi commoner, strapped to a metal chair, watching nude men approach and depart through the far door. Some of the men—paler, middling height, their features shaped by hasty makeup—stopped a handbreadth away, and a soft, warm note played. The woman's embarrassment softened, and she lifted her lips to draw some drug or draught from the pipe mounted near her head.

But when other men—darker, taller, more muscular or more beautiful— came close, the cell filled with terrible harsh buzzing and a stink that filtered out beneath the door.

"She volunteered for fidelity conditioning to repair her marriage," the functionary explained. "Wise. Two of her social proximates reported on her behavior. She could have been found responsible for hedonic sociopathy or hereditary misconjugation."

"The method?"

"Simple conditioning. We pair pleasant stimuli with facsimiles of her husband. If that fails, we'll proceed to paired-icon behavioral coaxing, manual stimulation, or sterile proxy conjugation. The final option is a diagnosis of hereditary nonmonogamy defect and sterilization."

Baru found herself grateful for the mask. "What about surgical intervention?" she asked, thinking of Aminata's warning, of the nauseating threat. "To render conjugation joyless? Do you conduct those here?"

Tain Hu had looked into her eyes, smiling, her lips drawn like a recurve bow, the motion of her breath slow and assured in her shoulders and chest, and she had not seemed at all nauseated or afraid—

But that had been a trap. Baru stamped on the image and the thought with silent, urgent efficiency.

"I'm sorry, Your Excellence. The somatic intervention wing is closed to visitors without the Jurispotence's direct approval." She gave Baru a cool sidelong gaze, assessing, and Baru saw Xate Yawa's eyes behind hers. "Our behavioral work here is equally important. Aurdwynni family structure requires strict corrective action. Especially among the Maia bloodlines."

On the way out they went through the holding cells, full of men and women waiting to be processed and assigned to judges. Strings of stamps marked their charges, their risk assessment, the nature of their arrest:

COLLECTED BY SOCIAL HYGIENE PROFILE.
REPORTED BY SOCIAL PROXIMATE.

FAILED UNDERCOVER LOYALTY SPOT CHECK.
REPORTED BY SOCIAL PROXIMATE.
REPORTED BY SOCIAL PROXIMATE.
REPORTED BY DEEP COVER INFORMANT.
COMPLIED WITH ENTICEMENT CHECK.

In another conditioning cell, a man sat in a drugged stupor, manacled to a chair, moaning in chemical bliss, while a functionary in a bone-white mask stared into his eyes and recited: "Falcrest. Mask. Hygiene. Incrastic. Loyalty. Compliance."

A crash of hidden cymbals. The functionary raised a smoking censer to the man's face, poison-yellow, as the crash came again, again, again. "Rebellion," the mask said, as the man began to shriek. "Revolt. Devena. Himu. Wydd—"

The new carriage they gave her for the ride home had a drunken old man for a driver. Rattled, she barely acknowledged his greeting—"They call me Gray, for the beard. I know every street and sewer in the city."—and it took her minutes to realize he'd been driving her in circles.

"You should be more careful, Your Excellence," he admonished her. Passing lamplight caught his blue jungle-crow eyes. "I could've taken you into Northarbor and given you to a diver with a knife. The last Accountant I drove came to such a fate."

"Xate Yawa will hear of this," Baru hissed. Her mind was still fixed on the Cellar, and on the thought of Salm, taken in the night to some waiting camp, or pit, or the hold of a receding ship, to be remade with drug and knife, or (better? was this better?) snuffed out in agony.

Gray laughed like a madman at that, the sound flat, arid. "Yes she will!" But he took her to the Governor's House.

6

REAMS of the Cold Cellar haunted her. In the morning she hissed and grunted through Naval System exercises, trying to breathe and sweat the memory away, until she could at last make herself think of the audit again.

"Muire Lo!" she called, rinsing herself, buckling and belting on the accoutrements of her office, waistcoat and purse and sailor's boots, an armor of imperial devices. "Come! I need to walk and think."

They clattered down the accountant's tower in a busy racket, Muire Lo baffled by her energy but playing along. "This is what I need to find," Baru said, counting off points on her fingers. "What I need to pin the rebellion down and snuff it out. It's a pattern—a very specific sign we'll see."

Among the green gardens and stone walks of the Governor's House campus the garrison drilled at dawn. Baru strode off the other way, annoyed by the braying of the sergeants. "Check my logic. Aurdwynn sells lumber, stone, minerals, and cattle to Falcrest."

"Yes."

"Only a few of the duchies profit *directly* from that trade, primarily those on the coast. Unuxekome is one—that's the Sea Groom, the pirate, who's quite rich, I think, because he owns the Welthony harbor and access to the river Inirein. Another one is Heingyl Stag Hunter, Governor Cattlson's friend, who doesn't care about money—"

"Heingyl's daughter handles his accounts. She likes to stay in debt to the Fiat Bank, as a kind of bond of trust."

"Oh. Interesting. Maybe that's why she wanted my job. Who's her mother?"

"One of the sisters of the last Duchess Nayauru, I believe. Didn't survive the Fools' Rebellion."

"Interesting. Maybe a motive for sedition. Useful to know if we need to set Xate Yawa on her." They navigated a hedge maze beneath the north wall, Baru solving it inattentively. Bees made urgent bumbling sorties past them. "And the last major coastal duke is Radaszic, Duke of Wells, who seems to be something of a trifle—yes?"

"He's very happy," Muire Lo said neutrally. "Beautiful lands. Lovely vineyards. Nice orchards. Fostered from childhood in Heingyl's house. Actually, I believe it saved his life—"

"A man of wretched fiscal policy." Radaszic's books were a comedy of excess. The man seemed to operate on a drunkard's theory of loans: why not one more?

"It doesn't seem to trouble him."

"Well, it should. Look—" They passed the bonfire pit where Cattlson liked to arrange outdoor affairs. Baru plucked a burnt stick, staining her gloves, and pushed through a dew-soaked line of bushes to the white-washed outer wall. "The dukes compete against each other for strength. In peacetime, wealth is the only strength that matters—standing armies are just an expensive waste that turns no profit. And if only three of the duchies can actually get wealth *directly* off foreign trade, the others need indirect means."

"Radaszic might say joy and satisfaction cannot be bought. Heingyl might say the same of honor—Your Excellence, should you be doing that?"

Baru drew a big ragged box on the wall in charcoal. "There. Aurdwynn."

"A fine schematic, Your Excellence."

"All the duchies need to be rich, or they'll be outpaced by their neighbors. So they come to us, to the Fiat Bank, and say *give me a loan*. We're happy to oblige, since we have a great many paper fiat notes, and it's cheap to print more. We ask a little collateral—what do we ask?"

Muire Lo smiled patiently. "Gold, gems, land, livestock . . ."

"Right. Except they know they'll only forfeit the collateral if they don't repay the loan, so really they get to keep their riches, *and* spend a bundle of fiat notes we've given them. It's free wealth!" She drew a little smiling face next to the map, although it came out shaped like a broken egg. "And if you *don't* reach out for a loan, your neighbor will outspend you. Radaszic will buy more drink, Unuxekome will buy more ships, and you'll be left in the cold with all your people grumbling about your mi-serliness. So everyone has to loan. Am I wrong yet?"

"I'm Heingyl in this example?" Muire Lo's face pinched. "Can't I be Unuxekome?"

"You want to be a pirate?"

"Well, I'd like to be able to smile, at least."

"Radaszic, then?"

"I'd like to be able to do something other than smile, too."

"Don't distract me." Laughing broke her momentum. "I'm getting to the important part. As the duchies race to out-loan each other, the Fiat Bank comes to own more and more debt in their estates. In fact, we hold significant interest in nine of the thirteen duchies. Do you know who's escaped our net?"

"Unuxekome. Controls the Welthony harbor at the mouth of the Inirein and has a strong fleet. He can rely on trade revenue."

"Good. And?"

Muire Lo frowned crossly at Baru's awkward box-map and charcoal sketch of a smiling duke. "Oathsfire, Duke of Mills. North of Unuxekome, very business-savvy, controls most of the river Inirein and thus profits off trade between the north and the coast. And Erebog Crone, in the far northwest—she's just too old and grouchy to care about loans, I think. And . . . is it Vultjag?"

"That's right. Duchess Vultjag is too proud to take loans, so she's very poor. Aside from these duchies we've named, everyone else is deep in debt to us, and spiraling deeper. Now. How do we use this to detect rebellion?"

"I think you'd like it better if I pretended not to understand, so you could tell me."

"Very good. You're a fine secretary. Wait—let me be sure I have this right." Baru looked at her boxy map of Aurdwynn, drew a little roof on it, and then divided it into three floors. "It's like a fancy house, isn't it? The attic is cold and distant, but full of useful things. Erebog lives up there with Lyxaxu, bickering over clay and stone; Vultjag and Oathsfire, too, and Oathsfire has the stairs down. Then the Midlands, which are like the study and the sleeping rooms, because they're full of people and useful things—Nayauru Dam-builder controls Autr and Sahaule, giving her water and salt and excellent craftsmen, and Ihuake controls Pinjagata, giving her the finest herds and the best soldiers."

Muire Lo was chuckling at something. "What?"

"Oh, the bedroom simile. I thought you were mocking Duchess Nayauru."

"Why?"

"Well, it's just—she keeps to old traditions. A healthy dynasty comes from healthy fathers, and such. Thus Autr and Sahaule both . . ."

Ah. So Nayauru would have children who might say with pride things like *daughter of a huntress, and a blacksmith, and a shield-bearer* . . . But no: they would never say that, not under Masquerade rule. "Unless Nayauru's lovers are taxable, let's leave them to Xate Yawa. Where was I?"

"Aurdwynn is like a house. You were forcing the metaphor into the lower floor."

"Right. The lower floor has the rooms for going in and out, and the kitchens and storerooms, where they keep the grain and olives and such. And the armory: that's Treatymont, because Horn Harbor's where we keep our fleet."

"What kind of house has an armory? Did *your* house?"

"Hush. It's a good metaphor." Three floors to the house—one warm with olives and sea trade, one made of alliances and herds and reservoirs, one given over to forests and mines and wolves. "You're going to rebel. You're going to take over the house. What do you need?"

"I assume the Imperial Accountant believes the answer is 'money.'" *is that us?*

"Yes. Any rebellion not built on pure faith or rabid hate needs funding." She tapped the charcoal map with her burnt stylus. "And that's what will betray them to me. The rebels will be the ones trying to climb out of our trap."

"I don't necessarily disagree, but—"

"A very stupid rebel might take out an enormous loan and then go to war, assuming they'll never need to pay us back. But only an idiot tries to fight with enemy currency. People only believe in fiat notes because they know they can trade the paper for something valuable. Get on the other side of the war from the Fiat Bank, and confidence in your loaned paper collapses. That's our hook, right? The dukes bite on the loans, turn all their wealth into our paper, and we reel them in. So—how do you get the hook out?"

Muire Lo pursed his lips. "I'm still Heingyl? Heingyl wouldn't want to. Cattlson is his sworn liege. It's honorable to swallow Cattlson's hooks."

"No. You're Vultjag, say." Tain Hu with her dangerous eyes, her coiled mountain-cat motions.

"But she doesn't hold any debt. We don't have a hook in her."

"She's desperately poor. She needs to be rich to fund her revolt. How does she turn our paper into a rebel's wealth?"

"Buy hard goods, I suppose. Gems, gold, lumber, cattle, stone, ore, textiles . . ."

"Correct. The rebels will seek to convert their debt into stable wealth. The blood of rebellion. But!"

But the rebels would be up against the Masquerade, champions of economic war. What a *splendid* arrangement—what an incredible trap! The Fiat Bank loved to buy gold, silver, and gems at a loss. It sat on them, pleading: oh, we hold them as backing for the fiat note, so you can be sure your paper money has value. Help us help you! Why not pay your taxes in gold and silver? We'll give you a discount. Ah, now, are you *stockpiling* hard goods? I'm afraid we must assess a steep tax. Why not just liquidate those goods into fiat notes, and dodge the fee?

Baru saw the engine at work, drinking up Aurdwynn's wealth of gold and silver and gems, sending it to Falcrest, and replacing it with Falcrest-backed paper. She saw it and wanted to cry out in glee at the beauty of it. Not least because of the power it gave her, the power to pluck the rebels out of their camouflage, to offer them up as gift and proof of her own abilities.

"But," Muire Lo ventured, "you're well aware that money isn't the *only* factor in rebellion, and that the nobility is far less rational and calculating than you might think? You should read Heingyl Ri's monograph on the future of the Midlands Alliance—she predicts civil war simply because Nayauru has gotten heirs off Dukes Autr and Sahaule. It's a serious threat to the future of Ihuake's bloodline—"

"Heingyl Ri thinks that matters because Heingyl Ri was raised noble. She's too caught up in feudal pageantry to reduce the problem to its basic economic factors." Baru held up a hand to turn his protest. "When they try to turn their debt into wealth for their rebellion, I'm going to see them do it. They'll be buying hard goods, and that will leave a pattern in the ledgers. So." She snapped the charcoal stylus, dusted her gloves briskly, and wheeled back toward the accountant's tower. "The answers are in our books. In the numbers. We just have to hunt."

S HE sat down to work hopeful that she would have a map of the rebellion, its seditious dukes and secret-swallowing Jurispotences, by the end of the day.

(And found a full notebook page, written in Aphalone, tucked in among the books. Ffare Tanifel's this time, handwriting feverish. *They are coming at me from an unexpected direction. Calling me licentious, unhygienic—as if Cattlson did not indulge his own appetites, pluck generously from his own favorite fruit! If they take me into the Cold Cellar for this "physical" I will not get out. She says she cannot protect me*—Baru shuddered in horror and sympathy, and folded it away.)

Her hopes failed her.

By sundown she'd found nothing at all suspicious. The Fiat Bank tracked the income, expenditures, assets, and liabilities of every duchy in Aurdwynn. None of them leapt out as a prelude to rebellion. To all appearances, the dukes were scrupulously honest—reckless debtors, aggressive spenders, frankly a little stupid about money, but honest.

So what had Su Olonori been killed for? There *had* to be something. He must have come too close. And before him there'd been Tanifel, executed for corruption—so whatever the trick, whatever sleight of hand the rebels depended on to find their money, it must be visible to the Imperial Accountant. It might even require her complicity.

She barely noticed her own headache until Muire Lo knocked and the sound boxed her ears. "Come," she groaned.

"Lieutenant Aminata, Your Excellence, with the final tally from the bank vaults."

Baru knuckled her temples, feeling the oil in her unwashed hair. She'd been chewing on coffee beans and fought the urge to lick her teeth clean. "Send her in."

"Your Excellence." Aminata came down to the office to salute and set herself at attention. Baru cleared her throat and wished she could look so damn upright. She must have stopped and dusted her uniform, or had a spare brought off the ship. She looked immaculate. The years had kept her taller than Baru, and her duties had kept her graceful and strong, as forthright and ready as a good javelin. There were many reasons Baru had avoided her on *Lapetiare*.

"Don't sit. I've been sitting all day." Baru circled the desk. "Did you find any discrepancies?"

"No. The material in the vaults matches the Principal Factor's records precisely in both number and kind. We found no evidence of graft or misuse. Even the quality of the metal is superb." Aminata offered the palimpsest. "Our tallies, for your review."

Baru accepted the records wearily. "Thank you for the loan of your marines, Lieutenant."

"Of course. I'm happy to report that discipline held."

"Good, good." Baru felt the unaccountable need to lean on the other woman, her perfect bearing and spotless uniform and apparently inexhaustible patience. But she couldn't, because Aminata was a terrible confusion, a knot of hurt—her relentless swordsmanship, her furious reprimand (did she think Baru had been after—but she'd given no *hint*—), her formality and distance: all this spoke to anger. But then the offer of her own blade and her appearance with the marines, all seemingly in good faith . . .

"It's past sundown, Your Excellency," Aminata said. "You've worked too long. I wondered if . . ."

Baru probably did not manage to keep her surprise off her face.

"If you'll forgive my impropriety," Aminata said, "I haven't taken my shore leave yet, and—I thought we could reminisce about Taranoke before *Lapetiare* sails." *And we never see each other again.*

"I can pour some wine," Baru offered, her stomach clenched.

"Your Excellency—"

"Please, Aminata." All those stolen hours in the larder making codes. They must still count for something. "You can still call me Baru."

Aminata crossed her arms, cocked her weight on one hip, and smiled insouciantly. "I don't know if it's to your taste, Baru, but this is a seaport, and sailors don't take leave in an office with a glass of wine."

"Oh," Baru said, her stomach not relieved, her heart quite uncertain when and how to beat.

Cairdine Farrier had spoken to Aminata. Cairdine Farrier was here. Cairdine Farrier was watching her through these deep open eyes. And all it would take to save herself would be one phrase: *mind your familiarity, Lieutenant*—

But—one way or another, she would know more at the end of this night than she had at the beginning.

"I'll get my coat," she said.

THIS one tastes like piss," Baru said.

"How would you know what piss tastes like?"

She laughed into the mug. "I'm a savage, from a savage land."

"Please. If anyone drinks piss in this midden of a world it's the Aurdwynni." Aminata tapped the bottom of the mug, mischievous. "Go on, go on, finish—good! You want another?"

Baru considered the bottom of the mug and tried to deliberate. Instinct, for perhaps the first time in her life, felt easier. "Yes," she said. "Immediately."

"You're paying for all this," Aminata said, leaning across the bar, "because you have unlimited money."

"It doesn't work like that." Baru frowned deeply, certain she should be concerned about open discourse on certain topics, not quite sure if money was one of them. "There's inflation to think about, you know—and I haven't even written purchase orders for pens and ink—there's so much to *do*, Aminata! I thought it'd all be complicated figures and simple duties, but it's the opposite."

"Nothing's complicated for you." Aminata belched and took another pair of mugs from the barman, who shared his Falcresti fashion sense (apron, bare shoulders, loose-laced sport corset, striking makeup) with the exasperated Principal Factor Bel Latheman of the Fiat Bank. "You're brilliant, you know that?"

"I'm glad you think so." Baru considered the geometry of her upraised forefinger. "I am drunk. I think this is the first time." It would be important to remain cautious, even drunk, and say nothing that could betray her, like: "I missed you, you know."

"Don't get weepy, bird, we're barely past midnight. And I think we need to find you—" Aminata leaned in and bounced her eyebrows. "Company, hmm?"

At close range, Aminata's face became a geometric proof in bone and flesh, clean angles and perfect concentric topologies of sclera and iris and pupil. Baru braced herself on the bar and remembered her paranoia. *The Jurispotence is always watching.* "I don't know," she said, pleased by the subtlety and reserve of her own facial expressions. "It's just good to talk to someone. Everyone's listening to me—everything I say—but they're not—I can't—"

Aminata listened intently, nodding. Behind her a scar-faced woman shouted to a hushed table about her intent to murder Duke Sahaule the Horsebane, who'd done something terrible, presumably to her horse.

"I don't know," Baru said, choking on her own habits of silence.

"No, no! Tell me more! I'm leaving soon anyway, it doesn't matter!"

"I don't even remember how I was before I went into that school. I don't even remember being allowed to have feelings!"

"Like what?" Aminata shouted over the rising roar.

"Like—" Aminata had turned her uniform coat inside out, to signal that she was off duty, but Baru grabbed at its shoulder anyway and tugged. "You're a Masquerade soldier, but you're Oriati! You help the people who want to conquer your homeland! If there's another Armada War, you'll be killing your own blood! How do you feel about that?"

With drunken cunning she thought: they will expect these doubts of me, these questions of loyalty, so they are safe to offer up as chum. Whoever she reports to will eat them, and be satisfied.

"I don't know." Aminata's brow wrinkled. "They're fair to me. I'm going to be an admiral some day."

"No you won't! Look at who you are!"

"Please." Aminata rolled her eyes. "Seacraft has always been a woman's game. We're better at mathematics and navigation, all the hereditary science says so."

"I mean you're Oriati! They'll never give you a chance!"

"You're an *Imperial Accountant,* and look where you're from." Aminata stood sharply. "Come on, before you get too serious—let's go upstairs, let's give you a chance—"

"No, no, no—wait!" But Aminata had already left. Baru followed her unsteadily, surprised by how much the crowd restricted her vision. "Sorry," she said, deeply upset to be inconveniencing those she bumped into. "I'm so sorry. I'm very drunk."

Aminata led her up the stairs and into a dim lamplit space, crowded wall to wall with jostling shouting people. There were doors everywhere, and men and women dancing on a raised stage, mostly unclothed. "D'you know how to do this?" Aminata shouted. "You've got to tell them what you like."

"I don't want to rent!"

"It's safe! You tie a cap on him and it stops everything from getting through! I'll show you how!"

Baru, flushed and unsteady, took her by the shoulders. "I know why you're doing this!"

"What?"

"I said, *I know why you're doing this*!"

Aminata frowned at her for a little while, chewing her lower lip. Men brushed past them, jostling, but, seeing Aminata's inside-out coat—clearly an officer, clearly Masquerade navy, backed by a vengeful syndicate of seafaring women ruthless in their retribution for even small crimes—gave them no trouble.

"All right," Aminata said, "all right. Look: if it's really that way I just don't want to know, okay? Let's just not talk about it. It's safer for both of us."

Baru did not want to be silent, but she could find nothing safe to say.

"Let's go back to the bar," Aminata said, tugging on Baru's wrist, "and try something harder."

D'YOU think they're going to rebel?"

"Aurdwynn always rebels!" Aminata shouted over the roar of the crowd. "Either the dukes are happy, and the people rebel, or the people are happy, and the dukes rebel, or the dukes hate each other, so it's civil war. That's what the Admiralty thinks."

"So what do I do?" Baru had shouted herself hoarse, and now had to lean into Aminata's ear to make herself heard. "The Governor's a spineless romantic and I think the Jurispotence is on the other side."

"I don't know! I'm just a lieutenant!" Aminata laughed, as if this were really a joke.

"I want to go home." Baru slipped on the bar and caught herself on Aminata's stool. "To Taranoke. I miss it so much, Aminata—"

Aminata helped her back upright. "You can't go home."

"Why not?"

"I don't know. Because it's gone." Aminata frowned, finished her drink, and nodded. "You can't find it again. Even if you go back, it's not there anymore. That's history, that's how it works! Someone's always changing someone else."

She was right; she was right, of course, and more fool Baru for not having said it first—the Taranoke of her childhood was gone, had probably never existed; Halae's Reef had never cut the waves like smooth shark teeth, the water had never lapped *that* clear on luscious black sand. Pinion had not known the name of *every* star and Solit had never held her up to count them for an *entire* night and Salm had—ah, no, better not to think of that while drunk, not at all. And yet she couldn't seem to help it—

Baru caught sight of a face in the far corner, barely visible, cornered by the mass of an enormous Stakhi woodsman in a leather tabard. The face looked up, icy, speaking to the woodsman, a curse or a threat.

Muire Lo. "Oh," she said, "shit."

"What?"

"That man's my secretary. And probably a spy."

"So? You haven't done anything."

"If he saw us go upstairs together, he might think—he might tell someone that we were—"

Do you know what's done to a suspected tribadist, Baru?

"Oh fuck," Aminata said, bolting upright. "Do you know who he reports to?"

"That merchant, I think—you know the one, you've spoken to him—"

"Do we run?"

"No, we'd look guilty. I'd better go say something—Lo!"

The gigantic woodsman's bellow carried across the tavern as he took Muire Lo by the throat and pinned him up against the wall. People recoiled, shouting, a clamor of Stakhi and Urun and Iolynic and Aphalone. Baru and Aminata left their stools barely a moment apart, Baru trailing, Aminata shouting in Aphalone to those with ears for it: "Imperial Navy, stand aside, stand aside!"

Muire Lo pawed at the grip around his throat, eyes wide. The woodsman used his other hand to push an interloper away, politely but firmly, and continued strangling the life out of Muire Lo with calm inexorable strength.

Aminata reached him first, still shouting, and when the man raised his spare hand to fend her off she took it by the wrist, pulled it palm-up close to her stomach, turned on the balls of her feet, and tried to throw the man by the sheer pain of the joint lock. He was too big and too firmly set to move, so instead the lock snapped his wrist. He roared and dropped Muire Lo, and before he had time to do anything else, Baru snatched up a heavy mug and clubbed him in the back of the head as hard as she could. He was huge and angry and would probably be a match for both of them even with a broken wrist. She had no choice.

He crashed onto his back on the stone floor, his left arm raised rigid, his right arm flexing at his side. "See that? That's called a fencing response," Aminata said brightly, pointing to the way his arms twitched. "You gave him a concussion. Good. I said IMPERIAL NAVY! STAND BACK!"

Muire Lo looked up at Baru from where he'd slumped against the wall, mouth gaping fishlike. The room moved around her like a ship in chop and after a moment she decided to sit down beside him. She was drunk and terrified and it took her a moment to plan out the sentence: "What were you doing here?"

"I thought someone was going to kill you." His voice was a wheeze and as if that didn't hurt enough he sounded mortified. "I'm sorry, Your Excellence, I just wanted to keep watch—but I was never very good at this in train—in taverns."

"And him?"

"Oh," Muire Lo said, not glancing at the fallen man. "I told him who I worked for and he got angry."

Baru let that half-answer pass unchallenged. She'd sort him out tomorrow. "What do we do?" she asked Aminata.

"We pay our tab," Aminata said, kneeling to go through the man's pockets, "and if you're willing to explain what we were doing together in a Southarbor tavern to your Governor and your Jurispotence and my captain, we take this man in."

"He was watching you," Muire Lo said dully. He touched his throat, where bruises had already begun to rise.

"Who told you someone was going to kill me?" Baru waved off a bystander's hand. Off-duty Masquerade garrison soldiers had already begun to form a screen around them, their rivalry with the navy briefly set aside in the name of Imperial solidarity. "Muire Lo, who told you?"

"No one told me," he said, eyes averted. "But I thought if the Jurispotence would try, it would happen as soon as the Governor left to go hunting."

"Does he have a weapon?" Baru asked Aminata.

"No." Aminata frowned. "Just a notebook."

B ARU woke with her first hangover. Sniffling and cramped, she stumbled around her paneled room, hunting for a goblet of spring water before giving up and bringing a bottle of wine into the bath. The miracle of Masquerade plumbing called up hot water and the memory of drinking from the hot springs on Taranoke.

How far away were those springs? The sky printed in the still water? Dark young stone down in the deep like the shadow of caldera gods? She couldn't remember, couldn't manage the geography or trigonometry with her pounding headache. Forever far. Unreachable.

That's what Aminata had said. You couldn't go home.

A knock came from the stairway, first tentative, then insistent. Muire Lo, no doubt. "Come," she shouted, and then, out of deference to local modesty, "but I'm in the bath!"

"Your Excellence, Jurispotence Xate Yawa is in the waiting room."

Baru groaned.

"What should I tell her?"

"Make clever conversation for ten minutes. I'll be down." She put her head under the water and tried to drift, but the bath was too small and she was too long. After a moment she sat up rigid with a terrible thought.

Perhaps Xate Yawa was here to arrest her, as she had Ffare Tanifel. To drag her away and have her drowned. But if Xate Yawa was with the rebellion, surely she would have *protected* the traitor Accountant—

She says she cannot protect me, the note had said.

Perhaps Xate Yawa had discarded Ffare Tanifel to prove her own loyalty. Safeguard herself. Perhaps Cattlson had made a better offer.

I came to apologize."

Jurispotence Xate Yawa looked across the desk without a hint of judgment, her eyes and shoulders formally set, gloved hands flat on the redwood. Baru, barely presentable in a collarless laced shirt still loose at the wrists, tried not to squirm. Just as she'd noticed on the docks, Xate Yawa's eyes were the blue of a Taranoki crow. Baru was certain Yawa knew everything that had happened last night—the who, the where.

"Apologize?" Baru played for time, smiling, trying to figure out what she wanted. "For what?"

"For the man I had watching you. For his conduct toward your secretary." The Jurispotence straightened her gown's collar with absolutely convincing formality, a manner-perfect mime of what she was saying: *things between us are slightly out of order, and I will set them proper.*

So the Stakhi woodsman had been hers. The notebook had been hers. She knew that Baru knew what the man had been up to, and had decided to concede the play before it could go against her.

"I'm young," Baru offered. Beware, she thought to herself, beware the years she has on you, the games she's played. She used the Masquerade's invasion to gain herself high station and her brother a duchy. Beware that steel. You can't win. "I'm foreign. My two predecessors have come to a bad end. If I had some moral failing that you overlooked, and it damaged the welfare of the Imperial Republic in the province of Aurdwynn, you would be guilty of negligence. If you sent that man to watch me, then you were only doing your duty as the guardian of Aurdwynn's moral hygiene."

Xate Yawa slumped for just a moment in clear relief, hiding it almost before it showed. The acting was immaculate. "You're so wonderfully pragmatic. We waste too much time on politics here."

"I'll have the woodsman released and returned to you. If you trusted him with this job, he must be very useful to you."

"I'm grateful."

They smiled at each other in mutual respect and admiration for a few moments. Baru thought fixedly about Aminata and nothing else, because it seemed the best way to keep that smile glued convincingly on.

"I've heard you're performing audits," Xate said. "Have you found anything . . . untoward? I fear that some of the northern duchies are funding ykari cults. Oathsfire has grown obscenely rich on Inirein trade, and his friend Lyxaxu indulges in *thoroughly* regressive philosophy."

"The moment I locate an irregularity, I will be in your office, shouting for a warrant. I promise."

"Beautiful." Xate Yawa offered a hand. "Oh, this has been so much easier than I'd feared. Please—don't think I did this out of anything but a sense of duty to the Imperial Republic."

"Of course. A good day to you, Your Excellence." She kissed Xate Yawa's hand and smiled all the way until Muire Lo opened the office door for her, let her out, and let himself in.

"If you're going to listen at the keyhole," Baru suggested, "you should pretend you don't know she's leaving until she knocks."

Muire Lo's flush rose above the ring of bruises around his throat. "You're *letting him go*? Just like that? You didn't even ask why he—"

"He attacked you because you told him that you're a Falcresti spy, which makes you a grave danger to the rebellious plot Xate Yawa is involved in." She waved away his protest and clapped a hand on her desk for attention (he twitched visibly at the sound). "Listen! Did you hear how directly she played everything? How honest she was? She's afraid of me— she's only putting the strictest truths into play, so I don't have room to turn anything back against her. She knows I have Falcrest's favor, she knows I'm closing in on something that could harm her, and those two things together are a real threat to her. The man who attacked you isn't important. *His notebook is.* Do you understand?"

"If she had the book, she'd have the notes he took while watching you."

"And written evidence is everything. If she had a reliable eyewitness account of me vanishing into a brothel with a beautiful woman"—his flush said so many different things—"I would be one mistake away from a terrible and permanent fate. She controls the courts. Given reason and motive, she can destroy me. If she's with the rebellion, she has that motive. If she had the notebook, she'd have the reason. Could she have that woodsman fabricate a copy?"

Muire Lo nodded along, sharp and engaged, apparently not on unfamiliar ground. He *had* been trained, Baru thought. "Not without a lot of trouble. She'd have to get forged seals and time stamps. He'd miss telling details. Review would detect it."

"Good. The woodsman was an urgent option, an expedient. That means her plan is happening too soon for her to take more subtle measures." Baru let herself go, trusting the analytic trance to spot riptides and shoal water. "So her next step could be murder. She has power over Aurdwynn's criminals. She could turn them loose on me. It worked on Olonori."

"We should move you back aboard *Lapetiare,* then." Muire Lo turned to the door. "They're above her reach."

"No. If I'm locked up on a ship I might as well be dead—I won't be able to hunt for the rebel gambit." Baru put her steepled hands to her mouth, her brow, the back of her neck, thinking furiously. "I need to be somewhere where it's too risky to strike at me. Somewhere that would unavoidably link my death to her or her allies. Can I move my office to the Cold Cellar? No—no, she'll see everything I do, it has to be far away from her—"

"Tain Hu," Muire Lo said.

"What?"

"Vultjag. The Duchess of Comets—Tain Hu." He grinned, excited, caught up in his own idea. "Tain Hu's late aunt was married to Xate Yawa's brother, Xate Olake, the Phantom Duke of Lachta. Everyone knows Tain Hu was the first to challenge you, out on the ballroom floor—everyone knows she's the one who tried to draw out your sin where Xate Yawa could observe it. If you were close to her, and you were killed, *everyone* would see Xate Yawa's hand in it."

"If I were close to Tain Hu . . ." Baru traced the logic. Tain Hu, clearly seditious, could not kill Baru without drawing Cattlson's full wrath. Xate Yawa would want to keep attention away from their connection—

It was perfect in every way, except that it would put her right in the grasp of a woman who might not share Xate Yawa's subtlety. Who might reach for a knife instead of a writ.

But she had told Cairdine Farrier she would stop the rebellion. Cairdine Farrier was the way to Falcrest.

She would accept the risk.

Baru began to open drawers. "I'll get all the records I need to keep working. Find Tain Hu and inform her that I'm going to her estates in Vultjag to look over her records. Tell her that I would be more than honored by her company."

WHEN Muire Lo had gone to make arrangements, Baru went back up to her rooms to find country clothes—riding jodhpurs, heavy coats, hard-soled boots. While she worked she thought, trying to be remote and cold about it, calm and deliberate. But it hurt her heart to consider these things, and soon she found herself tearing clothes from her cabinets, piling them unfolded like a child in a snit.

She sat on the corner of her bed and put her head in her hands.

Even on the best roads, by the best carriage, Tain Hu's Vultjag estates were hundreds of miles and many days to the north, up the long cause-ways through Duchies Heingyl and Ihuake. *Lapetiare* would sail long before Baru could make the trip and return. She would lose the marines aboard, her only trustworthy hand in Aurdwynn. She would lose Aminata, her only friend.

She could order the ship to delay its passage, and bring Aminata and some of her soldiers along as security. But that would be sentimental and, worse—so much worse—stupid. She couldn't ignore the fact that Aminata had brought her to that tavern, had drawn her upstairs on drunken pretense with one of the Jurispotence's men watching. It might have been unhappy coincidence. Or Aminata could have been thinking of her career, and all the ways that the favor of a provincial Jurispotence could help it.

When Muire Lo returned later, he said, "All the arrangements have been made. Will you need me to carry any messages to *Lapetiare*?"

She wrote a terse and official set of orders, commanding vigilance during her absence, ordering the ship to sail on schedule. She couldn't risk reaching out to Aminata, couldn't even offer a formal good-bye. It would only provide more evidence of some unsavory connection.

So be it, then. She could go forward only with what she absolutely needed.

"You won't be coming," she told him, unsure how he would take it. "I need you here."

The word *need* made him smile, not unpleasantly.

TAIN Hu sent a carriage and a column of horse, twenty riders carry-ing the comet banner. Baru expected to ride alone in the carriage, the duchess aloof on horseback. But when she stepped up into the cab she found Tain Hu waiting within, sprawled along the length of one passenger bench like a satisfied cat.

"Yours." She gestured to the other bench.

Baru set her bag of papers and palimpsest down carefully. "Your Grace. Thank you for attending to my request so promptly." Her lips really *did* look a little like a recurve bow, didn't they? Always drawn in mockery . . .

"I'm not unaccustomed to Masquerade scrutiny. They send their creatures to keep the North reined in." Tain Hu wore riding breeches and
there was mud on her tall boots. She had the noble height, raised on good
meat and citrus; Baru was glad to almost match her. "I'm sure we'll make
an occasion out of it. Aren't you bringing anyone? Where's your little
chaperone?"

It was hard to read Tain Hu's age: older, clearly, but not much older,
which made her contempt all the more grating. (How young had she
inherited Vultjag?) She could remind the Duchess Vultjag of the appropriate honorific, but it would only seem petty. "I don't need any staff,"
she said, smiling back. "I expect the audit will go smoothly, and I am
assured that your men-at-arms can provide the finest security on the
road. The safety of your estate, of course, hardly needs praise."

Tain Hu drew herself upright with slow control. "Aren't you afraid,"
she said, the corners of her mouth and eyes drawn ever so faintly, "that
if you find something wrong with my finances, I'll cut you apart and bury
the pieces in the woods?"

Yes I am, Baru thought, but she let none of that thought into her
face. "Am I afraid that you're a fool? No."

"Su Olonori was killed in his bed. The murderer was never brought
to justice."

"You will have to protect me even in my bed, then."

Tain Hu sat back against the bench and considered her with what
seemed like genuine bemusement. Her reset nose was a little crooked
from the front, which seemed a good flaw to fixate on. "Why are you
here?"

"Simple. If I'm to do my job, I need to know where the money goes."

"Money isn't everything."

"I'm an accountant." Baru offered a wry shrug. "As far as I'm taught,
it is."

Tain Hu set her hands on her knees and leaned forward, her lips
parted over her incisors, disgust or challenge or something else in her
eyes. "As far as you've been taught. And now you want me to teach you
the rest?"

She heard the memory of their last meeting, her own words thrown
back at her. *All the paradoxes of Aurdwynn bound up in one woman. I
think I could learn a great deal from your lessons, Tain Hu.*

"Would I be here if I didn't?"

"Then watch. Understand what you're part of." Tain Hu reached behind her and opened the driver's shutter. "Take us to Northarbor before we leave the city. I want her to see the purge."

IN Northarbor, where dockside architecture gave way to the arches and arcades of old Stakhieczi stonework, they found a riot underway.

The sound reached them first, a roar, a surf that wouldn't ebb. Then they met lines of Masquerade regulars in blue and gray working in cadence to move barrels of diluted acid. And, last—from the vantage of a rooftop, because neither Tain Hu nor her armsmen were eager to press deeper into Masquerade lines—they saw the riot itself.

The mob wore iron-mordant green. Baru had expected to see them on the attack, pressing on prison gates or carrying torches for a tax collector's home.

But it was the garrison that had cornered the riot, cordoning that roaring mass against the north edge of the square, where they stood in defense of a lime-washed warehouse without window or label except the Aphalone script NORTHARBOR SPICE. Baru strained to hear their chant, but it reached her only as a desperate thunder.

"It's a secret temple," Tain Hu murmured in her ear. "To Wydd. Defended by its followers."

"A god?" Little in her studies had mentioned faith in Aurdwynn except as a political problem.

"A human being. Someone who practiced a virtue completely enough to become the name and the trait. To speak of acceptance or obedience, winter or pneumonia or erosion or time, is to speak of Wydd. Wydd stands across from Himu and Devena stands between them." Tain Hu touched her brow, in reverence, or just after an itch. "Not that anyone of worth believes these old forbidden superstitions, of course."

"They don't look very accepting to me." Baru searched the garrison lines and found the barrels of acid, passed hand over hand toward the front. Sappers waited with spades and gloves and rag-stuffed masks to pry them open.

"They are very poor followers of Wydd, it seems," Tain Hu said dryly. "Perhaps Himu moves them today."

The sappers opened their barrels and drenched the crowd in acid with slow underhand throws. Screams reached them on the harbor wind. "Don't be too concerned," Tain Hu said. "Pacificant-process acid only burns the eyes and membranes. On skin it leaves an itch and a red rash. Blindness is rare, but the burns will mark the guilty for days to come, so they can be rounded up. A just and gentle method, I'm assured."

A lock of Tain Hu's hair had come free from her braid and set itself wiggling in the breeze. Baru fixated on it, preferring it to the chaos below. "Why build a temple to Wydd in a warehouse? Why defend it?"

"The ykari cults are illegal. They speak to the transience of worldly authority, you understand, and thus promote anarchy and dissent. So—" Tain Hu found the loose lock of hair and tucked it absently away, her eyes still on the crowd. The garrison had advanced behind the acid, dividing the mob. "You have a clever technique. You permit the ilykari to build a quiet little conclave in a hidden place. You permit word to spread that the faithful may gather for worship or divination. Sometimes, I think, you start the cults yourselves."

"A honeypot."

"Just so. Why stamp the cults out in their infancy, when you can watch who comes, who overlooks the gatherings, who accepts the bribes to permit it, and then sweep them all up at once?" Tain Hu gestured to the spread of rooftop all around them. "Down there, in the streets, other soldiers are making arrests. The ilykari will be imprisoned or drowned. Their cultists and accomplices will face the judgment of the Jurispotence and her kind. She will be busy tonight, and for weeks to come, with all the acid-washed guilty brought before her."

Baru remembered glances in the ballroom, suppositions of conspiracy. Foolish to say it too directly, but foolish not to probe at their alliance: "You know the Jurispotence's methods so well."

"Xate Yawa does what she believes must be done to hold her power. Her techniques are quite sophisticated. She tells me that in Falcrest—did you know this?—in Falcrest prisoners are permitted to escape their cells, permitted to reach the streets, only to be recaptured. Again and again. So that they will learn that escape is always an illusion." Down in the square, a second wave of acid barrels moved to the front. "So, then—look on this. Do you believe that this is what must be done?"

"I am an accountant." Baru wished she could close her ears to the screams of the sectioned, smoking crowd. "I deal in costs, not faiths."

"But you are part of this." Tain Hu was a little taller and she moved with purposeful force. Her words, no matter how soft, were not unintimidating. "This *is* a cost. This is the cost we pay for broad roads and hot water, for banks and new crops. This is the trade you demand." And there was no doubt who she meant, for she used Aphalone's singular *you*.

"This resistance is meaningless," Baru said. "If they want change, they must make themselves useful to Falcrest. Find a way up from within."

"A people can only bear the lash so long in silence. Some things are not worth *being* within."

"Order is preferable to disorder," Baru said, speaking words she had mocked on Taranoke, under the dark hangings of the school beds.

Tain Hu turned away.

THEY went north across cream limestone blocked over beds of shattered pot and concrete, over gravel and lime and pounded Aurdwynn earth. There might come a day, Baru thought, when the Empire's roads were made of Taranoki tufa.

Tain Hu rode with her armsmen and left Baru to work in the carriage. She struggled to focus on her papers, battling a rising unease she couldn't name. Maybe the memory of the riot. The thought of those acid-stained desperates vanishing into the Cold Cellar. Or the knowledge that Tain Hu could kill her and dump her body for the coyotes and she would never be found.

Worrying at a palimpsest, she tried to focus herself. Tain Hu's estates at Vultjag would have their own accounts. She would open the books and search for signs of seditious behavior—enthusiastic loan taking, aggressive investment in old coin or hard resources, purchases of weapons or grain to feed and fight a rebellion.

And if she found something? If Tain Hu *believed* she'd found something? What then?

If she vanished or died on this excursion, surely it would be obvious that Tain Hu had killed her. Surely Tain Hu would know this.

But as Baru studied the passing olive orchards of Duchy Heingyl, squares of silver and green and black rich earth, wood and oil already machined into money and influence in her mind, she found her eyes drawn to the rising land ahead, the redwood sentinel forest that stood guard over the valleys and crow-colored Mount Kijune and the high white peaks beyond. This was Aurdwynn, the wolf land, and perhaps here the rules were not the same. Perhaps here cleverness was not a strength at all, compared to the knife. (Perhaps, a wary part of her whispered, Muire Lo had maneuvered her out here, to be disposed of. . . .)

They made camp that night beneath cold stars, a sky of tilted foreign constellations. "Are you uneasy?" Tain Hu asked.

Baru drew her cloak around her and watched the duchess across the campfire, uncertain whether to take the question as a threat.

Duchess Vultjag opened her hands to the brush around them, the shadow of the looming forest, and smiled. The firelight gilt her eyes like an eagle's. "All I meant to ask was: isn't this the farthest you've ever been from the sea?"

B Y the day they reached Vultjag, Baru understood why Parliament was so greedy to own Aurdwynn. More than just a shield against invasion, it was an asset of incalculable worth—forests, fisheries, coastal farmland, stone and mills, and even its feudal craftsmen, whose technique had been folded and hammered by years of ducal war.

Aurdwynn would be good for the Empire. Aurdwynn would also be very, very profitable to whoever controlled it.

But the dukes and duchesses kept the land divided. Their jealous tariffs and guilds prevented free commerce and created vast inefficiency. Baru found herself wandering across an imagined map of the land, smoothing out the borders of the thirteen duchies, erasing the keeps, making an Aurdwynn without lords and tabulating the results.

What could she do with her own rebellion? Tear it all down and rebuild it? Would the daughters of Aurdwynn look on her with the same curious awe as she had looked on those sails rising off Halae's Reef?

The road climbed up through high forest and came to the crest of a pass. "Ride ahead to the fellgate, and have it opened," Tain Hu ordered, and brought her charger alongside the carriage. "Come with me. Look on my land."

Baru took her hand, glove in glove, and with some difficulty sat astride Tain Hu's horse, gripping the back of the saddle rather than the rider, as her books had taught her. The horse moved beneath her in a way that was utterly unlike a ship.

"Easy. Keep yourself relaxed." Tain Hu brought them forward, through gates of stone and redwood, between sharp-eyed armsmen with shortbows and comet tabards, and then they looked out over the dale, over Vultjag.

The forest filled it, wall to wall, and the shadows of the clouds shivered on the treetops as the wind moved through the boughs. Down the center like a crooked bolt ran the river Vultsniada, white and racing, and along its banks crowded mills and villages and—to the north, on the lowest steps of the mountain—a limestone keep which bridged the torrent and admitted, through open sluice gates, a great waterfall.

But for all the beauty of it, Baru's eyes went to the crows and hawks and harriers soaring on the thermals, high above meadows and clearings of stone, the birds gathered in towering kettles that seemed to stretch from canopy to cloud.

She had not even begun to make a count when Tain Hu cried a word in Urun and spurred her horse onward, plunging down the steep road and into the forest, her armsmen carrying her banner ahead and behind. Baru held herself against the saddle, clinging to safety and dignity, trying to stamp on her sudden inexplicable joy.

8

BARU spent one cold night in her guest quarters in the waterfall keep, listening to the mountain wind howl through the towers. Then, after a breakfast of smoked salmon and watered wine, she went on a horseback tour of the Vultjag estates and determined at once that there was corruption afoot.

This was what she saw:

In the first of a string of villages along the river, she met hunters bringing deerskin to a tannery, their cheerful Iolynic banter instantly silenced when they heard her speak, her tongue betraying her where her face and skin had not. They would not answer her questions, but she made note of their numbers, and the size of the tannery.

At the quarry, the workers and their families turned out to cheer at the sight of her carriage and its ducal banners. But by the time she walked among them some word had gone out, and she heard the whispered Iolynic *mask, mask, mask* as they scrambled to hide their children from an agent of Treatymont, a pawn of Falcrest hunting social sin. She passed through them in stiff silence, observing their brawn and skill.

They were not all afraid of her. A few were willing to give interviews, in rough Aphalone or through a translator. "My family has worked the stone for a hundred hundred years," a pale green-eyed mason told her, passing her squalling son off to a wet nurse. "My ancestors tunneled out mansions for the Stakhi and now, just this last year, I finished work on the duchess's new keep. Look at the boy—he'll draw more chalk dust than milk from me, and probably turn out better for it." She spoke with love, unafraid of winters, of dead sons.

Armsmen drilled in their village square, long spears and gleaming shields and great bearskin coats, a disciplined phalanx. "The Sentiamuts," she was told, "a family known even in Treatymont for their faithful service to our duchess. They guard the pattern of those bear coats jealously."

Ah, she thought. I know that family.

All of these things Baru fit into the greater riddle, the puzzle of Tain Hu's estates. The puzzle was this: there was no famine.

Vultjag had a quarry, and quarrymen needed food to stay strong. But the valley could not feed itself. The forests could be hunted and foraged, the river fished and the take salted for winter. But that would only be enough to feed a few villages. Without agriculture or livestock, the crafts-men and masons and their families would starve.

So Vultjag would need to bring grain and olives and fruit upriver from the great Inirein (beautiful name for a river, Baru thought—it meant *Bleed of Light)*, or overland through the narrow pass, which probably closed during the winter. To do that, Tain Hu and her serfs would need to barter or buy. They could barter stone, lumber, gems, hawks and fal-cons, and pelts taken from hunting the forests. But barter was inefficient and unreliable, so, more likely, Tain Hu bought her food wholesale, praying every autumn for a kind market and easy transit.

And to buy wholesale, she would use fiat money, money she raised by selling her stone and lumber and gems and hawks and falcons and pelts to her westerly neighbor Oathsfire, who would in turn move it down the Inirein to the coast and sell it at a profit. Vultjag had to use Masquerade fiat notes because she had to deal with Oathsfire, who had to deal with the coastal dukes, and those dukes needed fiat money to turn the best profit. The whole system was built to guarantee it.

So it went like this: the people of Vultjag worked their valley to create goods, and they sold those goods for food. So Vultjag should have been poor, a subsistence economy, getting by season to season. Masquerade economics taught Baru that real wealth came to those higher up the production chain.

And yet she saw development.

Money changing hands everywhere. The snap of paper fiat notes in the village square markets and the stables, at the mills and the lumber-yards. New walls and fences going up around the riverside villages. Bucket gangs paid to bring sewage to the river instead of dumping it in the streets. *Where,* Baru kept asking herself, *where does the money come from?*

Vultjag was richer than she should've been. New mills? New barracks for new quarry labor, and wages for them? An entire new limestone keep, built with ambitious daring around the waterfall itself?

And when Baru returned to Tain Hu's house of stone and clear water

and asked for the ducal accountant to be brought before her, she found
another thing that was not as it should have been:

"I present the ducal accountant," said Tain Hu, her hair unbound on
the metalwrought shoulders of her tabard, her boots loud on the stone;
and she bowed mockingly low.

"*You?*"

"The law says each duchy must have an accountant. Nowhere does
it say that the accountant cannot also be the duchess." Tain Hu carried
a leather-bound book under each arm. "And I am literate, if only in
Iolynic. An uncommon talent here, Your Excellence."

Baru took the books and opened them in silence, silence because she
wanted to smile or laugh at the woman's cheek, or stand up from the little
redwood desk and demand to know what would happen when she found
the cheat, the hole in the books.

"You'll join me for dinner. The armsmen will show you the way." Tain
Hu paused at the door, looking back into the little chamber with a curious frown. "Is it true that you duel?"

She set out her own parchments and palimpsests and books, ignor-
ing the duchess. The notes were in Iolynic, which she could only barely
begin to read—but the numbers she understood, and the numbers would
do. "Bring me more ink," she said.

B ARU missed dinner. A yeoman brought her candles to work into
the night.

Her first line of attack failed. Duchy Vultjag's accounts had been pains-
takingly balanced. The simplest forms of fraud and corruption betrayed
themselves here, in the balance of payments, but Vultjag's payments—
on food, on iron, on wages, on interest—had all been drawn from legiti-
mate taxes, sales, loans, and the duchy's own capital reserves. Tain Hu
could manage her own arithmetic.

But Tain Hu was of Aurdwynn, and Aurdwynn had known of fiat currency and accounting for not nearly long enough to master them. She
must have made a mistake somewhere, a mistake that an Imperial
Accountant could sniff out.

Surely.

Unless there was no treason to conceal. No brewing rebellion in need
of coin.

Baru took a long sip of watered wine and ran a finger down the itemized list of the duchy's transactions. "What?" she said, and then, setting down her wine, "*What?*"

She'd been looking for the fingerprints of rebellion—the use of aggressively loaned fiat money to purchase gems and precious metals, land and goods.

But Vultjag had done just the opposite. Tain Hu had *sold* her quarries and her forests for fiat notes. She'd unloaded the gems and gold that her ancestors had stockpiled for generations, all in the name of gathering more paper. And it had been done so strangely, so unambitiously—no sweeping bargain, no great financial maneuver. Just a blizzard of tiny little transactions, chipping her own estate away piecemeal.

Pieces that added up. Tain Hu had done well in these sales. The rates were very generous.

But sales to who? The names on the ledger weren't other dukes, not neighboring Oathsfire, who'd nipped at Vultjag for so long, not Lyxaxu come down from his high hold. No sales to the Fiat Bank or the Imperial Trade Factor, who would be overjoyed to buy productive land. Just a run of little undistinguished names, without title—

"Oh," Baru said. "Oh-ho."

She opened the Vultjag census and ran through it, and *there* were the names—the Awbedyrs and the prolific Hodfyri, the Alemyonuxe who had spent whole generations building mills riverside, the bear-coat Sentiamut who had made their small fortune ranging north into the Wintercrests from whence their ancestors had come.

No nobility here. Just the common families of Vultjag.

Tain Hu had sold her duchy to her own people. She'd liquidated her estate.

But where could those commonborn families, hunters and masons and rangers, have found the capital to *buy* it? Where had they earned enough Imperial fiat notes to purchase Tain Hu's estate out from under her at generous prices, arming her with enough liquid capital to buy other duchies wholesale, debts and all?

Money had to come from somewhere. This only pushed the question back a step, from Tain Hu to the people of Vultjag.

Baru got up and paced the geometry of the room, the carpet dancing underfoot, chargers and spearmen and threaded blood beneath her boots. *Why* do this? Well, because Tain Hu needed a way to get money that didn't draw a lot of attention, apparently. Like selling her holdings to her people. But why would *they* go along with it? What could the Sentiamuts do with a stretch of land in the Wintercrest foothills, or the Awbedyrs with a thousand acres of forest? Sell the land to the Fiat Bank at a slight profit? They were feudal serfs, not the kind of landlords and rentiers who dominated the Midlands duchies. (Alone of the northern powers, Duchess Erebog had allowed landlords to rise, and found that the hardscrabble land made them unbiddable and tightfisted.) No, the Vultjag families wouldn't know where to begin.

Baru put her fists on her temples and pressed.

Why would Tain Hu's vassals buy her estate from her with fiat notes they couldn't reasonably have? If they had taken out loans, the Fiat Bank's records would have noted it. So *where had the money come from?* And what was it good for, anyway? Tain Hu could not reasonably expect to spend all these fiat notes on things like spears and horses, or even use them for wages during wartime.

So the money had to be useful *before* the war.

Baru went to the window and looked out at the yawning dark silence of the forest and the valley beneath her, the worthless riches of Vultjag, all this wood and stone that couldn't be harvested or moved, trapped by distance and the cost of labor, by the cold fact that Duchy Vultjag was good only for providing the resources that others would profit from.

She closed her eyes and set her shoulders and tried to be Tain Hu, to wear her boots and mount her horse and ride the paths of her duchy thinking: *How do I unlock all this and turn it into power, power to use against the Masquerade? I cannot sell my wealth and land to them without feeding them—how do I escape their maze?*

How do I turn this valley into an army at the gates of Treatymont?

The money had to come from somewhere.

But the paper trail would end with these little families. Unlike the duchies, they were not required to keep their own accounts.

Ah. And there it was.

Su Olonori's scrap of a note: *V. much land sale?* He *had* been on the right track. V for Vultjag. Selling her land.

The woman Ake Sentiamut, in the bear coat, offering drinks, murmuring that Bel Latheman was blameless—Ake Sentiamut who was liaison to the moneyprinters—

The money had to come from somewhere. Unless it didn't. Unless it had appeared out of nothing.

THE next morning, she told Tain Hu that she had concluded her audit. "And all is in order," she reported, smiling. "Would that all the duchies kept their books as cleanly as you. If you'll give me a moment to unburden myself of this?"

She touched the chained purse of her station like it was a dead thing strapped to her belt.

"You'll stay a while, of course," Tain Hu insisted. "I've promised myself I'll teach you to ride before Governor Cattlson has a chance to butcher your technique."

The thought of *Lapetiare* came to mind unbidden, and Baru put it away just as quickly. Aminata's ship would sail before Baru could return, one way or another. There was nothing to be done.

She took a long swig of the breakfast wine and closed her eyes to savor the taste, to escape, for a moment, the pressure of Tain Hu's ceaseless watch.

"Of course," she said.

THE duchess taught her to ride, first two to a horse, then Baru on a phlegmatic chestnut mare that refused to hurry even when the winding forest paths carried them into the territory of a few violently displeased crows. Baru found the crows delightful, and tarried a while just to see how far their wrath would go. But after a while the birds decided on an airy unilateral truce.

"I have a theory," Tain Hu said, "regarding your attention to birds."

"Oh?"

"It's the only tongue of your homeland that you can still hear spoken aloud."

"We spoke Aphalone on Taranoke," Baru said, and let none of her surprise show.

"Not before they came."

"Before *we* came."

Tain Hu made a face of silent mockery.

The next day, Tain Hu brought shortbows and taught Baru how to shoot. The components were fascinating—fletching, limbs and riser, nock and fistmele, glue and sinew and horn—but making them work together required coordination that Baru seemed to lack. The same could not be said of Tain Hu. She moved and spoke decisively, sometimes with a certain impatience, as if the world dragged two steps behind her will and she found the friction grating. On horseback or with a bow, she performed with boastful mindlessness, her focus clearly elsewhere, on the conversation or the birdsong. But given a challenge—shooting backward from a gallop, answering a question of deep history or philosophy—her brow would furrow and some stiffness would pass out of her, as if she had forgotten, for a moment, to pretend to be someone else.

For a while Baru didn't notice how closely she'd been observing the other woman. Perhaps this was self-deception: once noticed, it would have to be controlled.

In the forest, riding without guard beneath the dark boughs and the impossible towering heights of the redwoods, they came to speak of dangerous things. Religion. Politics, local and foreign. Marriage—Tain Hu was young, but in Aurdwynn, where views on family often echoed the old bicameral Tu Maia ways, a woman of proven fertility could go farther. And, in the end, the Masquerade. First the questions dearest to Baru's heart—*Why do they rule us? Why are they so powerful?*—and her best answers: "Chemistry, and finance, and very clever seamanship," to which Tain Hu replied that the ancient Tu Maia had invented heavy cavalry and the horse-drawn plow, and that it had given them half the known world, but only for a time.

"What will we be, if you have your way with us?" Tain Hu asked. Around them the forest moved in the twilight, ancient, vast.

"You will be remade. Your blood inoculated. New ways to be wealthy and useful introduced. Your marriages will be—" Baru struggled briefly with the Aphalone words. "Adjusted. So that your children and all their descendants may serve the Republic best."

"We will be bred like cattle." Tain Hu bent to rub her horse's flank, as if in apology. "It's already begun. They have set quotas—no fewer than so many marriages between Stakhi and Maia bloodlines, no pure Belthyc marriages—"

"The first steps of the Incrastic program seek to quantify the natural strengths of the racial types and their various hybrids."

"And what do you think of it?"

"I am an accountant. Heredity is not my concern."

"You will never rule anything," Tain Hu said icily, "if you limit yourself."

"What?" Baru said, just to buy time against the chill of hearing Cairdine Farrier here.

"Money is only one kind of power. Faith is power, too. Love is power. Slaughter and madness are both roads to power. Certainly, symbols are power—you wear one wherever you go, that purse you carry. And you wear others when you decide how to dress yourself, how to look at men and women, how to carry your body and direct your gaze. And all these symbols can raise people to labor or war." Tain Hu looked down at her with regal distance, with no anger at all. "And *you* are a symbol. Look at yourself. Taken from one conquered land because you were young and bright, and set to rule another. How can you be anything but a challenge? A commonborn girl, given authority over a land of old noble men? You are a word, Baru Cormorant, a mark, and the mark says: *you, Aurdwynn, you are ours.*"

"I am Baru Cormorant," she protested, "accountant, and I earned my place by merit. I am a mark of nothing except myself."

"As long as you believe that is all you are, you will never be anything but a piece of the machine."

"A piece can change the whole. It may take patience, or sacrifice, but—"

"*This* machine? Better to break it, and build something new." Tain Hu spurred her horse on ahead.

LATER, on a high stone outcropping where the horses moved only gingerly, they watched the sun set. Tain Hu had not taken them home.

"You found it, didn't you?" Tain Hu asked. "In the books. You told me that all was in order, but it was a lie. You realized I've been forging fiat notes. Maybe you even understand the scale of it."

Baru could have lied again, and been caught in it. Instead she told the truth, because she thought it was what Tain Hu would respect. "Yes," she said. "I found your trick. You could kill me here, and make it look like an accident."

"And what then? They would send yet another clever foreigner, one less pleasing as a houseguest?" Tain Hu shook her head, braids scattering. "No. It was never an option. You protected yourself too well."

Baru bowed in her saddle. "I'm honored."

Tain Hu looked out into the forest. In the distance an owl called. "You won't be able to do anything to stop it. The rebellion will begin. Your helplessness against it will be an indelible failure, marked on you as surely as a scar. And for that I am sorry. You must have your own wants, and this failure will destroy them."

She would have been young during Aurdwynn's last rebellion. She spoke of no parents, no siblings. Perhaps she understood the cost of revolution well. "And what do *you* want, Tain Hu?"

Duchess Vultjag considered her estates from the high stone. "I am of noble blood, and like all nobility it used to be that I only wanted to rule, to be separate and above my people. Just as you now rule us."

"And now that we rule you?"

"Now the Masquerade has taught me the weight of the saddle. Now Xate Olake, beloved husband of my lost beloved aunt, has opened my ears to the cry of the commoner." She lifted her hand to cup her mouth and called back to the owl, a soft and perfect imitation. "Now I want to make my people free."

"Treason," Baru chided softly.

"Tell the Jurispotence, then." Tain Hu laughed.

"It was clever, using your own serfs to launder the forged money into your books. But there's one thing I'm curious about."

"Just one? You're so easily sated?"

"Two, then," Baru said, thinking back to her audit of the Fiat Bank, the terrified Principal Factor, and to Ake Sentiamut, who had brought her beer and protested that her beloved Factor *had never bent a rule in his life.* "I know how you got the pattern and the seals to forge the notes— the Sentiamut family is truly daring. But where did you find the labor talent? To copy one fiat note is an enterprise. To do it in such quantity, without detection . . ."

Tain Hu took up her reins and looked toward the perilous descent. "I have heard it said that the greatest love of the ilykari priests who worship Wydd and Devena and Himu is the study of their sacred manuscripts. And those manuscripts are very beautifully illuminated, whether the originals, or the copies they make. Some have even been taken to Falcrest, to be shown as art."

"Ah," Baru said, understanding. Xate Yawa's Cold Cellar was full of ilykari awaiting trial, and they could be set to work.

They found the path again as the forest fell into darkness. But although the stars here were foreign to Baru, they were not to Tain Hu, and she guided them with ease.

9

BARU went south again, back to Treatymont, back to the snake pit. Racing against time and the rebel plan. There might still be a chance.

On the road north of the crossroads freetown Haraerod, in the fang-shaped shadow of Mount Kijune, a band of soldiers blocked her way: a filthy phalanx bristling with steel. Vultjag's escorting armsmen muttered, sullen but not worried—*"It's Ihuake, taking toll on her roads . . . thinks we're all cattle, really, just another kind of herd. . . ."*

Likely not assassins. Not here, not now, not by this means. Vultjag's armsmen would have done the job themselves.

Baru dismounted, put on her mask, and marched straight into the teeth of the phalanx with a scowl and a mind to sow terror. Today was not a day for delays. "Stand aside," she called, raising one white-gloved hand. "Imperial business. I don't pay tolls." And then, when the wall of spearmen did not stir: "The Duchess Ihuake pays me tribute! Do you want to spend the rest of your lives eating slop in her pigpens?"

One of the fighters in the phalanx put down his long spear and shield and walked out to meet her. He was an old man, leathery, untroubled by the burden of his armor and helm. Angry years had worked his face with scars.

"Afraid they don't speak Aphalone," he said, and made a good case for his own honesty—his Aphalone was awful. He'd painted black makeup beneath his eyes to fend off sunglare. "Let me get a look at you now. Hm."

Baru drew up at an arm's reach, baffled. The old man squinted at her, working his jaw in a sort of disgruntled loop, and then shook his head in disgust. "Well, you look just like her, but she's a better rider. Take off the mask, then. I've got to be sure."

Curiosity beat out indignation. "Just like *who?*"

"The Duchess Nayauru. Word came she'd been sighted in disguise passing through Ihuake's territory. Young woman, very clever, round about your height. Possibly intent on seducing Her Grace Ihuake's son and usurping her lineage, or so Her Grace has warned me. Have you been seducing the Cattle Duchess's heir?" The infantryman noticed the chained purse at her side and his brows knit. "Ah, shit. Are you the Imperial Accountant?"

"I am."

The man chewed on this for a second and then spat into the road-stones. "Well. Duke Pinjagata, at your service. You're Ffare Tanifel? We met at the—that damn affair in the big house, you recall?"

Baru did her absolute utmost to look unflappable in the face of compounding absurdities. The Duke of Phalanxes turned out on foot to patrol for illicit lovers—it was like something out of a prerevolutionary romance. Or one of Muire Lo's monographs. "Ffare Tanifel's dead."

"Fuck me, that's right, Xate got her. So you're Su Olonori, the replacement. I don't think we've met." Pinjagata extended one gauntleted hand. "I also thought you were a man. Or—are you? I know the Oriati are flexible on that point. No place of mine to decide; just tell me which you prefer."

"He's dead, too." Baru took his hand and gave the best impression of strength she could manage through the mail. "I'm here to repair the situation."

"Dead too? Is that right?" Pinjagata eyed her with a kind of bemused respect. "So you came up here to unfuck the situation between these two?"

"Between Ihuake and Nayauru? That's not a priority now." Xate Yawa could solve the hereditary bickering of the great Midlands duchesses. Tain Hu's maneuver had to be countered. "I have urgent business in Treatymont. Move your soldiers and I'll forget this inconvenience."

"That's kind of you." Pinjagata gestured with his right hand and the phalanx behind him raised spears and began to split. "Glad you weren't Nayauru. Damned if I know what I would've done. Probably had to arrest her on some invented charge, and then her stallions Autr and Sahaule would've started another fucking civil war, which I'm damn well tired of winning. You kill the duke, that's fine and good, that's war, but then his relatives start vowing revenge and you've got to kill them all too. Personally, I've never felt easy about strangling some second cousin who hasn't even seen his balls drop, you know? But I suppose that's why Ihuake's got the dynasty and all the cows, and I don't. A certain ruthlessness. You ever had to kill anyone in the course of your duty? Someone cheat you on taxes, default on a loan, the like? I imagine they'd give the purse to a real killer, if the last two died."

"Mm. A compelling theory." Baru signaled for her guard to bring up her own mount and the carriage. "Aren't Ihuake and Nayauru allies?"

"Ah, don't ask me. They're both simmering—something about inheritance, or grazing land, or fresh water, or becoming queen. It's all beyond me. I just plan campaigns." Pinjagata clapped her on the shoulder. "Safe travels!"

LAPETIARE sailed before Baru returned.

She found Muire Lo waiting at his desk, official correspondence stacked to his left and a single letter sealed in red naval wax filed to his right. "Lieutenant Aminata?" she asked, unbuttoning her coat.

"Gone, Your Excellence. *Lapetiare* has sailed for Falcrest. Your coat—"

She'd meant the letter, and almost snapped the clarification at him. But if it were Aminata's, he would have understood, so it couldn't be. She hadn't written. Baru ignored his offer and kept the coat to fold, just so that she would have something to do with her hands and eyes.

Aminata gone, *Lapetiare*'s marines gone. Xate Yawa and Tain Hu working toward their endgame. And Baru had only Muire Lo to stop them, to satisfy Cattlson, to earn her way to Falcrest and the salvation of Taranoke.

"There was some unrest in your absence, Your Excellence." Muire Lo, stumbling over her sudden cold, fussed with the papers on his desk. "A number of riots, several local functionaries arrested on charges of sedition and conspiracy, temples to the ykari Wydd and Devena uncovered and dispersed. And a number of requests for audience, which I've recorded here. Duke Lyxaxu in particular seems eager to discuss philosophy."

"Have you hired a staff for me?"

"No, Your Excellence, although I've gathered suitable candidates. Jurispotence Xate's office has yet to return any of my requests for social review."

She tapped the sealed letter. "What about the letter from Cairdine Farrier you're holding there? Do you already know what it says?"

It came out harsher than she'd meant. Or had it? How could she have meant that as anything but an accusation?

Muire Lo sat back down behind his desk, eyes on his hands, and made a visible effort to say something both decorous and honest. He did this for long enough to make himself flush, and then pushed the letter across the desk to her, the unbroken seal framed between his long fingers.

"He's gone now, I presume." Baru took the letter from the desk, judging its weight (light) and quality (diamond fold, marble cream paper, choice naval wax). "Which means that you'll need to become more talented at slipping your reports to him, because if I find one, I'll have no way to avoid sacking you. Is that understood?"

She didn't expect the eruption that followed. Maybe it had been building while she was gone, while Muire Lo, left alone to manage her business in a city tearing itself apart around him, sat in her cold tower and made excuses for her. Maybe her careless impropriety left him no choice but to lash back.

It was a slow, purposeful outburst, delivered in silent gesture. He opened a door of his desk, hinges creaking, and (eyes appropriately downcast all the while) drew out a book, the Stakhi woodsman's book, the book that had earned him the bruises that still marked his neck. Page by page he leafed through it, licking his finger deliberately, reading nothing, until he found the last page with any writing on it at all. Then he set the book down on the desk, open to the place—Baru could not read it, of course, but nonetheless—where the man had surely recorded: *she went upstairs with the sailor, into the brothel.*

"A canny politician would certainly have kept careful track of such a potentially compromising item," he said. "Especially with the city in such a fevered state."

Baru took the book, snapped it shut, tucked it under her arm, and then—after a moment's silent regard—gave Muire Lo a nod of gratitude, of acknowledgment.

"Of course," she said. "We can be sure of the loyalties of so few."

He stood and opened the door to her inner office, bowing at the waist. She touched his shoulder on the way in, her throat warm, her mind working. The notebook could have gone with Cairdine Farrier, on to Falcrest, to her permanent file. But it was here.

She could trust him.

Or Farrier could have left it for Muire Lo, so that he could use it to buy her confidence.

Muire Lo cleared his throat. "Was your trip to Vultjag productive?"

"Thoroughly." She set out her ink pots across her desk. "You'll be interested to know that all those ilykari priests the Jurispotence has been sentencing to death are using their final days to print counterfeit fiat notes for Tain Hu. She's selling her estate to her serfs in order to launder the forged notes onto her books."

The secretary stared at her for a moment. "I *am* interested to know that. Should I arrange a meeting with the Jurispotence?"

"No, there's nothing to be done. Xate Yawa is part of the arrangement, she owns the prisons, and at the first sign of discovery she'll bury the proof." She unlocked the drawer and found her master book. "We need to map out the connections. Tain Hu already has the money she needs, but in order to make a rebellion she has to spend it."

"I'll find the books of grain merchants and smiths."

"Good. And get me an urgent appointment with Cattlson." Baru frowned. "Tain Hu may have something more direct in mind."

The letter was from Cairdine Farrier, as she had suspected. It said only this:

> *Order is preferable to disorder.*
> *Remember the Hierarchic Qualm.*
> *I am not their only agent.*
> *You are not the only candidate.*

GOVERNOR Cattlson's hunting expedition with Duke Heingyl had done him well. "Your Excellence!" He swept out a chair for her. "Returned to us at last, and the whole city clamoring to meet you. Heingyl insists you will undermine and betray me—he's very insistent!—but I suspect he's simply jealous that we've found a wit to rival his daughter, Ri. You, boy, bring us mineral water and then lock the door. Governor's business."

Time to make her case. To prove her value as an instrument of the Mask. Outside the great window she could see the color of sails in the harbor mist.

As Cattlson bustled about, boasting of the stag he'd taken and the experimental marriages he'd arranged—"For improved endurance in the forests, I think it best to mix only northern bloodlines, diluting out the rest"—she opened her chained purse and drew out the map she'd made.

"What's this?" Cattlson frowned down at the table.

"This is the conspiracy to raise Aurdwynn in rebellion." She'd worn her whitest gloves, to make the act of tracing the web more striking. "It begins here, in Treatymont. Jurispotence Xate Yawa cracks down on the ykari cults, giving the imprisoned ilykari priests reason to cooperate with the rebellion. Tain Hu's agents, quietly overlooked by the Jurispotence, use the ilykari and their artistic talents to forge Imperial fiat notes of unsurpassed quality." She touched Treatymont, the roads north, and then Vultjag. "The notes are moved to Duchy Vultjag, where they are laundered into Tain Hu's accounts through transactions with her own serfs: she sells her property to them for a pittance, then pretends they've paid her enormous sums in return. While the other duchies sink deeper and deeper into debt to the Fiat Bank, Tain Hu accumulates her war fund—"

Governor Cattlson put his ramming-prow chin in his hands and sighed. Baru, expecting horror, stumbled to a halt.

"I don't mean to steal your sailing wind." He smiled gently, a paternal expression, trying to cushion her against everything he thought she didn't understand. "It's a clever little story. Perhaps it's even true. I know Xate Yawa permits certain indiscretions, where she thinks it best—and I overlook those indiscretions, just as she overlooks mine. Perhaps there's a counterfeiting scheme in the Treatymont prisons. Perhaps that brigand bitch Tain Hu profits from it. But it doesn't point to rebellion."

Baru felt like a diving bird meeting an unexpected sandbar. "Aren't you going to ask for proof?"

"You're Cairdine Farrier's favorite, and I know what he likes. I'm sure you've proven everything in triplicate."

"Money is the blood of rebellion." She tried to make herself take up more room, to look big and broad-shouldered like one of his damnable hunting companions, like something he took seriously. "Money is the only thing Tain Hu needs to turn this tinderbox into a—"

Governor Cattlson laughed at her. He tried, visibly, to stop himself, but laugh he did. "You're an accountant. Talented, eager, of course, but—surely you see how that could slant your perspective? Even if Tain Hu has made herself rich, what of it? She still needs to buy weapons, find loyal armsmen, and provision her army. It'll take years, and in that time her neighbors, Oathsfire and Lyxaxu, jealous and wary, will come whispering to us. Even if she suborns them as well—and I won't deny, Your Excellence, that money can sway a mind just as well as wine or secrets—we have spies to watch them. I mean, come now! We're the Masquerade. We won't be taken unaware."

She wanted to scream at him, and the urge made her think of Diline, the social hygienist at her school, and what he had said: *it is a scientific fact, an inevitable consequence of the hereditary pathways that have shaped the sexes . . . the young lady is given to hysteria. . . .*

Or had that been Cairdine Farrier?

"She can use her money to destroy you and everything you've tried to build," she insisted, quiet, thin-lipped, speaking more from pride than hope of getting through. "The Federated Province of Aurdwynn will slip from Falcrest's grasp. Parliament will not have its fortress or its riches. You will be held responsible."

She would lose her road forward.

Cattlson sat back, exasperation unconcealed now. "You're so sure there's a rebellion coming. You've snatched this whisper out of the air and made it your own temple and creed. But you have no sense of history. The dukes of Aurdwynn have been fighting each other for *centuries,* Cormorant. Nine years ago they tried to revolt, and they still remember our reply. We've given them an excuse to rebuild, ride their estates, hunt their forests, and sate their lusts. We are not so harsh on them—surely you've heard Duchess Nayauru bragging of her lovers? Hardly hygienic, but she still rules half the Midlands. We've given the people safe roads and the promise of inoculation. Even a blind man could *smell* the ways we've made their lives better. Why would they rebel?"

He thought she understood nothing but coin, that she'd neglected the rest. And perhaps he was right—surely, thinking rationally, she had to consider that he might be right. He was older, more experienced, selected for merit and ability, and from Falcrest as well, the seat of all knowledge—

No. She had learned from Tain Hu, of politics and of defiance. "The Jurispotence uses harsh tactics to suppress their faiths. We dictate their marriages and customs, we tax their lords and they pass those taxes on to their serfs. You said it yourself: they live hard lives. These are all reasons."

The corners of Cattlson's lips told her that he took a certain pleasure in correcting her naiveté. It was not vindictive, exactly. Perhaps it was satisfaction, or relief that he did, after all, have things to teach this savant girl. "The Jurispotence does what is necessary to satisfy her more zealous overseers back in Falcrest. What if we suppress their faith? What does it matter? No one cares about the old books except the ilykari and their acid-stained congregations. The people want beer, medicine, meat, and games, and if we offer those we can ask a little Incrastic discipline in exchange."

It would be better to withdraw now. Regroup and reconsider. But he had spoken *down* to her.

She pushed her map at him, her web of transaction and sedition. "Your Excellence, I—I *exhort* you to consider the position of the people with respect to—" She gave up on presenting it academically. "The people of Aurdwynn have been kept like cattle. Taught to love their duke and fear everything past the horizon. You told me yourself that the Masquerade does not fear the discontent of the people, it fears the discontent of their lords. When the rebellion comes, the people will follow the nobility."

He waved her away. "Your disregard for the common people of Aurdwynn troubles me. This is a land built on the ruins of three different cultures, complex and divided. The dukes cannot unite their people—"

She was on her feet now, fists on the table, leaning halfway across. "The dukes don't rebel because they're all enormously in debt to the Fiat Bank, to *me*! They owe me their prosperity! They draw loan after loan just to keep up with each other. I could call that debt tomorrow and destroy them, but if Tain Hu uses her counterfeit liquidity to buy up their debt—if I try to call the debt, and Tain Hu bails them out—do you understand?"

Cattlson huffed. "You can buy *debt*?"

"You can buy anything! Tain Hu doesn't need to raise an army or hire a spearmaker! She can buy the other Duchies themselves, Nayauru and Ihuake and the whole Midlands with all their armsmen and all their cavalry, Radaszic with all his olive fields and grain that feeds us here." She put her closed fist down on the coast, white glove on black ink. "Once she's bought up their debt, she'll hold the controlling stake in their wealth, not me—and instead of racing each other for paper loans to keep their commoners and landlords happy, she'll have them buying gold, grain, and spears. She'll subvert our own economic system to prepare Aurdwynn for revolt."

He sighed. "But now you know that her money's counterfeit. So you won't let her buy anything."

"She laundered it into her books. Xate Yawa will back the transaction. Xate Yawa will refuse to prosecute on any of this. I can't stop Vultjag without your help. She'll be *me,* you understand? She'll be the new Fiat Bank!" She hammered on the map. "She'll make herself rich, she'll offer them wealth and freedom, and they'll all rebel. They'll have us bottled up in Treatymont within the year. Any relief from Falcrest will either need to come overland—and you *know* they'll drop the bridges at the river Inirein—or risk the winter storms at sea. We won't last that long!"

Cattlson looked as if he had just discovered a terrible problem right in his lap. For a moment she thought she might have convinced him of the danger. But no: it was just his realization that she would make his life complex and miserable. He'd liked her better when she was just a girl with a purse and no ear for riding innuendo.

She found herself expecting to hear: *"Is it true that you spent the last fortnight out in Vultjag?"*

"Perhaps you're right," he said. He had a good smile, open and happy; he looked like a man who preferred to smile, whenever his life allowed him. "Why don't you assemble a case, and you can present it at the next meeting of the Governing Factors, where we can all evaluate your warnings fairly."

Where Xate Yawa, alerted by Tain Hu, would be waiting to make a mockery of her, destroying her authority before she'd ever properly exercised it.

She left the map on the table when she departed. On her way out she passed Cattlson's secretary, carefully watering a glass of wine.

"He'll be in a foul mood," she warned him. He raised the glass in thanks.

WHAT to do now?

There was a preposterous amount of work to be done, an appalling amount. Even with the Fiat Bank's records—which she would have to review in great detail, trusting no other eye—she still needed to request copies of the master book from every individual duchy, then cross-reference and hunt down every discrepancy. And every day she spent on that work left the daily business of the Imperial Accountant piling up: preparations for tax season, rates and structures to modify, request after request after request from merchants and duchies and the Fiat Bank to review one policy of Olonori's, or another of Tanifel's. Would she continue to demand this milling fee or forbid that river tariff?

Not with a staff of a hundred and a sleepless year could she bring this under control. And her meeting with Cattlson had left her too angry to work. After a while she gave up, set her gnawed pen down, and rang Muire Lo in.

"Your Excellence?" He peered around the door.

"Do you duel?"

"Not with you, Your Excellence!"

The incident with the woodsman's book had made him brave. It might not be wise to like it. She liked it anyway. "I've had enough of this. Get the wine and sit. There are questions I should've asked you by now."

He poured with deft efficiency, hesitated, sat. "You'll want to know if I have a family, I expect. Whether there's anyone I need to find."

She tucked her legs beneath her and took the offered glass. "Astute."

"I've made a few inquiries. A visit or two. But by and large, I've found the results . . ." He drank, a short draw and incurious swallow. "If my family misses anyone, it's the boy they lost to Falcrest. Not the man they got back."

"They don't recognize you."

"That's the intent of Masquerade education, isn't it?" He shrugged, eyes averted. "To remake."

"Did Cairdine Farrier train you personally?"

He considered her over the rim of his wineglass. "I met him on Tara-noke. When he attached me to your service, he was satisfied I'd been thoroughly prepared."

"Good." She approved of both his training and his canny deflection. "The moment we've found an effective staff, I'm going to ask you to gather some information for me. You're wasted on this—" She gestured to the ceiling and her chambers. "Housework."

"It has its charms."

"So there's nothing to you but your service." She chuckled, just to take the edge off her words. "Nothing I can dangle as a prize. You want only what I want."

"What *do* you want?"

"I want to understand where power comes from," she said, without any hesitation. "And how it can best be used."

It wasn't what she'd said when drunk with Aminata. But being drunk did not, she thought, really make her more honest.

"I went out on the streets while you were in Vultjag. Walked the Arwybon Way and talked to the fishmongers and dockworkers. Everyone's whispering sedition." A clinical cast to his voice and Baru thought: *he was trained for this, to listen, to report.* "They whisper that their husbands and wives are going to be taken away. That Duchess Vultjag's going to murder Duke Heingyl in a duel and kidnap Heingyl Ri, so she won't have to marry Oathsfire herself. That Xate Yawa will put her on trial and have her lobotomized." He took another sip, his eyes cast over her shoulder, through the bay window. That watchful cold went out of his voice. "I was here during the Fools' Rebellion, when sister killed brother for collaboration and fathers disowned daughters for fratricide. I don't want to see Aurdwynn return to that. So"—he smiled self-consciously—"if you can learn anything about power—perhaps put a finger on the scales for me."

"You *do* want what I want."

"A secretary must consider such things. My mother was a loyalist during the Fools' Rebellion; so was my father, although his loyalist was the other kind. They both called themselves *loyalist,* you see. What I mean is—" He frowned at his wineglass. "What I mean is that I became very talented at considering the wants of others."

She drank, sifting the dark dry wine between her teeth. "Tomorrow," she said, "I'm going to go to the Fiat Bank, and I'm going to stop Tain Hu from starting a rebellion."

"Just so?"

Baru grinned at him. "You doubt me? Cairdine Farrier's precious savant?"

"It's just that—" He set his glass down and grappled, briefly, with some gesture he couldn't quite complete, a caution, a care. "In matters of rebellion, I always expect a price."

"Oh," she said. "Yes." She was warm with the wine, with the shape of the plan she'd begun to form, and could not keep the merriment from her voice, the joy of reaching out into the world and altering it. "There will be a price."

10

THE plaza and the Fiat Bank swarmed with soldiers.

Baru dismounted, purse and papers rattling under her left arm, heart in her throat. "You!" She pointed to the first garrison officer she saw. "What's all this?"

"Honor guard, my la—Your Excellence." He bowed at the waist. "The Jurispotence is visiting the bank."

"Well, so's the Imperial Accountant. Spread the word." She gave him a moment to step away before she allowed herself to panic. Xate Yawa here now? Coincidence or countermove? Impossible to know. No matter, though, no matter, no matter. She just had to walk in and pass the orders that would defeat Tain Hu. How could Xate Yawa prevent that?

She went in through the ranks of blue and wave-tip gray, her head high, wondering if the soldiers would respect her more or less if she'd worn her sword. "The Imperial Accountant!" an officer bawled, announcing her, betraying her. The doors of the Fiat Bank opened for her and she passed through into the hall of clerks and stag heads. Then left, along the wall, toward Principal Factor Bel Latheman's office—

Where Xate Yawa waited, sipping from a tin mug. And the Principal Factor, who looked up crossly and began to say, "My secretary will—" But his eyes fixed on her purse, her face, and recognizing Baru he sat back in his chair with ill-concealed despair, his hands checking his high collar.

"Your *Excellence*!" Xate Yawa cried. "Please forgive me if I don't rise. It's such an unexpected pleasure to find you here."

"Likewise, Your Excellence. Perhaps more unexpected, in my case, as this is a bank rather than a court." Baru took her hand and kissed it. Her eyes, those jungle crow eyes—impossible to avoid. How practiced she must be at staring into guilt.

There had been time enough for Tain Hu to alert her that Baru was on to them.

"I've been running down these degenerate ykari cultists. Bel Latheman has been invaluable." Xate Yawa smiled at the Principal Factor, who ducked his head in respectful reply, eyes twitching between the two of them. "They need property to set up their temples, after all, and every piece of property has its owner. The guilty and the negligent alike must be held to account."

Baru favored Bel Latheman with a smile. Cosmopolitan, Falcresti, and—by the curl of his lip, the sweat on his brow—clearly unhappy with his position. Perhaps she should've had a dinner with him before raiding his bank with marines. "I'm glad my Factor could be of assistance. Please, never hesitate to come to me directly."

Her Factor. He must be remembering: the last two Imperial Accountants he'd served under hadn't survived.

"Of course I'll come to you! But your secretary told me you'd gone to Vultjag." And Xate Yawa winked outrageously, as if Vultjag were a brothel or an assignation, rather than the heart of her own conspiracy. "I'm sure you have business with the Factor. Will it need privacy? I can wait for these records out on the floor."

"Oh, no," Baru said, desperate to avoid the appearance of secrecy. "Changes in monetary policy, loans to approve—just housework."

"Should've sent your secretary," Xate Yawa clucked. "That's what he's for."

Bel Latheman had spoken not one word, and his grotesque pasted-on smile nearly sent Baru into a fit of nervous laughter—*just how I feel*, she wanted to say, *just how I feel*. But she drew the orders out of her purse, sealed with the Accountant's mark, stamped with signs for urgency and secrecy. "Your Excellency," she said, extending them to Latheman. "Please see that these are implemented at once."

He smiled cautiously as he took the letters, and she saw hope—that it was not another search, not another esoteric order from an Accountant wrapped in intrigue, but a simple chance to show his capability. "At once," he said. "Of course."

"Does that mark say *secret*?" Xate Yawa set her mug down delicately. "And urgent? Your Excellency, anything worth those marks should be discussed with the Governing Factors, and I certainly haven't been part of any such conversation. Has Governor Cattlson approved these orders?"

"Ah, well." Baru smiled and screamed inside. How had she *seen*? The marks were miniscule. Those *eyes*—"The Governing Factors don't meet for nearly a month, and I'm afraid the mess left by Olonori and Tanifel can't wait that long. Word will need to be ridden out to all the ducal branch banks, you understand."

"It must be quite a sweeping policy change, then."

"Purely of technical interest, I'm certain." Baru tried to turn away but Xate Yawa's eyes caught her. Perhaps she had looked at Ffare Tanifel that way, as she watched the old Accountant drown.

"As a judge, I take great interest in technicalities. Please." The Juris-potence tried to rise, pretending infirmity, and obliged both Baru and the Principal Factor to reach out and help her up. Her grip on Baru's wrist felt warm and dry, perfectly relaxed. "Let's review these orders together. If Cattlson objects, you'll have me as an ally."

Baru's heart thundered in her chest.

She had two choices. She could order the Principal Factor to keep the letters sealed, insisting that any review of her missives required written and court-reviewed authority from an Imperial Justice. Xate Yawa would point out that she could issue this authority, so surely they might as well review the orders now. The Principal Factor would resent being trapped in the middle. Certainly Xate Yawa would go to Governor Cattlson and alarm him with stories of Baru Cormorant's secret orders.

Or she could say: "Of course. Please—unseal them. Secretary!"

Ake Sentiamut, the woman who had stolen the fiat note patterns for Tain Hu's forgers, leaned in through the door. She was not wearing her bearskin. "Your Excellency?"

"Lock the office and permit no visitors. Secret business."

The Principal Factor unsealed the two envelopes with visibly trem-bling hands. Xate Yawa craned over his left shoulder. "To the Principal Factor of the Provincial Bank," he read to her, "from the Imperial Accountant, Baru Cormorant, assigned to the Federated Province of Aurdwynn—"

"Yes, thank you, Bel." Xate Yawa clasped his shoulder. "Just set the pages down and I'll read them myself."

Baru found a seat and waited.

"Curious." Xate Yawa frowned at the letters. "You've ordered the Bank to print a new run of fiat notes in order to fund a series of loans to the dukes. And you've authorized the ducal branches to make small loans di-rectly to private citizens . . . but only in gold and silver."

Baru nodded, not trusting her tongue.

"Well, it's all very irregular, and quite against what I understand of the Imperial Republic's policy." Xate Yawa straightened without any pretense of age or infirmity. Fury, Baru thought: she is furious. "But you're the Imperial Accountant, and allegedly a capable mathematician, so you must know what you're doing. I recognize that when it comes to matters beyond the names and varieties of sin, I have little authority."

And with that she left, her gown swishing in her wake.

The gasp of relief Baru made might have been audible. Across the desk, Principal Factor Bel Latheman stared at her in bewilderment. "Do you understand what you're doing?" he hissed. "Does *she*? I cannot let these orders stand."

"Oh, yes, I understand." Baru gripped the lion-headed arms of her chair. "I've just destroyed the value of the Imperial fiat note in Aurdwynn. I've set us back ten years, ruined the provincial economy, and bankrupted most of the dukes."

Her orders would be catastrophic. The Bank would print more paper fiat notes than it could possibly back with gold and silver. That money would enter the market through seductively generous loans, new wealth conjured from ink and paper. The dukes would claw over each other just to sign first.

The Aurdwynni dukes probably didn't know the term *inflation*. Didn't understand that a glut of money supply would kill the value of the currency. But when the Aurdwynni woodcutter found that the duke's mill could now purchase his entire stock with the windfall of a generous loan, he'd raise his prices. So would the fishmongers and the miners, the quarrymen and the estate dealers, the hunters and tanners. Everyone who worked for a wage would face those rising prices and demand a raise in turn, just so they could still manage to buy food.

The purchasing power of the fiat note, the amount of anything real you could buy with it, would plummet as commodity prices skyrocketed. It was monetary suicide. Confidence in the fiat note would collapse, and in short order, Falcrest's favorite weapon would be useful only as toilet tissue.

Which meant that all those loans and debts Tain Hu intended to leverage to build alliances—loans issued and debts held by the Fiat Bank, in fiat notes—would be worthless.

So would her own counterfeits.

Everything measured in fiat money would be wiped clean. There was nothing Xate Yawa or Governor Cattlson could do to stop it.

Tain Hu's rebellion would die along with the debts.

And in the meantime, the gold that the Fiat Bank had been stockpiling for all these years would be loaned out in little parcels. Not to the dukes—Baru had made sure of that. The gold loans she'd authorized would go to the olive farmers and fishermen and woodcutters. The masons with their chalk-dust sons.

Aurdwynn would slide back into its preinvasion economy, driven by gold and commodities. Except that the gold would now be in the hands of the commoner. She'd watched the Masquerade remake Taranoke's economy, and now she would do precisely the opposite to Aurdwynn.

And every one of those gold loans, those loans that would save a hundred thousand serfs from starvation and debt, would be signed on paper that read BY THE GENEROSITY OF THE IMPERIAL ACCOUNTANT, BARU CORMORANT. Every one.

Most Aurdwynni serfs couldn't read. All the better. Someone would have to speak the contract aloud. *By the generosity of Baru Cormorant.*

Remember her name.

"We should be seen at dinner," Baru said.

The Principal Factor goggled at her. "*Excuse* me?"

"My work leaves me no time for courtship. I need an ornamental man to shield myself against unseemly whispers. We have a professional relationship to hide behind, which will make the affair all the more believable. Are you married?"

"No," he said. His shoulders slumped with profound fatigue. "But—"

"That's a shame. It would be a more convincing scandal. But we'll make do." She smiled and clapped the desk. "Write my secretary. He'll make arrangements. Oh—and—"

He put his head in his hands. "Yes?"

"Your secretary in the bear coat. She's a Sentiamut? Down from Vultjag?"

"Ake? Born Hodfyri. A Sentiamut by marriage. Though her husband is in the Cold Cellar for sedition." His eyes widened. "No! She's indispensable."

"Fire her," Baru ordered.

* * *

WHAT happened next was simple economics.

"It's my fault," Baru told the actress. "I did all this."

A fence of shot glasses divided their territories at the bar. The actress had spilled water or whiskey on the redwood, and as she listened she drew rivers between the droplets with her bare fingers, so that they would flow together.

"You can't have," she said. She had a rich Urun accent and she wore a fine damask gown in red and gold. "All those dukes and merchants ruined? How could one woman do that?"

Spring had turned to summer. For a little while, Baru's new loans made the market euphoric. Then the economy gorged itself on a glut of fiat notes and finally began to choke. Prices spiked. Inflationary collapse kindled in the dockside markets and rolled out like paper thunder.

Baru's counterplay. Tain Hu and Xate Yawa held in check.

And all it had cost was this breed of devastation—

"Entirely my work." Baru set another empty crystal glass in the dividing wall. "The poverty. The riots. The curfews that came from the riots. The merchants dumping their fiat notes in the harbor because they're not worth their own space in the cargo hold. The columns of starving people leaving the city. All this—" She laughed, meaning to sound hollow, regretful, but it came out a husky boast. "All this was by my craft."

The actress exhaled softly, surprised or impressed. The rivers of whiskey in her territory trembled in their candlelit course.

A careless observer might have taken the actress for Baru's sister— a little shorter, a little less severe, untrained by Naval System exercise or day labor, but close enough that Baru felt she could use the similarity as camouflage. She had presence, too, a kind of wordless needless authority, torchlike, contingent on no approval or loyalty. That might have drawn Baru to speak to her, if she hadn't come to Baru first. She was new to this tavern—a recommendation from her cousin—and maybe she had seen something of herself in Baru, too.

Baru spent too much time in bars now, to be drunk, to be near the sea. She wore sailor's garb, and if the curfew patrols challenged her in the streets, she showed them the technocrat's sign. Tonight she had gone to a place near Atu Hall, to get away from the divers who drank harborside, long-legged swimmer women with ankle knives and instincts keyed up on mason leaf. They were dangerous in too many ways, and damnably distracting. Actresses were safer.

"So you have more power than, say, any given duke." The actress made a decisive finger stroke, connecting two beaded reservoirs of liquor. Her eyes weighed Baru sidelong, curious. "That's your claim?"

"They only rule by blood. My claim is higher."

"Ah—such noble blood, though."

"Is it?"

"Every day Duke Heingyl rides patrol with his cavalry to save the refugees from banditry. Truly an honorable man."

"They say Duke Radaszic rides patrol, too, to save the refugees from Heingyl's company. Noble in his own way." The actress laughed, delighted and affronted. Baru put a coin on the bar and beckoned for another drink. "What use is noble blood to them? I only needed one letter to destroy their wealth, and I am—" She touched her own cheekbones, the bridge of her nose. "Vulgar."

The actress raised a hand, gestured with two fingers, a motion of decisive negation. "No. They still have wealth."

"Not in my books."

"Then your books are incomplete."

Baru put one finger down on her side of the wall, as if to pin something invisible to the wood. "Show me the error. Show me Radaszic's secret wealth."

"Radaszic is a fop—to think the Duchy of Wells is ruled by a man who doesn't understand irrigation! But he has sons. Duke Heingyl will never be anything more than Cattlson's dog, but his daughter is brilliant. Have you read her monographs? Duke Lyxaxu and Duke Oathsfire both have daughters. Duchess Ihuake has a son and a daughter, and badly wants more." The actress touched the wall of glasses between them, selecting one, then another, correcting their alignment. Her eyes followed Baru's, guarded, intent, trying to offer something, or ask for it. "They have family. They have heirs. The line is secure. No trick of ink can take that from them."

Baru took another shot of rough whiskey. It went down hard. "More mouths to feed," she said, looking for a gap in the wall to fill. "If Xate Yawa doesn't take them. If the Charitable Service doesn't send them to Falcrest."

The actress took the empty glass from her and found it a place in the wall. "Ah," she said.

Baru, considering the geometry of whiskey-damp glass, the spray of light from the candles and lanterns that refracted through them, made a small adjustment. "Ah?"

"You told me something about yourself, just there."

"I doubt it."

"When was the last time you took any notice of a child?"

"Children pay no taxes."

"Can you name a single ducal consort? Lyxaxu's, perhaps?"

"I don't bother with trivia."

"Do you know the story of Xate Olake's marriage to Tain Ko? Could you tell me why Heingyl Ri has only one living cousin, and who it is? Can you name the dukes who lost all their children in the Fools' Rebellion?"

Baru brushed the challenge away. "Touching stories, I'm sure. I'm not a playwright. If it mattered, I would learn."

"You rule a nation of the bereft. That matters. It changes how we think."

"I keep my mind on my work."

"You don't have children, I presume?"

"No." Startling how quickly her company had become tiresome, really. "Do you?"

"I could. I could rule Aurdwynn with them."

Baru laughed at the thought. "Mothering your way to empire?"

The laugh struck something, an edge of pride or defiance. The actress leaned forward, hands on her knees, and Baru found something in her eyes, maybe offered, maybe revealed by the defeat of the camouflage that had kept it hidden: a distant horizon, a movement of wind across an imagined future, not Cairdine Farrier's mechanism, not so cold or certain—instead a passion, a want, and a powerful will fixed upon that want. Her voice carried the charge of it. "I would get children with the dukes and the sons of the duchesses. I would marry my blood into theirs and hold their loyalty by passion and shared joy. Once I had my heirs aligned, my rivals bound to my flesh, I would tear up the borders and stitch our lands together. I would irrigate the herdlands and make them rich with wheat, I would feed the cattle and make my people fat on milk and beef, I would guard my roads with the broad-backed sons and daughters of women free to love. Against our ancient strength the pale chemistries and mincing edicts of a younger people would be as a child's tantrum, and they would pass away into the east to be forgotten. I would issue forth a dynasty. And my blood would make a place in the world for the Urun songs to sound again, for the imperial line of the Tu Maia to find its lost glory and in time surpass it. This is the power I claim."

The fire went out of her eyes, and the breath from her chest. She looked at the dripping shapes she'd drawn on the wood for a moment, and then back at Baru. In the silence after her voice, she looked terribly young.

"Sounds expensive," Baru said, to cover her response. "Do you need a loan?"

The actress laughed, a wild unbroken sound, and here after the stage-searing monologue and that laugh, Baru had to admit that perhaps she was not safer company than a diver at all.

"A loan," the actress said, "of course, who doesn't? And noble blood, to make the claim I need. So I suppose I'll stay in Treatymont, pretending to be people I'm not."

"You're very good at it." Baru meant it: it was a stirring monologue, in its way. "What play was it from?"

"An original, actually." She shrugged. "I'm still working on it. I think it risks being called seditious."

"It is my Imperial duty to support the arts. I'll pay your tab."

"Truly, the power of coin surpasses all others." The actress stood, checking the hems of her gown. "I'll tell my cousin she chooses interesting bars."

BARU drank and sang and learned some Iolynic and some Urun and sometimes sat alone in silence. On another night, an entirely separate actress, drunk, ample and beautiful in the way that Maia culture preferred, said: "Why do you hide everything? I want to see laughter, or tears, not a second sort of mask." And Baru thought: if I am going to Falcrest to win the secrets of empire, I must be entirely devoted to it, outside and in. I must be able to hide any emotion, pretend to be anyone.

If there is rebellion in my heart, a rebellion of huntress mothers with man-killing spears come to find their vanished husbands, well, I must be ready with acid and steel mask.

But she answered: "I spend too much time with numbers."

Passing in different worlds became second nature. First nature, perhaps: what else was she? What loyalty did she really have behind the mask?

She had crushed Tain Hu's rebellion in the name of her own advancement. She needed to get to Falcrest. Needed to play the Masquerade's game in order to reach the top.

There had been no other choice.

In a wharfside tavern, watching merchant sailors pass dice and news, she set eyes on a tall, feline Maia man in a hawk-feather mask. Her interest piqued by his solitary discomfort and the peace-knotted sword at his side, she took her wine and pulled him out of the crowd, not sure what she would do with him but eager to hone her deception.

"You're Baru Cormorant," the man said. He had a smoky voice, not very deep, perhaps affected. "I recognize you."

She put him down on one side of a battered table and took the other. "Tonight I'm not," she said. "Tonight I'm from Aurdwynn."

"You could pass for Maia, if you wore a mask." He rolled his shoulders and stretched, arms hairless and sinewy. Baru did not disguise her interest in this trait. Perhaps it even gave her a little relief. Her occasional dinners with Bel Latheman were colder than Governor Cattlson's attitude in council (the poor man had seemed utterly lovestruck at first— Latheman, not Cattlson—but Baru decided very quickly that he was, thankfully, lovesick for someone else). "But you'll need a new name."

"I'm open to suggestions," Baru said.

"Fisher," the man suggested. "A forest weasel beloved of commoners, and a play on words."

"A play on words?" She frowned, not following the pun in Aphalone.

"A cormorant is a fishing bird. In Iolynic *fisher* means *a weasel who fishes*. They're a symbol of ykari Devena, the Fulcrum."

"Ah. Clever. Baru Fisher, beloved of a forbidden god." She nodded to his blade. "There are people who want to kill me, you know. Dukes I bankrupted, rebels I frustrated, Parliaments I disappointed. You could collect quite a prize. I don't even think the Jurispotence or Governor would object, after what I've done to the fiat note. Falcrest's tax ministers are in an uproar."

"My blade," he said dryly, "is knotted, and will take some work to extract."

Baru considered him as she drank, judging his accent and voice, his knowledge of woodslore, the crooked set of his nose. A ranger, maybe? He had Tu Maia blood, that much was obvious.

Or—

She tilted her head, considered the man's eyes for a few moments, then reached out and took him by the chin. He did not draw away, even when she squeezed as if to test the familiarity of his bone. She leaned across the table, drawing him in. Saw his lips part, his eyes half-close. Felt his chin lift in her grip.

Disappointed him, perhaps, by whispering in his ear instead: "Tain Hu. What a determined disguise."

Duchess Vultjag laughed huskily. "Spotted at last. So slow! I thought you'd know me by more than my face."

"Have you come to kill me?"

"Your countermove is cast. The fiat note has collapsed. I have no answer." Her hair, cut so short since last they'd met, brushed Baru's ear as her head moved. "You've ruined yourself to ruin us, you realize. Liberated us from the shackles of the fiat note. Burnt ten years of the Masquerade's economic conquest to the ground. In a way, I've still won."

"But I've stopped you."

"For now. But consider your own future."

Baru drew away, fell back in her chair, and drank again. Tain Hu, taking it as the consideration she'd asked after, laughed.

What a strange position they found themselves in. They'd cast their spears, and now they sat together, wounded and bled dry. More than anyone else in Aurdwynn, she knew Tain Hu's wants and secrets. She had already destroyed them as thoroughly as she could.

Perhaps that meant Tain Hu could trust her.

"I have some advice for you," she said. "A clever idea I read about. Something the Oriati devised."

Tain Hu lifted her glass. "Go on."

"Every summer you buy grain and fruits for Vultjag, to stockpile against the winter. When the price spikes, you suffer—and all your families, the Sentiamut-Vultjags and the Hodfyri-Vultjags and the others, they suffer, too. When the price is unexpectedly low, the grain merchants suffer. Both of you would prefer a happy middle. So—" She'd drunk enough wine to make drinking more feel like a good idea. "Set up your contracts in advance. Buy next summer's grain now."

Tain Hu frowned. "I suppose that I should say it hasn't been grown yet, and so we can't know if the crop will be large and cheap, or small and expensive."

"That's exactly why you set up the contract now—to protect yourselves against uncertainty. The merchants give up the chance at an unusually high price. You'll give up the chance of an unusually low one. But you'll both reduce your risk. You'll be able to budget better and guarantee grain to your serfs. They'll be able to rely on a solid profit."

Tain Hu pursed her lips beneath the feathered fringe of her mask. "Your last economic policy ruined thousands. There are people who'll starve and die this winter because of you."

"Nonsense and hyperbole." Some venom in Baru's voice; at night she flinched from these fears. "Only the nobility, the landlords, and the merchant class invested in fiat money. They were the fish the Masquerade wanted to net, and they were the fish I gutted. I am a champion of—" She laughed into her cup. "A champion of the common people."

"Yes. I've heard that said. Your gold loans have made you a name in the cattle pens and quarries. But you don't understand Aurdwynn, Your Excellence. When a duke suffers, he extracts the compensation from his people."

Baru brooded in silence, her eyes flickering around the tavern, across the sailors, past a man with hair the red of rowan fruit who had just ordered an extravagantly old drink and drawn admirers for it.

It was Tain Hu who broke the silence. "Tell me about Taranoke."

"I can hardly remember," Baru lied, and then the lie spun itself off her tongue, full of little pieces of the truth. "Just the colors. How dark the earth was, how clear the sea. We were alone with the stars and the waves and I used to think . . . when I stood with my fathers to watch the merchant ships go out, I used to think the ships would fall off the edge of the world, and we would remain. I didn't know about harborside, or plainsmen, or currency trading, or masks."

"Your fathers. More than one?"

"We were savages," Baru said, stomach leaping—just to speak of this was taboo, surely, and now she would have to make excuses. "We didn't know better. In the Masquerade school I learned—"

"For sodomites, hot iron; for tribadists, the knife," Tain Hu recited. "I know the codes of hygiene, the names of sin. They ordered me to post them on every door in Vultjag. They set neighbor watching neighbor."

"I had so many aunts and uncles," Baru whispered. Oh, to speak of this to her foe—so unwise, so poor a move. But this was her weakness: drink, and the chance to pretend she lived in a warmer world, where secrets could be shared. . . . "On midsummer days, when the stars were bright, we would come out of our houses and join hands. We could make a chain all the way from the sea to—to—"

Her voice broke with the memory. She decided that silence would be wiser.

"When we rise," Tain Hu said, "I'll make it known that I want you alive, Baru Fisher. I've already asked the Phantom Duke to spare you."

"You murdered Su Olonori when he came close to stopping you." The Phantom Duke again, Xate Yawa's vanished brother. The rebel spymaster? Make note, Baru, make note—Tain Hu lets her secrets slip as well . . . "Why spare me?"

"Because you won't stop us."

"I can't let you win." Baru shook her head, dizzy with the wine. "You were born to rule your home. I have to win the right to rule mine. I—I have to go to Falcrest."

"You will find no power behind the mask." Cold, rooted conviction in Tain Hu's voice. "It will wear you. It will eat your face away. You would do more for your home if you tore it all down."

"How could I? How could anyone? They rule by coin and chemistry and the very words we speak. Falcrest's power is vast, patient, resilient. No little rebellion will last." Baru shook her head. "The only way forward is through. From within."

"You will pay a terrible price. You will lose yourself."

"Any price," Baru rasped, each word a debit, a loss in her account books: secrets given for no advantage, for no reason except that her heart moved her to speak them. Her traitor heart. "Any sacrifice. It is the only way to take a piece of their power for our own."

Tain Hu sat across from her for a short while, as if waiting for her to say something that had been left unsaid, or take some chance still untaken. But in the wine and the heat Baru could not say or see it, and later she would not remember when exactly Tain Hu had gone.

INTERLUDE:
CRYPTARCHS

THAT next night, Baru finished a book, a history of revolutionary Falcrest, the days of *The Handbook of Manumission* and *The Antler Stone*. Regicide days; days when old bloodlines ran across Commsweal Square or burned out in the bitter mouths and ungrown gonads of royal children fed sterilizer. Days of terror, as the uprising turned on itself in a glioma of constant cannibalistic treachery.

It had been a nightmare, of course, a self-perpetuating atrocity. But it had also been an opportunity. Those who had survived the bloodbath had set the course of the Imperial Republic, and the world.

How would she have done it, if she'd been there? She sat in the dark, chin in her hands, and wondered—how would I have weathered the revolution?

Trust, like money, needed a guarantee to back it. She would need allies with secrets. Secrets that she could hold over them. If she wanted to build a web, well, she would make it out of people already full of hooks.

Yes—that would do it. Everyone poised to destroy everyone else, and thereby held in check. A trust governed not by love or simple fear, but by the assurance of mutual ruin, by the delicately balanced threat of certain annihilation for anyone who stepped out of line. Mutual blackmail.

It was the power Xate Yawa had come so close to holding over her.

"Muire Lo!" she called. He had been staying late to oversee the work of rebuilding the books, and sometimes fell to napping in her office. "Lo, come up here!"

He peeked warily around the banister. "Your Excellence?"

"What's the Aphalone word for . . ." She considered. "Rule by secrets?"

"Oh. Hm." He frowned. "I don't know."

"Fetch the dictionaries," she commanded. But she went down to the office with him to help, barefooted on the tiles, laughing with him as they opened volume after volume, papering the floor with their hunt.

But the word would not come. "We're going about this wrong," Muire Lo said, sitting in a circle of abandoned thesauruses and rubbing his temples. "What should the roots be? If you had to invent the word now, from first principles—what would it be?"

"Crypsis," Baru said, "for secrets." She sat beside him, leaning back on her hands. The lamps made their shadows dance. "And the suffix?"

"For rule? -Archy."

"Crypsarchy?"

"Cryptarchy. And the rulers would be cryptarchs."

Baru thought of the Masked Emperor, silent and mindless on the throne. Of Cairdine Farrier laughing behind the mask. A chill took her, and she trembled, making a small uncomfortable sound. "A draft," she said, to explain it and, at Muire Lo's skeptical sidelong glance—"I'm cold!"

"Did you expect otherwise? You're in a nightgown."

"You're no help."

He considered her dryly. "I could fetch you a blanket, though it would be patronizing. My other options all seem wholly improper."

She laughed, and then considered herself through his eyes, sprawled beside him, immodest and foreign and powerful and laughing. It was a strange thing, even after all these years of Masquerade conditioning, to look at herself through other eyes, to think: I cannot act this way, even though he is my ally, my advisor. It will make him feel things I cannot afford.

She drew herself upright. "I'll help you with the books."

"It's all right." He stood to bow, and waved her off as she began to gather the scattered dictionaries. "Please, Your Excellence. The draft will make you sick."

WARLORD

A S the repercussions of the fiat note's collapse rippled out to Falcrest, Baru's dreams of a career crumbled down around her.

She spent her days on work, managing a tower full of new and untrustworthy staff, fighting to rebuild the books ruined by Olonori's tenure and the economy ruined by her own. At night she retired with her books or her blade. Muire Lo moved into the tower's cellar after someone burned out his apartment—men from Duchy Radaszic, Baru suspected; the cheerful Duke of Wells had seen his wealth gutted by the fiat note's collapse. On some days Baru took dinner with him. On others she made appearances with Principal Factor Bel Latheman, whose reputation she'd destroyed by mere proximity.

But he was a shield, the poor man, a vital shield.

No word came from Cairdine Farrier. No acknowledgment that she had quelled incipient rebellion. No sign that Parliament felt anything but rage and astonishment at her policies. Her letters mostly came from Duke Lyxaxu, one of Vultjag's neighbors, who wrote long articulate opinions about phenomenology and the philosophy of rule that she dwelled on and always *meant* to find time to reply to.

She began to think she had imagined Farrier's mysterious influence, his shadowy colleagues with names like Hesychast, his intimations of the apparatus behind the Masked Throne.

And so it went for the next three years.

Three years while Aurdwynn's dukes grumbled in impoverished discontent, and the Fiat Bank bled its hoard of gold back into the Midlands and the valleys of the north, and little dale-rebellions guttered out under acid smoke, and Tain Hu introduced Aurdwynn to futures contracts, and Muire Lo made a theater out of his failure to conceal his letters back to Falcrest, reporting, as he had to, on her successes and missteps. Three years of work and no sign of progress.

She went to the harbor and drank, scrupulously alone, mindful never to establish patterns, except for the obvious pattern of drinking more and more.

And then came the day when a ship anchored with news that Taranoke had been renamed Sousward, and while Baru drank away her feelings on this topic, a man with red Stakhieczi hair curled over pale Stakhieczi cheeks came into the tavern and ordered something well beyond his apparent means.

He came to her lonely table and sat. When she looked at him in irritation, trying to remember where she had seen him before, he smiled brilliantly and said:

"Do you know the Hierarchic Qualm?"

THE man's hair was absurdly, outrageously red. Dye, perhaps—or pure Stakhieczi blood in his veins, freckled on his pale cheeks, written in the color of his eyes.

"The Hierarchic Qualm." Of all the strangers Baru had met in these taverns, none of them had ever opened with something out of Falcresti revolutionary philosophy, from the old *Handbook of Manumission*. "I know it. Why?"

"It's a test, of course." The man waved past her, into Treatymont, into Aurdwynn. "Tests behind you, and tests ahead. I'm not sure I believe you know it."

"Oh," Baru said. "I'm crushed." Her mind circled back, again and again, to the news that had just come: *Taranoke renamed Sousward; the Sixth Fleet will be built and harbored there; plentiful lumber and labor available, so long as unrest among the population can be controlled—*

All as she had foreseen on that last day on Taranoke, walking to the harbor and *Lapetiare* to say good-bye.

The stranger leaned into the conversation. He smelled of salt fragrance. "Itinerant told me that you were always eager to display your masteries. But that was three years ago, when you still hoped to be a technocrat in Falcrest. Perhaps you've wandered from the path he saw for you."

Baru set down her cup and regarded the man with cold disinterest, trying to hide the stab of panic he'd aroused, the sick fascination. At last, at last, here it was again—the conspiracy of strangers who watched and

judged her, the cabal who made Governor Cattlson treat an undistinguished merchant like a superior.

"Farrier," she said, connecting the dots. "He's the one you call Itinerant. And he mentioned his colleague, Hesychast. Do I have the pleasure,
then?"

"Ha! No." The northman took one sip of his outrageously expensive
drink and made a face of bliss. He wore a stark, loose-fit shirt and a short
jacket. He looked a little like a dandy playing sailor, and that might
have fooled someone born elsewhere; but he kept his neckerchief in a
grief knot, which Baru knew as a sailor's joke. "I don't share Hesychast's
preoccupation with the science of who fucks who. They call me Apparitor,
which makes me the one they dispatch. And here I am, bearing a message. Now: the Hierarchic Qualm?"

"The sword kills," Baru recited, trying to remember the *Handbook
of Manumission,* its arguments for revolutionary zeal. "But the arm
moves the sword. Is the arm to blame for murder? No. The mind moves
the arm. Is the mind to blame? No. The mind has sworn an oath to duty,
and that duty moves the mind, as written by the Throne. So it is that a
servant of the Throne is blameless."

"Come," the man who called himself Apparitor said. "Walk with me."

They went out and circled the evening harbor where the water murmured on copper and barnacle and quay-timbers and the evening light
rusted the white merchant sails with hints of Navy red.

Apparitor spoke:

"What you did to the fiat note three years ago destroyed all our progress in Aurdwynn. We meant to use the province as a tax base for war
against the Oriati federations. Now we take losses on Aurdwynn. Half
of Parliament has been baying for your blood—and the rest demand
the head of whoever installed a Taranoki girl as Imperial Accountant. They
had great expectations for Aurdwynn, as a source of easy wealth and a
shield against the Stakhieczi invading south across the Wintercrests. But
with all the dukes free of their debt and the gold reserves bleeding back
into the land, we've lost our hold." He looked at her, the masts of a dromon at his back, its sailcloth a canvas for his exotic color (so *pale . . .*),
and he smiled impishly. "But the question is, Baru Cormorant, did you
destroy the fiat note in service of the Throne? Are you thus blameless?"

"Parliament doesn't understand Aurdwynn. I did what was necessary to preserve the Imperial Republic's rule here." She'd written no letters to Falcrest in defense of her policy. How could she? They would demand Xate Yawa's corroboration to prove that Tain Hu had been using the prisons for forgery.

Apparitor studied her with open interest, and she used the opening to study him in turn. He was young—not much older than she—and slight, but he moved with unhurried confidence and a kind of high-headed pride, a strange subtle cant of nobility. It vexed her, that carriage, because he spoke like Cairdine Farrier, but somehow in a distant way his motion rhymed with Tain Hu.

He spoke again. "Parliament understands little except its own interest. But *we* understand Aurdwynn. That's why we sent you here."

"You." She'd spent so much of the last three years wondering about this. "You and Cairdine Farrier and Hesychast? The power behind the Masked Emperor on the Faceless Throne?"

"There are others, too. We—we *are* the Throne. The . . ." He hunted for words, and Baru thought: this is not something he commonly explains. "The steering committee. We keep our eyes on the horizon while Parliament squabbles over the wealth of empire." He made a gesture of self-deprecation. "Just a few philosophers and adventurers, delicately balanced, who happen to sign their position papers with the Emperor's name. Held in careful, mutual check by our shared secrets."

"And you put me here? You were behind my placement exam, behind my appointment?"

"Itinerant championed your potential as a savant. It has occurred to us—" He opened a hand to the distant Wintercrests marching across the horizon. "It has occurred to us that the saying is true. Aurdwynn cannot be ruled. The dukes are a useful way to keep the people in line. But the great problem with these dukes is that they are not all loyal to us, hmm? If a storm comes down on the Empire, some of them will cast their lot with us, and some with the enemy. If that enemy is a united Stakhieczi invasion, or a renascent Tu Maia empire out of the west, or the menace from across the Mother of Storms—well, we cannot risk division in a moment of crisis. So how to draw out the disloyal, we wondered? How to address the trouble of the dukes? How to purge Aurdwynn of its illness, before that illness sickens our Empire? We have a favorite method."

Baru understood at once, and the weight of it, the callous crushing sweep of what they were, took her breath away: this quiet committee hidden away in the bureaucracy, plotting out migrations and conquests, transfers of wealth or culture or plague across decades and leagues, with the cold assurance that it was all scientific, all properly Incrastic, that they understood best what prices would need to be paid.

What price she would pay.

"Civilization must endure," the Apparitor said, as if reading her thoughts in her eyes. "At all costs, the Empire must survive. The lives our sanitation and discipline will save, the victories we will win against disease and disorder in the centuries to come—they justify any brutality. We must have control. Control by any means." *Nazism?*

"I understand what you want me to do," she said, stunned by her own calm. Perhaps she had always known, since the moment in the cabin with Muire Lo when she had realized the power she had. "But what do I obtain from the bargain?"

Apparitor clapped his hands. "Ah, now, that's the good bit. Itinerant and the merit exams are in agreement, Baru Cormorant. You *are* a savant, a savant not merely at figures but at the understanding and the exercise of power. You are Taranoki, bred from the lineages of the Tu Maia, who ruled half the Ashen Sea, and Oriati Mbo, which produced the finest thinkers of the last millennium. The things you know in your blood are the key to understanding a piece of the world that has so far escaped our grasp. To understand is to master, and it is mastery we seek." *emphasis on pure blood-lines, race*

"You would make me—"

"Do this thing for us, survive it, and yes." The Apparitor's face became abruptly solemn. "We will give you what you most desire. What you have craved since childhood."

She wanted to laugh, and call his bluff: This is what you offer me, in exchange for collapsing the fiat currency? Or, perhaps: why not let me rise through your bureaucracy, season and prove myself? You're lying, lying to make me do this thing for you, to use me as an instrument, foreign-born and expendable.

But she had known, these past three years, that she would never rise up through the bureaucracy. She had ruined too many with the inflation trick. Ruined herself.

She remembered Cairdine Farrier's favorite declamation, the value of merit and merit alone, and realized what he had been trying to prepare her for.

"So." The Apparitor straightened his neckerchief and smiled. "Will you execute the will of the Throne?"

THE next day she visited Census and Methods, the bones of Imperial power: ream upon ream of records cataloging everything valuable in Aurdwynn, stone and gold, salt and lumber, flesh and blood. Demographic projections of the available workforce. The tax base and the export rate. The relative concentration of Stakhi, Belthyc, and Maia blood.

The department fell under Xate Yawa's purview, and the Jurispotence's eyes watched Baru as she worked, as they watched Baru on the street, in her tower, in the meetings of the Factors. She did not so much as dare to make eye contact with women here. Ffare Tanifel had been brought down on charges of licentiousness—an unacceptably overt fondness for men. Baru carried higher sins.

She worked in silent, taut fury.

She'd had enough. Enough of compliance. Enough of quietly playing her role. As far as Parliament was concerned, collapsing the fiat currency had marked her ineptitude not just on her permanent record but on her very heredity. Her dream of Falcrest, of telescopes and academies, of the Metademe or the Faculties or even Parliament itself, was dead. There might be recriminations against other Taranoki in the Imperial Service. They might even have punished Pinion and Solit.

She would not save Taranoke by excelling as the Imperial Accountant. She would never be a technocrat or a scholar or a member of Parliament.

But another way had opened.

The power of the Imperial bureaucracy lay in its ability to quantify and understand the world, so that those quantities could be turned into the wise expenditure of money and armies, the optimal extraction of tax and treaty.

Baru wanted to know how to quantify what the people of Aurdwynn thought about her.

She combed the census riders, the simple poll questions the Governor—and sometimes the Imperial Accountant—could attach as a *not at all democratic*

way to pretend to care about public opinion. Frowning in frustration, she read: *census riders shall be reviewed and approved by authorized factors of the Governor.*

There was no way to get the information she wanted out of the next census without alerting Cattlson.

She made a show of frustration in her exit. Later tonight, someone in the Jurispotence's employ would read the report: *Baru Cormorant displeased, as usual.*

At the Governor's House, climbing through the many murmuring rooms of her tower, she hit on the solution to her census problem. "Muire Lo!" she called, sweeping past his deck. "My office!"

They'd had three years to fall into a routine with each other, a routine that had to fit all the things he had been to her—nursemaid, guide, tailor, functionary, notebook, ineffective watcher—and all the things that she had done to him: his ongoing solitude, his cramped little quarters in the base of the tower, the ill-hidden discomfort that they both felt at his reports to a distant man in a distant city, the sharp dislike he had taken to the "unforgivably rude" Principal Factor Bel Latheman.

"Your Excellence?" He closed her office door, for privacy, and made a theater out of pouring wine, chiming glass against glass. "Another bank run?"

She went to him. "I want to add a little annex to this season's common tax form," she murmured in his ear. "It should tell the commoner that ten notes of their tax will be allocated among their local duke, Governor Cattlson, Jurispotence Xate, and myself, for use in our own personal projects. It's up to them to decide how to split the ten."

"What possible reason could I give?" Muire Lo looked at her in bewilderment.

"They'll invent their own reasons, I'm sure. What's important is that Cattlson has to approve the census rider—but he *never* reads the tax form." She clapped him on the shoulder. "See to it."

"And shall I make arrangements for these ten-note distributions?"

"Oh, no." She went to the stairway door up to her quarters, pleased with herself. "No need for that. I just want their answers."

She would make a map of Aurdwynn's loyalties. A map of the new road forward.

*   *   *

BARU sat at the window with her knees tucked under her chin and considered the city.

If she did this thing, this would be the last moment of real peace she'd have for a long time—perhaps for the rest of her life, and no telling how long that would be. She'd been comfortable here, for all her failures, for all the currency she'd debased and merchants she'd ruined, all the letters from Duke Lyxaxu she'd left unanswered. She had a room in a high tower with a hot bath and a clever secretary. She could rise every day and set her eyes to the parchment, testing all her wit and learning against the unending disaster of Aurdwynn's financial collapse.

Had she been happy, all this time? Had the endless meetings of the Governing Factors, the men explaining her own job and policies to her in slow simple words, been a fair price for a taste of power? Had all the harborside nights, disguised in the dress of another woman with another homeland, another accent, another taste, been a delightful game, a proper challenge?

Beneath her window, a squad of garrison soldiers made a sweep of the streets, masked and gloved, checking the beggars and petitioners for signs of plague. Xate Yawa maintained a sanitarium on the eastern edge of the city, outside the walls, where Masquerade doctors of the Morrow Ministry studied the effects of ailments foreign and domestic on Aurdwynn's races. Some marked it as the finest experimental clinic on the Ashen Sea. Those with natural resistance would be bred widely—in this respect, men were preferred, as they could conceive more offspring in less time. Especially virulent carriers would, it was whispered, be whisked away on special ships to Oriati Mbo, where they could be released into the enemy's cities in the event of war.

You are part of this. Tain Hu's voice, three years past, still close enough to make her shiver.

Hadn't she wanted to be able to change things, at the beginning? Hadn't she looked at the red-sailed ship in Iriad harbor and begged mother Pinion to explain?

But she'd had so long to learn since then—how could she forget all those lessons in Incrastic philosophy and directional history? She'd been made to understand that the Imperial Republic was a new and better mode of civilization, dictated by rational rules, rules that recognized the different and specialized abilities of the sexes and races, rules that could sniff out unhygienic behavior in the halls of power and the cribs and bedrooms of distant lands, before that behavior could crawl into the hereditary line and derange the blood. The libraries of the Imperial Republic brimmed with enough knowledge to make the hundred thousand stars of Taranoke's sky seem like a child's scrawl, a dim wonder from a less masterful world. The Justices and Incrastic scholars had named more varieties and consequences of sin than the children of Taranoke could ever have imagined.

How could she forget that? How could she weigh cousin Lao and Father Salm more heavily than the fate of nations?

Surely that would be irrational. Surely it would be better to walk the narrow, safe path. To remain an Imperial Accountant, rather than daring everything on this incredible gambit.

Her thoughts ran in cannibal circles. She rang for Muire Lo.

"Your Excellence?"

"If I want to change something," she said, "but I don't know what, exactly, or how—what is the logical way to proceed?"

"Emperor Unane Atu Maia, *The Dictates*. In the absence of direction, claim and expand the freedom to act as you will." *what does this mean? If you don't know what to do, do what's*

"Good," she said, reassured somehow that they were in accordance, *right in* that he would understand: *get more power, so that you can remake the your own world*. "As I thought. I need you to make me an unusual appointment." *eyes.*

She would go through with it, bind herself to this gambit, swallow this secret of secrets. This would be the first step down the new road.

She would give up her place in the Accountant's Tower, and take an awful chance.

Muire Lo had given her the connection three years ago, when they'd expected revolt at any moment. *Tain Hu's late aunt was married to Xate Yawa's brother, Xate Olake, the Phantom Duke of Lachta.*

The man who'd killed Su Olonori.

"I need to speak to the Phantom Duke. To Xate Olake," she said. "Wherever he is, find him and bring him to me."

Muire Lo looked at her in silence for a little while, bowed, and left.

12

I'VE had enough of this," Bel Latheman said.

Baru held up a hand to ward off the waiter. "Pardon me?"

They had met to be seen together, as they did monthly, in places Baru chose so it seemed she was making an effort at discretion. Lately it had been fashionable for members of the provincial authorities and the Trade Factor to eat in open longhouses, served by rare pureblood Belthycs, stolen out of the forests, who smiled and minced and offered trimmed venison marinated in citrus and barded with beef fat, or albacore, or sea bream grilled on redwood charcoal. With Aurdwynn's native wealth so terribly battered, luxury establishments had learned to cater to the foreigner.

Baru and the Principal Factor had gone to one of these longhouses, finely dressed, to eat in curt silence and vanish together in a carriage for a pretended liaison. She'd grown to enjoy the display of tailored gowns and underdone jewelry, the sly comparisons and jealous asides of dining technocrats. Bel Latheman had been meticulous in his makeup and dress, always leading the local fashion. In this as in his work, he was diligent and competent.

Somehow three years of mock assignations had lulled her into the assumption that he'd accepted this as part of his job.

"I said, I've had enough of this. I will not play my part any longer." He cut his venison into small squares as he spoke, his eyes on his plate, knuckles white on his knife. "I'm quite certain, Your Excellence, that I need not describe the damage done to my reputation, both as a financier and a marriageable man, by our—our—"

"Arrangement," Baru suggested, pressing the irritation out of her tone. Oh, it was unjust to think this, but why now? Why would this man make a scene *now*, with so much about to happen—but that was unjust. He'd been a perfectly pliant and useful instrument, both at the bank and at the dinner table. "And of course, of course, you needn't describe the damage."

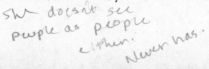

"Perhaps I do, though. Perhaps it is unclear to you that once one—mingles—with a very young and very foreign woman, one has established an entirely new and irrevocable reputation." Latheman set his knife down with decisive force so that his plate rang like an annunciation bell. Everyone in earshot pretended not to pay rapt attention. "There are certain proprieties that you seem unfamiliar with—understandably, given your upbringing. One of them is the impropriety of coercing a subordinate into a personal affair. And another, many might assert, is the impropriety of granting Imperial authority to an untested youth when other suitable candidates are available!"

Her temper flared—how long had she expected to hear that from him? And yet it still struck home. With great difficulty she bit back her first retort, a Falcresti quip about the unsuitability of a man, concrete-minded and tactile, for matters of abstract figures and books. Better to take the opportunity: that speech would be a wonderful excuse to stop seeing each other. "Bel," she whispered. "I will happily provide you with a graceful exit. You've done enough for me."

He leaned in to hiss in return, his mock-mask eyeshadow meticulous and fascinating in its precision, his speckled-egg fingernails trimmed minutely. "There is no graceful exit from this embarrassment. I expect reparations, or I will—" He swallowed and pressed on. "I will alert Governor Cattlson to the rider you have introduced to the new tax form, this matter of *dividing ten notes,* with all its seditious implications."

She counted five breaths. "What do you want?" Somehow she could hear the accent of her own Aphalone, as if drawn out by her anger.

"A lifetime pension, given that my career in Imperial service will likely never advance." His lips thinned with determination. "And a marriage permit from the Office of the Jurispotence, for a courtship I intend to pursue."

Could this be a honeypot, one of Xate Yawa's tricks? "No," she said. "I won't have corruption on my hands. I'll sack you and give you generous severance. You can go to Xate Yawa yourself."

He restrained a shout and it came out as a tremulous whisper. "You *will not dictate terms to me*! You've ruined me! Xate Yawa will never permit my marriage to Heingyl Ri without your pressure—"

Heingyl Ri. Interesting. Someone else found those sharp eyes charming, too. "The rider is an empirical trial, a harmless piece of research. I've nothing to fear if you bring it to Cattlson." She shrugged with calculated calm, as much for herself as for the eyes on them. "And I've no idea why you expect to succeed in courting the daughter of Duke Heingyl. Marrying into aristocracy is a regressive game for a good citizen of the Imperial Republic."

"She deserves your post. You ruin the fiat note, you overlook Duchess Nayauru's licentious games—what have you done to stop her? Do you even see the danger? The Lady Heingyl is not so blind."

"Listen to you." A careless sip of wine, calculated to infuriate. How like him to fixate on Duchess Nayauru and her lovers as some kind of grand menace. "Tangled up in fever dreams of kingdom and inheritance. Where did you go wrong?"

Latheman sat with great propriety and composed himself for a moment. She had underestimated him, she realized, and realized it again as he spoke. "You will help me, Baru. Or I will go to Xate Yawa and sign a sworn statement that in three years of courtship you have never shown so much as a *glance* of interest in me or any other man. And that—that truth she will hold over you forever."

She could not help her reaction. It was the wrong threat for him to make, a real and revolting one, and it drew her to her feet, drew one glove halfway off her left hand before she stopped and made herself think. Murmurs rose around them as Bel Latheman stared in appalled shock at her aborted gesture.

"You wouldn't," he said. "You've no one to stand for you except that spineless secretary."

"Latheman," she said, "I don't *need* anyone to stand for me."

"I would refuse," he said, chin raised. "The duel is a contest for peers."

Her mind raced, testing possibilities and consequences. She could manufacture such an outrage, such a ruinous storm of whisper and counterwhisper, such an incredible spectacle—love, jealousy, corruption, impropriety, scandals of race and age and hygienic behavior. Everyone in Aurdwynn would hear of it.

And it would be perfect, wouldn't it? It would be exactly what she needed.

She stripped her left glove the rest of the way off and threw it on the table. "To first blood," she said, loud enough for the whole longhouse to hear. "For the honor of Taranoke, my home, which you have insulted. You may name a second. I stand for myself."

He stood stiffly, gaze locked, incredulous. "Last chance," he said, meaning, she was sure, *before I go to the Jurispotence, and tell her you are a tribadist.*

She crossed her arms and stood there in her white gown, the chained purse at her side, waiting for him to answer the glove.

"Don't be hysterical," he said, although his heart was not behind the insult, although he looked as if he wanted to apologize. Everything was theater now. "Think of what Xate Yawa did to Ffare Tanifel."

It was a misstep even though it chilled her. "And you *dare* imply I am treasonous as well? You, who conspired to print our currency for the rebellion?" She smiled haughtily—it did not come so hard. "You who've been planning another courtship under my nose, as if you want an old-blood aristocrat more than a merit-tested savant?"

Their audience sat rapt. Baru, suddenly stage-frightened, felt the onset of a tremble. But she held herself still, thinking: he cannot refuse now. I have made this about his honor. If he walks away he will leave my story unchallenged.

And he needed his honor to show Duke Heingyl.

Bel Latheman picked up the glove, his jaw hard. "You made me fire my favorite secretary," he said, as if unable, even now, to stop playing his part as her neglected lover. "You never could let me have my way."

BARU began to tremble during the long climb up her tower, emptied for the night. "You *can* control yourself," she hissed, leaning against the stone centerpole, the fabric of her gloves creaking as she balled her fists. "That's part of your job. *Control.*"

What had she done? What could have driven her to such hasty, un-subtle action? A *duel*? She'd never used a blade in anger—and that aside, it would be every bit the spectacle she'd envisioned, which meant that neither Xate Yawa nor Cattlson could ignore it. She'd kept herself cloaked in dull, diligent, loyal work for three years. She could have gone forward into this mad gambit carefully, deliberately, every maneuver subtle and well-planned.

Instead she'd risen to Latheman's bait.

What if he'd been put up to it? What if he were Xate Yawa's creature?

She locked the doors to her office and quarters, cursing her hands, and sat to pour herself wine with meticulous precision, spilling not one drop. It went down bitter and she began to pour again, humming to herself, a star-spotting song that must have come from mother Pinion or some aunt or their whole extended family gathered on the mountain to draw new constellations in the old stars.

"It's poisoned," said a voice from her bathroom.

She'd read in *Manual of the Somatic Mind* that the character of a man could be divined from how he startled—toward a door, toward a weapon, or toward nothing, a prey animal's petrified freeze. Whether it was the wine or all the dreams she'd had of a moment like this, she only drew a sharp breath and set the wineglass down.

She discovered that she could still think through her fear. He would have killed her already if he wanted to. He wouldn't have revealed the poison if he meant for it to work. She was safe.

Unless this was an act of cruelty rather than calculation. Unless he was here to harm before he killed.

"Come out," she said, sliding her chair back, making ready to stand.

The man had Xate Yawa's blue eyes but more gray in his hair, in his long beard. He wore common-cut boots and tunic, deerskin and wool, and his teeth were commoner-rough. She checked his hands and belt and found him unarmed.

She recognized him. From where?

"Well," he said, "here I am. Your secretary made an awful racket trying to find me. So I came."

She stood slowly, measuring the distance between herself, the man, and the place where her scabbard hung. "Where's Muire Lo?"

"Perfectly safe. Wore himself out barking and yapping all day. But you're right to be afraid." He approached her table as she retreated, keeping the space between them open. "Your tower guards are unreliable. You should have had all the locks changed. What I've found to be the case with you technocrats"—he took up her wineglass and sniffed at it—"is that you respect subtlety overmuch. You obsess over whispers and rumors and intangible marks of authority, and fail to consider what will happen when a man with a knife breaks into your rooms and cuts your throat. Aurdwynn is not civilized enough for subtlety."

"I half expected such a man," she said. Her scabbard was only a little ways away. "Never a duke, though. What drives you to these theatrics, Xate Olake?"

"You have, of course. Young folk respect theater more than death." He drank from her glass, frowning and sniffing. "Ah. I believe I overdid the dose. Let's be quick, then. Why did you call for me? The city knows I'm a recluse. Why seek me out now?"

Had her heart just skipped a beat? Was that pain in her stomach just a cramp, her clammy palms just nerves? "How do I earn the antidote?"

"With the truth." He drummed impatiently on the table. "Do I look like a man with a great deal of time? Why did you call for me?"

She drew a breath and took the leap. He had no pen and no parchment, could hardly hope to indict her by written record. But his sister was Xate Yawa, and if she wanted, she would find a way to make the charge stick.

These could be the words that drowned her, as Xate Yawa had drowned Ffare Tanifel.

"You killed Su Olonori," she guessed, "in order to conceal Tain Hu's counterfeiting plot. But I discovered that plot and destroyed it."

There were surgeons in the Masquerade who cut away the vocal cords of dogs so they couldn't howl. They made for terrifying guards—silent and maddened. Xate Olake's dry aspirated laugh brought them to mind. "I suppose that *is* technically the truth. But it doesn't answer my question. Why have you been loaning gold to ducal commoners? Why have you alienated Governor Cattlson, whose favor could still send you on to Falcrest and a higher station? Why did you call for me?"

"I've considered rebellion," she said, "and because you're the rebel spymaster, I needed you as an ally."

"And now that you've told me that," Xate Olake said softly, "I will tell Xate Yawa, and she'll have you boiled alive. They'll keep your skin for study."

"Xate Yawa won't touch me." Oh, that bluff of confidence, confidence she desperately wanted to feel. "She wants a free Aurdwynn—the Masquerade is only an instrument to her, and she helped crush the Fools' Rebellion only because it was doomed. She's playing her role so that she has power enough to make a difference when the moment comes. I am that moment."

"Perhaps you ascribe too much patriotism to my dear sister. Perhaps she'll back the sure victor, rebel or Masquerade."

"I can *make* your stillborn rebellion the sure victor."

"Ffare Tanifel struck the same bargain. But she overstepped, playing her pieces too clearly and too soon, and made her treason obvious even to Cattlson. My sister had no choice but to try Tanifel and issue a death sentence in order to protect herself." Xate Olake steepled his hands. "Why would you do better?"

"I can rally the people and the dukes—"

Again that harsh silent laugh. Again that sense that something within her had skipped a measure. "You'll *rally* them. Do you know the Traitor's Qualm?"

"No," she admitted.

"At least you're honest. Well. I devised it in the model of those Incrastic qualms you people are so fond of. It killed the Fools' Rebellion, and it goes like this. If you are a duke in Aurdwynn and you see an insurrection rising, you face a choice." He took another sip of poisoned wine. "You cast your lot with the rebellion, or with the loyalists. You are ruined if your side fails. You hold your position, maybe even benefit, if your side wins. But the thing about rebellions is that they involve a great deal of treason, mm? The traitors cannot condemn treason. So the safest bet is to remain a loyalist at first, and then switch sides if the traitors seem certain to win, pretending you're terribly clever and have been hampering the loyalists from within. You see the difficulty?"

Even here with this man in her quarters and poison in her veins, she could not resist a puzzle. "You gather dukes to your cause through success, but you can't score any success without the backing of dukes. If the rebellion doesn't begin with a decisive and spectacular victory, no one will gamble on it. It gutters out."

"Good. I always wondered if those Masquerade schools taught anything real." He nodded and stroked his beard as if they were carrying on this conversation in a tufa-walled classroom. "No rebellion can succeed without winning over the cautious and the self-interested. The zealous rebels and firm loyalists must attract the middle. Given that the Masquerade is the status quo, and a seemingly insurmountable one at that, the loyalists have quite an advantage."

"The people are ready," she insisted, though against his age and confidence it felt so hollow. "There is such outrage—"

"The people cannot make use of their outrage. I should know: I was commonborn, and my sister and I clawed our way into nobility only by playing the Masquerade against the rebels. No, we need dukes, and the dukes are trapped in the Traitor's Qualm. It is too soon." He sighed heavily. "What you did to the fiat note helped us, certainly. But conditions have changed since Tain Hu's gambit. The dukes are afraid of serf rebellion, landlord mutiny, bankruptcy and winter, not the Masquerade. We must allow the deadwood to build up for another decade before we strike a spark."

They have renamed my home, she wanted to shout. They have banned the marriage of fathers and made Iriad into a shipyard. And you would have me wait a decade?

"You've no choice," she said, thin-lipped. She saw Xate Olake's eyes glow in the candlelight as he looked up sharply. "I've committed. I'll be fighting a duel with Principal Factor Bel Latheman in the next few weeks, and I've made it into a matter of national honor. It's the perfect moment to declare myself."

"My sister will prevent it. Duels are a judicial tradition, and she has power over the Judiciary. You'll never have your stage." Xate Olake stood, shrugging, and finished the rest of the wine. "Bide your time, child. We'll signal you if we want you, and destroy you if you move against us. Perhaps my sister and I won't live to see the rebellion. But Tain Hu and the others are young, and can afford to wait. The Fools' Rebellion was well-named. We will not see Aurdwynn ruined by an uprising that cannot win quickly and with decision."

She took up her scabbard from its hook on the wall. "The antidote," she said. "Now. Or I'll kill you as an intruder in my home, and take my risks with the poison."

Xate Olake, at the door now, tutted softly. "I counsel patience and control," he said. "Perhaps I've poisoned you. Perhaps not. But if I have, it will be a slow variety. And if you want to survive it, Baru Cormorant, you will make yourself *worth* an antidote."

13

BARU roused Muire Lo and together they wrote orders to change the guards and the locks. She permitted him a few details. "Slow poison?" He took the news with alarm, of course, but practiced familiarity, too. "The dose was low? We should screen your food and drink. He might have agents in the kitchens."

"It might be a bluff." Her life was already full of things that could kill her any day. "Take measures, Lo. I'm going to sleep."

If Xate Olake had poisoned her, it was a gentle admixture. She slept easy, woke fresh, and took breakfast at her desk, thinking intently about Bel Latheman, duels, taxes, the Traitor's Qualm, and—with less purpose, and more anger—that damnable word *Sousward*.

So long since father Salm had gone. So long since she'd wondered exactly who had done it, and how. Had he been killed? Likely. Could the murderer—murderers?—be an officer now, a garrison commander, a town watchman? Could mother Pinion have tracked him down over the years? Could they be stalking each other now, looking for an opening, a moment to use the boarding saber or the man-killing spear?

Your daughter is one of us, he might taunt. *She serves in Aurdwynn. Very poorly.*

In the waiting room Muire Lo began to shout.

Baru had an instant to compose herself before Cattlson burst in, wolf's head cap snarling, trailing armored garrison troops and a slim man whose milky skin barely showed past mask and glove. "Cormorant!" the governor roared. "You've done *enough*!"

"Your Excellency." She made herself nod and smile, though the ranks of armed guard set her heart racing. What did he know? What *could* he know? Had Bel Latheman gone to him? "Is there some concern?"

Cattlson waved his guard back and marched down the length of her office in a dull thunder of hobnail on rug. The pale man shadowed him noiselessly. "A *duel*?" Cattlson roared. "With your own *banker*? And the first I hear of it is from Duke Heingyl, who tells me everyone in the city, every peasant and franklin between here and Haraerod, has already started making wagers?"

"He insulted my honor," Baru said, fighting the urge to stand (it would only make her feel shorter than Cattlson). "I had no choice."

"*Your* honor? Tax season is almost on us, and you're making a theater out of your affairs! If you cared about your *honor* you'd have some mind to overturning the reputation of Taranoki women!" He slammed his fists on her desk. "You are an embarrassment to my government, a catastrophe for our rule—"

Cattlson arrested his rant mid-word and sucked down a few breaths. The pale man took station at his shoulder. Baru found herself trying to cringe, and trying harder not to. It was so hard to beat back the school and the teachers, the etiquette of subservience.

"I care deeply for the opportunities we provide to those of less fortunate birth." Cattlson tried to smile. He had that easy-smile face. It was somehow sad to see him struggle. "I genuinely want you to succeed in your post. I understand—oh, I, of all people, understand!—that youth is full of passions that may sway better judgment. But if Falcrest takes the slightest issue with this year's tax season, if you make the *smallest* error in the harvest, then I will be recalled, and Aurdwynn will fall into the hands of a less generous man, a man who will make Xate Yawa look forgiving. I cannot permit that, you understand? I have worked too long to build an understanding with the dukes. To build a future for their sons and daughters. I cannot allow you to ruin this province. Can you acknowledge that as a peer?"

So this was what it took to rob her of her cool, of the careful deliberation that had carried her through ballrooms and plots and sorties with her enemy. Just a powerful man shouting in her face.

"One duel will not ruin you," she managed, more defensively than she'd wanted.

"I cannot take further chances with you. You lack the—the *gravity* your station demands. You are too young." Cattlson's wolf's head flopped as he shook his head. "I've been told that you found an intruder in the tower and demanded a change of guard. Here it is, then. Captain Lodepont and his men will keep most vigilant watch as you work in your office. And to guard your person . . ."

The pale man at Cattlson's side, the man who was not by his uniform or conduct any sort of captain at all, nodded properly. Small muscles in his neck slithered against each other.

"I have charged one of the Clarified with your personal safety," Cattlson said. He glanced at the pale man with a troubled disquiet that frightened Baru more than any of his bluster. "He will accompany you at all times."

No. Unacceptable. She reached for her leverage. "You have no authority to arrest me. If you want an untroubled tax season and a happy Falcrest, you'll permit me my freedom. And if I don't have that freedom—"

He threw up his hands in exasperation. "Don't be petulant—"

"If I don't have that freedom, I think you'll find your tax season quite *thoroughly* disrupted." She leaned forward, to hide her hands. "You can't afford to lose me right now."

Cattlson touched his brow. "I gave you every opportunity. Every chance. But you've forced my hand. I must give your duty to a more reliable servant of the Imperial Republic. Perhaps Bel Latheman."

She smiled and made a sound of doubt and tried desperately to think what his next move would be. "I'm a merit appointment. I'm not yours to remove."

"You will be given every chance to display your merit." Cattlson's grip made something in the corners of her desk creak. "But if you proceed with this rash and ill-advised duel, you will be—injured. Your physical and emotional health will fail in the wake of this whole affair of wounded passion. I will have no choice but to appoint Latheman as Accountant for the season."

"Oh," she said, not displeased. "Injured? You have great faith in Bel Latheman's swordsmanship."

Cattlson tugged at his jacket and shook his head with the air of a man unable to believe in the state of his world. "Bel Latheman has designated a second to stand for him, as the codes permit. A second who will better satisfy the requirements of peerage, and one who will assure the people of Aurdwynn that my government supports Bel Latheman's union with Heingyl Ri as an honorable and proper alliance between the technocracy and a noble line. Aurdwynn loves to see a test of arms, and if you insist on going through with this pageant, well, I must ensure that the outcome is constructive."

Baru mapped the plot in her head as Cattlson spoke. The Governor would back Latheman in a gambit to steal her station, and back Latheman's marriage to the daughter of Cattlson's closest ducal ally and friend. A move to consolidate his control over the Accountancy, and to bring the loyal dukes closer to him. A good play. She wondered who'd given him that advice.

"Who will I face, then?" she asked, to play for time.

Cattlson squared his shoulders and lifted his chin. "You have one week. Then we'll meet in the plaza outside the Fiat Bank at noon. No armor. To first blood."

"But who will I—" Abruptly she understood, and clapped her mouth shut to hide her surprise.

"As I said." Cattlson shook his head with paternal regret, the heaviness of a man who believed he was the only stanchion of sanity in sight. "We'll meet."

THE pale man attached himself to her like a remora and could not be removed.

She tried to talk to him, but he was mute. She tried to work, but although he kept a discreet distance, she found herself certain that he was watching—and besides, it was impossible to focus with the ruin of everything she'd hoped for so near ahead. Muire Lo practically tiptoed around the remora man, seized by the same fear (or, perhaps, by some secret knowledge of his capabilities and loyalties).

When the sun set and Baru went up to her quarters, the pale man followed her. She crossed her arms and blocked his way, and he spoke for the first time. "I cannot harm you." He had a soft and reasonable voice. "I am an instrument. I have eyes for danger and a mind for tactics. Nothing else."

"I won't have a strange man in my rooms," she insisted, voice thick with frustration—because how had this happened? Hadn't she felt, just yesterday, that she could bend even the unexpected to her will, that she was on the verge of a new and precipitous journey? How could Cattlson march in and smash it all in one conversation?

What was the power of purse and coin worth if she couldn't keep an utter stranger out of her own private quarters?

"I am not a man," the Clarified said patiently. "I am an instrument, conditioned from birth by drug and bell. I must obey my purpose."

His purpose allowed her not even one moment's privacy, not to bathe, not to change. She hadn't been naked in front of a stranger since physical exams at school—ah, no, there'd been the washes on *Lapetiare*, but at least there it had been a raucous crowd. Not one watchful stranger who barely seemed to breathe. As she changed into her nightgown she wanted to issue some proud defiance, some assertion of Taranoki immodesty—*it is my body; so?* But shame had come into her over the past few years and she could not even face him naked.

But she tried to consider it pragmatically: clothed or unclothed, he did not seem to look at her any differently.

He stood silent guard. Eventually she fell asleep.

On the next day, she tried to go out, and Captain Lodepont's guards would not let her. For her protection, Lodepont insisted, she should remain in her tower until the mysterious interloper could be arrested. Even the technocrat's mark wouldn't move him, although he looked contrite. The frustration made her want to fence. She performed exercises on her office floor instead of working, grunting out her exasperation under the empty watch of the Clarified man.

Muire Lo came to her bearing salvation. "A letter, Your Excellence. From—ah, from the urgent mail stack." His eyes flickered to the pale man. The sense of scrutiny that rolled off him was incredible, oppressive, a one-man panopticon. "For your eyes *only*, the mark says. Captain Lodepont went to great pains to confirm this."

She unfolded the cheap rag paper and read:

They are <u>bred</u> and conditioned in Falcrest. They came on the same ship that brought news of Sousward. They are the governor's, but I am given my own words of authority over them, as a <u>check</u> on his power.

This one's word is "suspire." He will not break his orders, but with that word, he will listen to you.

We need to speak. Find a way.

Baru read it again twice, nodded, and passed it back to Muire Lo. "Destroy it. I'll have a reply soon."

They came on the same ship. The remoras were in Taranoke, too. Hunting sedition, perhaps. Sniffing out disloyal mothers and their sodomite husbands.

THE remora followed her up to her quarters for a second night. She'd considered saving the word until some key moment, where it would have the strength of surprise—but what was the point? Cattlson had locked her up, powerless to do anything but send letters and read accounts.

She drew a breath and spoke. "Suspire. Tell me your name."

"Purity Cartone," he replied, unhesitating. His stark black half-mask could have been printed on the cream of his skin.

"Tell me what authority I have with this word."

If the sudden fact of her command startled the remora, he gave no sign of it. "You may command me within the bounds of law and conditioning. You may not negate orders from Governor Cattlson." And then, like a sail tearing under a brief and powerful wind, he smiled. "You may loosen or constrain my freedom to speak."

She perched on the corner of her bed, fascinated and a little thrilled. What had they done to this man in Falcrest to make him respond like a puppet to a single word? Was it a code of honor, the secret creed of some chivalric order dedicated to Imperial service? No, that hardly fit the Incrastic philosophy. They would want a scientific hold on him, some treatment or condition, some surgery or plague from foreign lands. . . .

A new and obedient race, bred in Falcrest, specialized for service. He was the face of the destiny of the Empire, and there was no question in Baru's mind that Cairdine Farrier and his ilk had a hand in his making. *Hesychast*: it meant *one who makes a temple of the body*.

What could she do, she wondered, if she had her own race of men like Purity Cartone? What justice could she pursue? And then she felt a little sick at the thought, at the thrill she'd felt. There were such secrets to be had in Falcrest—

She tried to question him about his orders from Cattlson. After that she asked every question she could imagine about men named Hesychast and Apparitor and Itinerant, about the Faceless Throne, about secrets of the Imperial Republic. But he refused the questions with a simple phrase. "I am bound by higher command."

But he'd smiled at the mention of his own constraints. She tried a different tack. "I revoke any limit on your speech and expression not explicitly bound by higher command."

The remora (was it his paleness, his plain features, the slow serpentine way he moved, that made her still think of him that way, instead of by his strange name?) inclined his head in gratitude. "You are a ranking servant of the Empire in Aurdwynn," he said. "I am grateful to be allowed the chance to serve you as well as Governor Cattlson, where that service does not explicitly conflict."

How could she bend this new instrument to the task of getting out of Cattlson's cage? She'd planted things—the tax rider, the duel, the greater purpose behind them—that desperately needed tending. "Stand for me in a duel," she ordered.

"I cannot."

Damn. Well, if that wouldn't work—"Will you carry messages for me?"

"Yes."

"Will you read them and report the contents to the Governor?"

"Yes." He smiled broadly at that, and after a moment spent in consideration of that eerie awkward expression, she understood: by revoking the limits on his expression she had allowed him to signal his pleasure and displeasure to her. Perhaps he was not so loyal a creature—or, no, that was the wrong way to think of it. He was a *literal* creature, eager to obey the letter of orders. Given his own way, he would seek to satisfy as many authorities as he could.   human ⸗ animal

He had been conditioned to take pleasure in obedience, like a dog. He had no preference for her or Cattlson, but inasmuch as she could offer him more freedom to obey—to obey her *and* Cattlson, rather than merely Cattlson—she could work him.

"You're bred and trained for intellect," she ventured. "Yes?"

"For all the capabilities my mission requires."

"And you prefer to exercise that acuity in service of the Masquerade?"

"The Imperial Republic, please," he said, a flash of pain crossing his face, the discharge of some conditioned trigger. "I prefer to serve the Imperial Republic in all possible ways. I am made to advise and inform as well as protect and obey."

"Judge me," she said, instantly curious. A man of intellect, without ego or agenda of his own: how could she resist knowing what he saw? "Tell me what I am, so I can better serve."

"A woman of Sousward. As a woman you are disposed to abstract thought and numeracy, but weakened by potent emotions and hereditary maternal instincts that soften judgment." She let that bit of Incrastic doctrine pass unchallenged. "As a Souswardi, your bloodline carries the factors that promoted Tu Maia imperial success, but also the inherent promiscuity and savagery of the same race, exacerbated in recent centuries by unhygienic mating practices." He smiled as he spoke, a less broken smile, one of quiet satisfaction at the exercise of talent. Observation made him happy. "You are a measurably gifted mathematician, a potential polymath, and a prospective Imperial-grade savant in disciplines of control. Your dedication to your work and the utilitarian nature of your few known social relationships indicates a useful degree of pragmatic instrumentalism, but also the risk of full-blown sociopathy. You are likely, but not certainly, a latent tribadist, which may require corrective conditioning."

She found herself fascinated by the litany, and a little infuriated—infuriated enough that it slipped out of her sidelong in a meaningless demand: "Taranoke. Call my home Taranoke."

"I cannot."

Stupid of her. No reason to waste time on triviality. "Tell me what mistake I've made. Tell me why my authority has been hobbled."

"Your tactics are self-centered. You have forgotten that you are not the only player on the board, that inherent talent speaks for no more than experience, and that others around you seek to expand their authority and constrain yours. Your error is fundamental to the human psyche: you have allowed yourself to believe that others are mechanisms, static and solvable, whereas you are an agent."

So easy, so satisfying, so sickeningly sweet to use him like this. To find in her hands this pale and pliant oracle, this man who would speak with authority and intellect on any topic she pleased without demands of his own. And hadn't his jaw relaxed a little? Hadn't his breath smoothed and deepened like a man on opiates? He had served her by informing her, by using his talents to help. It had brought him real joy.

Was it really slavery if the slave was grateful? If that gratitude had been hammered into the alloy of his being?

Deep in her heart she suspected that the Masquerade sought to make the whole world in Purity Cartone's image. To breed a future of grateful human automata. They had crushed their own inbred aristocracy, crying *poison in the heredity, weakness in the germ*. But even after the Old Lines died, that obsession with better blood had carried on. In the Metademe they had determined that behavior and experience altered the hereditary cells. Hygienic behavior bred clever disciplined citizens— and social sin bred licentious, hedonist parasites.

"And my next move? What do you suggest I can do to secure my position?"

"Take a lover." His expression betrayed no lechery, no particular interest at all. "Arrest on charges of unhygienic behavior is the most powerful weapon that can be used against you. My word to Governor Cattlson that you had a male lover would be taken as fact in any Imperial court. You would be secured, at least a little, against these allegations."

Her stomach filled with a seasick buzzing not very different from what she had felt when she realized her authority over him—a powerful sensation, but utterly unlike lust. Maybe that was what made her dismiss his suggestion at once: her body did not agree with it, for all his composed Falcresti looks, for all her queasy interest in the thought of someone doing anything she ordered. Or maybe it was something more intellectual, inherited from her conversations with Aminata about the navy: a stubborn and recalcitrant sense that using her body as a political tool, in even the slightest way, was a form of surrender or compromise.

Why should she be punished for her chastity? Why should her bedroom matter more than her books and coin?

But the man before her was a kind of answer.

"Go," she said, troubled and uncertain, petrified suddenly by the fear that she spoke in her sleep and that Purity Cartone listened. "Go guard the bottom of the stairs while I sleep. Suspire. Go."

She told herself the next morning that she'd dreamed of Taranoke filled with clockwork people, brilliant men and women who built beautiful things at her command and offered cogent truth without fear. Dreamed of the whole Ashen Sea ringed in them and made reasonable, like a well-

yes - you take away a person's ability to choose. You confiscate or decimate their will.

kept account, everyone set in their ordered chosen place as the stars in constellations.

But it was a lie and she knew it. It hadn't been a dream. She'd prodded at the thought over and over again with the nauseating fascination of a child pulling scabs, unable to decide if what she felt was pain or glee.

The duel was coming. She only had a little time before Cattlson cut her hand off, or worse, and left her bedridden and impotent. Only one course remained: answering the letter that had carried the trigger word.

So she acted.

Purity Cartone watched her write the note, watched her pass it to Muire Lo. An innocent thing: *I would like to meet to discuss planning for tax season.*

Xate Yawa came that afternoon.

14

THEY took coffee and small cakes drizzled in date syrup under the eyes of Purity Cartone and Muire Lo, two silent attendants reporting to distant authorities, two men that Baru felt she could trust completely—within narrow, defined bounds. Bounds she was about to depart.

Xate Yawa eyed the pale man with fascination. "He's a spectacular specimen, isn't he? Remarkably capable. When the Governor showed him off, I had him repeat the whole conversation word-for-word. He could replace all my recorders."

Baru heard the warning there, and almost smiled. She'd set Muire Lo to transcribe the whole conversation, to be sure that Xate Yawa understood how scrutinized it would be. She should've trusted the old judge to know. "With a dozen of him I could've sorted out Su Olonori's books in a week."

"I doubt there are a dozen Clarified in all of Aurdwynn. They're bred in the Metademe, where they've built these ingenious cribs out of levers and bells—oh, but that's all rumor." She chuckled with polite mirth. "I shouldn't pass it on."

"Rumor is all I've had these past few days," Baru said, marking Purity Cartone and then the door with her gaze: *the guards?*

Xate Yawa's bright eyes followed hers intently. "Yes. The matter of this . . . protective detail. Were it a formal house arrest I could lift it at once. But as the Governor sees the, ah, unknown intruder as a matter of provincial security, he has the right to conduct military action in your defense. If he can justify your confinement as short-term protection, I am—for the moment—powerless."

Not that she or her brother saw any reason to let Baru out of her tower. Not so long as they believed a rebellion had no chance.

That was what Baru had to change. They'd backed Tain Hu. They could be swayed again.

She spun her coffee cup on its plate and flopped back in her chair, overly at ease, screaming to Xate Yawa: *now, this, this is the important part*. "No matter at all. It's given me a chance to focus on our tax program."

"How dutiful of you."

"With our collectors on the road and the coffers beginning to fill, I've started to worry about matters of security. In lean times like this, taxes put the people in a mood to revolt and the dukes in a mood to defraud. And Governor Cattlson—" She flicked her gaze to Purity Cartone. "He is most concerned that we offer Falcrest a healthy season. Parliament is frustrated with its losses here. They expect war with the Oriati federations, and that war will cost them."

Xate Yawa examined the decor idly, her gaze tracing a long anchor-and-chain motif. "I've made an example out of the fraudulent the past few years. Taught them that lean times are the times that most demand brotherhood. I think you'll find rich yields."

What she really said: *Play your role. Don't make trouble.*

Muire Lo's pen scratched away at the parchment.

"Quite." She caught the older woman's gaze and held it. "But it's occurred to me that we risk a different disaster. Rumor of the new Imperial fleet being built in Sousward will push pirates north along the trade circle. Their old haunts in the southwest of the Ashen Sea won't be safe. They'll be looking for new targets."

Xate Yawa's gape of astonishment might have seemed a fake to anyone who didn't understand her real allegiance, anyone who hadn't met her brother in the night. Baru knew that it was real. That she'd intuited where Baru was going.

Xate Yawa took a moment to regain her composure. "The tax ships headed to Falcrest, loaded down with a nation's worth of gold . . . but surely the navy will guard them diligently. Surely these pirates will be turned away."

"I am confident no disaster will befall them. But I'd like to take steps to raise that confidence to surety." Baru smiled blandly. "The markets run on confidence, you know."

In the background, Purity Cartone stood statuesque, his eyes focusing here, there, relaxed and inattentive and screaming danger from every pore.

And Baru, too, wanted to scream: for in this instant she could feel her whole life, all her dreams and ambitions, every painful perfect memory of Taranoki water and seabirds calling, every hope of imperial power and subversion, balanced on a knifepoint, and that knife in the hands of Xate Yawa.

I am a fool, Baru thought. She will keep to her brother's word. It is too soon.

He'd said: *she'll have you boiled alive.*

Xate Yawa sat in silence for a moment, and spoke again.

"Of course we must take steps. I'll have Admiral Croftare's liaison bring you the necessary paperwork so that you can examine the schedules and reassign ships as you see fit." Xate Yawa sipped at her coffee. "Perhaps the tax ships should be held until they can sail together in convoy. So they cannot be taken piecemeal."

"Just what I'd thought."

The Jurispotence frowned sharply. "There's another matter to attend to, however, and one less pleasantly constructive. I am gravely disappointed that you and Governor Cattlson alike have elected to go forward with this juvenile challenge. I've worked for years to end Aurdwynn's affection for trial by combat. Now here you are, stirring up the country with rumors of the commoner's favorite gold-lender taking up sword against the Governor. I would insist that this ridiculous dispute be settled in court, but the Governor is fixated on the duel."

"As am I. It's a matter of honor." Baru tried not to overplay, tried to go along with Xate Yawa as she sailed the conversation smoothly away from the offer that had just been made and accepted.

Xate Yawa tugged at her gown with convulsive irritation. "You could be badly injured. I insist that you find someone to stand for you. We can't afford to lose your service."

"Or the Governor's."

"Or the Governor's." She rolled her eyes. "I forgot. You are a duelist, too."

Baru spread her hands, helpless. "I'm in no position to search for a second while I remain under—" She laughed, spontaneously and genuinely, amused by the irony. "Under the Governor's protection."

"Well, then." Xate Yawa smiled irritably and gave not one hint of satisfaction, not one smug silent tic to indicate the pleasure she might feel at this deal so rapidly done. "I will have to find an appropriate swordsman to serve as your second. One who can ensure that neither party is damaged."

And surely Xate Yawa could—Xate Yawa, who in years long past had murdered the old Duke Lachta herself, who controlled every criminal enterprise in Aurdwynn by the fact of her station.

Muire Lo and Purity Cartone made their respective records, pen and silent mnemonics, marking down the words and with any luck at all missing entirely the great pivotal stroke that Baru had ventured, the twin irresistible prizes she had offered to the twin masters of Aurdwynn's simmering rebellion: gold and blood, arranged before them, waiting only to be seized.

It was done. All the power had gone out of her hands. In a few days Xate Yawa would destroy her, or see the first spark of rebellion lit.

And then Baru's real test would begin.

THE day of the duel broke rainy and hot, the whole city steaming from pavestone and cobble after a midsummer squall. Baru came down to her office, already stretched and limbered, dressed in riding trousers and a heavy surcoat, to find Muire Lo standing at the windows behind her desk.

"Cartone's gone," Muire Lo said, smiling out at the city. "The Governor recalled him to report on your activities. I've brought breakfast."

"I didn't notice him missing," she said, surprised at herself. Muire Lo had cooked fresh cod in olive oil, and onions for Aurdwynni luck. She wished she had an appetite. "He's like furniture. Just slips right out of attention."

"Not mine." Muire Lo spidered his hands against the windowpane, staring into the mist. Baru felt a little pang at the look on his face: a soft, graceful melancholy, as if he had decided he would do something that hurt. "I remember mornings like this used to smell like shit. We had awful sewers, and everything would back up into the streets when it rained."

"And now?"

"The Masquerade rebuilt them while I was gone." He shrugged. "No more sewage fog on summer mornings. But you have a hot bath at the top of a tower, so I suppose you're not impressed."

"You can go on," she said, picking at the cod.

"Mm? About plumbing?"

"With all the things you wanted to say while that man was attached to my side."

He set his brow against the glass and closed his eyes. She watched him, wanting to understand even as her thoughts circled back to the duel, to Cattlson's plan to see her crippled and taken out of play. Would it hurt? Would she lose a finger, a hand?

"What are you doing?" Muire Lo murmured, softly, as if to escape some hidden eavesdropper.

"Well." She swallowed and lifted her knife. "I can't back down from the duel without issuing an official apology to Bel Latheman. If I do that I'll compromise my ability to hold office, and I'll be pushed into resignation. Cattlson sees the duel as a chance to repudiate all the harm I've done to his government. Xate Yawa doesn't seem to care enough to stop the whole affair. So neither of us have a way out, and we have to fight."

"That's not what I mean." He peeled himself away from the window and the abstract slithering shapes in the fog (Baru thought, with a chill, of Purity Cartone's slim muscled neck). "The tax rider. Your cryptic arrangement with Xate Yawa. Your meticulous scheduling of appointments six months in advance, like you're trying to prove you'll still be *having* appointments six months from now." He came to the other side of her desk and stood there, hair sleekly oiled, his surcoat buttoned to full formality. He didn't look so much like a finch now. Maybe a crow. "I know you. You wouldn't stake your standing and career on this childish duel without some reason behind it. What are you doing?"

She took another piece of cod, to buy herself and her heart a little time. "I'm going to need your help with a great deal of paperwork afterward."

"Or you'll need me to nurse you." His lips twitched, and then the smile fled. He spoke harshly, as if forcing himself to go forward. "If you're going over, if you're planning to cast in with them, I want a chance to warn my family before it happens. Enough to get them on a ship and out of port. Do you remember that huntsman who strangled me when I told him who I spied for? That wrath will come down on them, too."

Her heart cried out in her chest, full of sudden want to save this child of rebellion past, to warn him what was to come. And from where did that want come? He was older, a trained operative, a native. He could manage himself. But he was tethered to her, wasn't he, under her power. He had been bound to her by Cairdine Farrier.

She spoke in calculated defense: "I won't hear treason spoken in my office. I'm under scrutiny enough."

Muire Lo bowed his head. "I am at fault. Forgive me. I presumed to know your mind." He stumbled on his words. "I thought that if—in the event of—that is to say, under such circumstances, I thought you might need my . . ."

Whatever he was after, he hadn't found a way to say it yet, and Baru couldn't do it for him. She pushed the tray away. "I want to be early. Call a carriage—and if the Governor's already arranged one, have it changed."

Whatever he had wanted to venture, whatever confidence or daring, he packed it away in an instant. "Of course, Your Excellence."

Baru found Aminata's boarding saber and buckled it on alongside her chained purse. If she needed it today she had already lost.

Xate Yawa hadn't written a letter about finding a second.

THE crowd roared like storm surf.

It wasn't productive to think about losing. To imagine that she might lose a hand, or take a festering wound, or faint from the unexpected immediacy of the pain. No, Xate Yawa would have a second ready to stand for her. She wouldn't have to fight. If she fought she would lose to Cattlson, who had reach and strength and experience and confidence with a blade.

But she wouldn't have to fight.

She stepped down from the carriage into the middle of the plaza and half the city shrieked their hate or adoration at her.

A coded riot. Ranks of garrison blue trying to hold back the crowd. Banners of coin and mask flying on redwood poles, merchants hawking beer to ragged dock laborers and hollow-eyed rangers with scurvy teeth and Pinjagata spearwomen who stood shoulder to shoulder crying in terrible enthusiastic Aphalone: *Gold from a fairer hand! A fairer hand!* Even men under Ducal banner, Oathsfire and Lyxaxu and Unuxekome, knotted in uncomfortable separation from the common crowd, raised the same cheer.

Cheering for her.

She'd made her loan policy as a calculated move to buy the affection of the commoner. She'd made Bel Latheman's insult to her honor public as a calculated move to buy their outrage.

Apparently she'd calculated well.

A fairer hand!

But of course there was the opposition.

Toward the Fiat Bank side of the plaza, horses jockeyed in the crowd. The riders wore armor or ducal finery. Baru found the stag banner of Duke Heingyl, and then the duke himself, armored and rigid on his black charger. He'd lost so much during Baru's inflationary collapse that Governor Cattlson had stepped in with gold to prop him up. But his loyalties ran deeper than that. He'd pledged fealty to the Masquerade when Aurdwynn first fell, and his sense of honor ran so strong that he'd stood with Falcrest during the Fools' Rebellion. His word was iron.

He lifted a hand to her, and then drew something out of his saddle: a white seabird, bound but twitching. At her shoulder Muire Lo sucked in a sharp breath.

Heingyl snapped its neck and threw it into the crowd. A volcanic roar erupted from the people there, and then a chant, overwhelming in its volume: *she comes too cheap!*

"Crude," Xate Yawa sniffed, coming to Baru through a file of steel-masked garrison soldiers. "What would his daughter say? I will stand judge today."

Baru tried to smile, tried to present calm. Her knees wobbled and her stomach turned storm-sick flops. "My second?" she asked, as quietly as she could manage.

"Pardon?" Xate Yawa frowned, leaning in. "My old ears fail me when it's warm."

Baru's heart sank. Bile washed the back of her throat. There was no second.

Courage, now, courage, courage. She'd been a good fighter in school. She'd kept up with her forms. Perhaps—perhaps—somehow—

"Come, come." Xate Yawa tugged at her wrist. "There's a doctor standing by. Best to confront the pain, and find a way through."

Her offer had been rejected, coin and blood and all. Xate Yawa must have spoken to her brother, and they still judged the time too soon.

The roar of the crowd fell away into nothing and she walked across rough cobblestone to the chalked circle at the center of the plaza, where Governor Cattlson waited in his wolf's head mantle and sleeveless dark leather, a long two-handed blade at his side.

"Cormorant," he said. He tried to smile, as he always did, but there was regret in his voice. "Have you counted the crowd?"

"It must be half the city."

"I had the docks closed and a holiday declared. The mob loves nothing like a show of strength. Aurdwynn must know who rules it, and why— it'll do them well to see that their Governor can win on their terms." He passed his blade to his left and offered his right hand to shake. "I'll cut you light, if I can. And—I apologize for the chant. It wasn't mine, or even Duke Heingyl's."

Behind him, Bel Latheman stood with his chin erect and his hands clasped behind his back. Anger felt better than fear. She almost spat at his feet, but the chant—*too cheap!*—made her think of Latheman's words in the longhouse. *Don't be hysterical.* Whatever emotion she showed would be turned against her.

She clasped Cattlson's hand and shook. He frowned. "You've forgotten your mask."

She'd left it behind as a symbol. She'd left it behind because she wanted her Taranoki heritage to be an issue in this duel. Her second could fight masked.

But she had no second. She had only the Naval System against Cattlson's reach and strength.

Muire Lo nudged her and pointed. She found the remora Purity Cartone, who stood among the Governor's masked retinue, pale and obvious now that she noticed him.

But whatever he was about to say was cut off.

Xate Yawa raised her hands and the garrison troops pounded their shields. The crowd's roar died and the plaza fell silent but for the nicker of horses and a low murmur. "I stand judge over trial to first blood," she called. Garrison officers repeated the chant, word for word, a booming chorus that spread out through the lines. "Today Her Excellence Baru Cormorant of Taranoke, the Imperial Accountant, challenges His Excellence Bel Latheman of Falcrest, Principal Factor of the Fiat Bank. Baru Cormorant, what grievance do you bear?"

She'd practiced it a hundred times and it came up just as easily as spit, as the bile of fear. "Bel Latheman is faithless in duty and in love. He used his station to better himself at the expense of Aurdwynn, and he used my affection as entertainment while he pursued Lady Heingyl Ri. He insulted my blood, my sex, and my homeland. That I will not countenance, not from a man of Falcrest or any other nation."

Keep it simple. Keep it personal. The woodsmen and the dockworkers were the audience. The rumormongers who would carry her words north, up the roads and the river Inirein and into every duchy and freetown. Even Duke Pinjagata would hear the story of the sharp-eyed woman who looked like Nayauru standing against Cattlson, and even Pinjagata would remember her name.

"Bel Latheman, how do you answer?"

Now the officers and the ranks echoed Latheman. "Baru Cormorant forced herself on me by authority. She ruined the dukes of Aurdwynn with her disastrous policies and allowed the blame to stain me. She is unfit in mind and heredity for the station she holds, and I will have my freedom from her authority and her repute."

He hadn't made one allegation about tribadism. Maybe he thought it wouldn't play well. Maybe Cattlson's paternal concern had overriden him. Maybe he couldn't stomach the thought of Xate Yawa's surgeons circumcising Baru's womanhood.

Baru tried to count her own breaths and factor the count. Primes at one (depending who you asked), two, three, five, seven—

There were words Xate Yawa could say now, passages of law that described the fallibility and irrationality of duels. She skipped them, of course. She was here to see Baru wounded and taken out of play. "Let this combat to blood judge the truth of these allegations. Baru Cormorant, will you apologize and withdraw?"

Not here. It was impossible. She had to chance the blade. "No."

"Bel Latheman, will you?"

"I will not."

"Bel Latheman, will you name a second to stand for you?"

"I name His Excellence the Governor."

The Fiat Bank side of the crowd, Duke Heingyl's side, roared and clapped. Horses reared in unison. Cattlson opened his arms to the crowd, claiming in his triumphal grasp the chalked dueling circle, the cobblestones, the arcades and scaffolds around them draped in urchins and commoners.

Xate Yawa turned to Baru, who tried to think of nothing but father Salm, wrestling in the firelight, so sure and strong, and instead found herself thinking of father Salm, gone to war and never returned. There was a hint of apology in the purse of the judge's lips, but just a hint. "Baru Cormorant, will you name a second to stand for you?"

She opened her mouth to seal her own ruin.

"I stand for Baru Cormorant."

The crowd gasped, hushed, roared like a wave rising and retreating.

And the duchess Tain Hu stepped into the circle, hobnailed boots ringing off the limestone cobble, hair shorn, cheeks slashed in lines of red. She lifted her blade to Cattlson, her eyes to Baru, and touched her brow in salute.

"My lady," she said, as Xate Yawa tried to disguise her fury, as the garrison officers repeated everything the duchess Vultjag said to the plaza. "Command me."

And Baru cast the first dart at hand, the words that set the coopers and the fishmongers and the bannermen of Lyxaxu and Oathsfire and Unuxekome roaring: "Show them who should rule Aurdwynn, and why."

Vultjag! the poorer parts of the crowd screamed, a raw astonished sound. *Vultjag!*

THE *Antler Stone* was full of swordfights, sweeping romantic duels in prerevolutionary Falcrest. Scholarship had been written (and she'd read it) on the remarkable transparency of the Second Book's prose, absent all the meticulous descriptions of arms and armor and lineage that filled the old epics. But the fights still went on for pages of parry and riposte, footwork, feint, maneuver. Everyone adored the fights in *The Antler Stone*.

Baru had trained in the Naval System. There were no parries or ripostes. Every response was also an attack—a counterstrike timed to intercept and displace an opponent's blow, bind and leverage it into a grapple or a wound. "On a ship, in a storm, in the dark," Aminata had snarled, rapping her knuckles, "while drunk and surrounded, and there's six of them to one of you!"

It had always felt right to her, even though she'd never been as good as Aminata.

But Tain Hu did not know the Naval System. And Baru had no idea what Cattlson knew. Maybe it wouldn't matter. Cattlson was taller and bulkier, armed with reach and strength.

The fighters took their places and the plaza waited in silence. Jurispotence Xate Yawa stood with her hands flat on her thighs, the parchment of her face pressed still and flat.

"Watch the feet," Muire Lo whispered in Baru's ear.

Cattlson took a square stance, left foot forward, and put his long blade up in the Naval System's ox guard, hands at the cross and the pommel, blade level with the top of his head and aimed straight for Tain Hu like an accusing finger. His bare arms bunched, the blade held perfectly still—an incredible display of static strength. A boast.

Tain Hu shrugged out of her jacket, back turned in insult (the bankside crowd jeered), and with laconic confidence set herself toward Cattlson in a half-lunge, bent a little forward at the waist. Her tabard bared arms and knotted shoulders slick with sweat. She gripped her pommel with her left, the cross with her right, and leaned the blade of her longsword back against her shoulder like a laborer carrying a pole.

Cattlson's prow of a jaw twitched and his supporters jeered again. "Put the blade up!" someone cried.

"She could've picked a stronger guard," Muire Lo muttered.

"It's a fine guard." Baru had chewed most of the skin off the right side of her lower lip. She switched sides. "It doesn't mean anything."

Xate Yawa raised her hands and held them a shoulder span apart. "First blood," she intoned. "Ready."

As a child Baru had watched the birds as much as the stars—watched the beat of their wings in flight, and tried to decipher the technique.

Someone behind Tain Hu clapped and barked, high and mocking. Duchess Vultjag didn't twitch. The muscles in Cattlson's calves bunched at the sound.

Xate Yawa clapped her hands and stepped back out of the circle. Cattlson struck.

It was a thunderously powerful stroke, an incredible piece of reach, checked at the end of its arc (down in the tail guard) by pure strength. Tain Hu stepped back, hind foot, then front, her blade still on her shoulder, and got out of the way in time. Surrendering the space Cattlson had attacked.

Jeers and raucous shouts answered her retreat. The Governor reset to high ox guard, began to circle with long smooth steps. Tain Hu matched him, expressionless, her breath almost invisible except in the slow roll of her shoulders.

"She can't afford to attack." Muire Lo wrung his hands at the edge of Baru's stinging unblinking vision. "He's too—"

Cattlson's stance dropped abruptly, as if about to leap. Tain Hu did not respond. The Governor chuckled, grinned.

"Do you think she'd still have ruined you," Tain Hu drawled, "if you'd had your way, and put your sword in her back when she—"

She erupted mid-sentence, a hydraulic uncoiling from her toes up through her calves, her sword coming up off her shoulder to strike cross-wise and down.

Cattlson struck back, meeting in the cross, strength absorbing the shock, stopping her cold. Their swords rang and shrieked. He roared too. And followed through, stepping into her, pushing her back by the force of their locked blades—

Tain Hu, off balance, arched back past her own center.

(Baru watched the wing beats—)

Tain Hu turned her body and her blade, declining the lock, passing all the fury of Cattlson's press off to her right. His blade went over her right shoulder, sliding down the length of hers, and he stepped forward to keep contact, to overpower and disarm her.

Steel screamed where the swords crossed.

Tain Hu's shoulders bunched in sudden anatomical relief as she turned, letting the energy of Cattlson's step carry him forward into—

(Baru caught the movement of her hands: one glove wrapped around the blunt base of the blade, for the leverage she needed to aim—)

—the pommel of her sword. She smashed it into his brow with a sharp grunt, as if Cattlson's ferocious bind and disarm had only been a convenient way to get his sword out of position and punch him with the back of her own.

He fell on his side on the cobblestones, stunned. The crowd howled. Muire Lo made a raw sound and leapt a little on his toes.

Tain Hu cut the skin of Cattlson's brow with a flick of her blade, a shallow mock lobotomy just beneath his wolfshead cap, and stepped away. Her eyes met Baru's and she grinned without calculation or mockery, a wolfish and exultant sign.

It had all lasted a second. Perhaps two.

"It goes to Baru Cormorant!" Xate Yawa cried into the silence.

The garrison troops, fearing riot, began to bang their shields before the crowd even started to roar. Muire Lo gripped Baru's shoulder as she stood, stunned, gaping—Purity Cartone went to the Governor's side, kneeling to help—Bel Latheman put his head in his palms and began to shake—

"The carriage!" Muire Lo hissed. "Quickly, while they've still got the road open!"

He pulled on her hand, but she reached out, toward Tain Hu's lopsided grin and badly reset nose, to draw her after them, up into the carriage and safety. All around them the crowd boomed: *A fairer hand! A fairer hand!*

NOW would be the moment for rash countermoves, for sealed orders opened in the event of Cattlson's defeat, for Xate Olake's unsubtle men with their inelegant knives. She had won the duel, won the heart of Aurdwynn. But she had lost the last vestige of security in Treatymont.

Which could be fatal. She'd counted on Xate Yawa's protection while the rest of her design went forward—little chance of that. And she certainly couldn't go back to her tower, swarming with Cattlson's guards.

"Duchess," she called, shouting over the roar of carriage wheel on cobblestone. "I need a safe harbor."

Tain Hu sat with her scabbard in her lap and a wolf smile that hadn't faded since they left the plaza. "My men quarter at Duke Oathsfire's estate in Northarbor. He's a rival in the North, but an ally here. If you need to flee, he can get you on a ship to the mouth of the Inirein, and Duke Unuxekome can take you upriver to my keep in Vultjag."

Where she could be pocketed and held like a coin. But at least it was an option. "Good. Muire Lo?"

"I'll tell the driver." He went forward.

"How long have you been waiting to do that?" Baru asked the duchess. It was impossible to keep herself from grinning back.

"Since that self-satisfied prick sailed into harbor." She stretched her arms across the back of the carriage bench and sat like a warlord for a portrait. "He didn't know how to fight, back then, and neither did I—I was barely a grown woman." Her lips quirked. "But it seems my learning outpaced his."

"It seems so." It was so easy to be giddy. "Where did you—with the sword, I mean, how did you learn?"

"Woodsmen. Rangers. A few real skirmishes." She shrugged. "Stakhieczi poachers from the Wintercrests come south into Vultjag in the autumn, and we fight them off."

"You've killed," Baru said, queasily fascinated.

"The man with the iron circlet," Tain Hu replied, referencing, perhaps, some legend or intimate mark of memory. Her smile flickered, and Baru, thinking again of rashness and countermoves, reminded herself that Tain Hu was not safe, was not a known quantity. *You are not the only player on the board.*

She leaned across the bench to whisper in Tain Hu's ear. Duchess Vult-jag smelled of sweat and leather, of victory. "Shall I pretend to believe that Xate Yawa chose you as my second? That she meant for me to win?"

"It won't matter," Tain Hu murmured back. "She and her brother be-lieved it was too soon to back you, even after you offered them the tax ships. They wanted you wounded and taken out of play. But I've broken ranks and put my vote behind you. If we can show them that we have a chance, they'll come along."

"Why?" she asked, meaning not *why will they come along,* but—

Tain Hu's lips kept careful distance from her ear. "Because I think you've realized that who you are will forever hold you back from what you deserve. Because I know you're selfish, calculating, and farsighted, and when you find no way forward through the Falcresti maze, you'll resort to tearing it down. I knew it even when you ruined my counter-feits. I knew you'd tire of the chains." She gripped Baru's shoulder and bore down painfully, her gloves studded, her strength obvious. "But my support will come at a cost."

THE riots that rocked Treatymont over the next few days ran the gar-rison out of acid wash. Xate Yawa's courts declared an amnesty and set up clinics where the burned could put down their names and collect soothing ointment. Baru imagined the judicial clerks diligently copying those names into hidden ledgers, referencing them against known pseu-donyms, building tables and matrices of the guilty. Recrimination would come. The Masquerade never failed to punish the smallest insurrection.

Despite his careful protests, she sent Muire Lo back to her tower to make excuses for her absence. He wrote, mornings and evenings, but the businesslike brevity of his notes—*tax yields on target; Governor Cattlson occupied with great unrest and his own private matters; Xate Yawa asks about your health*—made it clear his letters were being watched.

And Baru, too, knew she was being watched, watched and judged, though the means were not secret. Tain Hu had chosen her price carefully, made her instructions clear. She would wait in Oathsfire's estate, and Tain Hu would send for her.

One morning soon after, Baru came down the stairs to find a Stakhi woman in a simple wool dress, her long straw hair braided and coiled. "Your Excellency," she said, and bowed.

Baru recognized the bow. It caught her and held her frozen between two steps. "Ake Sentiamut."

The woman smiled courteously. If she remembered what Baru had done to her—that offhand order, disposing of Tain Hu's agent in the Fiat Bank, that callously simple *fire her*—it showed only in the tightness around her eyes. Without her bearskin she was rail thin, almost emaciated. Perhaps it was not the bearskin alone she had lost.

"The duchess sent me." She carried a small case of inlaid wood. "I will be your guide to Treatymont's slums."

"Why?"

"As a lesson. The duchess wants you to see the plight of the commoner." She offered the wooden case. "You'll need this. Your face is too well known."

It was full of Falcresti cosmetics, of the kind Bel Latheman had used so expertly. Beneath the lid was an etching of a deer in its antler morph. Baru considered the powders and jars with skepticism. "I think," she said, "that it will be very difficult to disguise me as a man."

Ake's lips twitched. "We will leave that art to Her Grace, Your Excellence. Cosmetics can be a woman's disguise as well as a man's ornament." She paused delicately. "I know their use well. And I am not unpracticed with Maia skin."

Baru, curious, uncertain, offered her the case.

Ake took her into the drawing room and made her sit very still. Baru tried to speak without moving her face, as if her skull were a porcelain mask. "Did you learn cosmetics from Bel Latheman?"

Ake chewed on the tip of her tongue in concentration, applying some mark or line to Baru's forehead. "No. I taught him."

Baru frowned, making Ake cluck. "But it's a Falcresti art, and he was always so fashionable."

"He was a shy man, poorly raised. He struggled with the expectations of his station." Ake's brush tickled Baru's eyelashes. "I helped him become a man Cattlson could respect."

Baru's curiosity drove her past propriety. "But how did *you* learn?"

"My husband worked as an entertainer on the docks. Oriati ships came in to harbor. There were lamen in the crews who taught him."

"Ah." Baru's upbringing armed her to understand this, at least; when lamen went among societies with only two sexes, they often chose to pass as a man or a woman, and became expert at it. "And was your husband ever released?"

Ake did not pause her work. "So you remember."

Baru wished, now, that she had taken the conversation somewhere else. The starved shape of Ake's body said that her last three years, the years after Baru had destroyed her, had been unhappy. But it was done. "It puzzles me that you would help Bel Latheman master his station, even while other Falcresti held your husband for sedition. Even while you were Tain Hu's agent in the Fiat Bank."

Ake finished and began to put her instruments away. "It puzzles *me*," she said, "that you would crush Tain Hu's rebellion, and then make yourself into a rebellion of your own. But I am a commoner. Perhaps I have no mind for games of power."

Her eyes were evasive, deferential. But perhaps, Baru thought, this was her own art, to hide herself behind propriety. They all had their own arts of passage. "Show me what your duchess wants me to see."

Ake Sentiamut took her out into the streets in common garb. "Hide your teeth," she warned. "They will break your disguise. These parts of Treatymont are not friendly to the noble."

They walked north and east, out of Northarbor and its brawny salt-caked arcades, into Little Welthon where dockworkers and divers and laborers all kept their families. "I work for a chemist now," Ake explained as they went. "A Falcresti man."

"Out here?" Falcresti expatriates kept to the neighborhoods near Southarbor and the garrisons, where they could hide their children from the Iolynic tongues and Maia temptations of the broader city, lining their streets with hired mummers whose job was simply to fill the air with Aphalone—long quotes from revolutionary manuals, ambient Incrasticism for the infants and the youth.

"There's money to be made." Behind Ake's deference, a spark of anger flared. "Do you understand the writs of hereditary hygiene?"

"Those are the Jurispotence's business, and the Charitable Service's. Not mine."

"Here," Ake said, "they are every woman's business. They cannot be otherwise."

She explained how children of impermissible racial mixture were seized, how unlicensed marriages were punished by sterilization or (Baru's stomach knotted) reparatory childbearing. "So you see? Mothers need Falcresti chemistry, or their bodies will be taken by Falcresti laws. The market—" Ake laughed harshly, shaking her head. "The market is rich for chemists."

Reparatory childbearing. Women confiscated and sown like repossessed earth. Baru had known about it, of course—she hadn't dozed through all those meetings of the Governing Factors. But it was one thing to think on it, and another to confront it.

And the policy would be implemented on Taranoke. *Had* been implemented, while Baru sheltered in her school.

As they went they heard the laughter and the screams of children, but met none on the street. Baru didn't need to ask why. The Charitable Service's agents would come for clever children, and anyone could be one of those agents. She had seen the contracts herself: *you will be rewarded for children of merit, and rewarded further based on their placement in the service exam in years to come. . . .*

Muire Lo must have been one of the first. A child promising enough to send on to Falcrest. Whoever had given him to the Masquerade must have been richly repaid.

He'd never seemed eager to see his family again. Could they have—?

"There will come a time," Ake said softly, "when this city will not remember a time before the Masquerade. They will be in our language, and our homes, and our blood."

Baru's ears rang with a strange memory: the sound of Aphalone spoken at the Iriad market, like a new verse in an old song.

It's not what the Masquerade does to you that you should fear, she wanted to tell Ake. It's what the Masquerade convinces you to do to yourself.

There were other strange things to see in the slums. Falcresti families came here to hire wet nurses, so their children could drink immunity factors from a native breast—a shield, they hoped, against the bitter winters and the plagues that killed so many of their children. Some of them even sought illegal blessings from the ilykari. A whole industry of milk and blasphemy had risen here, complete with its own criminals, baby poisoners, mystic protection rackets that cursed households and demanded gold for the undoing. And other kinds of crime, too, guilds of yellow-jacketed plague survivors who cleared the dead and offered their very flesh as a cannibal inoculant. Graft and corruption and illicit love.

None of it could be reduced to something as simple as *invader* and *invaded*.

Baru saw in the city what she felt in herself. The two-faced allegiances, the fearful monitoring of self and surroundings, the whimpering need to please somehow kneeling alongside marrow-deep defiance. One eye set on a future of glittering wealthy subservience, the other turned to a receding and irretrievable freedom.

The liquor of empire, alluring and corrosive at once, saturating everything, every old division of sex and race and history, remaking it all with the promise and the threat of power.

When the sun reddened and fell west, Ake Sentiamut took Baru's wrist. Her deference had gone. "You've seen enough today. The duchess will meet you."

"We return to Oathsfire's estate?"

Ake smiled, as if at some joke Baru had unwittingly told. "Duchess Vultjag has never rested well under an Oathsfire roof. She will wait at my home."

It was one room in a narrow stone building. There were no accommodations for a husband. Tain Hu drowsed on a wooden bench, long and feline, and opened only one eye when Ake led Baru in. "You look like a painted gargoyle. What did you see?"

"Hope," Baru said.

"Oh?"

"The people can still see their shackles. The Masquerade rules them, but it has not yet made them *want* to be ruled. The chains are not yet invisible."

Tain Hu sat up. "You've thought on this a long time, haven't you?"

"The hope I see in your city is the hope I hold for all of Aurdwynn."

"*Your* people made this city. The real Aurdwynn is out there with the trees and the hawks. Not bound up here in this awful tangle." She rolled to her feet. "Tell me what this city makes you want."

Here she could be honest. The truth worked to her advantage. "It makes me want to save my home from what has been done here."

"Save them? Even from the new sewers? From the inoculations and the futures contracts?" Tain Hu taunting, seeking for doubt. "Is that your endgame—roll back the years? Burn everything the Masquerade brought?"

"No." Baru stripped her gloves, finger by finger, considering her words carefully. "I want to steal their secrets. Make them our own. Turn them back against their makers."

Tain Hu went past her, to Ake Sentiamut. The Stakhi woman lowered her eyes, but it was Tain Hu who knelt.

"Ake," the duchess said. "You have given me enough. Go home."

"Your Grace, you will need me."

"I will need you in Vultjag. You have burnt enough of your life in this pit." Tain Hu kissed Ake's slender, translucent hand with regal courtesy. "Go back to the forest. The other Sentiamuts will welcome you. Nurse your strength, and I will call on you there."

Her lips curled as she rose and looked to Baru. "Perhaps I will come with a guest. Perhaps not."

B ARU came back to her bedroom in the Oathsfire house to hear two men speaking inside, their Aphalone accented, northern, hushed.

"Vultjag's had her ear too long. She's been poisoned against me."

The second voice was softer, the accent less pronounced. A man of letters. "Then you will draw the poison out."

"I don't have your charm."

"Or my wife, or my wit, or that, or this. You've spent too much of your life telling me what you don't have, friend. Why not look to your strengths?"

"A mountain of coin? Though Himu knows the Cormorant woman nearly poisoned that, too. What if I have no strengths she respects? What if Vultjag told her about my failed suit?"

"Out," Baru ordered, noticing their wolf-trimmed silks and half-capes too late. She halted, boots sliding on the ceramic tile, startled and unready. They were high nobility.

"Certainly," said the duke on the right, straightening from the doorframe—a rugged knoll of a man, bearded and armed, his eyes indiscreet but at least not lingering in their attention. "At once."

"But we'd be pleased to have your company when we go, Your Excellence." The taller duke was a pale man with a narrow mouth, a mantle of red marten skin, and calm eyes. He had the smoother and more educated Aphalone. "Tain Hu is satisfied with your character. It's time we invited you in."

"Oathsfire, Duke of Mills, at your service. I hope you've enjoyed my home in the city. I paid for it in spite of your best efforts." The bearded man bowed deep. "Our leaders have called a convocation, and you'll be the toast of it."

"The reason for it, too, I should say," his redwood-tall companion added. "I am Lyxaxu, Duke High Stone, Vultjag's westerly and more mannered neighbor. I hope Duchess Vultjag has been kind to you?"

"She's notoriously—" Oathsfire made a flapping bird wing with his hand. "Mercurial."

"Not about you, though." Lyxaxu's eyes sparkled.

"No, she's always been quite steady there—"

Baru found them immediately exasperating, and resolved not to be charmed. "I need a few more weeks as loyal Imperial Accountant before I begin anything. Go tell your convocation to wait."

"Cattlson is hunting you. Dangerous to leave this waiting." Lyxaxu peeled himself off the wall and checked his gloves for bits of plaster. "Dangerous both spiritually and practically. The siblings Xate—"

"—May we be spared forever from their attentions—"

"—feel that it's time to bind you to the rest of us."

"We've every reason to distrust you, you understand."

Lyxaxu frowned at his companion. "Are you really going to list them?"

"I am."

"Well, go on, then."

Oathsfire rapped his knuckles against the wall, a slow martial beat. "Foreigner. Populist. Masquerade technocrat. Secretary a known Falcresti spy."

"Ruined me quite thoroughly," Lyxaxu added, smiling wryly. "Even worse than Radaszic. I'd bought so much of that idiot paper . . ."

"Hard assets, my friend. I really did advise hard assets." Oathsfire reached up to clap him on the shoulder. "So, Your Excellence, you have the rare favor of our neighbor Vultjag, the thorn of the North. Come with us, and we'll tie you into our great sedition."

"Wait, wait, old friend. Let's not be shy about our purposes." Lyxaxu stepped between Baru and his bearded comrade. "We're here to speak to you before you go through with this. I know Vultjag must have mentioned us—our personal histories, perhaps, or our predatory attitude toward her little vale?"

Baru crooked an eyebrow, taken aback by his directness. "She's hardly mentioned either of you."

"Oh," Lyxaxu said, his brow furrowed. "But she's usually so—"

"Plainspoken."

"I might call her tactless, even."

"You're boring Her Excellence, old man."

"Ah. Yes." Lyxaxu cleared his throat. "There's a topic we want to broach. Seeing as you're a woman—"

"I concur, seems plain—"

"Shut up, Your Grace. Your Excellence, I have daughters." Lyxaxu straightened to his full height. "As does my friend here, in fact. I'm married for love, and he's divorced for lack of it. We've no desire to see our children bound up in the Masquerade's breeding plans. We're not all occupied with hunting and honor like that idiot Heingyl, you understand? Some of us have a mind for philosophy, for children, for other such—"

"Womanly things," Baru enunciated, startled by her own iciness. Was she irritated by the way he'd brought it up, sidelong, like a shameful thing? By the possessiveness of it—*we'd hate to see our women under their control*?

Oathsfire again: "What he's dancing around, Your Excellence, is a certain argument we've had. What would it mean if Aurdwynn looked to a foreigner for its salvation? How could we reject all the Masquerade's notions of heredity if we needed foreign blood to free ourselves?"

She'd wondered this herself. Imagined some Oriati Prince liberating Taranoke, smearing himself in the volcanic earth like he'd been born to it. How would mother Pinion take that? "Some might say that Aurdwynn is a land of foreigners, a scar carved by invasion after invasion. Surely one more foreigner would make a fitting liberator."

"A fairer hand!" Lyxaxu cried, in imitation of the chanting crowd.

"A hand too busy to answer all my letters, though." He laughed. Baru, by student's reflex, felt immediately contrite.

Oathsfire did not join Lyxaxu's laughter. His beard hid his mouth, but his expression spoke to marshaled will. "When this is done, this rebellion that you and Vultjag push us toward, we will be victorious or we will all be dead. If we are victorious, Aurdwynn will have to stand united. That will mean one ruler, set over all the dukes. That was how the Stakhieczi repelled the Tu Maia—one Necessity to unite the mansions. It's how we'll repel the Masquerade, when they come again."

Lyxaxu nodded solemnly. "One king. Or queen. This is the unspoken prize that preoccupies us all. Nayauru Dam-builder is closest, and hungriest to rule—she has gotten children on Autr and Sahaule, and if she can marry those heirs to Ihuake's or produce a child from one of Ihuake's sons, she may be able to usurp the Cattle Duchess, claim old Pinjagata, and unite five duchies under one throne. With her reservoirs and Ihuake's herdlands at last combined, she would have enough good food to feed millions—enough to build a kingdom that might trouble even Falcrest. But we would stop her, you see? There lies the key."

"We've had centuries to build up our hates, after all. Decades to engrave our little squabbles in bone. When one of us rises, the rest grow jealous. A foreign-born queen, without stake in Aurdwynn's grudges, might be the only one who could command us all." Oathsfire looked to Lyxaxu, seeking some shared memory, a ghostly scar of troubles past, or an understanding of those yet to come. "The Midlands Alliance will break soon. Ihuake fears Nayauru's fertility and ambition. In the North we have made our own mistakes. Lyxaxu here bickers with Erebog. Erebog has given her landlords too much power, and cannot wrest it back. And in my greed for land and stone I've found my hands full of Vultjag's quills. We need someone to unite us."

Baru blinked at him. "You're asking me to be queen of Aurdwynn. When we haven't even started a rebellion."

"Nothing so hasty, really!"

"We're just suggesting possibilities you might pursue." Oathsfire offered an open hand. "Offering our conditional support."

Lyxaxu cocked one eyebrow. "A foreign queen *would* profit from an Aurdwynni king. It's indisputable."

"Shame he's married." Oathsfire chuckled. "I know he's prettier." He went past her, to the door, his boots clattering on the tile. "If you'll come with us, Your Excellence, the convocation waits."

Baru caught tall Duke Lyxaxu's eyes. "I read your letters," she said. "All of them. I always meant to reply. But there was so little time—"

"I understand." He held up his hands. "Praxis must come before philosophy."

THE rebellion in Aurdwynn began in a hidden temple, a place built of paper and oil and old faith.

Baru dismounted the carriage into warm summer rain and followed the two dukes into a lamp workshop. The storerooms smelled of olive oil and clay. They walked between rolls of hemp and half-washed pottery kilns left to air in the dark. "Closed until the riots are over," Lyxaxu explained. "Up these stairs, Your Excellence."

Some small sentinel in the back of Baru's head ticked through a list of fears: *a trap, a honeypot, Xate Yawa's means of disposal, Cattlson's revenge, a trick of the Cold Cellar—*

She wished for Muire Lo's company, his shy pragmatism. She never should have taken him for granted.

At the top of the stairs, a plump Belthyc woman in white who smelled pungently of onion guarded the door. Her smile was full of warmth. "Ykari Himu welcomes you," she said, her Aphalone liquid but still clear. "This is a temple to the Three Virtues. You're dressed richly, Your Excellence, and should therefore be careful, as the oil will stain."

The woman—an ilykari, surely, one of the outlawed priest-emulators of the Virtuous—unlocked the door with two small shining keys.

Baru shivered at the cold, and at a stab of awe.

The second floor of the workshop had been an office. The ilykari had knocked down the interior walls and made an airy space of white partitions and cedar poles, golden with lamplight cast through paper. Everything paper: the meditation cells, the little side rooms, the dividing walls that sectioned the space into small energetic arrows, as if demanding the visitor move somehow, act with vigor.

It all reeked of olive oil. She stripped one glove off and touched the nearest cedar beam. Her finger came away slick.

"So we can burn it in an instant," the ilykari woman said, still smiling, "if they find us. Come."

In the central space, on a ring of mats, waited the other conspirators.

Xate Yawa and Xate Olake, steel-gray hair and beard, Jurispotence and Phantom Duke side by side like two roosting doves. Tain Hu, in her riding costume, the longsword she'd used to defeat Cattlson scabbarded on the floor beside her. Another man in noble finery—Baru caught her breath in pleased surprise. It was Unuxekome, the Sea Groom, the coastal duke who owned a full quarter of Aurdwynn's privately held ships and yards, and was furthermore rumored to be a financier of pirates. He looked back and smiled.

No one spoke. Behind Xate Yawa, a small trickle of water ran down a waxed paper chute and into a silver bowl. Baru knelt on a mat as Oaths-fire and Lyxaxu took the positions beside her.

The weight of the risk here pressed the breath from her lungs. Every-one gathered in one place, under Xate Yawa's eyes—and in an ilykari temple, at that. It would take only one whisper to set the garrison on them . . .

Perhaps that was why they had done it. All the conspirators bound to-gether under the imminence of ruin.

The ilykari priestess went to sit in the center of the circle, sandaled feet whispering. She carried a small pot of ink and a palimpsest in a cedar frame, stretched taut by cord. "In our silence we exemplify Wydd, who gives us patience to endure. In our will to act we exemplify Himu, who drives us to war. In acting now, when the time has come, we exemplify Devena, the middle course, who tempers these extremes."

Baru caught Xate Yawa shifting in subtle impatience, her lips drawn down. She hadn't thought the time had come, had she? She wouldn't be here at all, given her way. But her accomplice Tain Hu had acted, and she had been drawn along.

Surely she was too old and canny to go in without a fallback. . . .

"I will read now from the missives I have been given, anonymous and unsigned." The priestess lifted the palimpsest and Baru saw old Iolynic characters, columned and incomprehensible. She spoke with apparently infinite calm. "Let me serve as a conduit for the fears and hopes of all those gathered, that we may hear what they cannot voice. This they have written:

"I fear this Taranoki woman is an instrument of the Masquerade. I fear the people's love for Baru Cormorant may outstrip their loyalty to us. I fear we will not have the strength to overcome the Masquerade, even with her. I fear we will fail to act, and that the opportunity will never come again. I fear her youth and rashness."

The silent calm of the place came over Baru, and although she did not believe in ancient men and women who had practiced their virtues so perfectly that they subsumed and became them, she found all her knotted-up wariness pressed flat and still. Water, and oil, and light through paper, and somehow the words spoken were true without being dangerous.

But still she tried to match each sentence to one of the circled faces. Her curiosity remained.

"I hope for a free Aurdwynn for my daughters. I hope the Taranoki will be the spark we need. I hope—" The ilykari smiled gently, as if moved. "I hope for her hand and a throne. I hope for freedom, and no more. I hope for freedom. I hope for freedom."

The wind outside blew against the walls and small clear drops of water seeped in through the roof to tremble against the waxed paper and the oiled cedar poles. The caged light of the lanterns danced and flickered.

"Some of us are enemies outside this place." Now the priestess spoke with the wind behind her. "Xate Yawa hunts and kills my fellow ilykari. Baru Cormorant wears the mask of the tyranny in Falcrest. Dukes Oathsfire and Lyxaxu bicker with Vultjag over marriage and land. Duke Unuxekome consorts with the pirates that trouble our waters. If we are to unite in rebellion, we must bind each other close. I have tied that bond between you, and now I will tie another. Baru: come forward."

Tain Hu's dark eyes glimmered gold in the candlelight. Baru had to will herself to move. The stillness of the place had seized her bones.

"I am here," she said.

The priestess offered the ink pot, the pen, the palimpsest. It had been filled with small square provinces of old Iolynic script. "On this palimpsest I have written the secrets offered to me by all those gathered here. Secrets of deadly power. You will offer a secret to me, and I will write it here, so that you too will be bound."

"What if," she said, the smell of olive oil in her nose, her eyes, "I lie?"

"I will know," the priestess said, and then, whispering in Baru's ear, close and soft as clay, "just as Cairdine Farrier knew the potential in your eyes, just as Devena knows the divisions in your heart. I will know."

Baru drew away with a start, her spine prickling. Duke Lyxaxu chuck-led softly and murmured inaudibly to Oathsfire.

The priestess held the pen low and tight like a woman gripping a snake. "You don't know Old Iolynic. But I do. Whisper your secret to me, Baru Cormorant, and Wydd will hear."

The secret of secrets rose in her like a rotten thing trying to retch itself up, and just to stop it, to head it off, to do anything but say it or feel it like a pole of obsidian strapped to the curve of her spine, she seized the priestess by the back of the neck and held her close to hiss a different secret, her lips against the ilykari's small dark ear: *I want to fuck women.*

Why had she done that? Oh, no, why had she *said* that—what a fool, what a gullible fool—what desperation could possibly have driven her to vomit that truth up, that truth she struggled every day to hide—

The pen scratched in short geometric arcs. "Is it enough?" Xate Yawa asked, breaking the silence. "Something of power?"

"In the Masquerade, it is enough to end her life," the priestess said. "She will never go back to them."

"Good!" Unuxekome, the sea duke, clapped his hands against his knees. "Then we have a rebellion to begin."

A ND so they began: the circle now a war council.
        Xate Yawa spoke first, to claim her primacy. "I stay in Treaty-mont." As if this were the simplest and most trustworthy duty. "Play my part as Jurispotence as long as I can. If I learn something vital it will go through my brother."

So eerie to see Xate Olake sitting alongside her, those jungle-crow eyes twinned and sharp. What did they see when they looked at each other? Could any secret survive? Was there, perhaps, a sort of compact of vigi-lance, a mantra or instinct that kept them from ever blinking at the same time, so that one Xate or another always watched—

But Olake was speaking. "My spies will do their work. We must de-termine which of the dukes will join us, who will go with Cattlson, and who can be courted. Heingyl is Cattlson's, of course, but although they were once as brothers, I have hopes we will turn Radaszic—he dwells on the books Lyxaxu gave him, and the ruin Baru Cormorant made of his estate. Now he chafes against his chains."

"The Midlands?" Lyxaxu asked.

"Nayauru Dam-builder and Ihuake could fall either way—or both, if their split grows deeper. With Nayauru comes Sahaule and Autr, good soldiers and good salt. With Ihuake comes Pinjagata, and we all know his worth."

"His worth," Oathsfire murmured to Baru, "is that he and all his people are mad bastards who spilled out of a rabid bear already clutching spears." Baru grinned, remembering her baffling meeting with Pinjagata, and then hid the grin, so that Oathsfire would not be misled.

Olake set them all aside with a gesture like a bucket poured. "But the Midlands can wait. Your neighbor is the real priority, Lyxaxu. We must buy Erebog to secure our hold on the North—and we must keep her from falling to her own landlords."

"Why the North?" Baru wondered, as she spoke, how long and how carefully these plans had been considered. She had come late to their council—in the span of the night, and of years. "You won't begin by seizing Treatymont?"

"Treatymont is a trap." It was Unuxekome who spoke, the Sea Groom's voice smooth, eager, full of long-checked need to act. "Heingyl Staghunter will rally to his friend Cattlson with a frightening count of cavalry. Radaszic may not turn to us. He loves and fears Heingyl."

"With or without Radaszic, the move would still destroy us." It was lamplight that put the hawk-gold in Tain Hu's eyes, but Baru imagined it as an inner fire. "If we took Treatymont we would be bottled up. Powerless to defend our duchies from reprisal when reinforcements came from Falcrest."

Xate Olake's murmur brought the taste of wine to Baru's tongue, the memory of maybe-poison. "If we act too suddenly, we cannot untangle the Traitor's Qualm. We must display endurance . . . make a case to Nayauru and Autr and Sahaule, to Ihuake and Pinjagata, that we are a safe investment. We need them for triumph."

"That endurance depends on accomplishing three tasks before winter." Tain Hu rapped on the floor, her eyes circling the conspiracy. "First, build a base of power in the North, a place that will tell the people"—her eyes flickered over Baru—"that we can offer them a fairer kind of rule. When the time is right, we will declare open rebellion and drop the bridges on the Inirein. My neighbors and I are agreed?"

To each side of Baru, Oathsfire and Lyxaxu nodded and made sounds of assent. "The other dukes know they can't root us out of the woods," Lyxaxu said. "High Stone itself is beyond siege. Oathsfire's longbowmen are peerless, and Vultjag—well, we all know the difficulty of troubling her."

Unuxekome raised a hand. "My friend Oathsfire here is marriageable again, if we're desperate to sweeten the pot with Nayauru or Ihuake. They are unwed—Nayauru, of course, keeps the old Maia habits, but she might accept a political marriage so long as it didn't bind her to one bed."

Oathsfire sighed. "My southerly neighbor is always thinking of my happiness."

"She's quite lovely—"

"And she knows it too well."

"I'm sure your heart would win her."

"Against Sahaule, it's not my heart that needs to impress her—"

"Our second need." Tain Hu cut them off with admirable curtness. "Our serfs will only leave their families and fight if we can give them food, protection, and salaries. We need money for all of these. Once open rebellion begins, that need will only grow."

Everyone looked at Baru. She nodded, offering confidence, *feeling* confident. This web of money and terrain and treason felt familiar, tractable—easier than sitting in an office drinking wine and folding sedition into polite words. She'd been so pliant for so long. A joy to act at last. "I can give you the tax ships. With Xate Yawa's help, I'll arrange for them to travel back to Falcrest in convoy, where they can be taken together." She considered Unuxekome, struck by his enthusiasm and by the respect in his eyes. What had she done to earn that? "We only need a fleet to seize them."

He nodded. "If you can disrupt the naval escort, my ships can do the rest. But how can you be sure Governor Cattlson will let you have any authority over the tax ships, after—?" He gestured to Tain Hu, to the duel that had thrown Treatymont into havoc. "Surely he suspects your loyalties have wavered. Last time an Imperial Accountant strayed toward the rebellion, he killed her. Why would he let you near the tax harvest?"

Xate Yawa smiled a thin efficient smile. "Because I won't let him constrain her. He may not trust his Accountant, but he cannot overrule the Jurispotence without a writ from Falcrest. That writ will be some time coming."

Tain Hu rose from her crouch, her scabbard whispering across the flooring as she moved. "Our third objective follows from there. Once we seize the tax ships, Cattlson will call for reinforcements. They'll come sailing against the trade wind and the currents, hoping to put down the rebellion quickly, but they'll be racing the end of summer and the storm season. Duke Unuxekome, your ships will be the only means we have to head them off. Can it be done?"

The sea duke's confidence suggested to Baru that perhaps he knew very little about the Masquerade navy. But then again, she knew very little about him. "My ancestors sailed this coast for centuries. We know every inlet and harbor, every trick of current and wind. There are pirates coming north, driven out of Taranoki waters, and we have gold to offer them. Yes, I think we can make a fight of it."

Tain Hu looked to Xate Yawa. "You doubted the time was right."

Xate Yawa shrugged slightly. "Soon all doubt will be erased."

They all stood together, Baru missing whatever silent signal brought the meeting to an end. "We leave separately," Oathsfire murmured to her. "At intervals."

"I can't imagine why." She stepped away from him, irritated by his condescension, her irritation springing from some deeper restlessness, an eagerness to begin. "Unuxekome, Your Grace. A moment."

The Sea Groom walked with her as she stepped away from the circle. Above his gloves the black cords of his lower arms were raw with rope burns. He'd spent time sailing rough waters, not long ago.

"You called them Taranoki waters," she said. "Not Souswardi."

"My maps say Taranoke." He had a comrade's smile, wry with the knowledge of shared suffering. "As long as I rule, they always will."

"I'm grateful." And she was.

"Is that why you're doing this?" The candles behind him moved softly in their glass as the wind hissed outside. "Because of what happened there? The pirates told me how Taranoke fell."

She felt the test, and hesitated. He spoke into the silence: "I dreamed of liberating and ruling Aurdwynn, you know. I think we all did, in the years after the occupation began. I had the ships and I had the hate. But I couldn't find the way. It was all so—" He grasped at something, gloves tight, like an invisible knot in windblown rigging. "So *complicated*."

"I want to show you that way," she said, seizing on that hope, that truth. "I have been a servant too long. I want to help make something free."

He bowed his head in acknowledgment, perhaps in gratitude. Behind him, Oathsfire watched their conversation with hooded eyes.

CATTLSON'S retaliation fell swiftly, in the shape of a letter, copied to every organ and factor of the provincial government.

It was Unuxekome who slipped her away—out of the Horn Harbor on a little mail ship called *Beetle Prophet,* past the burnt towers, between the torchships, and east toward his home at Welthony, where the river Inirein joined the sea.

"Tell me a story," the duke Unuxekome said. They stood at the prow, early in the afternoon. Baru was reading her letters.

"A story. Hm. There are riots in Treatymont." Duel riots—Baru's riots. The cauldrons of Little Welthon and the Arwybon finally spilling over as all the rage of poverty and stolen children boiled and flashed into steam. Garrison troops swarming to the Horn Harbor to protect the shipping. They'd left too much unguarded: a cadre of woodsmen in green wool had led a mass breakout at the Cold Cellar.

"That's not a story, Your Excellence. More of a report." He stood balanced on the ship's bowsprit, hands light on the ropes. "It's hard to find good stories now. I can't read Aphalone, you know—really I'm a very poor—"

An exocet fish leapt from the bow wave and Unuxekome lunged, trying to catch it by its silver wings. Baru snatched for his tunic to pull him back, startled, thinking already: the idiot, the child, they'll say I pushed him—

But the duke kept his footing, bare toes curled on the wood, hands spidered in the rigging. The exocet glided away. "Ah," the duke sighed, and then, turning, "You thought I'd fall?"

She hid her embarrassment. He was maybe ten years her senior, salted and authoritative, a captain on any ship he cared to sail. She would have to match him. "I planned against the eventuality."

"And here Vultjag warned me you thought only of yourself."

She permitted a soft *ha.* "Even so. Cattlson would've been pleased to charge me with the murder of a duke."

"Oh? But you're already a wanted traitor, aren't you?"

"No. Suspected seditionist. It means—" She grappled for a moment with the exactitudes of Masquerade law. "He doesn't have the power to arrest me without the Jurispotence's backing. But if he marks me as a se-ditionist, he gains the power to review all my orders, which lets him counterplay them. And if he still had me in Treatymont, he'd lock me in protective custody."

"Hmm." He rested his head in the rigging, as if the ship were all his hammock, and stared up at the circling shearwaters. "Still sounds more like a report than a story. Needs a hero."

"An illiterate duke captaining a mail ship?"

Unuxekome looked at her like he'd been stabbed, and then laughed. "I'm sorry," he said. "I must seem like a vain bastard, preening up on the bowsprit."

"I'd never question the bloodline of a duke of Aurdwynn."

"Oh, no, please do. I used to dream I was a bastard. My mother sailed with the Syndicate Eyota, see? All those dashing Oriati buccaneers, raid-ing and adventuring . . ." He rolled his neck, squinting in the noonday sun. "Better than a father who loved harbor dredging and river trade."

Baru had an idea what had happened to the duchess Unuxekome and her consort. The same quiet disaster that had left so many duchies in the hands of young people with sparse families and graveyards full of noble bones. But she didn't ask about the Fools' Rebellion. "You may go bucca-neering yet," she said. "If I have my way."

He lifted himself a little ways off the ropes to watch her intently. "And will you have your way? Can you possibly arrange for the tax ships to be taken, even with Cattlson dogging you?"

Cattlson had tried to countermand Baru's order to the Admiralty—that vital order, the key arrangement: *sail the tax ships to Falcrest in a sin-gle convoy, for security.* And that might have been the end there: but Xate Yawa protected her. Baru had won a legal duel, after all, without any firm violation of Imperial law. The protocols of that same law gave Cattlson no cause to relieve or countermand her. He needed the Jurispotence's consent to destroy Baru's authority. And she would not give it.

"Let her manage the remainder of the tax season," Xate Yawa had counseled Cattlson (or so Muire Lo reported). "She'll work to excel in her duties so she can look better than you in Falcrest's eyes. It won't be enough. By midwinter, Parliament will order her relieved."

No need for Unuxekome to know how close it had been. Baru brushed his concern away like a circling fly. "The tax ships will go where I want them. I have the law on my side."

His jaw hardened, as if to bite. "You have Xate Yawa on your side, in the same way I have the sea on mine. The sea takes no side. Be careful about pinning all your plans on her."

"I'm pinning all my plans on *your* fleet, Your Grace."

She meant this as reassurance, even flattery. But Unuxekome rose from the rigging and walked down the bowsprit to her, swaying against the wave motion. "And I'm pinning my hopes on you, Your Excellence. Tell me how to take these ships. Tell me where they'll be, and with what escort. I will see to the rest. If you trust anything, trust in me. But give me what I need to do it."

And he really thought he would, this barefoot sweat-soaked duke of waves. He had shown Baru something vital, trusting or uncaring (perhaps this was a habit of the nobility, born into power, unconditioned to secrecy and meticulous self-containment—a habit of those who never had to earn their station). Unuxekome loved stories. He loved them much more than plans. If he could be the saga-captain sailing into death and legend, he would.

But Baru had heard stories of her own. Aminata's boast: *a single Masquerade frigate can fight four Oriati war dromons and leave them burning. . . .*

The Imperial Navy ruled the Ashen Sea. Unuxekome would never take the tax ships by main force. Not even with the help of the pirates he'd call up out of the south. Baru had to arrange for his victory.

But how?

Everything she sent to the Admiralty in Treatymont would be opened and read. Every order she gave would be scrutinized for some excuse Cattlson could use to reject it. She had to betray the tax convoy to the rebels without betraying herself first.

How?

Unuxekome watched her closely, waiting for her to share her great plan, the masterstroke of manipulation that would give him his chance at heroism. She smiled at him, an easy confident smile laced with secrets, a smoke-screen smile, and said, "I think I'm going to climb the rigging. I need exercise, and space. Would you take my coat down below?"

And she did, wondering if Unuxekome watched her, considering his own bloodline, his mother climbing in the ropes of her own swift ships, and perhaps some day his children, too. That was a duke's story, wasn't it? Noble ancestors, and noble heirs . . .

She would need to use all the leverage she could find. But it bothered her to think of Unuxekome like this. He was easy to talk to, dangerously honest. And deep down she liked stories too.

Up at the top of the mast, arms burning, she realized how she would take the tax ships.

BEETLE *Prophet* stopped to take on reports on the progress of tax season. Baru read them nervously. She was certain that Bel Latheman had told Cattlson about her tax rider, the innocuous question she'd asked every noble and commoner in Aurdwynn: *whom do you love best?*

Muire Lo's reports were full of numbers, small tiles prised out of a vast buckling mosaic. Unrest sputtered across Aurdwynn—serfs rebelling against dukes, mobs snapping at tax collectors, garrison troops dealing harsh retaliation. In particular there was great tension in the Midlands, where Nayauru Dam-builder and Ihuake the Cattle Lord each suffered terrible raids by mysterious bandits that withdrew back into the other's territory.

The weave of rule beginning to fray.

Baru unrolled a map of Aurdwynn and began to paint it in her secret knowledge.

Her tax rider asked the payer to divide ten notes between the local duke, Governor Cattlson, Jurispotence Xate, and herself. She pulled the results from Muire Lo's reports, quite pleased with her instrument, and painted her map in colors of loyalty—

The red of Imperial Navy sails for towns or duchies that slanted toward the Governor. (Mostly this was Duchy Heingyl).

Forest green, Aurdwynn green, for areas that kept loyalties to their own dukes. Vultjag's people loved her, and Unuxekome's, too; but not those of gentle Radaszic or (*hm!*) clever Lyxaxu and, most of all, Erebog, the Crone in Clay, all of whom suffered in deep debt. . . .

And then blue, great runs of sky blue and sea blue, whatever excited inconstant blue she grabbed from her paint pots, for the areas that loved *her.*

No one favored Jurispotence Xate, of course. But her power did not require popularity.

So Baru had what she wanted: a map of Aurdwynn's loyalty, as seen through the lens of one kind of power, the power she best controlled. Now all she needed was an empirical test, proof that she could turn the blue on the map into shouting commoners on the streets. . . .

When *Beetle Prophet* came to the mouth of the river Inirein, the mighty Bleed of Light that ran down from the Wintercrests and marked the eastern border of Aurdwynn, she went ashore with Duke Unuxekome and walked the streets of Welthony, his capital. On the map she'd painted it blue and green.

Word went out through the streets ahead of her, first by whisper, then by shout, then by riders up the river to the duke's house. She strode up the riverwalk with her chained purse at her side, and the people of Welthony, no friend of Cattlson or the Masquerade, turned out from their labor to cry in Iolynic and Aphalone: *A fairer hand! A fairer hand!*

Unuxekome walked with her, smiling, bare-headed, his Maia bones proudly unmasked. "My ship has brought good news," he told his gate guard. "She's not here on audit!"

"I grew up in the sea," she told the armsmen, invoking Taranoke and her own Maia blood. "But I never thought to meet her groom."

And the watching crowd roared approval, as blue as the map predicted, pleased that this foreigner knew the meaning of their duke's name.

"Have you found a way?" Unuxekome hissed in her ear, as he drew her in through the gate, as his armsmen closed them off from the crowd. "The tax ships sail soon. How will we take them?"

"Simple," she said, clapping him on the shoulder, like a brother, a friend. "I give Cattlson what he wants. I offer to resign my post."

By the time *Beetle Prophet* sailed from Welthony, headed back west to Treatymont, Baru had written and sealed four letters—to Cattlson, to Tain Hu, to Xate Yawa, and the last to Unuxekome himself, who would bear it south by ship to the pirates and Oriati privateers.

She stood at the prow and watched the dawn, trying to see the curve of the world, to imagine it turning beneath the sun, the great patterns of trade and sickness and heredity and force moving on its face. The very ink and grammar of history. Driven by and made from and ultimate master of hundreds of millions of people. The question and the answer:

Mother, why do they come here? Why do we not go to them?

Why are they so powerful?

She hadn't written to Muire Lo. She hadn't given him the warning he wanted. If she tried, the letters would be opened, the warning discovered—

Surely he'd understand. Surely. He would get his family out. He would save himself.

Everything had a price.

O N the way into the Horn Harbor, following the buoys between the torchship *Egalitaria* and the burnt towers, Baru picked out the shapes of the tax flotilla waiting to sail. Twelve great ships riding low in the water, heavy with gold and silver, and the escort—five frigates with red sails, their decks lined with marines at drill. The prize.

The Treatymont garrison was waiting to arrest her.

They couldn't call it an arrest, of course. In her letter to Cattlson she'd been careful to define it as a *voluntary self-recall*. Until she arrived in Falcrest and submitted herself to the judgment of Parliament, she would still be Imperial Accountant of Aurdwynn, with all the powers and responsibilities vested in the title. But to Cattlson, the difference was a formality. Baru would be locked up on the tax ships, isolated from mail or money, consigned to the judgment of a higher power. He'd be free to hunt and drink and marry Heingyl Ri to Bel Latheman without the trouble of Taranoki women ruining economies and winning duels. Muire Lo would take command of her office until Parliament could either (ha) return her with her authority reaffirmed or dispatch a new Accountant.

She'd offered Cattlson a way out.

As she'd written the letter she'd tried to put herself in Cattlson's place, to don his obsessions and fears like his wolf's head cloak, remembering what Purity Cartone had told her—*you are not the only player on the board*. Cattlson would wonder why she'd given up so soon after her victory in the duel. He would go to Xate Yawa to ask about the legalities of the offer. She would help him understand that Baru had realized her impotence: she had no real power without the Governor's backing, and the mercy of Parliament offered her only hope for a continued career.

Too proud to beg to him for forgiveness, *of course* Baru would pretend she was going over his head, traveling to Falcrest in search of exoneration rather than clemency. Cattlson, paternalistically merciful, would understand that her pride offered her no other surrender.

But Cattlson was still careful.

So he set his garrison soldiers waiting for her at the dockside, seabirds in blue and gray. Xate Yawa stood between them, her lips pursed sourly, the black robes of her station like a trespassing corvid. "Your Excellence." She gestured to Baru, drawing her in—*walk with me.* "Perhaps with your departure, Aurdwynn may find some relief from the disquiet that has seized it. The Governor offers these soldiers as escort to the frigate *Sulane,* which will carry you to Falcrest."

Baru followed her down the row of soldiers, minding her carriage, keeping her head high. Only by pretending victory could she pretend defeat. "I will not travel on *Sulane,*" she said, as they'd planned, as she'd written in her letter from Welthony. "Nor will I tolerate an armed escort. I'll spend the journey aboard the transport *Mannerslate,* organizing my papers and preparing testimony for Parliament."

"The Governor commands these troops," Yawa reminded her.

"The Governor commands the *garrison.*" Baru tipped her chin toward the flotilla gathered in the harbor. "Once they set foot on a ship, they fall under naval authority, and once the navy leaves harbor, I'll be the ranking technocrat aboard. That makes them mine. And I don't want an escort."

Xate Yawa conceded the point with a flick of one gloved hand. "I'll inform the Governor that you declined his courtesy. I took the liberty of having the papers and effects you requested delivered to *Sulane,* but I'm sure they can be transferred." She paused by one of the garrison officers. "Stand your soldiers down. The Accountant will travel without escort."

All as they'd planned—Xate Yawa's power used to strip away Cattlson's safeguards, to leave Baru the sole and unchecked Masquerade authority aboard ship.

The Jurispotence took her hand. Whether she gripped with formal delicacy or some meaningful strength, Baru couldn't tell. Their gloves masked too much. "I hope you have not become too rash," she said.

Baru considered the woman, her flint and cold, looking for some glimmer of assurance or fear or any human response at all. But Xate Yawa offered only composed, polite concern.

She had betrayed one rebellion to Falcrest because she'd believed it would fail. It could happen again.

A navy launch waited to bring Baru out to *Mannerslate*. Word of the Imperial Accountant's departure must not have spread, because there was no riot dockside (although perhaps, Baru thought, she overestimated her own celebrity—but no, she had the numbers now).

Something moved through the crowd. Baru caught the disturbance, a stiffness, a ripple of recoil. Cattlson, come to see her off—?

Muire Lo stepped forward, eyes downcast. He wore his secretarial coat buttoned to the throat and carried a small folio of loose papers in mindless disarray. At once Baru put her heart in ice. "Over here," she called, preempting whatever he might be planning to do. She'd left him in Treatymont because there was no safe or useful way to include him. She couldn't explain now.

He stepped forward. "I'm sorry," he said, eyes still hooded. He hadn't washed or oiled his hair. "I tried to draw him off."

And with a jagged pop of awareness like the first shock of a broken bone she saw Purity Cartone, the remora, the Masquerade instrument, standing at the edge of the gathered crowd, smiling blandly. "He's to be your bodyguard," Muire Lo explained, and at last looked up. His eyes were like river stones, still and smooth, and perhaps no one but Baru would have seen past them. "Is it true you're going to Falcrest? Leaving me in your place?"

She smiled through her shock, clinging to the necessities of the moment: to seem unconcerned, to give him strength, to succor the splinter of pain in her own breast. His *eyes*—"It's true," she said. "I need Parliament to sort out this . . . unpleasantness before I can continue my work."

"Your Excellence." He stepped forward with abrupt, unconsidered haste, as if trying to catch something falling. "Is there—is there anything that I can do? Any instruction you'd like to leave for me?"

Purity Cartone's mild gaze followed everything with appalling languid precision.

Baru smiled bravely at Muire Lo, lying, shutting him out, closing him like a book of things already known. There was no warning she could give that would not risk the whole plan. "No special instructions," she said. "Keep the office in order while I'm gone. I'll write if any business strikes me."

She thought he might do something rash.

But Muire Lo squared his shoulders, drawing himself up against the weight of everything she hadn't said. "Your Excellence." The constancy of a clean decision sharp in his voice. "All will be just as you require it when I see you again."

He watched her launch go out. Purity Cartone sat in the stern, the wave motion of the Horn Harbor rippling through him, as if he were only another medium, another vessel on the water.

17

THE Imperial Republic's frigate *Sulane* led the tax convoy east with the trade winds, racing along Aurdwynn's coast.

The twelve transports sailed in a column after *Sulane*, chasing her stern lanterns under aurora skies. High-sailed twins *Juristane* and *Commsweal* ran wary guard abeam. *Welterjoy*, heavy-helmed and formidable, carried astern, ready to raise full sail and ride the westerly trade winds down on any attacker. Around them darted *Scylpetaire*, swift, hungry, a torpedo-bearing sheepdog free to search for trouble and trouble it in turn.

The navy would not give up Falcrest's due.

And what a due. The gems and precious metals aboard these ships— excised, resentfully, from Aurdwynn's dukes, the treasuries of distant Erebog and cattle-rich Ihuake and briny Autr and all the rest—could finance seasons of open war.

Baru Cormorant was at last, however briefly, on a ship to Falcrest.

She took dinner with Rear Admiral Ormsment aboard *Sulane* on their first night out of port, and found it, at least at first, oddly pleasant. Ormsment was an urbane Falcresti woman with a limitless and apparently genuine curiosity about Taranoke. "What concerns me the most," she said (the topic of the new name had come up, that ugly word *Sousward*), "is just this—that in making your culture ours we have overlooked some strength, some primal vitality that might have bettered us. What use a republic of nations if we make them all the same?"

"It's practically incestuous," Baru agreed, taken in, for a moment, by the notion. Perhaps she would find this sentiment popular in Falcrest. Perhaps the Parliament would realize that Taranoke could offer more to the Masquerade on its own terms, as a partner rather than a conquest—

But she wasn't going to Falcrest for a long time. And Ormsment, for all her charm and authority, seemed more fixated on *primal vitality* and treating Baru like a wayward daughter than answering her questions about astronomy.

And in any case, it proved impossible to relax with Purity Cartone smiling behind her.

THE first pirates struck too early.

Baru had taken a bunk on the lead transport, *Mannerslate*. Instead of an office (what had she expected?) they gave her a hammock down among the stinking swearing marines who guarded the cargo. The papers she'd brought as a pretense of business proved impossible to keep out of the damp, and although she could have let them rot, years of school habit brought her up to the deck to try to dry them in the sun. Frigate birds taunted her.

Two days from the mouth of the Inirein, two days before the arranged time, she woke in the night to bells. Fought her way up onto deck through swarming marines and shouting crew to see:

Distant fireworks. The arc of rocket flares falling into the sea. Sharp sunrise flash as *Scylpetaire,* in the middle distance, fired two more. Light on the water like a drowned moon.

And a pair of ships pinned in the glare, their lateen sails taut, straining. Oriati-pattern dromon galleys. Bannerless.

Two raiders closing from astern, riding the weather gage.

Maybe they'd thought to slip into the formation and take one of the transports in silence. More likely they'd sighted one of the transports and one of the escorts, and—thinking that the tax ships would sail one by one, as insurance against a devastating early storm—they'd assumed the escort was out of position, and made an attempt.

Scylpetaire had caught them.

Fireworks popped above *Scylpetaire,* then *Sulane,* red, blue, white white white: signals passed to the flagship, orders relayed on to the rest. Baru watched in anxious fascination while *Mannerslate*'s captain brayed for calm and a steady course.

The navy frigates made dark avian forms in the night, *Scylpetaire* shadowing the raiders as they turned off, cutting sails to go against the wind. Day-bright for an instant as she launched volleys of flares to keep the raiders in sight.

And then *Welterjoy*'s sails caught the aurora light, running full on the wind, crashing through the wavefronts as she raced to intercept. She sailed dark, trusting *Scylpetaire*'s flares and *Sulane*'s signals to guide her in. Baru, engrossed and exhilarated, lost in the mechanics of wind and chase, pointed and called to the crew. They shouted to each other in the rigging, excited. Only the marines kept their silence.

Light kindled at *Welterjoy*'s prow. Two white rockets leapt forward like exocet fish. The wind grasped them and smashed them into the water astern of the fleeing raiders.

"They'll have the deflection now, Your Excellence," Purity Cartone murmured. Baru leapt in surprise.

Welterjoy fired again: eight rockets at a more confident angle. One of the fat steel tubes tangled in the lead raider's rigging and, after an instant of furious incandescent sputtering, popped into a shower of grease fire.

The raider's rigging and deck began to burn. Whatever the crew tried as an answer only spread the inferno. The mainsails and the masts burst into sheets of fire. Baru watched, not horrified, thrilled on some fundamental level to witness at last the Navy Burn, the Masquerade's chemical edge. The wind carried the smell: acrid, ferociously artificial, a cremation of linen and hemp and flesh.

When *Welterjoy* had finished with the other raider (the fire burned even when wet, spread across the water, a less gentle aurora) a string of fireworks went up from *Sulane*. "No aid to survivors," Purity Cartone read, eyes gleaming with reflected starburst. "Resume formation. Convoy proceeds."

They couldn't have been Duke Unuxekome's ships. Not two days early. Not in such paltry strength.

But it didn't matter, did it? Unuxekome's flotilla would never take the tax ships, not with a two-to-one advantage, not four-to-one. The navy couldn't be beaten on the open sea.

It would be up to Baru to win the battle. And to do it with Purity Cartone fastened to her flank.

BARU called Rear Admiral Ormsment aboard *Mannerslate* before Admiral Ormsment could invite her to *Sulane*. For this to work, Baru would need to command—not only in title but in practice. Ormsment had seen her as a Taranoki, a daughter, a troubled careerist fighting for vindication against a hostile authority: all appealing to a flag officer who'd come up in the naval culture of women officers tutoring their young protégés.

But Baru didn't need Ormsment's maternal advice. Baru needed Ormsment to pull her escort from the tax ships. Baru needed to be one of the three most powerful technocrats in Aurdwynn, not a troubled Taranoki daughter.

Mannerslate's captain offered her cabin for their meeting. Baru took the map room instead. "Stand here," she ordered Purity Cartone. "Taller. Can you look more serious? Good."

He obeyed, clearly pleased. Cattlson *must* have ordered him to dog Baru, to prevent any last gambits on her part. But he still wanted to serve her, too. His conditioning demanded that he make himself as useful as possible to agents of the Imperial Republic.

Baru found the maps she needed and pinned them to the plotting table.

Ormsment arrived with her retinue, sooty and harried. Her brow furrowed for a moment when she saw Cartone, posed half in shadow, the lamplight illuminating his jaw. "Your Excellence."

"Rear Admiral." Baru touched her brow. She'd dressed in her coat, her chained purse, her white gloves, even the half-mask. "Your crews performed commendably last night. My report to Parliament will make specific note."

"Hardly worth a note." Ormsment chuckled softly, stripping her own heavy canvas gloves. Her aides murmured to each other, barely attentive. "Last night's visitors were opportunists, Your Excellence, trying to seize a few scraps before the real feast. Just harbingers."

"As I'd feared." She snapped her fingers, calling for attention, and leaned forward across the plotting table. She could guess the path of Purity Cartone's gaze by the way the aides in the back row stiffened. "What news from *Scylpetaire*'s scouting? Have we sighted the main enemy force?"

Ormsment cocked a brow in slow, understated compliment. "You expect pirates to travel in force?"

"I certainly expect Oriati Syndicate Eyota privateers under false flag, forced north by our new strength around Sousward, dedicated to covert interference in the Republic's trade, to travel in force." Baru touched the map, stroking the coastline, the dotted fan of the Inirein's plume. "They're sailing up our wake, I'm sure, and in some strength—at least fifteen ships. We can't turn back for Treatymont without fighting through them, and they'd have the weather gage on us if we tried. A significant disadvantage in naval combat, correct?"

Ormsment nodded and drew breath to speak. Baru talked over her.

"We can't outrace them without abandoning our transports. Similarly, if we wait for them to attack, your frigates will lose the advantage of speed and agility. The tax ships are shackles you can't afford in a fight."

The Rear Admiral crossed her arms, mouth curled in amusement. "They say seamanship runs in the Taranoki bloodline."

"I am the Imperial Accountant," Baru snapped, giving a little rein to real anger. Purity Cartone made some small motion behind her that lifted Ormsment's chin. "Blood or no, I know how to keep my taxes safe. Here are my orders, Rear Admiral: detach your frigates from their escort. Engage and destroy the force trailing us."

The slow exhalation among Ormsment's aides made it clear they'd come expecting to beg for just that chance. "And if another force of raiders attacks the transports while we're gone?" Ormsment asked. "If they're hoping to draw us away?"

Her first question had been tactical. Not an assertion of her military authority. Not a reminder of Baru's precarious political stance. A tactical matter.

Good.

"We'll make harbor at Welthony, where the river Inirein meets the sea." Baru rapped her knuckles against the map. "Duke Unuxekome's ships and armsmen can provide security until your return. You'll have the freedom of the open ocean to make your attack."

"You trust Unuxekome?"

Here she would bluff, trusting in Ormsment's unfamiliarity with Aurdwynni politics and its many species of duke. "With twelve transports of your marines in harbor, and my Clarified to keep an eye on him? I don't *need* to trust him."

After a moment, Ormsment gripped her corners of the plotting table and bowed her head. "You understand," she said, "that this is a risk."

"I'll assume full responsibility."

"That's just what I mean. If I'd proposed these tactics—and I would've—and they failed, you could feed me to Parliament. I have the backing of the Admiralty and all the allies and favors a long career has earned me. I might stand a chance. But you're a foreign child already falling rapidly out of favor." She looked up, speaking softly. "You understand what it will mean for you if something goes wrong?"

"Rear Admiral Ormsment." Baru held her cold Falcresti eyes. "I am the Imperial Accountant of Aurdwynn, the ranking authority aboard this flotilla. You will execute my will."

M ANNERSLATE'S navigator, a lissome harelipped Oriati man who spent his nights writing an original translation of the *Handbook of Manumission,* seemed torn between irritation and terror at Baru's constant presence. But she found the current and wind charts, the tenuous cartography of sea and star, too fascinating to avoid. The circular winds made coastal voyages during the trade season easy, but off-wind or away from the coast, the Masquerade's navigation corps provided the first and only defense against storm, shoal, and the constant, overwhelming threat of dehydration.

She'd wanted to be a navigator, if accountancy didn't work out.

When the navigator judged them twelve hours from the mouth of the Inirein, Rear Admiral Ormsment's ships began to split away, red sails close-hauled, heeling as they went against the wind. First *Scylpetaire,* then *Juristane* and *Commsweal,* and last of all *Welterjoy* and *Sulane* herself.

Baru imagined Aminata on one of those ships, snapping at the deckhands, terrifying the crew with stories of what might go wrong if they let fire get to the rockets and torpedoes. Of course Aminata would be far away, on *Lapetiare,* or at some new post.

And there would be no fire, no battle. The pirate flotilla tailing the tax ships would try to draw Ormsment further away, then break south, out of the trade circle, and flee. Unuxekome wouldn't have his moment of piratical glory—not yet.

All that stood between the rebellion and the tax ships were the marines still aboard.

The sea changed color as they sailed up the Inirein's plume. Fishing birds wheeled and dove in silt-rich water. Baru paced the deck and irritated the navigator with questions she could have answered herself.

Past noon the lookouts called land. Baru beckoned for Purity Cartone. "Pass the word to the marine lieutenant and the other ships. We'll conduct a formation review in the town square. All our marines will go ashore. So the duke understands what we have, and knows not to give us trouble."

He nodded without apparent suspicion and went.

Baru stood at the stern rail, closed her eyes to the wind, and thought: soon everyone on this ship will be the enemy. Soon Xate Olake's men will walk out into the Treatymont night with knives and torches for the Unmasking. Soon Muire Lo will—oh, Muire Lo—

"Cartone," she called.

He paused at the stairs to the main deck. "Your Excellency?"

"What were Cattlson's orders?"

"I am bound by higher—"

She waved him off (and he smiled, even at that small compliance). "Under what circumstances will you need to kill me?"

He gave her a child's wide-eyed bafflement. "You serve the Faceless Throne. Why would I kill you?"

"Perhaps if I ceased to serve it."

"How?" He smiled rapturously, some trigger hammering the strings inside him. "The hand of the Throne moves us all."

FOR all her gentle tides and sheltering bluffs, Welthony harbor had never been dredged of river silt, and her shallow bottom made the deep-draft tax ships nervous. They anchored in carefully selected spots marked on a harbor map, Baru at the captain's ear the whole while, needlessly micromanaging every maneuver and making strident protest when it seemed they would damage a fishing buoy. *Cordsbreadth* moored out of formation and Baru insisted she raise anchor and reposition, a dreadful hour-long exercise that required great effort at her oars.

They had to believe she was controlling enough to put the whole marine complement ashore at once. Had to believe the Imperial Accountant cared more about an intimidating parade than the physical safety of her collected coin.

She should've known it wouldn't hold.

Mannerslate's marine lieutenant, red-faced, unschooled in the proprieties of addressing technocrats, came top deck shouting—"and *fuck* the promotion board!" She listened to him, chin up, nodded in agreement at the end—under no circumstances, of course, could they send the *whole* marine complement, leaving the ships unguarded. "You're right, Lieutenant," she said. "I'd thought we'd need our full strength ashore in case of any attempted indiscretion. But perhaps it would be best to delay the inspection until tomorrow morning. I'll take the night to visit Duke Unuxekome and get a sense of his disposition. You can put scouts ashore."

The lieutenant's flush receded, revealing a ladder of shaving nicks. He was very young, younger than Aminata, as young as Baru. "Your Excellence," he said, remembering the honorific at last. "Very good."

Baru pressed her lips together and tried not to scream. The inspection had been a trap, of course, a key element of the plan. But it had been a trap meant to save lives. They couldn't get the wealth off these ships while the marines were still aboard.

Duke Unuxekome, tacitly experienced in piracy, had warned her it wouldn't work. He'd been right.

She took a launch ashore at sunset, Purity Cartone rowing—guard enough, she'd insisted—until they got halfway to shore and her nerves overwhelmed her. "Go sit in the prow," she snapped, and took up the oars herself.

Duke Unuxekome and a lightly armed honor guard met them dockside. Salutations were curt and tense, as they'd agreed, though Baru suspected Unuxekome hardly needed to act. He stared in undisguised alarm at Purity Cartone.

"One of the Clarified," she explained, following his gaze. "My bodyguard."

Unuxekome, his wrists freshly rope-burned by recent acts of seamanship, frowned. "Some Falcresti order? I've never heard of them." His gaze flickered to her, back to Purity Cartone. "Is he well? He seems . . . remote."

"Don't worry," Baru said, not daring to make even the little sign they'd agreed on to mean *a complication*. Cartone saw too much. "He's loyal."

Maybe Unuxekome would understand. Maybe he would have some way to pry the remora from her side before the sun set and Cartone realized what she had planned.

But no: they were still at dinner when the transports began to explode.

THE mines had come from Oriati Mbo—from Segu, specifically, naval weapons meant for blockade against a Masquerade invasion, smuggled out by Syndicate Eyota privateers and then brought to Aurd-wynn. Oriati chemists had never matched their Falcresti rivals, never replicated the vicious Navy Burn or the whispered breeding factors of the Metademe.

But they could, given a large enough casing, make a prodigious bang.

The mines had been tethered to the harbor floor at the last low tide, their lift bladders and wooden casings straining for the surface. Now Unuxekome's divers, women hand-picked from loyal pearl and spear families, oiled and nose-clipped and racing the sunset, only—only!—had to cut the right mines free, the mines beneath the anchored transports.

Baru had studied the designs, particularly the firing mechanisms, the spring-and-spike systems that would spark detonation when the mine pressed up against a ship hull. She believed they would work. Masquerade torpedoes were more complex and temperamental, and—allegedly—*they* worked.

Maybe it would have been easier to board the transports. But Baru wanted no part of a plan that required a successful attack on a shipload of marines. Even outnumbered, they could hold the transports until their water ran out. Ormsment and her frigates would return long before then.

If the marines couldn't be drawn off the transports, they would have to take the transports out from under the marines.

The duke's River House, upstream and upslope, looked down on the harbor. The duke's men had served dinner on a seaward-facing balcony.

They had a clear view when *Mannerslate* buckled in half and began to sink.

Purity Cartone, seated with his back to the harbor, reacted first—seeing, perhaps, some shock in the duke's face, some sign of surprise or fulfillment that had not even had a chance to become action. He turned and looked at the harbor: nothing more.

Baru trusted herself only enough to say: "What?"

The mines were designed to detonate directly beneath a ship's hull. The blast was too weak to lift or crack the vessel—at best, it could punch a hole in the copper jacket and the wood beneath. It did, however, displace an enormous amount of water.

The same water that the ship's hull usually displaced. The same water that supported a transport's vast weight.

Mannerslate did not so much explode as fall into the void that had opened beneath her; did not so much suffer a blast as break under her own oaken mass. The sound that reached them on the hill was soft, a low cough, a distant splintering. The ship's masts began a graceful crumple into the harbor.

"What's happening?" Unuxekome said, keeping up the bluff. His arms-men were already raising their weapons to kill Cartone.

But he was Clarified.

Purity Cartone drew a knife and leapt up onto the dinner table in one run of motion as easy and natural as a diver falling.

Behind him in the distant harbor *Cordsbreath* rolled sharply to star-board.

"Cartone! Wait!" Baru ordered, trying to stand, the table banging her hips. He was so *fast*—

Cartone hooked a plate (stuffed pheasants in hot butter) with his foot and flipped it into Unuxekome's face. The Sea Groom fell onto his back and Cartone leapt down onto him, expressionless, blade already de-scending.

Baru threw her knife at him. It spun wide. She had never thrown a knife before.

A mine bobbed to the surface and exploded with a booming thunder-clap.

Purity Cartone's knife cut into Unuxekome's throat and then one of the ducal armsmen shot him right in the chest, the feathers of the cross-bow bolt abrupt and absurdly colorful, hunting-bright. Cartone reared off the fallen duke, blood and butter spattering from his hands, and leapt from the balcony, straight down into the river.

"Find him!" Baru shouted, hoping the duke's men would listen to her. She tore at Unuxekome's collar, his stubbled neck slick with blood and cooking oils. He deserved better than this—not how he would have wanted to die, far from a ship, flat on his back, with pheasant in his face—not any kind of story worth a duke—

One selfish part of her noted: *Cartone didn't go for me—he didn't know I was part of it—or he did—*

"Mail," Unuxekome rasped. "The mail turned the knife."

Baru's fingers found the duke's armored collar. The blade had skipped off it and made a shallow but bloody cut all the way up to his ear. She stopped the gush with a linen napkin. "Clever," she said.

He smiled up at her with an incredible kind of delight. "I am not a duke of fools."

Armsmen shouted around them. Someone fired a crossbow down into the river. In the harbor the transport *Inundore* snapped like kindling. One of her masts broke halfway and speared the deck as it fell.

"It's begun?"

She helped the bloodied duke to his feet. "It's begun."

Unbidden, she thought of the harelipped navigator and his beautiful charts.

18

THE slaughter in Welthony harbor ran through the dawn.

Aurdwynni spearmen patrolled the shore and, laughing, cast from boats at the sailors in the water. Most of the Falcresti drowned before they made it to shore. Others swarmed up the nets of the four surviving transports—spared by mines that missed or failed to detonate. Duke Unuxekome's archers took their own sport with them. Pitch arrows started fires on the decks and rigging, but disciplined Masquerade crews with sand, knives, and jars of old urine kept them from spreading.

The harbor's collective shriek—the victors, the dying, the bells and drums of Masquerade officers trying to rally, a desperate atonal music—carried to the ducal house.

Mannerslate had exploded first. Baru obsessed over it, probing the fact like a sore. She'd sailed with *Mannerslate*'s crew knowing they were all going to die. She'd lied to them, a terrible kind of lie, a *nothing unusual will happen* lie: the treason of banality. She'd acted as if all were as it should be.

And she would have to do it again, and again. . . .

She'd mapped out her schemes from here to Falcrest. Everything had been put into its place, every detail considered. So why had *Mannerslate* exploded *first*? Why not second? Why not third? It had to *mean* something—

Of course it didn't.

Baru tried to exhale the whole tangle. Chance, coincidence: they would have their say. She had to remember that.

"They'll try for a breakout," Duke Unuxekome murmured.

But there was no way out. Unuxekome's dromons and tartanes, waiting in coves and inlets nearby, had blockaded the harbor mouth.

Cordsbreath, one of the four survivors, took on water and eventually sank. Unuxekome's elite dive sappers—middle-aged women in loincloths, chewing young mason leaves to dilate their pupils—swam out into the starlit harbor, crying prayers to ykari Himu. The handheld mines they planted brought down two more transports.

The last tax ship tried to run the blockade, hit another Oriati mine, and sank prow-first.

When the sun rose on a harbor bloated with wood and corpses, the recovery began. The whole plan came down to one differential: marines could drown. Precious metals couldn't.

Eight transports had—as planned—split in half, spilling cargo across the harbor floor. The chests were bright red, heavy but designed to be moved long distances on land, by foot if necessary. Divers (still all women—coastal Aurdwynn held to the Tu Maia tradition of diving as a woman's work) went down into the harbor with ropes and stones. Some vanished into the wrecks for heart-stopping minutes.

Chest by chest they fixed ropes and buoys, and chest by chest they began to raise them. Some came up by pulley and muscle, hauled by boat teams. Swarms of divers went after the rest of the easy targets, descending with bundles of air bladders weighed down by rocks, fixing the bladders to the chests, and cutting the ballast free.

Baru itched to go down to the harbor, to help make a tally of the recovered wealth or count the dead, to pin her sick anxiety to some real number. But they'd agreed that she would pretend, for the moment, to be Unuxekome's prisoner. Keep up her charade a little longer, in case her authority could still be used.

Purity Cartone's boots had been found drifting in the harbor.

"The divers," she asked the duke. "Where do you get them all? There must be hundreds."

"Devotees." His surgeon had bound his wound with linen. "Every coastal village in Aurdwynn has its divers, and among those divers are many ilykari—with the discipline of the body comes discipline of the soul. Mine are the finest. They have always been a strength of Duchy Unuxekome."

Baru watched another pod of divers leap from a fishing sloop, trailing ropes and bladders. "Mason leaf to help the vision. Clips and cotton on the nose and ears for the pressure change. But the pace, the depth, the cold—"

"The ykari give them strength." Neither of them had slept, but Un-uxekome managed a wry smile. "Believe it or not. I do."

"Ykari Himu," Baru guessed, thinking of the temple convocation, of oil and light. "For vigor."

"And Wydd, for patience of breath. Devena, to balance pressures and keep them from losing the surface. In matters practical, it's good to invoke all three." The duke yawned, and looked briefly appalled with himself. "Pardon me."

The clatter of footmen bringing a late breakfast came from the stairs. "I hope you haven't pinned the rebellion on help from your gods," Baru said.

"Not gods. Aurdwynn has known too much war and change to want gods. We believe in the transcendence of human virtue." He smiled, a strange, peaceful strength in his face. "They're old, you know. The ykari were Belthyc. They lived here long before my ancestors or the Stakhieczi began their invasions and counterinvasions. And they still endure."

"The Masquerade would see it otherwise. Would see the ilykari exterminated."

"And the woman charged with that task is one of us." His smile flickered, as if the thought of Xate Yawa had reminded him of the other conspiracies now underway, the distant gears in motion. But he spoke with quiet hope: "See? They find their ways to endure."

DUKE Oathsfire, Duke Lyxaxu, and Tain Hu all sent barges down the Inirein to gather shares of the plunder. They would take the gold and hide it in the Wintercrest foothills. The rebellion would have its northern stronghold, its winter nest.

Two days after the massacre in the harbor, the frigate *Scylpetaire*'s sails broke the horizon. Baru rejoiced at the timing: she knew Admiral Ormsment used *Scylpetaire* as a scout and advance guard, and since she had taken two days to return, Ormsment must have chased the pirates deep south before turning back.

Scylpetaire sent up signal fireworks. No one in Welthony, Baru included, knew how to read them, so Baru ordered Duke Unuxekome to take her down among the few Masquerade prisoners they had fished from the harbor. Among the caged survivors, Baru found *Mannerslate*'s captain, a round-cheeked matronly woman with bloody fingernails. Unuxekome held a knife to Baru's throat, and Baru, playing along with the charade, tremulously ordered the captain to translate the fireworks.

Enemy routed. Six destroyed. No losses. Returning at best speed: eighteen hours. Report.

"Tell us how to reply," Unuxekome demanded.

Mannerslate's captain straightened her uniform and, after some consideration, spat. They debated sending a message, or a prisoner, or a corpse. *Scylpetaire* sailed too soon, concluding, perhaps, that the silence and the empty harbor screamed disaster. Duke Unuxekome ordered his fleet into hiding along the coast, hoping that Ormsment would sail her frigates into the remaining Oriati mines, or come too close and let herself be surrounded. But when the other frigates arrived, they kept a cautious distance. *Scylpetaire* broke away from the rest and sailed west, toward Treatymont, carrying the news.

The rebellion's first success touched off a string of disasters.

In Treatymont, Xate Olake's operatives struck—ilykari cultists, pirates, rogues, fanatic convicts plucked from his sister's Cold Cellar, all executing the long-whispered Unmasking. Garrison soldiers were already thin-stretched and exhausted. Many of them burned or suffocated in their beds when a laundry chemical fire swallowed the dockside barracks.

The assassins who went after Governor Cattlson met two Clarified disguised as maids. None of the assassins escaped. (No maid in the Governor's House ever suffered disrespect again.) The team intended for Bel Latheman couldn't find him; by odd coincidence, the Lady Heingyl Ri had gone traveling to call on the duchess Nayauru.

Worse misfortune came in the Horn Harbor. Here a team of ilykari divers set out to destroy the two torchships moored outside the towers. They would carry incendiary grenades into the perilous Burn stores, setting both ships alight and annihilating the navy's core strength in Aurdwynn.

But Province Admiral Croftare, unnerved by "the smell of the air," ordered her most precious ships to reanchor a mile offshore. Some of the divers made the long cold swim anyway, using mason leaf to navigate in the night. The first woman to reach *Egalitaria* began to climb. Grief befell her. *Egalitaria*'s captain, a veteran of treacherous Oriati harbors, had ordered the hull studded with broken glass.

The diver cut her fingers and fell. The splash tipped off an alert marine, and flares went up. One diver, shot by crossbow from *Kingsbane*'s stern, fixed her grenades to the ship's rudder and burned it. Another climbed *Egalitaria*'s anchor rope and actually made it belowdecks before a disregarded challenge got her stabbed.

Scylpetaire arrived at a city in an uproar. The garrison couldn't contain the riots; Falcresti citizens were murdered nightly. But the navy still held the harbor. Any hope of a blockade by Duke Unuxekome's ships had died in the crib.

Governor Cattlson met *Scylpetaire* and received the news that the taxes had been lost and Baru Cormorant taken hostage with weary credulity. "I wish," he told Xate Yawa, "that I'd been even a little surprised." He ordered the frigate to wait before sailing for Falcrest, hoping to learn whether Unuxekome's mutiny would gutter out or spread.

It spread. But not as the rebels might have hoped.

THE closest Dukes to Treatymont were Heingyl, Cattlson's constant companion, and Radaszic, the fop.

The Duke Radaszic sent a letter to the Duke Heingyl, as a way to explain his choice. Xate Yawa's agents intercepted and copied it. Later Baru read the intercept, and understood a little of what had happened, even as she wanted to tear it apart in frustration.

To the Duke Heingyl, Lord of Stags.

(This had been written with a broad space behind it, as if Radaszic wanted to include more honorifics, or something else—Heingyl's personal name, perhaps.)

I will write this plainly, as you prefer. By now I've broken my oath of fealty, declared rebellion, and marched on Treatymont. You will not read the words of oathbreakers, so I ask that you give this letter to your daughter, whose perfect character, we will both agree, cannot be stained or diminished by the understanding of traitors. She will find a clever way to tell you the rest. May she one day rule all of Aurdwynn, as I know you desire.

You are my brother—I said it enough while drunk; now I will say it sober, and in writing. Your family raised me when mine could not.

Even after we were men you kept me close as kin. In the Fools'
Rebellion it was your counsel that kept me from the drowning pit. I
remember making arguments to you, pleas for uprising, and so, too,
I remember your constant reply: we swore an oath.

The rest of the Radaszic line chose revolt, and was extinguished.
I alone remain. That is to your credit. My life is an honor to you.
My errors are my own.

I am a duke known for grain, and excellent cheer, and debt. I
want to leave my sons a name that means more than bread and
excess. You have what I want, foster brother: a name that makes men
think of conviction. I want that class of name. So in recent years I
have taken to books of philosophy.

In these books, emperors and learned women speak of Truth as
a high star beyond the rule of any lord. Foster brother, I believe that
if you swore an oath to a lord in a porcelain mask, and if that lord
told you that the sun was black, you would walk blind in summer
light. You deserve a better lord. The sun is good and golden. That is
truth, to which we owe our first and highest loyalty; and if I hope to
be a man of any worth to anyone, that is the loyalty I must now obey.
They will say that treason is in the Radaszic blood, and must be bred
away, like spots from a dog. But that is a lie too. Truth does not need
a mask.

Thus I ride on Treatymont, so that my children will never stum-
ble beneath a black sun.

Duchy Radaszic fell northwest of Treatymont. He had grain, and
horses, and a great many farmers rioting in support of the unrest in
Treatymont, all crying: *A fairer hand! A fairer hand!* He had never mentioned in his letter that his people were sharecroppers, that he had taxed
them dry trying to pay down his own debt, and that gold loans had been
their best relief from starvation. But perhaps this was also part of his guilt,
his desire to be more than a duke of bread and revels and famine.

Radaszic took all his armsmen and his rioters and marched on
Treatymont. Xate Olake asked him to go east instead, to conquer Heingyl
and link up with Unuxekome, bringing almost the whole coast under
rebel control. But he would not strike at his foster brother.

At Finnmoelyrd Henge, sacred to the ilykari, nestled among the orchards and the beehives, his column paused to graze their horses. There Duke Heingyl found him, Duke Heingyl with all his heavy cavalry, and although Heingyl hadn't seen the letter, it hardly seemed to matter, because he had to come to do his duty and that was all there could be.

Heingyl led the first charge, which killed Radaszic's sons and drove into the heart of the column. And there upon a lance tip, maybe Heingyl the Stag Hunter's lance tip, maybe not, the line of Radaszic ended, and went into the ground to feed the flowers that would feed the bees.

With Radaszic died the rebellion's best ally on the coastal plains. Heingyl spent one day at the henge resting, surely not in meditation with ykari Wydd, as that would have broken his oath to Falcrest.

Reading all this at Unuxekome's River House, where the swarming divers still battled debris and cold to raise more coin, Baru felt Xate Olake's specter at her side: the Traitor's Qualm. The rebellion seemed disorganized, incoherent, doomed. No Midlands duke would declare for them—not Nayauru, who could command Sahaule and Autr by will and by the children she had gotten on them, or Ihuake, who could bring Pinjagata and his spearmen, and her own vast herds of cattle and cavalry. That meant no easy access to grain before the winter. No cavalry to ride south in the spring. They would be bottled up in the North with no way to break out.

The rebellion needed a focus, a central hope. It did not need the pretense of a hostage Imperial Accountant.

It needed the truth of a turncoat, a renegade prodigy, Falcrest's very finest gone over to lead Aurdwynn's native-born.

But before she could find a way to do this best, to ignite all that blue on her map like one of the Oriati mines, Tain Hu came down the Inirein and interrupted her.

Y ou should've gone north already."

Tain Hu spoke in Baru's ear and the force of her presence snapped Baru from her work trance in a galvanic jerk—the coiled weight of her bent over the chair as if to draw Baru away from her writing, one arm braced like the preface to strangulation or embrace.

Baru managed not to gasp aloud. "Duchess Vultjag. You weren't announced." Perhaps Unuxekome's guards outside the study had assumed Tain Hu was expected.

"Cattlson won't believe you're an innocent hostage. He'll send his Clarified to kill you. You'd be safer at Vultjag." Tain Hu circled the desk, her hawkish profile bent in curiosity. "What have you been writing?"

She'd been writing drafts, a whole midden of scribbled parchment, now mostly torn up in frustration. All of it in Aphalone, at least, which Tain Hu could speak but not read. "I've been trying to figure out disbursement plans. For the money we've seized." She began to gather up her papers, trying to look finished. At least she hadn't had the loyalty map open. "Just an accountant's habits."

"I may not know Aphalone script—" Tain Hu pinned one rag of parchment beneath her splayed fingers. The gold darkness in her eyes startled Baru. "—but I know the signs for your name. You've written them too many times for mere accounting."

"You know the signs for my name?" Baru leaned back, to project insouciance, to escape those eyes. Why had Tain Hu come? Why hadn't Unuxekome announced her arrival? Surely the conflagration swallowing Aurdwynn would have called her elsewhere. . . . "What a curious place to begin an education."

For a moment only the candle fire moved.

Then Tain Hu came around the chair, her hobnailed boots clattering on the hardwood. Baru began to rise, and the duchess took her by the throat and hooked a heel behind the leg of her chair and threw her down thunderously on her back. The chair splintered beneath her.

Tain Hu drew her sword.

"Guards!" Baru shouted, head ringing, sight a red glare. "Guards!" She felt, more than anything else, a strange childish outrage—had she not whispered in the ear of the ilykari woman? Had she not bound herself to the other rebels in trust?

The blade that had opened Governor Cattlson's scalp tickled her brow. "You gave us too much," Tain Hu said, her voice distant, thin, agonizing, like a glass cut. "I saved you from Cattlson so that we could bargain with you, and you gave us too much. Do you understand?"

"You still need me." The duchess wheeled in Baru's sight, an osprey circling. How had she forgotten? How had she made *the same mistake*? A game of dukes and nations, decades of occupation, centuries of betrayal and realignment, a ledger filled with the transactions of power, and she had thought she could be the center of it—that she could step in and rearrange the pieces and not in turn be played. "The tax ships aren't enough. We still need to break the Traitor's Qualm."

The tip of the blade pricked her skin. "I spent years listening to Xate Olake plead the Traitor's Qualm. Years bowing to Xate Yawa's protestations that it was too soon to act. Now the time has come and Aurdwynn will rise. Tell me why—" The blade trembled with her mocking shrug. "Tell me why we need you. Why we would not all be safer without a Masquerade technocrat among us."

"The fisher," Baru said.

Tain Hu's blade stilled. She looked down at Baru and her lips parted for one curious breath. "What?"

"The name you gave me. On the docks, three years ago. Baru Fisher, the Fulcrum, beloved of ykari Devena." Baru pushed herself up, pushed herself into the sword fighting screaming instinct, and Tain Hu drew the point away. "Has the word reached you? Have you heard Radaszic break the gates of Treatymont? Seen the red sails burning in the Horn Harbor? No! You never will. The rebellion is stillborn—the other dukes won't join us. Nayauru and Ihuake will watch us drown and divide our land and riches. But listen, Tain Hu, listen to your serfs calling—"

"A fairer hand," the duchess Vultjag murmured. "Even the Sentiamuts in the foothills know the chant."

Baru had never killed anyone face-to-face. Never faced real, imminent death—Xate Olake's poison had been an invisible game, and she'd been saved from Cattlson and the duel before the moment of reckoning. The slaughter in the harbor had been a trial of her stomach, not her heart.

So now she found herself trembling as she drew herself up the side of the desk. Her hands shook as she tried to seize the papers, to lift them and offer them to Tain Hu. A coward after all.

"I will lead the rebellion," she said. "In name if not in deed. I have ruined Aurdwynn's dukes once already—they fear and respect me. I have taken up the sword against the Governor and made myself beloved to the people. *I* will break the Traitor's Qualm. Do you see what I have written? Do you see the signs for my name? *I am Baru Fisher, the Fairer Hand—*"

"And what," Tain Hu hissed, "if that is what I came to stop? This rebellion must be Aurdwynn's."

"The dukes are not Aurdwynn, Vultjag! The dukes have failed Aurdwynn again and again! *I* am the commonborn, the foreigner, the newborn hope!" Baru struck the table, rustling the parchment, the still-wet ink. "I am your last and solitary chance!"

Duke Unuxekome's voice came from the door. "Enough, Vultjag. She's right."

The smoke in Duchess Vultjag's voice spoke to all the things Baru had forgotten, had hidden from behind the schoolyard walls—the rage of a nation brought low. "Once she is in us we will not get her out. She will be like a tick. She will grow fat on us and we will never dig her free."

"She's earned her place." Of course Unuxekome would speak up for her—they had sailed together, taken plunder together. They were comrades now. "She wants what we want. And she only has to be a symbol, Vultjag. Nothing more."

The tip of Tain Hu's blade described one small analemma in the air, and Baru remembered her words, three years ago, spoken into the forest, into the birdsong and the silence: *Symbols are power. You are a word, a mark . . .*

And it pierced Baru's heart to realize that no matter what Tain Hu chose in this moment, she would regret it to the end of her life.

"So," Tain Hu said, sheathing her sword, suddenly wry. "Have you already joined the court of would-be kings, Unuxekome? My bearded neighbor in the north is all atwitter. He's finally found someone less interested than me."

The Sea Groom smiled in shared mirth. "I think Oathsfire's wealth makes his solitude more lonely."

"Are you done, then?" Baru looked between the two, her lips pressed thin. "Was the secret I gave the ilykari not enough? Must I make some other proof?"

A split silence.

"There's a prisoner waiting for you at the harbor," Unuxekome said.

I will not do it," Baru said.

The captain of the *Mannerslate* knelt in the harborside mud. Two of the Sea Groom's armsmen had dragged her from her cage, silent and rigid, and beaten the backs of her legs until she'd fallen. She'd left a print of her face, like a mask, in the wet earth.

She spoke no Urun, but then again, she had been asked no questions. The test was not for her.

Tain Hu offered Baru her sword again, for Baru had not worn the boarding saber. "You have betrayed them already. You've led hundreds of them to die. You will be the traitor queen of a rebellion that will slaughter tens of thousands more." Her mailed shoulders caught the evening light and broke it into rings of reflected fire. "Kill her. Make it true with blood."

Everything she said was true. Baru had already killed this woman— led her to her death. Beheading her would only be correcting an error, a mislaid mine, a malformed charge, an errant spear.

But Baru turned away.

Tain Hu's mocking voice took an edge. "Have you forgotten what you are? You are a *traitor*. No home will ever love you. No one will ever call you *good* or *just* again without thinking of what you did to those who raised you up. You cannot avoid this price."

The woman in the sand, weary, uncomprehending, spat between them. "Fuck yourselves," she said, in Aphalone, and brushed some of the sand from her uniform.

No place for sentiment here. And she had already killed, hadn't she? Destroyed Aurdwynn's fiat economy, driven the dukes to tax their vassals into malnutrition. Murdered the sickly and the weak. One more life would weigh no heavier—

But it did.

She turned back to the duchess Vultjag.

"This I will not do," Baru said, though she could only manage any courage by speaking softly. "It is too much."

"The reparatory marriages forced on us. The children taken by the Charitable Service. The murdered ilykari. The sodomites they execute with hot iron rods—did you ever watch it, Baru?" Tain Hu's voice fell to a hiss. "Did you listen to the screams? Take revenge for all that evil."

And in a convulsion of aimless doubt, a cannibalistic self-destructive exercise, the breaking pains of the white porcelain mask she had worn, the first cold claws of the test she'd swallowed, Baru found herself thinking of a rebuttal, of all the lives the Masquerade had saved—*the innoculations, the sewers, the roads, the schools, the wealth*—

She raised her hands, as if in panic, or as if to take the sword.

"Vultjag," Unuxekome murmured, and only his murmur saved Baru from the choice. "Enough. We've seen enough."

And Tain Hu sheathed her blade again. "The prisoner lives," she said, and smiled with what, after a moment, Baru saw as relief.

Another test.

Her outrage—*is this not* enough?—must have reached the duchess, who said: "We had to see what you would do."

"I know," Baru said. Better a woman of divided loyalties than one of no loyalty at all. Better a reluctant traitor than the terror of a true sociopath.

"No more tests." Tain Hu raised one gloved palm to ward off her anger. "Tell this captain what you have written. Unless—" She raised her brows and the red ink war-lines written on her cheeks moved over the high bones. "Unless you need a few more drafts."

The harbor surf lapped up at them, peaked, receded.

Baru stepped between the two Aurdwynni lords and the kneeling captain. The Aphalone words came easy to her tongue, but she hesitated at that ease.

She had been pretending loyalty for so long.

"Go to Treatymont," she told the *Mannerslate*'s captain. "Go to the Governor's House. Tell Cattlson that I renounce my name and station, that I repudiate his false Republic and all its power. Tell him that I am Baru Fisher, the Fairer Hand, and that I will set Aurdwynn free."

She watched the woman's incomprehension kindle into hate. Above the harbor the gulls shrieked and squabbled and dove for corpse meat.

19

THEY dared one meeting at Welthony, though Purity Cartone's corpse had never been found, though the Stag Hunter's cavalry or the Masquerade's ships could sweep east and come upon them in days. They needed the certainty of voice and face before they scattered.

To the balcony of Unuxekome's house, where the harbor wind already prickled with the end of summer, came Tain Hu and Unuxekome and Baru Fisher. Then, down the river from the north, Duke Oathsfire, the Miller, and Duke Lyxaxu, High Stone.

The others were beyond reach. Xate Yawa still played her part as Juris-potence in Treatymont, and Xate Olake wouldn't break cover to come. Somehow this troubled Baru less than the final absence—the ilykari priestess who'd bound them all together. Baru wanted her presence. A terrible guilt had been rankling her in the night, something worse than the feverish insomniac hunger to *think,* to know what the Masquerade would do before even they did. A loyalty she'd betrayed.

"I thought we'd agreed she would only be the bankroll." Stout Oaths-fire had chopped off most of his beard, perhaps to look younger or more flattering. Chance had betrayed him there—he had an awful cold. "She gives us a few ships and in exchange we let her say she rules us? We all know she'll be important afterward, if we win—but so soon?" He didn't look at Baru here, although she expected him to. Maybe his pride couldn't bear to touch on their last conversation, the delicate matter of kings and dynasties. "Are we already so desperate for a figurehead?"

"More than a figurehead." Unuxekome's casual glance and smile carried a hint of defensiveness—possessiveness, even, though Baru didn't trust her sense for it. "She's the only one we can rally behind. An Imperial prodigy, certified by their merit exams, turned back against them? She refutes everything they offer."

Lyxaxu, pale and towering, his marten-skin mantle loose about his shoulders, put a hand on Oathsfire's shoulder to restrain him. "The choice is made. The word has gone out. Whether we want it or not, this is Baru Fisher's uprising now."

Tain Hu leaned against the railing in her riding leathers, her back to the sea. "And yet," she said, her eyes on Oathsfire, "you're all very reluctant to let her speak."

Baru took the opening—any chance to get out of the cage of ducal politics. She slapped her map of Aurdwynn down on the table, weighted by the coins bound to each corner. "Thirteen dukes of note. Four of them are here and openly committed to the rebellion." Her eyes circled the table: the mismatched northern men, Unuxekome, Tain Hu. "And we have Xate Olake as spymaster in Treatymont, though he has no vassals or political presence. That gives us five. As for those who'll declare for the Governor—Duke Heingyl's lands are north and east of Treatymont, and we all know he'll stay loyal to Cattlson even when we have him dangling from a noose."

She touched the coastal farmland directly to the west of Heingyl's duchy. "Radaszic is dead. We needed him, his horses, the food he could have offered us. But he leapt too early." She slid her hand to the northwest corner of the map, imagining the miles racing beneath her, the land fracturing as it rose toward the Wintercrests. "Duchess Erebog, the Crone in Clay. Lyxaxu's neighbor to the west. With her alliance we'd have the whole North, from Erebog in the west to Oathsfire and the River Inirein in the east. If Treatymont keeps her, they'll be able to turn our flank, maybe even send troops into the Wintercrests to envelop us. If she doesn't declare for us before winter, we'll be lost."

They stared expectantly. "And the rest?" Unuxekome asked. "The five in the Midlands? Nayauru Dam-builder, Autr Brinesalt, and Sahaule the Horsebane? Ihuake of the thousand thousand cattle and Pinjagata Spearforest? Nayauru can't keep two lovers and expect to be a friend of Cattlson or Falcrest. Ihuake's too proud to accept anyone's rule. Surely they'll come over."

"The Traitor's Qualm," Baru and Tain Hu said together. They made apologetic looks at each other, began to speak again, and—Tain Hu shrugging—finally Baru continued. "Just as Xate Olake thought. Until we prove we have a real chance, they'll hold back and pretend loyalty."

"What if they don't?" Lyxaxu cocked his head in curious challenge.

"Nayauru's ambitious. Defiant. She wants a throne. She might take the chance for her own gambit."

"I'm confident she won't." Lyxaxu's intellect was useful, dangerously sharp, but sometimes it led him into useless abstraction. "Nayauru's every bit as bound by finance and logistics as the rest of us."

"Her bloodline is rich, her consorts strong—"

"Her bloodline means nothing. She doesn't have the coin for war." Baru held Lyxaxu's eyes, facing down thirty-five years of study and all the weight that carried, until he blinked. "We have time to court Nayauru and the rest. The Midlands dukes will wait out the winter before they move."

"Send Oathsfire," Unuxekome said.

"What?" said Baru, as Oathsfire huffed, as Tain Hu grinned and chuckled.

Unuxekome shrugged and put his hands behind his head. His shoulders bunched impressively (Oathsfire glared). "We need Nayauru. We lose the war in the spring if we don't win the Midlands to our side, and Nayauru is half of that alliance. So send her what she treasures. Another noble father for another heir."

Oathsfire bristled. "I am not a brood stallion."

"She's quite lovely," Tain Hu offered. "Exactly your type. Your new type, I mean." Unuxekome made a little choked sound of mirth.

"Perhaps I'm not the best choice. Whoever we send will have to distract her from Autr and Sahaule. Someone with a laborer's build." Oathsfire adjusted his gloves. "A sailor might do. If we can find one with a working cock."

Unuxekome shrugged with his upraised elbows, as if to offer the shape of his arms in answer to the jab. He'd never married. Baru supposed that was Oathsfire's target. "Whatever the Fairer Hand prefers."

Save her from noble men and their games of position. "What I *prefer* is that we leave the Midlands be until spring. Winter is our chance to make our case to them."

"We need a bold victory, then," Unuxekome said. "A raid. Before the autumn storms lock my fleet in harbor."

"No. We need to withdraw." Baru set her palm on the map, fingers aimed north. "The best thing we can do is consolidate our hold and wait out the winter. It's the only way out."

Unuxekome crooked a brow. "Persuade me."

Baru stabbed Treatymont with her forefinger. "The Masquerade's control is economic. I know—I enforced it. Their garrisons are small, their outposts undermanned compared to fortresses like Ihuake's Pen. Falcrest has never trusted its army, because they know that republics are the natural prey of a professional military. But they are patient, thorough, methodical. They've never relied on the sword to conquer.

"They'll draw their strength in to Treatymont, abandoning the Midlands, securing the coastal plains and the harvest. Bandits will take the roads they abandon. Poverty will fester in the absence of their banks. They'll leave Aurdwynn to rot through the winter, to feel the cold of life without the Masquerade, while they keep the harvest for themselves. Come spring, when the marines land from Falcrest, when the trade winds are ready for easy shipping again, they'll come north in campaign. Marching up through Duchy Nayauru into Duchy Erebog, then into our western flank, through Lyxaxu and Vultjag to Oathsfire. Unuxekome, you will be the target of a second thrust." She sketched a spear thrown inland from the sea. "A naval assault on Welthony, then a push up the Inirein to meet the other column at Oathsfire's keep. And thus we will be erased."

Lyxaxu measured her. "It would be an error of rigor if I didn't ask: when did you become a general?"

Blessed Lyxaxu, asking the right questions. "I'm not. I know money, logistics, shipping, and infrastructure. And those are the weapons they'll use to defeat you."

They were all watching her now, silent, respectful, and it gave her the same thrill she had felt auditing the Fiat Bank, speaking to Purity Cartone, hearing the adulation of the crowd—the shock of power.

"Until spring," she told them, "most of the Duchies in Aurdwynn will, for the first time in almost a quarter of a century, be left to their own governance. Pulled between the rebellion in the north and the Masquerade to the south. We'll have a few cold, desperate months to court them. And we have one advantage that Falcrest and Treatymont never foresaw: we are *rich*. We can keep our troops fed and armed through the winter. We can step in wherever the Masquerade has left them to crumble. Hold the roads open. Buy out the banks. And if the Masquerade tries to stop us—you are Northmen, are you not? If they cross the Midlands and come up into the vales and the woods, into the land we know like our fathers' hands, struggling through the snows, we kill them."

Tain Hu set her fists on the table. "Is this how you think we should fight, Baru Fisher? With coin and open roads?"

"No war has ever been won by slaughtering the enemy wholesale." Baru found skepticism in Unuxekome's eyes, on Oathsfire's face. Only Lyxaxu looked thoughtful. "Come, Your Graces. Surely you have read it in the *Dictates*—war is a contest of wills. The will of the people breaks when war makes them too miserable to do anything but acquiesce. We can turn that will to us."

"It may work," Tain Hu said, slowly, thoughtfully. "What we need in spring are healthy cavalry and sturdy phalanxes. Cavalry rules the coastal plain, from Unane Naiu to Sieroch. If we can find enough forage during the winter, if we can keep our own armies from being pinned down or bled dry, if we can convince the Midlands to declare for us . . . in the spring we can ride in force."

"They could come at us in winter across the Inirein, from Falcrest's western reaches." Oathsfire looked to Lyxaxu, as he always seemed to. "One march could take you, I, and Vultjag at once."

"Not once we destroy the bridges. The river may freeze enough for a northerly crossing, but they'll never march an army north from Falcrest to the Inirein without losing most of it to the snow." Lyxaxu offered Baru an open palm, upraised. "I'm convinced. This will be our strategy."

"Why not one strike before the winter?" Unuxekome pressed. "One raid on Treatymont harbor. I could take *Devenynyr* and gather my fleet."

Tain Hu shook her head. "The other side of the Qualm. If we seem too strong too soon, we'll force the undecided dukes into a choice. And they will choose the surer bet."

"There's one other matter," Baru said, speaking, at last, the guilt that had been gnawing her. "A weakness I want addressed. I'll need a ship and a way to pass a secret message to Xate Yawa."

They waited in silence.

"There's a man in Treatymont who needs to be smuggled out. One I couldn't move without betraying my real allegiance."

"No," Tain Hu snapped. "You'll risk Xate Yawa's cover if you pull him out. You'd court disaster, and for what gain?"

"I want him here." Baru stared the duchess Vultjag down, wishing, incongruously, that she still had her white mask, the impassive glaze of her station. It had gone down with *Mannerslate.* "He's a liability in Masquerade hands. And he's my responsibility."

"Saving him would be a worse betrayal than abandoning him," Tain Hu insisted. But her eyes roamed the other dukes, and following her, Baru saw what Vultjag must already know: Oathsfire and Unuxekome leaned in, jockeying for a chance to offer their help.

Tain Hu raised her eyes to the distant Wintercrests and said no more.

"My secretary, Muire Lo," Baru told the men. "He's the only one who knows my books as well as I do. Without him, Cattlson will have no way to set his accounts in order, no way to conceal his mismanagement from Parliament. He will call on Bel Latheman, who is clever—but it will not be enough. We can make it worse for them if we find and destroy the books."

I was here during the rebellions, he'd said. *I don't want to see Aurdwynn go back to that.*

Surely he'd realized what she was about to do when she sailed with the tax ships. Surely he hadn't believed she was actually returning to Falcrest for judgment.

Surely he'd found some way to protect himself, his family—

"Xate Olake arranged for the removal of Su Olonori," Lyxaxu said. "He could do it again."

Baru cut him off with an upraised hand, an unwise desperation seething within her, the terrible fear that she had just caged herself. She had forgotten something vital, something that Tain Hu might know, something that Xate Yawa certainly did, because three years ago she had sent a burly Stakhieczi woodsman to watch the new Imperial Accountant, and in a smoky tavern beneath a brothel that woodsman had met Muire Lo and—

And tried to kill him, driven to rage by the knowledge that Muire Lo was an agent of Falcrest, a watcher set to guard the new Imperial Accountant. A trained spy.

What would Xate Yawa think when she learned that Baru had tried to bring Muire Lo into the rebellion? Would she go to the ilykari woman in her temple of air and light and say: *tell me the secret that would destroy Baru Fisher?*

Tain Hu's eyes had left the Wintercrests. Tain Hu's eyes dwelled on her.

It would be safest, Baru realized, to order Muire Lo's death. It would prove her loyalty to the rebellion in the eyes of the twin Xates.

The tests would never end.

"I cannot betray him," she said, talking at Lyxaxu, speaking to Tain Hu. "I cannot abandon him, not when I have made him seem so complicit. Permit me this one loyalty."

"A dangerous loyalty," Tain Hu murmured. And Baru knew that she knew, that Xate Yawa had told her about the woodsman, about Baru and Aminata in the tavern, about Muire Lo's letters to Falcrest.

Had she ever really assured herself of Muire Lo's loyalty? He'd kept the book with its incriminating notes, rather than sending it to Falcrest— but couldn't Cairdine Farrier have made a copy and left the original with him—couldn't the Masquerade in all its love of subtlety and deception arranged Muire Lo's vulnerability and need for a moment such as this? A way to send him into the heart of the rebellion?

No. She had known him. She had *known* him.

"Send word to Xate Olake," Baru told the council, her voice hard, insistent. "Tell him I want Muire Lo alive."

Lyxaxu watched her blankly, impenetrably; but Oathsfire and Unuxekome looked at each other, a brief silent challenge, a contest.

JURISPOTENCE Xate Yawa ordered a bulletin posted on every door in Aurdwynn and read to the illiterate in every market and square:

> *We will execute all those who provide succor to the Imperial
>   Accountant Baru Cormorant.*
> *We will sterilize their families and the families of their husbands
>   and wives. We will seize their property and award it to the
>   loyal.*
> *Inaction is succor. Negligence is succor.*
> *Collaboration is death.*
> *Give us Baru Fisher.*

It was the most powerful endorsement she could have offered. Xate Yawa, sister of the forgotten Duke Lachta, the Jurispotence of Aurdwynn, killer of ilykari, arbiter of marriages, had devoted her life to building her own cult of hatred.

Now it was time to leverage that investment.

And she had created one other precious resource for the rebellion. Her years of methodical, ferocious persecution had forced the ilykari priests and their devotees to scatter and adapt, to don subtle camouflage and speak in secret new tongues, to send warnings that could outpace the Masquerade's own sealed directives. From the oil-drenched temples in Treatymont the ilykari sent the word out through the quietly faithful, to every vale and peak, every granary and olive field and trapper's post: *justice comes from a fairer hand.*

Aurdwynn had so many divisions. Consider these two souls, examples Baru plucked from tax record and Incrastic report—

An Iolynic-speaking Stakhi woodsman, gone to pray to ykari Devena for his wife's love at a secret henge in high cold duchy Lyxaxu, where the Student-Berserkers grew their strains of mason leaf and studied philosophies of fearless death.

And a Maia olive farmer who worked in Duchy Sahaule and sang the Urun of her warlord ancestors, sang of the duchess Nayauru and her many proud lovers, of her sons and daughters who would one day rule. Sang, lately, of the cruel Duchess Ihuake, whose jealousy was thick as pus.

All they shared was this:

The sullen memory of a time more than twenty years ago when the gate to Treatymont had read AURDWYNN CANNOT BE RULED, and the understanding that one could go to the Fiat Bank and get a loan in gold from someone named Baru Cormorant, who, very recently, had won a duel with that dry tit Cattlson. (These things and, of course, a hatred of Xate Yawa.)

On this common tinder the rebellion hoped to build its fire.

And the fire spread. In the freetown Haraerod, at the heart of the Midlands, the outraged crowd seized the masked messenger who read Xate Yawa's notice and cut out his tongue.

In Duchy Erebog, the farthest northwestern reach of Aurdwynn, a column of ghost-pale spearmen and archers overwhelmed and massacred the Masquerade garrison at Jasta Checniada, leaving the duchy's landlords and merchants full of panicked conviction that Duchess Erebog had cast in with Baru Fisher and that the Masquerade would come for all their wealth and blood. They rose up against their duchess. Erebog spent two months putting down the uprising, and lost so much money she found herself unable to purchase food stocks for the winter. The Crone in Clay had seen seventy winters. She knew what came next—madness, cannibalism, the death of children.

The rebellion pounced. Lyxaxu sent word through the forest to his neighbor:

> *Erebog, old foe:*
> *You taught me cunning. You disciplined my errors. Above all else*
> *I value a rigorous teacher, and above all others I know your strength.*
> *Now the time for lessons is over. I want you as an ally.*
> *Cattlson cannot save you. But we can. A loan can be arranged.*

A loan stolen from the tax ships. Treasonous by nature—irrevocably bound to the uprising. But how could she refuse? She had already purged her land of the disloyal. Starvation bayed at her door.

Old Erebog declared for the rebellion.

When the report came to Tain Hu, she burst in on Baru past midnight, wild-haired and flush with wine, crying: "We have the North!"

Baru blinked up at her. "Erebog?"

"Lyxaxu bought her." She gripped Baru's shoulder, then the curve of her skull, that grip ferocious and exhilarated. "Well done. It was your gold. Well done."

And so it was: all four northern duchies gathered in the rebel camp, a solid strip of forest and stone that commanded every approach to the Wintercrests and the long-silent Stakhieczi mansions beyond.

In the south the Masquerade built its reply. Xate Olake, at the center of his web in Treatymont, passed sly reports:

Duke Heingyl took counsel with Cattlson. Together they devised a solution to the riots in their capital. Heingyl's armsmen took command of the occupation, filling the streets with Aurdwynni faces, familiar Stakhi freckles and proud Maia noses. The Masquerade garrison formations traded places with them, marching northeast to seize the late Duke Radaszic's precious fields and granaries. The riots didn't stop—cries of *traitor!* greeted Heingyl's men—but without steel masks to hate they were starved for fuel.

Outside the city, the Masquerade's forces staked out a great defensive semicircle.

The western flank met the sea at Unane Naiu, ancient fortress of the Maia conquerors. The circle swept east around Duchy Radaszic and Duchy Heingyl, keeping Treatymont safe at its center, until it met the western edge of Duchy Unuxekome. There Heingyl positioned his elite cavalry, a threatening arrowhead aimed toward Welthony and Unuxekome's land on the Sieroch floodplain.

The cordon kept the rich coastal fields of Duchies Radaszic and Heingyl under Masquerade control. They were Cattlson's best weapon—a lance of starvation thrown north.

The Governor recalled every garrison that fell outside the cordon. Abandoned the Midlands and the North. Even Xate Yawa's social hygienists closed their offices. Methodical, defensive, patient, the Masquerade strategy left most of Aurdwynn to its own devices. "What are they doing?" Oathsfire asked, writing to Baru about matters of finance, scribbling questions in the margins. "Why not use their strength to hold the Midlands? Ihuake and Nayauru could deal them so much harm, and Cattlson needs to go through one of them to reach us. Why abandon all that land?"

And Baru replied as Xate Olake would have: "They are playing the Traitor's Qualm. Leaving the undecided dukes room to consider their loyalties."

Leaving them to weigh their choice while swift *Scylpetaire* raised anchor and set out for Falcrest, bearing the official declaration, two months after the loss of the tax ships: *rebellion in the Federated Province of Aurdwynn.*

And the first storm of autumn howled in off the Ashen Sea.

20

THE storm crashed ashore.

The rebels called it a blessing from ykari Himu, whose virtues included spring, birth, genius, leadership, war, hemorrhagic diseases, and cancer, all the forms of energy and excess, including the hot open water of the Ashen Sea and the storms it spawned.

As long as there had been sailors on the Ashen Sea, ships obeyed the law of seasons: in summer, ride the trade winds clockwise around the sea, from Falcrest to the Oriati Federations to Taranoke and onward past western lands until you come at last to Aurdwynn. Or voyage against the wind if your oars and sails and seamanship permit it, accepting the costs in time and labor, trusting in your navigators if you venture away from the coast.

But once the autumn storms begin, get your ships to harbor. No voyage, no matter how swift, no matter how close to shore, can be considered safe. The trade winds will betray you and vicious new currents will cast you up on the rocks.

Whether *Scylpetaire* made the journey to Falcrest no agent of the rebellion could say. But with the early storm they had won a powerful victory. The easy ways between Falcrest and Treatymont were cut.

Any reinforcements would have to come by land, through snow and rock and frozen marsh, across the Inirein. And Oathsfire had dropped the bridges there, blocked the risky fords with his phalanxes. The marines, Falcrest's lash, would not arrive until spring.

THE storm reached Vultjag, scattering the kettles of birds that circled the forest, swelling the river Vultsniada that ran through the valley, spilling its last rain against the slopes of the Wintercrests and Tain Hu's keep. Baru stood on the battlements and let herself soak, shivering in wet broadcloth, trying to feel cold and small and insignificant.

Like an idiot. If she fell ill there would be no saving her, not here in the north of Aurdwynn, far from Masquerade medicine. She had left the coast and Unuxekome's house behind and gone into the farthest north. Safer, yes, but easier, here, to feel far from things, to pretend she could hide and be small, to deny the burden she had lifted.

Rebellion.

From *The Antler Stone* she'd come to imagine rebellion as a creature of banners and fields, riots and mobs, secret signs and families divided. Swift and harsh as wildfire.

It had been two months since Welthony harbor, since Radaszic's disastrous march on Treatymont. Except for the uprising in Erebog, there had been no great battles, no dramatic betrayals. Just a slower, more powerful unrest, a movement of the earth, a stirring disease.

The Masquerade's most powerful military discovery had come early in its history: battles didn't kill soldiers. Plague and starvation killed soldiers, the slow, structural forces of conflict.

Maybe rebellion was the same. A change in structures. Like a bridge bending under wind and wave.

Tain Hu moved flags and symbols around the maps in her plotting room with agonizing imprecision. Here, the shape of a mask, going south: Masquerade formations withdrawing, raiding granaries and fields as they went. Farmers and ducal levies turning out to oppose them in a thousand tiny skirmishes that stoked resentment and hate. "We win these," Tain Hu said, "even when we lose."

Letters reported a string of peculiar assassinations. Ducal secretaries, freetown ombudsmen, ilykari priests, trade factors. Someone chiseling at the bridge between serfdom and nobility. This troubled Baru because it was so clever. It spoke to real talent in the Masquerade command. Cattlson had his strengths, and one of them was his instruments, the Clarified, the web of technocrats around him. . . .

The rebel dukes readied for war.

Like the others, Tain Hu had levied her able-bodied men and women— they appeared on the map as little pins, each one a phalanx ready to march. But the levies were temperamental creatures, their loyalty kept by salaries and the promise of reward. Fighters would set down their arms and go home if payment came late, or their families needed them, or morale fell, or an omen struck, or this, or that. So there were two other kinds of soldiers: professional cavalry, terribly rare in the North, and the all-important rangers who would rule the winter.

Baru left the soldiering to Tain Hu.

Soldiers were an Aurdwynni duke's answer to the problem of war. But Aurdwynn had not conquered the Masquerade, which meant that Aurdwynn's answers weren't enough. Baru turned her own attention to the greater problems, the problems a Falcresti would address.

Reports came too slow, and often proved inaccurate. This drove Baru mad. (Only now, deprived of its vast sprawl, did she fully appreciate the Imperial Accountant's subordinate bureaucracy). So she ordered every duke to detach a section of their cavalry—yes, she'd insisted, I don't care how precious they are to you, how badly you need them to prance around to herald your arrival, news is more precious still—to form a messenger corps.

A problem there. Most of the cavalry were illiterate.

Fucking hell, but of course, of course—no one raised in a white-walled Masquerade school would ever become ducal cavalry. After a few cups of wine Baru hit on a solution—incorporate the scattered ilykari priests as scribes. They knew old Iolynic and they had their own ecclesiastical codes. Once the protocols reached Erebog and Unuxekome, Baru hoped they could deliver a stream of secure information from the full reach of rebel territory.

"Is this how you'll lead?" Tain Hu sometimes came to her study to mock her. "Bolted up behind a desk, ink-stained and often drunk?"

"This is how your conquerors overcame you. This is their strength." Baru shook a cramp out of her wrist. "And I'm nowhere near drunk."

"I can correct that."

"Go *away*," Baru said, laughing.

As ever, there was the money.

The dukes wanted to split up the tax plunder. The very idea panicked Baru—separate treasuries, separate policies, mismanagement and graft. So she cornered Duke Lyxaxu at a council in his home, High Stone, leaving Oathsfire and Tain Hu to trade barbs while she herded him out into a marble-floored rotunda with a breathtaking view of autumn forest below. The towering Student-Berserkers he used as bodyguards waited at a polite remove.

"How are the accounts?" he asked.

"Too fat. We need to buy food and war material. We have the crafts-men we need to make weapons, and the granaries to survive the win-ter. Now we need to feed that engine." More than anything else, the rebels needed to turn their gold and silver into spears and bread.

"I understand the need." Memory of desperate winters in his eyes. "How can I help?"

"I need control of the money," she told him. "Every coin."

He arranged his mantle against the chill, taking care with each crease and fold. He was graying and slim, and up here the wind sang dry and cold as starlight. "You think I can give you that?"

"I'm certain you can."

"But I only have my own share." There was a kind of curiosity in his eyes when he spoke to her, as if he expected strange words and foreign connections, ligatures of philosophy that he could savor and tug at and try to take apart. "How will I take Oathsfire's? Unuxekome's?" A spark of wicked delight in his eyes. "Do you have another trick of finance? I came out quite poorly from your last maneuver."

"They look up to you." Maybe he wanted her to say this. "You're the philosopher-duke with the books of ancient wisdom. When you act, they watch your example. When you give me your share they will know their best mind has faith in me. And if they aren't persuaded—" She smiled dryly. "I know how persistent your letters can be."

"Mm. It might be so. Oathsfire takes my counsel, when it suits him. Certainly others have done well for themselves by mimicking my successes . . . and avoiding my failures." He turned away, stepped to the edge of the rotunda to consider the forest far below. "You want me to help you be more than a figurehead. And in exchange?"

"In exchange?" Lyxaxu, of all of them, should understand why she needed this. "I do my job. I guarantee the fiscal security of the rebellion."

"Yes. You preserve the common good." Here the trees were not all co-nifers. Lyxaxu watched the wind peel the forest canopy of its autumn dead and throw the leaves up toward the mountains. Baru caught a little sigh of appreciation. "But we're bargaining, aren't we? Wouldn't I be a fool to do this for you without some personal gain?"

Baru would have caught his shoulder and pulled him around if it weren't for his height: she would only be emphasizing the difference and giving him a kind of power. "If you insist on playing the rebellion for your own benefit then we will all go into the Cold Cellar together. Is that how you want this to end?"

He looked at her over his shoulder, eyes narrow above the silver marten-skin. The great storm of leaves blew across the sky behind him, troubling birds. "I miss the man who would rise to that argument. I miss Lyxaxu the philosopher-duke, moved by grand selfless ideas; he was a good man to be. But that man—I hesitate to call him a duke at all, knowing what I do now—led his people into starvation. That man watched his neighbor and student, his boorish venal ill-read goat of a friend, grow wealthy and fat by being very selfish indeed. Can you imagine how that felt? To counsel a man out of boyhood, only to see him surpass you? To see his people prosper while yours wept and ate their rags?"

The wind fell off. Baru spoke softly, to show respect for the confidence Lyxaxu offered. "Perhaps it means you counseled him well."

The marten-skin mantle tricked her. For one instant she saw not a man but a rabid fox, his eyes sharp with wit, hot with rage. And she sensed the things he might have said, an arsenal of plain pointed words to remind her that she faced an equal, a mind that would not be turned by flattery or indirection.

But part of that cunning was restraint. Lyxaxu did not lash out.

"No," he said. "It was my turn to learn a lesson from Oathsfire. No philosophy will feed my daughters. No common good will buy grain for my serfs."

The cold made her shiver, but Baru held his eyes and offered terms. "I can arrange for some of the money to vanish. How much will you need?"

"I don't want money. I want a promise—better: a contract." He lifted himself from the rail to turn back toward her, and again something in the motion of leaf and wind fed Baru an illusion, as if Lyxaxu were unwrapping the man from the marten-skin, or concealing the fox. "Play the others as you must. Lead Oathsfire and Unuxekome around by their dreams of dynasty. Feed the Xates with blood and poison to keep their teeth from your neck. All this I understand: revolution is a filthy business, and prices must be paid. But Duchy Lyxaxu is not your coin. Do you understand? My home is *mine*. When it comes time to sacrifice— spend another."

A deeper cold moved along her spine, like the ghost of an obsidian blade. Lyxaxu saw too much. "They will all ask me this. Who would not?"

"And you will lie to satisfy them. But not to me." He held out his hand. "This will be the truth."

They shook. Lyxaxu looked over her shoulder. "We should go back in and see to Oathsfire," he said. "Before Vultjag kills him."

BARU got her money. Lyxaxu gave his share, and as she'd expected, all the others followed. She went back to her study at Vultjag and made arrangements.

The rebellion had touched off a crisis of confidence and a spectacular crash in the Masquerade fiat note. This was ideal—everyone now preferred silver and gold, which meant a little rebel coin could buy a lot of wheat or flour or salt.

"Oh," Vultjag said, following Baru's explanation. "So we've gotten wealthier just by sitting here? No wonder you became an accountant."

Baru had to be wary; Cattlson would try to trick the rebels into buying poisoned or weevil-ridden grain. So she arranged for Xate Olake's agents to steal a set of official seals from Treatymont. With these she could forge purchase orders from the Masquerade government.

Her instruments were ready. Time to provision the rebellion for winter.

For this she reached out to Oathsfire. He'd made his fortune trading along the Inirein, running goods up from Duchy Unuxekome and into the North, dodging taxes and playing arbitrage. He gave her the cutout agents and smugglers she needed, her own makeshift Imperial Trade Factor. She wrote contracts backed with rebel gold, payable on delivery, and even delighted the smugglers and merchants with the first insurance policies they'd ever seen.

"*I have concerns,*" Oathsfire wrote, "*that they may insist on such generous terms in the future, making business difficult.*" She ignored him.

Food, wood, and metals began to flow north, filling out the granaries and stockpiles. The need for salt, their only reliable preservative, was desperate—Duke Autr would not sell to the rebellion without the consent of the duchess Nayauru, leaving the rebels dependent on sea salt from Unuxekome.

Desperate, too, was Baru's need for a staff. Coordinating purchases and transit from Vultjag's isolated valley posed an impossible challenge.

She needed a trustworthy agent, someone she could send south to Wel-thony to manage Unuxekome's ports, someone who would understand what she wanted without needing a letter to confirm it.

A secretary.

At the southern pass, Vultjag's armsmen at the fellgate raised a ban-ner: unknown riders coming.

N O," Baru said, and then, more softly, her mind taking better mea-sure of it, "oh no."

"You can't see him," Tain Hu said, and took Baru's shoulders, to stop her from bolting toward the carriage.

Baru let herself be drawn to heel. Stared, hollow, at the mud-splattered carriage that had come to a halt just beneath the gates of Vultjag's water-fall keep, at its veiled windows, its pus-yellow warning flag. At the yellow-jacketed drivers.

The yellowjackets were survivors, immune. The flag predated the Masquerade occupation, but it still meant the same thing: *plague*. Some Aurdwynni sickness, some ferocious hybrid, brewed in this cauldron of bloodlines and cattle, the rats and fleas of five civilizations.

An infected passenger.

"I'll call to him from outside," she said, toneless, her detachment in-voluntary and inadequate. "He'll hear me."

"No one gets close." Tain Hu's boots made wet phlegm noises in the mud. She circled Baru, to stay between her and the carriage. "He's trav-eled in quarantine all the way from Treatymont. If he passes one flea, one breath . . . you understand? The winter keeps us huddled close. I had this pox when I was a child. My parents had it, too. I became duchess very young."

"A note, then," Baru begged. "A palimpsest. We'll wear gloves. Let me write to him."

Tain Hu's eyes softened. "I'll carry it between you. I have immunity."

"You could give whatever he writes to me—"

"No. You can't touch anything that's been near that carriage."

"You could hold it up for me to read."

Anger folded the corners of Tain Hu's mouth, softened, after a mo-ment, by a stroke of something warmer that passed almost instantly back into irritation. "He'll have to dictate the message to me. *Nothing* leaves that carriage. I'll read your messages to each other. You'll write what you want me to say—"

"But I can't write anything you can read to him," Baru said, amazed at the incredible, stupid injustice of it: Tain Hu couldn't read her Aphalone script, and Baru couldn't write in Iolynic.

The irony of it almost ripped a wild laugh from Baru. The plague signs were Aurdwynni, but the paranoia, the doctrines of quarantine, were Masquerade, were the basics of Incrastic hygiene.

The liquor of empire. Everywhere.

"Dictate your messages to me," Tain Hu said, taking command, plucking the simple solution out of Baru's grief. "I'll take them down in Iolynic. Or, if you prefer, I can bring a translator."

An armsman brought a palimpsest. Baru stood beneath the overhanging battlements, huddled against the cold and rain, and wrote in runny black ink:

To His Excellence Muire Lo, the acting Imperial Accountant, once secretary to Baru Cormorant: Baru Fisher sends her regards. She knows no finer candidate for the position. No more capable or deserving mind.

She began another sentence, at first an apology, then a thanks, and then, in the end, just a sharp strikethrough. She could say something else after Muire Lo's reply. The translator came out of the keep, bowing to her duchess and the Fairer Hand, and did her work swiftly.

Tain Hu went to the carriage, walking into the invisible potentiality, the immanence of plague. Could she be sure it was the same pox she'd had, and that she was immune? Perhaps so. She spoke to the drivers, poised on the balls of her feet. Accepted something from them—a letter in a horn case—read it under the rain-shield of her cloak, and then returned it. Went to the windows of the carriage, lifted a veil, spoke softly to the glass.

Baru's stomach felt glassy, a decanter, an acid flask.

Tain Hu returned, her head bowed, stopping a long shout away. The mud caked her boots. "I'm sorry," she said. "The nurse says he's asleep. I think I heard him coughing, but he didn't reply."

"Ah." Baru swallowed. "The letter the drivers gave you? Is it from Xate Yawa?"

"Her brother, I think—it used one of his ciphers. Xate Yawa seized Muire Lo for interrogation so that Cattlson couldn't get to him first. He was too close to you to escape suspicion, and he would have been given to the Clarified if she didn't put him in the Cold Cellar. When the Xates had a chance, they arranged for him to escape prison and leave Treatymont. But the prisons are unsanitary, the old sewers backed up by rain, the drinking water not always properly boiled . . . there was sickness among them. . . ."

"Ah," Baru said.

"He was lucid when they passed through Haraerod. But he relapsed." Tain Hu took a step back, as if afraid her words would be infectious, too. "Nothing can be done for him in the North except what the yellowjackets have already done. We can only wait."

Wait. As Baru had waited to warn him. And look what that had done.

Baru turned away and went back into the keep, her steps filthy, accretive, heavy with mire. At the portcullis she stopped and began to kick the stone, trying to get herself clean.

Tain Hu did not call after her.

She went up to her high tower and ordered the servants to draw a hot bath and then leave her to her work. Tain Hu, delayed by the need to bathe and smoke her own clothes, was not there to tell the yellowjackets to wait when they next checked on their passenger, was not anywhere her servants knew to look for her when they tried to send word. And so it was the next morning when Baru learned that the body of the man in the carriage had been taken out into the forest and burnt.

WHEN her control faltered it let slip rage: jaw-splitting, teeth-breaking, thought-killing anger, minute and obsessive in its detail, omnivorous in its appetite. Anger at every choice and circumstance that had brought the world to this unacceptable state.

Fury against causality.

And as she traced the chain, the knot, the map of all the roads that had brought Muire Lo to ash in the forest—at the center of the map, between the thickets of empire and revolt, she came, again and again, to herself. Her fury had nothing else to eat and so it began to eat her. She sat at her table with her trembling pen and wrote nothing.

Into the fire came a knock.

Tain Hu stood at the door of the study, her boots immaculate. She held two scabbards in the crooks of her arms.

"I don't want to duel," Baru said, absurdly self-conscious of her loose gown and bare feet. She'd plundered Vultjag's wardrobe. Everything was too long.

"So be it." Tain Hu stepped past and set the two scabbards on Baru's worktable, covering the notes. "I'll leave them there. You can use them when you want to make me leave."

Her gaze was direct, but she picked at a loose thread on her tabard, at first with a slow, considered rhythm, and then in impatient yanks.

Baru poured a glass of unwatered wine, and then, after a purse-lipped pause, a second. Tain Hu accepted with a nod and a murmur. They waited in silence for some externality, a falling book or a crash of thunder, to give them permission to speak or act.

"He could have been very useful," Tain Hu said.

"He always was." The dry benediction felt like satire, a cheap joke, a pretense of mourning come too early. She wondered if Tain Hu could hear the bitterness in her phrasing: "He'll be missed."

The angle of Tain Hu's gaze deflected a few degrees, a rudder bracing against an expected gust. "You were close to him."

A range of lies and misdirections, careful admixtures of the truth, diluted by implication: *I cared about him. He helped me come this far. We were friends. I never thanked him.*

But they felt stale, pointless, rotten. Instead she said the harder, truer thing: "I trusted him. Unwisely. But I did."

And Tain Hu frowned and nodded, as if she understood. "Trust is precious," she said. "And hard to share." She twisted the loose thread around her fingers. "I'm sorry they didn't trust him. I'm sorry they didn't trust you with him."

"What?" Baru frowned for a moment, puzzled, and then stepped back, her weight on her right heel, stumbling in place. "Xate Yawa? Her brother? No. They didn't."

They had known Muire Lo's letters went to Falcrest. Xate Yawa's woodsman had made sure of that.

"I don't know." As Tain Hu spoke, Baru wished that she would stop being honest, so that she would find nothing new that hurt. But she continued, merciless: "I might have done it, in their place. I might not have trusted the Imperial Accountant's secretary in the heart of the rebellion, out of my reach. He had been to Falcrest, and he was sent back. They would have suspected his purpose as a check on you, and marked him as a threat. Perhaps they thought they were helping you."

Baru saw her own reaction reflected in the taut muscles of Tain Hu's neck and shoulders, the readiness of her stance. But even in the face of Baru's fury Tain Hu did not speak in anger.

"It is very dangerous," she whispered, in sympathy, in warning, "for those in our position to admit emotion. It will always be taken as weakness."

Baru nodded, a cold acknowledgment, a recognition from strength, passing over in that instant of conversation all the admissions and disclosures that might have unfolded, the shapes of the invisible cages around them.

Then she said, just as she realized it: "But if I had never asked them to send Muire Lo . . ."

If she had never called for him—

"I don't know," Tain Hu said. That awful honesty. "Maybe the sickness in the jails was real, and you were the best chance he had to get out. Maybe it *was* them, and if you hadn't asked, they would have let him live. I don't know." She jerked the loose thread out of her tabard and considered it as if seeing it for the first time. "Will you look for revenge?"

"No. It would be an error. None of us can afford an error." Baru set down her rattling wineglass. "Not one mistake. The stakes are too high."

"No," Tain Hu murmured. "Too high."

Baru raised her hand to smash the wineglass. Checked herself, checked even her trembling, and stood there in absurd pantomime, too firmly in control of her anger to move, too deeply angry for anything but stillness.

Tain Hu stepped closer, her own hand raised, as if to save the wineglass, or Baru's fist. "At Welthony I knew I wouldn't have to kill you," she said. "I knew you'd pass the tests. I always had faith."

"There is no one," Baru said thinly, bitterly, "in whom I can place my own faith. Nowhere I can show myself unmasked."

Tain Hu shook her head reproachfully. "A man died. Think of his loss, not your own."

Baru nodded, chastened, infuriated, paralyzed.

The Duchess Vultjag stood close by. For a moment Baru thought of their confrontation in the ballroom of the Governor's House, of Tain Hu's lure, her fierce dark eyes, her parted lips, her slow breath, and she felt that in some way Tain Hu stood unmasked, and was the more dangerous for it. But she was not afraid.

"He brought you something in the carriage," Tain Hu said. She averted her eyes midway through the sentence, to protect Baru or herself. "A notebook. The yellowjackets say he'd kept it hidden and safe, even in prison."

Baru's heart skipped. "What did he write?"

"He'd shredded all the pages." Tain Hu shook her head. "They were just pulp. Perhaps he was feverish. I wanted you to know, before we burned it too."

Ah. *That* notebook.

"Go," Baru choked, pushing clumsily. Static snapped when she touched Vultjag's shoulders. "I—please—go."

Tain Hu hesitated at the threshold, as if reluctant, hungry, craving still something left unsaid or unwitnessed. But she left and closed the door before Baru put her head down and, broken by this last loyalty, by Muire Lo's scrupulous destruction of the Stakhi woodsman's book and the sins it implied, at last began to weep.

WHEN she descended from her tower and went through the whispering passages of the waterfall keep to the greathall, she found the war council waiting for her, Tain Hu at the foot of the table. "The Fairer Hand," Tain Hu called, and the armsmen and ranger-commanders, men and women from the families named Sentiamut and Awbedyr and Hodfyri and Alemyonuxe, murmured with her.

"We're leaving Vultjag," Baru said. "Gather the woodsmen and the hunters. Make ready to march."

A ripple of unease. "Why now?" Tain Hu asked, though her eyes were curious. "Surely it is too soon."

"We will not spend the winter in our keeps and valleys while the Masquerade readies the ground for spring and war." Baru took the back of the high chair at the near end of the table and moved it sharply across the stone, a terrible sound. "We'll move through the forests. Travel light. Live by forage."

"To what end?" Ake Sentiamut asked, as the others muttered about starvation and cold, about an islander woman ordering them to march in winter.

To what end, indeed? To the end she had found in her grief, in her obsessive study of the tear-spotted maps. A way to reach the scattered vales and hamlets, the commoners and craftsmen and, before the spring, make them part of the revolt.

A way to become formless, ineffable, beyond the reach of the Masquerade and its spies, its clockwork plans and careful schedules of recrimination. She'd provisioned the rebellion, arranged investments and lines of communication, because that was the way to victory—and now she had a way to extend that strength, a way to build the logistics of rebellion on cold dangerous ground. A way to win the Traitor's Qualm by showing the Midland dukes a power more real than the enemy's, older yet more immediate, an Aurdwynni power, a power born not of coin and calculation but from the land.

And a way to get past those dukes and go directly to the people who had filled out her tax rider, who'd painted so much of her map blue.

"To show the people of Aurdwynn that we have the initiative. To prove to them, and their dukes, that we are real. That even in winter we fight for them." She met the eyes of each fighter at the table, one by one. "Leave to the Masquerade the keeps and the roads, the sewers and the ports. They are summer lambs. It will be winter soon, and we will be as wolves."

Tain Hu rose from her place and drew her sword. Those gathered around the table looked to her, silent, breathless.

"The Fairer Hand," she intoned, and setting her blade flat across her knee, she knelt. "This is my vow: in life, in death, I am yours."

"You will be my field-general." Baru reached down to draw her up, and Tain Hu took her hand to rise, glove in glove, her grip fierce, her eyes golden. "Choose your captains and lieutenants."

The gathered fighters rose, knelt, rose again. Baru looked across them, still hollow with grief, the hollow filled in turn with a cold exhilaration. She could survive this loss. She could make advantage out of any grief.

At her side, Tain Hu looked to the ducal armorer. "She will need a suit of mail. And a better scabbard for her saber." And then, whispering in her ear: "Before we march. Do you want to see where they burnt him?"

"Yes," Baru said. "Yes." And then: "Will you come?"

INTERLUDE:
WINTER

THE march began.

The word of their passage went ahead of them, carried by huntsmen and trappers, greatened by the mechanisms of rumor until it became a declamation, a prophecy. When they crossed from Vultjag forests into Oathsfire land they found the commoners calling them *coyote*. Tain Hu, stirred by the rhetoric of the war council, had wanted to be the Army of the Wolf, but Baru preferred the wisdom of the commoner's name.

Where civilization had purged the wolf the coyote still flourished.

They traveled by foot through the dark paths mapped by generations of woodsmen, light-armored and swift, armed with bow and hunting spear. The army split into loose columns, divided by family. When forage was lean they subsisted on beer, Aurdwynn's favorite source of sterile, portable calories.

They stopped at villages and ducal outposts to provision against scurvy, to buy salted meat and winter fare with stolen tax gold, spending more wealth than the common man saw in a decade. Wherever the villages had phalanxes, they offered training. Where there were woodsmen and hunters, the Coyotes accepted volunteers.

Tain Hu and her deputies kept harsh order. At every crossroads Baru met with riders from the messenger corps, taking their reports, sending out orders and missives to the other rebel dukes.

Autumn crashed down into winter. Snow covered the forests and made swan wings out of the boughs. Baru woke in the morning colder than she had ever been, her limbs stiff, toes absent, and stumbled out into the dawn desperate to move, to eat, to do anything warm and vital under the pale sun. Tain Hu laughed at her, and then sobered suddenly. "You've never seen a winter before."

"In Treatymont, of course. But—"

"Not enough." Tain Hu called out to her guard. "Ake! Ake, you will accompany the Fairer Hand. If she shows sign of sickness or scurvy—"

"I am not so fragile," Baru said.

"*We* are fragile." Tain Hu took her by the shoulders, so she would listen. "If we lose you, Baru Fisher, we lose everything. Remember that."

She could not stop herself from shivering. "I miss my office," she said, trying to smile. "It had better plumbing."

Tain Hu laughed, and swept an open arm to the forest around them. "Welcome to my home."

They doubled back through Oathsfire land, then crossed Lyxaxu into their newest ally, Duchy Erebog. Their ranks swelled. They foraged too widely, and the wolves bayed hunger behind them.

Sickness and madness struck with the cold. Men died trembling of scurvy or drew choleric water from fouled wells and froze in pools of their own bowel. They left a trail of unburied corpses on the frozen ground. Again and again Baru woke in the night from dreams of broken gears and empty-eyed masks and found herself so cold that she could not move, as if her will itself had frozen. It began to feel like creeping madness. The spells did not stop coming until Ake Sentiamut saw something feverish and rabid in her eyes, and began to take her out into the night to teach her Aurdwynn's constellations. Somehow this made sleep easier. But it did not warm her numb hands, or ease the sight of scurvied men whose bleeding gums left red trails in their porridge bowls, or comfort the parents of all the dead children they helped burn.

She had always loved the stars. But in the desert of winter it was impossible to forget that they were cold, and distant, and did not care.

Madness led to bloodshed.

A southern column under one of Lyxaxu's ranger-knights strayed into Duchy Nayauru and, finding itself unwelcome at a trapping camp, butchered the families there. Baru, desperate not to alienate the Dam-builder, sent emissaries to Duchess Nayauru to pay blood money. Tain Hu executed the column's commander. Outrage—at the slaughter, at the discipline—cost the Army of the Coyote good fighters.

They had to be liberators. Not bandits. The Coyote was an army at service, a reverse brigand, bursting out of the woods to raid the innocent with money and safety and hope.

In Duchy Erebog, where the Crone in Clay struggled to keep order after cremating all her rebellious landlords in the kilns, the Coyote patrolled the greatroads, hunted down brigands, and brought relief to towns enveloped by the snow. Here they met a strange ally.

A party of pale red-haired men and women met them on a north road in Erebog, saying in Stakhi: "We are warriors of the Mansion Hussacht. The Necessary King sent us south to find the rebel queen and watch her fortunes. We slaughtered the Mask at Jasta Checniada. Take us in, and we will slaughter more."

This news gave Baru Fisher wild dreams, and she invited their captain, Dziransi, to join her column, where, through translators, she questioned him about the Stakhieczi and the politics of the distant land beyond the mountains, so dreaded by the Masquerade. "Be careful of him," Tain Hu warned. "The Stakhieczi mansions have been silent too long. He was sent south with a purpose."

"Purposes are useful. Mutual interests give us ground for alliance."

"Or perhaps the Stakhieczi hope to complete the conquest they abandoned so long ago. They are stoneworkers. That makes them patient architects."

Baru smiled. "I am glad to have your vow," she said. "It takes two to keep track of all our fears."

Winter's bitterest months lay ahead. "We must find camp," the war council advised. "We must winter in a safe valley."

But Baru Fisher ordered them south, into the Midlands duchies, a trespassing army, an outrage and an act of war. They passed through abandoned Masquerade forts and raised their own flags: an open hand, for Baru, or a design of coin and comet, for the alliance between the Fairer Hand and the Duchy Vultjag. Word went ahead of them. When they came to Duchy Nayauru's villages, they found commoners waiting to give them beer, furs, shelter, and hand-sewn flags.

They marched through the Midlands, drawing new blood faster than they shed corpses, counting on their gold to offset the damage done by forage. At last, frostbitten and fierce, the Army of the Coyote met the phalanxes and horsemen of the duchess Ihuake, centerpost of the Midlands Alliance. The defenders ostentatiously blocked the way, denying access to the roads—but covered their eyes in mock blindness as the Coyote columns passed through the woods between them, and even sent five hundred bowmen and two hundred goats loaded with provisions "to ensure good conduct."

"The Duchess of Cattle knows your power," one of the Ihuake captains told Baru. "She is watching you."

Good, Baru thought, good—watch and judge. Weigh my strength. Consider the choice you will make in the spring.

Victory demanded that she break the Traitor's Qualm.

I N the darkest days of winter, too cold to snow, the transient sun glaring on the ice, Baru Fisher walked the length of the forage line, her moccasins whispering. At her side strode the ranger-knight and duchess Tain Hu, whose woodcraft was known in the North, where they called her *the eagle*, and in Treatymont, where they called her *that brigand bitch*.

The Fairer Hand and her field-general joined the hunters and showed their talent with the bow, their vigor, their keen eyes and clear level voices, their trust in the seasoned men who led the stalk. Wherever they went the weary wavering Army of the Coyote bristled with hope.

In warmer days of autumn they had slipped away together, Tain Hu exercising all her stealth, so that she could teach Baru how to string and fire a bow in secret, her tutorship harsh, often impatient. "You must appear a master," she insisted. "They would forgive an Aurdwynni a missed shot, forgive a man who struggled to string. But never you. Your errors will be written on your blood and sex. You must be flawless."

"The draw," Baru said, "is heavy."

"Many women lack the strength."

Baru, daughter of a huntress, a mighty spear-caster and a woman of strength, Baru who in moments of frustration or quiet always turned to the exercises and weights of the Naval System, drew with one easy breath.

Tain Hu touched Baru's elbow, drew her spine a little straighter, pressed at the curve of her back. "Fire," she whispered.

And all those months later in the ferocious cold beneath the pale winter sun Baru Fisher loosed an arrow with bright blue-dyed fletching and they all cried out in joy and leapt up to chase the wounded stag, crashing through the drifts, hearts pounding, lungs full of cold cutting ecstasy. When they brought the stag down Tain Hu opened its throat and helped the woodsmen dress it. All down the column they murmured of the omen, the fallen antlers, the stag of Duke Heingyl, the red of the Masquerade navy spilled across the snow.

Everywhere they marched they made it known: in the spring they would gain the loyalty of the Midlands duchies, the strength of Nayauru and Ihuake, and together they would push the Masquerade back into the sea.

AUTARCH

21

THE spring would bring tests—the decisive courtship of Nayauru and Ihuake and their clients, and greater tests beyond. But there was a little time for Baru yet.

The winter smeared her in Aurdwynn, caked her in its churned mud, filled her with its guinea-fowl curries and venison and salted fish, clogged her pores with the oils and scents of cumin and wild ginger and crusted salt. Her tongue mangled and then mastered the beginnings of Iolynic. She learned to swear in Urun and Stakhi, and to forgo the formal Belthyc word *ilykari*—a word now owned, it was felt, by the Masquerade, by Xate Yawa—in favor of the vernacular Iolynic *students*.

She learned the different tastes of cedar and redwood smoke. She laughed at fireside stories of Duchess Naiu and her four husbands, who had died heroes in the Fools' Rebellion. And she laughed harder when they mocked her for her nervous sidelong glances, checking for some frowning social hygienist ready to diagnose degeneracy.

"Men used to marry men," Tain Hu told her, as they crouched together over a fire pit to cook their venison. "And women once took wives. It was done by the poor, the starving, the desperate, by those who needed a business pact or a shared roof. By soldiers on campaign with no one else to turn to. Mostly it was done by those without needs or troubles—done for love. The words *tribadist* and *sodomite*, the things they mean and define, came later. Before those words there were only people."

Baru watched her warily, fearing some bait set out for the Taranoki savage. "But all this was long ago. Before the Mask."

Tain Hu tore a strip of meat, chewed slowly, and swallowed. "Long ago? Well." She grinned across the fire. "Ask around among the divers at the Horn Harbor. Or the actresses at Atu Hall. They will tell you how long ago it was. I am not quickly forgotten."

Curiosity came over Baru as instantly and powerfully as conditioned fear, and the mixture made her laugh. "You *didn't*. In Treatymont? Under Xate Yawa's nose?"

Tain Hu's eyes rounded in mock hurt. "You think I'd stop my work at the city gates? Please. I have Vultjag's tradition of conquest to uphold."

"There are *more*?"

"Oh, yes. It could take some tallying." Tain Hu made confused number-shapes with her fingers. "Might even require an accountant."

Baru began to cough on smoke, and dropped her venison in the fire.

S HE led the Army of the Coyote in a desperate form of war, a war without violence, a war with more casualties than any battle ever fought.

The steady Incrastic diet of her childhood made Baru strong and tall, healthier and more consistently able than many of the Coyote fighters. She helped them dig latrines, teaching them obsessive Masquerade hygiene, smelling more Aurdywnni shit than she'd ever planned on. Among the women she learned that a regular menstrual cycle in the winter was a mark of incredible prosperity—a noble luxury beyond ordinary reach.

She was common-born. But the circumstances of her upbringing made her nobility to them.

Her Coyotes ranged the forests of the Midlands, a ghost of order in a famished hungry land. The Masquerade's autumn retreat had pillaged the granaries and abandoned the roads, sowing anarchy: a message, a harbinger of life without Falcrest's glove and gauntlet. The Coyote fought back by opening routes north wherever they could, hiring ducal siege engineers to help with stonework, organizing bowmen and riders to patrol the roads. When the way was ready, they wrote to distant Oaths-fire and his swollen granaries, his stores of salt and meat: *send what you can*. Where they found excess stores, they paid outrageous prices to buy them and bring them where they were needed.

When they trespassed on the duchies of the Midlands Alliance, Baru prepared messages for them: *I am the Fairer Hand. I come to help.* But she never sent them. To leave written record of correspondence with the Midlands duchies would be to implicate them in treason. Even runners could not be risked. Better for the Traitor's Qualm if the Midlands dukes could pretend she wasn't there. It would be disastrous if they pushed Nayauru and Ihuake into acting too soon, disastrous for their strategy, and for Baru herself: she had assured Lyxaxu and the others that the Midlands would wait.

She studied the architecture of Aurdwynn's suffering. When they came to hamlets and freetowns, she took a translator and went among the houses, interviewing the sharecroppers and fletchers and smiths and masons, mothers and fathers, aunts and grandfathers, all tenants of the feudal landlords—recording their diets, their miscarriages, the birth weights of their children, the severity of their scurvy (bleeding gums and spotted skin and low spirits *everywhere,* universal, inescapable, synonymous with winter itself: *the breath of Wydd*), their fears, their small phlegmatic hopes.

She made a map of the feudal ladder, the rungs of duke and landlord, armsman and craftsman and sharecropper serf. During the shivering nights she considered how to smash it. Aurdwynn would never rise to match Falcrest until the feudal nobility could be torn down.

It would be a better land if only it could be ruled sensibly.

THE snows broke early and all the rivers, gorged on meltwater, began to roar. Baru dreamed of flight. Saw Aurdwynn from the belly of the clouds, sunlight reflected off spring rapids, off the mighty Bleed of Light, a fan of quicksilver bleeding out into the sea. She woke to birdsong.

Tired of oil and stink, she swam in a meltwater torrent, gasping every breath, the cold a sine of numbness and fire. Her armsmen—bearskin-cloaked Sentiamut rangers handpicked by Tain Hu—clapped and laughed, delighted by her defiant progress upstream and by the whole art of swimming, unknown in the North.

But when she came ashore shivering, the men averted their eyes, hesitating to step forward and offer their furs, as if they thought she would choose one of them, and signify something by it—and she, too, was suddenly hesitant, unwilling to signify, shackled by things she had never meant to learn.

"Be careful," Tain Hu warned her. "You have earned respect. But there are no men in Aurdwynn who can respect what they desire. I learned that from Oathsfire's courtship, when I was young."

"There are other women here. They are not all mistreated." Baru thought of the archers and fletchers, moss-pharmacists and astronomers, and the rangers like Ake. "Would you have me pretend to be a man, as you once did? Is that the only way to keep their respect?"

"Go to one of those women," Tain Hu said, "and ask her how she was spoken of when she left her lover, or took a second, or never had one at all."

"I have made brothers of these men. Not lovers."

The Duchess Vultjag, her hair unbound, her shoulders rolling beneath her leather and mail, shook her head ruefully. "You have been given a permit of brotherhood, Baru Fisher, and you have no say in when they will revoke it, or why." Her lips twitched, in laughter or regret. "I learned that from Oathsfire, too."

"Is that why you—" Baru could not make herself speak plainly of it. "Why you turned to divers and actresses? Instead of a husband?"

Tain Hu laughed aloud, delighted. "You think that I *turned*?"

Baru felt a little shame. It was a Masquerade question, the kind of question you learned to ask in a white-walled school. Her fathers had taught her better.

They walked in silence along the column, and came to a place where the canopy thinned and sunlight came down through the redwoods in the pattern of a fawn's coat. Meltwater roared in the near distance, and together they looked up into the warm divided light.

"I feel it," Tain Hu said. "The power."

"Is it ykari Himu?" She had never taken Tain Hu for *much* of a believer, but the duchess did believe.

"Change," Vultjag said. "Whatever you name it." She glanced sidelong at Baru. "You told me that there was only one road forward. That the Masquerade would never be defeated. Only subverted from within."

Baru looked away, as if in concession to pride. "You make me think otherwise." And although it felt colder than the meltwater to say or even think, it was true.

"What command, my sworn lord?" Not even a little mockery in Tain Hu's voice.

They'd made their case to the Midlands—shown their strength and resolve. Now it was time to win them, all their cavalry and wealth. Break the Traitor's Qualm and gather every last wavering maybe-rebel into one united force.

"Nayauru and Ihuake. We make them ours."

As they swung deeper south, Tain Hu resolved to test her courage by walking the cliff roads on Mount Kijune. This was where the war found them.

"It's not so far down," Baru said, and then, unable to help herself, began to laugh. Far below, the treetops moved in slow waves, tousled by the wind. The Coyote camps were tiny brushstrokes of cloth and smoke. North of them the Wintercrests climbed the edge of the sky, flanks as dark as ravenwing, peaks as white and unreachable as the clouds they pierced.

"Come," she said. "Just keep your footing."

Tain Hu clung to the chains that lined the walkway—a perilous narrow bridge shackled to the cliff face, high above Duchy Ihuake—and looked at Baru crossly. "I am not a goat."

Baru loved it. Like the black cliffs and volcano sweeps of Taranoke: wide spaces from a childhood before fear. "Come, Duchess." She beckoned. "We're nearly to the top. Come along!"

Tain Hu sucked in a breath and the wind gusted hard enough to set the whole walkway rattling and singing. She froze, clearly afraid to breathe, and made a face of frustrated misery while Baru laughed some more.

"Duchess!" the wind called.

Tain Hu looked downtrail, instantly alert, as if the word had touched a deeper part of her than the height. There was someone coming: strawhaired Ake Sentiamut, her bearskin coat bound tight, struggling up the chains from the stony notch below.

"Well," Baru said, as Tain Hu's brow furrowed. "*This* must be urgent."

The ranger-knight climbed to meet them. They went together up toward a sheltered saddle in the side of Mount Kijune, where they could hold council. Tain Hu moved quickly now, as if it was her duty to be fearless before her vassals—although she kept close to Baru and followed her footsteps.

They gathered in the flat lee of the rock, panting, all winded. Ake offered Tain Hu her coat, but the duchess graciously refused. Baru, chilled by the memory of winter carried in the wind, sat with Ake and huddled with her beneath the bearskin.

Tain Hu set her palms on the rock. "Tell us."

"There's civil war."

Silence for a moment, except for the whispering wind. "You mean," Baru said, "aside from ours?"

Ake unrolled a weighted map. The Midlands opened before them in ink and sheepskin—the second floor of Baru's allegorical house, full of craft and cattle. Baru laid her thoughts upon it, the shapes of tension and loyalty. The west was Nayauru Dam-builder's, Autr and Sahaule at her side, rich with clean water that glimmered in great reservoirs. The east was Ihuake's. Her herds were vast and thunderous, and she kept her soldier Pinjagata curled up beside her like a fist.

"Here." Ake traced a line from Nayauru's capital at Dawnlight Naiu, to Ihuake's at the Pen. "Our scouts found tracks in the mud."

Tain Hu exhaled slowly. "Whose?"

"Nayauru's soldiers. Marching east in great strength."

Baru found their own position, north of freetown Haraerod in Ihuake's heartlands. Haraerod the crossroads, where the merry came to sing, where years ago she had stumbled into Duke Pinjagata on a strange patrol. "Nayauru's coming for us?"

"Not for us. For Ihuake." Tain Hu spidered her fingers across the corners of the map and looked at it balefully. "Nayauru's always dreamt of rule—but the time is too soon, the heirs unready. She has no child of Ihuake's lineage to use as an usurper. Why now? Why not give us a chance . . . ?"

Baru's stomach turned. She'd insisted Nayauru wouldn't move. Stared Lyxaxu down and committed herself to it. They would never trust her counsel again. How to absorb this, how to turn this back into a strength—

A little movement of Tain Hu's chin said: *blame me.*

"Why didn't we see this?" Baru asked. "Duchess?"

"I hoped she'd turn to us. I respected her." Her eyes darkened. "The Fools' Rebellion swallowed her whole family. Why would she move so rashly? Does she remember nothing?"

Baru considered the map, raising her eyes once to look past Ake and out across the land. "I know what she's doing."

The two women from Vultjag watched her.

"Spring is here. Nayauru knows the Masquerade is going to attack us. She must expect Cattlson to march north across her duchy on his way to crush Erebog. She wants to be indispensable to the Masquerade by the time that offensive comes." Baru cursed herself as she spoke, remembering clues ignored, connections unmade, years of evidence that could have forearmed her against this choice—Bel Latheman pointing to Heingyl Ri, Heingyl Ri's notion of an inevitable crisis in the Midlands, Pinjagata's patrol for a woman who looked like young Duchess Nayauru. A whole web of intrigue, Nayauru's great design for a throne, and Baru had never bothered to tug on any of the threads. . . . "She knows Ihuake welcomed us into her land. That gives her an excuse to destroy Ihuake and take her herdlands, claim the strike as an act of loyalty to Falcrest, and win Parliament's favor."

And, from there, build herself into queen of Aurdwynn, mother of a lineage that might last the ages. A gambit of terrible audacity—like something from a play, an epic. Baru felt a chill of respect.

Tain Hu considered this, jaw set, fists balled against the stone. "That magnificent bitch," she said, using the Maia word for a mother wolf, not the Aphalone epithet. "Ake, if Her Excellence is correct—did the scouts see Masquerade regulars marching in support of Nayauru's armsmen?"

"They did."

Baru could only shake her head in wordless appreciation. The Coyote had hoped to use Nayauru and her consorts against Cattlson, and now, in turn, they had been used. All Nayauru had to do was claim the Midlands. Cattlson would sweep up her flanks and snuff out the rebels, and she would have her dynasty.

The same mistake Baru always made. Assuming that Nayauru was hers to court, a playing piece to be taken and deployed. Not a player of her own.

Ake shivered against Baru's side as the wind picked up again. "I spoke to the battle captains. They want to send word north. If Erebog, Oathsfire, and Lyxaxu all march their phalanxes south, we can reinforce Ihuake and save her."

"No!" Tain Hu and Baru shook their heads together. "We can't give them a target," Tain Hu said, as Baru pointed to Treatymont and the forces gathered there—Cattlson and Heingyl, waiting for the Coyote to present itself for extermination.

"My lords." Ake bowed her head. "All winter you've told us—no disloyalty intended, my liege, Your Excellence—that we would win the Midlands dukes to our cause. Now we find Nayauru turned against us. Where she goes Autr and Sahaule will follow. If we do not stand against them, then what? If Ihuake falls, the Masquerade rules the coast and the Midlands both. We will starve."

Tain Hu looked from her ranger-knight to Baru and waited.

"Give me a palimpsest," Baru said. "And ink." She needed her weapons.

When Ake found them both in her rucksack, Baru blew on her hands and explained her orders as she wrote them. "We will stop them ourselves. The Army of the Coyote will cross into Duchy Nayauru north of her march, cut south, sever her supply lines, and threaten her soldiers' homes. Nayauru's army will crumble without a single battle. See that the word reaches all our scattered columns."

"Winter left us ragged," the duchess cautioned. "The men need to rest their sores and eat away their scurvy. You would throw them from one ordeal into another."

"There will be no rest. The Coyote marches." Baru held her gaze. "There will be death before we take Treatymont. Let us make a companion of it."

On the way back down the Kijune Trail they stopped once more, at Tain Hu's request. "The air is clear up here," she said, "and I will miss the stillness."

Baru squeezed her shoulder, comrade to comrade. For a few moments Tain Hu leaned against her, in acknowledgment, or to get a little warmth.

NAYAURU'S soldiers marched east to conquer Ihuake. The Coyote began its answering maneuver.

A column of Oathsfire's yeomen-archers led the march into Duchy Nayauru. They shot dead a party of woodsmen, and found them carrying both Masquerade coin and ominous orders bearing Cattlson's seal: *Flush the woods. Kill the game. Burn the underbrush. Leave no forage.*

"Why?" Baru frowned, and looked to Tain Hu, the letters taut in her grip. "They can't expect us to starve now that spring has come. They must know that the people will feed us wherever we go."

Tain Hu oiled her blade with expressionless purpose. "They don't mean to starve us," she said. "They mean to *make* the people feed us."

Behind the Oathsfire longbowmen, the Vultjag columns raced west, then south, scouts reporting with breathless awe the strength and concentration of Nayauru's forces: cavalry and heavy infantry, supplemented by siege technicians and blue-gray companies of Masquerade regulars. The Dam-builder had hardened her armies into a thunderbolt. They moved with frightening speed and precision.

But their supply trains failed to keep pace. Wagons and mules bogged down on muddy roads. Spring rivers washed out the crossings.

Baru smelled weakness. Nayauru fought with a mix of professional soldiers and levies taken from their families before the crucial spring planting season. They might be powerful on the field—but they had to eat, they had to be paid.

She set her Coyote-men to feast on the supply train.

The Alemyonuxe-Vultjag families struck first, bowmen targeting horses and captains, making sport of killing the second man in every column. Nayauru's messengers, bogged down by the muddy roads, could not organize retaliation. When she sent her own rangers into the woods to strike back, the cunning Awbedyr-Vultjag hunters ambushed them in turn. Oathsfire's longbowmen, glory-hungry, attacked the rear of the main force itself, setting fire to the camps of the reserves in the night.

Nayauru had an army designed to win battles. The Coyote had learned how to win wars.

Then, entirely by accident, there was a battle.

Tain Hu, Baru, and the Sentiamut-Vultjags turned south too early, blundering into the friendly Hodfyri-Vultjag and Lyxaxu columns (all underforaged and hungry). This led to a day of great confusion, and on the next morning, misty and warm, some of the Hodfyri hunters walked right into the flank of Nayauru's northernmost column: a screen of the Dam-builder's skirmishers and bowmen, and behind them a full company of Masquerade regulars.

Tain Hu swore once, vilely, when runners came from the front of the column with news that they had found and accidentally attacked a force of nearly a thousand men on the Fuller's Road. "Tell the Hodfyri captain—" She glanced once at Baru, brow furrowed, and then looked away, as if seeking and then abandoning her input. "Tell him that the enemy does not know our numbers and intent. Tell him to throw fighters as far out to each flank as he can, and to set fires."

"The wood is wet," the runner protested, "and they have no way to start them—"

"Tell them to soak the wood in linseed oil. We want smoke, not fire. A screen for our movements." She whirled on Ake Sentiamut. "The Lyxaxu column must make all possible haste to join us. When the enemy sees the smoke they'll form an answering skirmish line. We will throw all our force against their left flank and see if we can get past and surround them. Send your best bowmen forward to kill their scouts. Keep them blind."

The runners scattered. Tain Hu gestured and a man brought her a shortbow.

"Will it work?" Baru asked, nervous, trying to tally their forces, the count and capability of the fighters. "Do we have the numbers?"

"Numbers won't decide this battle." Tain Hu hooked the bow behind her calf and bent to string it. "My aunt called it *jagisczion*. Forest war. The battle is won with confusion, deception, and ferocity. We will make them think that the woods are full of us and that they will surely die unless they flee. I need to be close to the line, with the reserves, so I can strike at the tipping point."

Baru, uncertain, heart in her throat, lifted a hand. "I'll march forward with you."

"No." Tain Hu raised the bow, testing the draw, throwing back her wool cloak. She did not look at Baru. "You're too valuable."

Baru couldn't argue. "Your Grace," she said, and then, haltingly, "Be cautious."

Tain Hu raised a hand in salute, and perhaps to silence her. Then the duchess Vultjag whistled and beckoned, turned, and at the head of a column of ragged red-eyed men, trotted away through the brush.

BARU'S guard found a fulling mill by a nearby stream. They brought her there to wait.

The terror that took Baru came from the deepest part of her soul. It was a terror particular to her, a fundamental concern—the apocalyptic possibility that the world simply *did not permit plans,* that it worked in chaotic and unmasterable ways, that one single stroke of fortune, one well-aimed bowshot by a man she had never met, could bring total disaster. The fear that the basic logic she used to negotiate the world was a lie.

Or, worse, that *she herself* could not plan: that she was as blind as a child, too limited and self-deceptive to integrate the necessary information, and that when the reckoning between her model and the pure asymbolic fact of the world came, the world would devour her like a cuttlefish snapping up bait.

The millwheel had been uncoupled from the machinery and it turned in useless creaking circles.

"Come," Baru ordered. "We're going forward."

They walked downslope, between the towering redwoods, through thin mist that thickened into acrid smoke. Distant shouts reached them, surging and receding, as if the rest of the world had begun to oscillate on a storm tide.

A man rushed at them through the smoke, shouting in Urun. One of the Sentiamut rangers shot an arrow over his head and then another took him in the gut. Baru, frozen by the man's scream (continuing, now, in new surprised tones), did not even draw her blade.

The man fell in the wet brush.

She thought of what would be said about this moment and, hoping to be courageous, went to the fallen man. Two of the rangers had already reached him. He screamed and screamed and clutched with huge strong hands at the roots around him, hammering his head into the mud, trying to draw himself away, or drown himself in the dirt, or somehow get free of the arrow in his gut. He'd tried to pull it out and its barbs had torn.

"Shit," one of the rangers said, speaking Stakhi simple enough for Baru to understand.

"Is that Ala Hodfyri?"

"No, he didn't have so many teeth—maybe Ora?"

"His cousin?"

"Brother, I think—"

"Ora always did get lost."

The fallen man's eyes bugged in shock. Perhaps, Baru thought (full of an empty resonance, a cavity like the hollow of an excavated eye), he had discovered a new variety of pain, a permutation of fear previously unimagined. His bowels stank beneath him.

"One of ours," she said.

The ranger who'd shot him doubled over to vomit. Baru watched this with expectancy, but nothing of her own came. He straightened, spat, and said: "Wish he hadn't called out in Urun. I don't speak much Urun."

The man on the ground was still screaming. Baru found all the guardsmen looking at her. She made a gesture of command, commanding nothing, knowing nonetheless what she had ordered.

"You want to do it, Ude?" a man asked.

The ranger who'd vomited took out his knife. "Ah," he said, looking at it. "No." And then, as if it were important: "He's got a beard."

"It's down in the well," the dying man rasped, then began to scream again, pounding at the earth, desperate, his eyes fixing on the men around him, beseeching them to understand. "I PUT IT DOWN IN THE WELL!"

They held him down and cut his throat.

"Who'll tell Ala?" the vomiter asked.

"I will," Baru said. The smoke had begun to thin. Through the trees she could see a canyon of light—the road, the battlefield.

"We shouldn't have come," she said. "Back to the mill."

FOREST war:

Nayauru's column saw smoke all along the treeline, a confusion of fog and bowshot. Captains roared command: *Line of battle! Get in line, you dogs!* The white-masked Masquerade regulars took the center, Nayauru's skirmishers the flanks, and their bowmen behind.

The Hodfyri Coyote-men took shots from the smoke and the trees, trying to fix the enemy in place. Tain Hu's battle plan was idiot-simple. It had to be: there was no other way to communicate it to all her scattered, confused war parties.

The Stakhieczi jagata charged first. Tain Hu's least-trusted command—but her toughest. Dziransi led his Mansion Hussacht fighters down on Nayauru's flank, pale, red-haired, roaring and shining with bitter steel plate. They struck Nayauru's levied hunters as ghosts. No one in Aurdwynn—commoner or duke—had forgotten the fear of a reunited Stakhieczi empire, an avalanche of steel down out of the Wintercrests. Now that fear came screaming at them.

They were the only line infantry Tain Hu had. The only Coyote fighters capable of standing in the open and trading blows.

But Nayauru's captains didn't know that. Nayauru's skirmishers with their leather jerkins and short spears saw an army of long lance and unbreakable plate. So they did what any sane fighter would've, the predictable thing, the ruinous thing—

They drew in toward the Masquerade soldiers at their center, and let the flank bend.

Tain Hu and her Coyote-men sprang through the gap. Bolted across the road, firing as they went, and got into the woods behind Nayauru's line. With them came another column, naked of shield, painted in red, trembling at their leash. Lyxaxu's Student-Berserkers.

Tain Hu gave them their word.

They screamed axioms of nihilist self-negation as the drugs in their blood peeled their eyeballs open. When they got in among the unarmored Nayauru bowmen the sound and spray that rose was abominable.

Nayauru's fighters, shot from ahead and behind, circled in screams, routed.

The Masquerade regulars held, shields up, boxed against the arrow fire. With grotesque determination they began to withdraw. But the light-footed bowmen harried them until Tain Hu, worried about running out of arrows or being drawn into reserves, ordered an end to the hunt.

She came to the mill and to Baru at the head of a cheering throng, and presented to the Fairer Hand a gift: a masked and severed skull, the steel of the helmet distressed where it had stopped arrows, one blue-fletched shaft protruding from the temple where it had not.

"We have prisoners," she said. "Shall we leave their heads to be found?"

"Tell them to go home to their families," Baru commanded. "Tell them to bear word to Duchess Nayauru: come over to us, and we may still be merciful."

"A fair fate for the fighters of Nayauru." Tain Hu lifted the head in offering. "But what of the men of Falcrest, the men in masks?"

"Slash their tendons," the Fairer Hand ordered. "Let Cattlson drown in his own cripples."

22

THAT night in camp, beneath the deerskin of her tent, Baru woke from a dream of a bird with an arrow behind its eyes and wings of blue fletching, circling the Iriad market, calling down to her: *I left it in the well!* From the dead peak of Taranoke came thunder and fire and she looked up to find the slopes covered in red sailcloth, rolling down on her, a scream in the air, a panic in the earth.

"My lady," murmured the armsman who had shaken her awake. "My lady."

"Ai." She caught his wrist. "What news?"

"You cried out." He averted his eyes, and she realized, with shame, that she did not know his name. "I thought you might prefer to be woken."

"Of course," she said, and then, seized by a sudden gratitude: "You did well."

THE victorious Alemyonuxe column, flush with the glory of the battle on the Fuller's Road, brought its wounded to a hamlet called Imadyff—Belthyc words, *a good grove*. When the village healer failed to save a favorite Alemyonuxe son from infection, his grief-mad father, a widower and a hard man, took the healer's own son as compense—unspooling his bowels through a slit in his belly. Two village mothers shot him mid-act, violence erupted, and the Alemyonuxe Coyotes, hungry and blood-mad, burned the hamlet down. Drunk on war they went south down the road into the nearest Nayauru vale, found storehouses of salt and meat in the village there, and made off with them, killing the guards and the party that came after them.

The weight of winter and the pace of the forest war had begun to tell. The men were scurvy-mad, starving, exhausted, and they had no loyalty or love for the people of Duchy Nayauru.

"We cannot turn on the yeomen and peasantry," Baru hissed, and the Vultjag war council nodded in agreement, looking to the coin-and-comet banner, the open hand. But Tain Hu, eyes dark, shook her head and gave grim counsel. The Army of the Coyote had grown too huge, too hungry for salted meat and beer and blood. There was no forage to be had. In order to fight on enemy land, it had to hunt.

"There is a balance," Tain Hu said, "seen everywhere in nature. It takes many prey to support a predator. We have brought too many predators to Duchy Nayauru."

And Baru saw the Masquerade's hand at work. They had sent their woodsmen everywhere, driven out the deer, burnt the underbrush, gathered the forage and taken it into their fortifications. Left the Coyote no prey but Nayauru's serfs.

They had a broad eye for war, a willingness to fight not just in the field with horse and spear but everywhere, with everything. They planned for the long run. She knew this, knew it better than anyone else in the rebellion. Knew the secret strength it gave them.

After the council she went to Tain Hu. Baru twice drew breath to speak, and twice released it, before at last saying: "I'm going to order the Coyote to start demanding tribute from Nayauru's villages. Food and clothing. Arrows. Goats. Only what we need."

"They will do that with or without your orders."

"This way," Baru said, "I can at least pretend to have control."

She'd checked her private maps, rolled in horn, guarded jealously. Duchy Nayauru was bright blue. The Dam-builder's serfs, addicted to Fiat Bank loans, all loved her.

But the Coyote had to feed.

NAYAURU'S shock columns reached Ihuake's frontier forts and laid siege. Scurvied, desperate, surrounded by the Dam-builder's elite siege engineers, Ihuake's garrisons would not last a month. When they fell, Nayauru would control the border and, by the Belt Road, threaten the Cattle Lord's capital at the Pen. She could offer Treatymont a safe road north to strike Erebog. Her ultimate victory would be very close.

(Looking over the maps and reports, Baru frowned at shards of drunken memory, years old—fragments of a soliloquy, a horizon glimpsed through dark eyes, a certain laugh—sprays of light on amber reservoirs—where, why? Was it important?)

But before the forts could fall, the Army of the Coyote intervened.

Lyxaxu scouts found a tempting target: a large convoy, heavily guarded, bogged down in the spring mud just short of a river crossing. Oathsfire's longbowmen burned the bridge and began to hunt the convoy guards, killing the pack animals and horses first, then working on the men.

The convoy guards might have outlasted the supply of arrows—Oathsfire's yeomen had been trained to attack in mass, not with precision. But they had no stomach to stand by their wagons and be shot apart. First in a trickle, then in clots, they abandoned the convoy and scattered into the woods. The Coyote raiders saw some of them pillaging their own wagons before they fled.

In the foundered convoy the Oathsfire Coyotes found sacks and chests of coin. Wages meant for the siege technicians and levies at the front.

"We've won," Baru said, thrilled by the news. "Nayauru's fighters already know that she can't keep their lands and families safe. Without pay they'll mutiny."

"That's what you said in autumn." Tain Hu huddled with her in the command tent, helping decode the encrypted Iolynic missives that came to them. "That Nayauru was bound by coin. She surprised us—she may yet again."

"She may surprise me. Her fighters won't. We've cost Nayauru her momentum. She'll make terms."

And she was right. The Duchess Nayauru sent riders to Ihuake to arrange a council, and to beg her to call off the Coyote loose in the woods.

In turn Ihuake sent riders to the Duchies Erebog, Lyxaxu, Oathsfire, Vultjag, and Unuxekome, petitioning the rebels to send emissaries to the Midlands, asking for the counsel of the Fairer Hand. A summit between the rebels and the great powers still uncommitted.

From Treatymont there came no word.

The rebels would sit in council with the Midland Dukes. The Traitor's Qualm stood poised to break.

As they marched back east into Duchy Ihuake, moving toward the council in stealth, Baru found herself writing it as if it had already happened, as an extract from the future history the rebellion wanted to make: *The Council of the Midlands would be remembered as the first great turning point, the triumph of the Army of the Coyote's winter strategy, the moment that Aurdwynn broke the Traitor's Qualm and made the rebellion real.*

Foolish and naïve. But so hard to stop. It was the way Unuxekome would see the future—as a story, a saga coming toward its climax.

They would meet at Haraerod, on Ihuake's land, in the shadow of Mount Kijune. So they came:

Unuxekome and Oathsfire together, marching west from the Inirein, sniping at each other about money and women and matters of pride as they crossed the Sieroch plain. Oathsfire brought ten companies of elite scouts and bowmen to stand sentry. Unuxekome came with a coven of ilykari from his harbors and diving towns, armed with the knowledge of truth and falsity, ready to sniff out treachery. Duke Pinjagata joined them on the road to Haraerod, marching utterly alone, confident that his duchy's strength at arms made him more valuable as an ally than a prisoner or corpse. He put a stop to the two men's bickering: his soldier's tongue proved a match for both of them, and they judged it better to withdraw.

Haraerod's merchants and brewers and clothiers welcomed the business, the lanky bowmen wearing Oathsfire's millstone tabards and the keen-eyed laconic mothers with a taste for mason leaf.

Next came Erebog and Lyxaxu, the Crone and the philosopher-duke, and if they remembered years of cold rivalry in the bitter north, well, they were wise and sagacious, and set those years behind them. From the high pass by Mount Kijune they saw the coming of the Dam-builder Nayauru: a glorious stream of armored cavalry pouring in from the west, Nayauru white-gowned at their head, her posture unbreakably proud. To her left rode Autr Brinesalt, broad and mighty, hammer-armed, loam-skinned, and to her right Sahaule Horsebane, who carried a spear caked in dark blood.

"She certainly has a particular taste," Lyxaxu remarked, watching the column through a spyglass. "Men with certain names."

"You have a Maia name too, boy." Erebog cackled at his reaction. "Your blood could go into Nayauru's great dream. Just tell your Mu it was a matter of state—she'll be forgiving."

"The Incrastic breeders would say the old blood of the West is thin in me. Diluted and made pale by so long marrying north." Lyxaxu lowered the glass. "I don't think it matters. We whisper about Nayauru, but the whispers lead us astray."

"Tell me your great theory, O sage."

"Nothing so sagacious." Lyxaxu folded up the spyglass with delicate care. "Only that she loves them, and they love her. That is what we miss."

Erebog looked away, eyes hooded. "Foolish to love a noble consort. Gets in the way."

Lyxaxu didn't press her. Telling, the way she'd lowered her gaze: avoiding Lyxaxu's eyes, of course, but the horizon too. Like the distant Wintercrests might cut her.

Duchess Ihuake arrived two days later in a column of warhorses so torrential in its passage it had to be followed by a roadwork gang. She and Nayauru made a guarded exchange of peace gifts. With the Midlands and the Rebel North gathered, the council waited only for the Fairer Hand and her field-general . . . or for word of the Masquerade army and Duke Heingyl's cavalry riding up the road from Treatymont to kill them all.

The Army of the Coyote came through the woods, scattered in its columns, wary, feral.

Baru, Tain Hu, the Stakhieczi brave man Dziransi, and their armsmen came to the bluffs above Haraerod and looked down on a valley flooded in color: a tartan of duchies, a glorious and voracious mass of horse and tent, the speartips of the drilling Haraerod guard phalanxes cutting the sunlight.

"Devena," breathed Tain Hu, and fell to her knees in awe. "See the Aurdwynn of old. See our ancient strength. Your Excellence—" She raised herself up on her haunches, balanced on her toes and one gloved fingertip, and looked back in wonder. "Look what we have made," she said, smiling, her red-slashed cheeks dimpled. "Look at the spring our winter planted."

They walked down into the valley, the coin-and-comet banner flying on a bent pole. The Duchess Ihuake sent her cavalry out as escort, and then Nayauru, not to be upstaged by her rival, sent her own, and Oathsfire rode out to them with horses for Tain Hu and Baru Fisher, but she refused to ride while her guards walked, so he dismounted to walk with them. His beard had flowered again with the spring and he spoke with profane good cheer.

They went into Haraerod through a roar of hooves and cheers. But it was a fearful adoration, Baru thought, uncertain, troubled.

They had gathered too much strength here. Charged the valley with too much power, uncertain of its loyalties.

23

I
T would be an error of rigor," Lyxaxu said, "if we didn't press Her Excellence on this point. She put great confidence in Nayauru's willingness to wait. She was wrong. That's all I mean to say—"

Tain Hu snapped over him. "That's not all you mean. You're undermining."

"Vultjag." Oathsfire, glaring over the rim of his beer. "You're not pissing in the woods anymore. This is a council of peers. Show some respect."

Tain Hu's mailed arms made an angry carillon on the arms of her seat. "Baru Fisher braved scurvy and starvation while you wasted her treasury on bowmen and fur. If you had a fraction of her courage or conviction you'd say what you want plainly—"

"We all want the same thing." Lyxaxu, laughing, raised his hands. "Vultjag, please."

"Is that so? Is that right, Lyxaxu?" Tain Hu came halfway out of her seat as she pointed to Erebog, as if the gesture came up out of the earth like a quake. "Let's check for an *error of rigor,* shall we? Erebog—you want what he wants? You'd like to palm the Fairer Hand and take her back home to hold until she's useful for kingmaking?"

Erebog sniffed at the inelegance of the question. "I share Lyxaxu's concern. Her Excellence misjudged Nayauru's intent. But it's clear to me that we owe our good position to the actions of the Coyote, and I understand that credit lies with her."

I wish, Baru thought, that they would all just shut up and do as I say.

The rebel dukes had all agreed to meet in a Haraerod longhouse to take counsel. Tomorrow they would need to speak to Nayauru and Ihuake with one united voice. Tonight—

Well, tonight they made Baru despair of the very possibility.

"You mean," Oathsfire said, "you owe *your* good position. There were Stakhieczi fighters in your land, weren't there, Erebog? This man Dziransi, emissary of the Mansion Hussacht, come south from their hidden fastness to speak with us at long last—how did he come to be there? Who would you have turned to for protection, if the Coyote hadn't come to open your roads and clear out your bandits? Would the Duchy Erebog be the Mansion Erebog now?"

Not without a certain sharpness, Oathsfire.

Lyxaxu shot Oathsfire a warning glare—cautioning him not to play that angle yet, perhaps.

No need: the Crone ignored him. "Immaterial. What matters now is that we court Nayauru away from Treatymont."

"Court her away?" Unuxekome laughed low in his belly. "We all know Nayauru. She'll get in bed with both sides, and then continue doing whatever she pleases."

"Tsk." Erebog flicked a speck of lint from the sleeve of her gown. "You mistake her appetites for her politics. If I'd had Autr and Sahaule as neighbors in my youth, I'd have gone hunting, too."

"We could have had Oathsfire's child in her by now. That would tie her to us." Unuxekome opened a hand to Baru, as if to pull on the rope of her regard. He'd greeted her like an old shipmate, and stayed late to hear her war stories. "It's not too late to arrange an alliance by marriage."

"You're as eligible as I am." Oathsfire scowled. "You think marriage would bind her? She'd get a child on me and set him in my place."

"Perhaps," Erebog said silkily, "you should be the last one in this council to speak to the trustworthiness of marriage."

Baru missed the ilykari priestess, her ledger of secrets, her hushed temple drowned in olive oil and perilous lamplight. This damn conspiracy was missing its keystone. All that remained were the unsteady arching ambitions of the dukes.

Ah, but—hadn't *she* volunteered to be that keystone, at that river house, on that bloody shore? Hadn't she declared herself the Fairer Hand?

"Enough." Baru leaned forward into the circle of redwood chairs. "I've read the ledgers—"

"At least I divorced mine," Oathsfire hissed. "Instead of arranging for a quiet disappearance far away north, in the mansion of someone I decided I loved more."

"I said *enough!*" Baru's voice set Oathsfire back in his seat and drew a little twitch of the lips from Erebog. "It's true that the winter ate our treasury. But we invested well. Our coin bought food and arms for thousands. The Coyote's efforts in the Midlands saved tens of thousands more from starvation. We have a commanding position. Now we need to leverage our gains."

All the dukes watched her in sharp attentive silence. Baru felt the greatest pressure from Lyxaxu—and Erebog, who had never sat in council with her before.

There was nowhere in the world, Baru thought, no collection of lords or lovers, that did not have its own politics.

"You know these dukes better than I." She would give Lyxaxu a little here, a sidelong acknowledgment of her error. "How can we set Nayauru and Ihuake at peace, and win them both together? Will their clients follow them?"

Control of Aurdwynn now balanced on the Midlands in every way that mattered: geography, trade, strength of arms. To win the summer, the rebels had to turn the Midlands against Treatymont, against the shadow of distant Falcrest and its rising retaliation.

"Not with our treasury, it seems," Tain Hu murmured. Oathsfire rolled his eyes.

Unuxekome rubbed his wrists. "She's right. We don't have the bank-roll left for a long war, especially if it comes to siege at Treatymont. The sea lanes are open—they can bring in relief by ship."

Baru had been gnawing at this problem. They needed revenue, and that would mean either harsh taxation—killing the very popular support that had brought her here—or pillage. Pillage would work in the short run, but it went against Baru's goals in the long.

"We must show our strength." Erebog's kindling-crackle voice touched on memories of Iriad elders in whispered council, in times before plague swept Taranoke. "Before Falcrest's ships arrive. A demonstration of force that will swing Ihuake and Nayauru to us."

"We have cavalry," Oathsfire said, and then, with a grudging glance at Unuxekome, "and many ships. Perhaps a sortie on the Horn Harbor—"

A cry of alarm came from the longhouse's door. Baru leapt to her feet almost as quickly as Tain Hu. Two of Unuxekome's ilykari, seal-shaped women in iron-mordant green, had seized an old man in the broadcloth cloak of an Ihuake ducal levy. They called out in Urun to their duke; Baru did not know the words.

Lyxaxu let go of his knife. "Well spotted. A talented disguise."

The gray-bearded man began to laugh. "Too talented," he croaked. "Harried all the way from Treatymont, hounded through wood and vale with but one loyal man to spot me, and for this? I should have stayed!"

He began to cough, a dry aspirated sound, not so different from his mirth. Baru recognized the cough with a thrill of fear.

"Xate Olake," Tain Hu breathed.

Baru reached the old man first, Tain Hu barely a step behind her. "Release him," she commanded the ilykari. "He's ours."

The spymaster-duke of Treatymont, twin brother to the Jurispotence of Aurdwynn, stumbled forward into the rebel circle. Exhaustion had carved the lines around his eyes deep, runes of mirth or fury.

I wonder, Baru thought, if you killed Muire Lo; and the thought had teeth.

Duchess Erebog leaned forward in her chair. "Olake? Is that you, you old fox? I thought you'd died three years ago."

"I would have died three *days* ago, if it weren't for that Stakhi cripple Yawa sent to guide me. Never seen a finer woodsman. The Phantom Duke, foraging and bolting like a deer!" He leaned on Baru and, pulling her along like a cane, limped toward a chair. "I lost Treatymont. Cattlson's given birth to a brood of these demons he calls Clarified. They ripped my network up by the roots. Like they could smell a spy just by a sniff of his breath." He collapsed into Baru's seat, drawing his cloak around him. "Yawa decided to 'arrest' me before they could. She tipped me off in time to flee. And—" When he smiled his eyes glittered like winter gems in the hair of his face. "She sent me with a gift."

From beneath his cloak he drew a drinking horn, uncapped it, and poured a stream of dark beer onto the floorboards. "This," he said, reaching into the horn, "is the fruit of all her subterfuge. Cattlson still believes she's loyal. Her cruelty is all the proof he needs. And that keeps her in his inner circle."

Xate Olake offered the circle a bead of wax and wood. "In here, written in our most private code, lies the Masquerade's strategy of retaliation. Their plan to crush the rebellion."

The dukes leaned forward in silent anticipation.

Baru, unwilling to let Xate Olake command all their attention, spoke. "What will we need to crush them in turn?"

Xate Olake's gaze met hers. She felt her palms prickle, and remembered the threat of slow poison, remembered his farewell: *make yourself worth an antidote.*

"The Fairer Hand." He passed the bead of secrets from one hand to the other and his eyes gleamed orange and blue in the torchlight. "We heard that you had made yourself queen of the rebellion."

"I made myself a rallying cry." (How wearisome it had become to see Unuxekome and Oathsfire meet each others' eyes at that word, *queen*.) "As I promised you."

"And it was well done. Come Falcrest's stroke, we will need a united Aurdwynn." Xate Olake looked around the gathered traitors with deep and unhidden weariness. "Governor Cattlson plans to end the rebellion in the first days of summer, with a single, decisive strike into the North. Nothing can stop him but the cavalry and phalanxes of the Midlands duchies. So tomorrow we must break the Traitor's Qualm, or see ourselves undone."

He grinned at them through the hush, filthy, hairy, matted. "You all remember the Traitor's Qualm, don't you?"

LATER, when at last the council broke, Tain Hu came over to them and knelt to murmur. "Duke Lachta."

"Vultjag." The old man ruffled Tain Hu's hair. "You look strong, niece. Visited Ko's grave on my way north. Had to pretend to be a madman to get in past the groundskeep. I wish the old warhawk could see us now . . . rebels again, at last."

"You were in Treatymont. I wondered if—" Tain Hu glanced at Baru, continued in a rush. "Word of our rebellion had all winter to spread around the Ashen Sea. Was there any sign of—by ship, perhaps, or even a letter, a symbol? Some mark left for your eyes?"

Xate Olake's eyes hardened. "No," he said. "No. I think we should be thankful for that."

Baru made a note to chase the matter, once the council was past, once the Midlands were won. But there was a rawness in both of them that seemed to beg for space. "I'll give you privacy," she said, and left Tain Hu to speak with this man who was her uncle by marriage to a woman now years dead.

Tain Ko. Why did she know that name? Who had mentioned it before? Why could she remember the voices of the Iriad elders but not—well: as a child she had never been quite so often drunk.

Erebog caught her at the door. In the street behind the old duchess a file of her guard waited with bright torches, their tabards red with the symbol of the clay-fired man. "Your Excellence."

"Your Grace." Baru caught herself against the doorframe.

"Fascinating to see you in council." How frail the Crone looked, snow-haired and spotted with age. How ancient and forbidding her eyes. Nothing like Xate Yawa's sharp brilliant stare—no, Erebog had eyes of dry bone, eyes of scurvy and desperate cold and rime on stone. "Lyxaxu told me so much about you. Interesting to see what he gets wrong."

Baru made to kiss her hand, as Xate Yawa had taught her. Erebog declined with curled fingers. "No pleasantries. We each have our own work to attend. I wanted to tell you—"

Baru, wary of yielding too much authority, wary too of her own instinct toward deference, arched a brow and waited.

"Do nothing out of love." Her smile had a little death in it: not a threat, not a warning. Only the sense that she had grown old, that she felt her fire burning low, and chose to speak plainly. It cost her nothing. "I loved a prince once, far away in the mountains. I loved him without any calculation or reserve. That error still dogs me."

Not personal advice, Baru understood now, not among nobility. Who—it was driving her *mad*—who had tried to tell her about this other sort of power, the power of blood and line? Tain Hu? No, she would remember that, she always did. Someone else . . .

"I have the instruments I need to go forward. I ask for no king yet."

"But you will. I want a future for my lineage in Aurdwynn, and that future needs a ruler who can command these hungry rabid men. So." Erebog drew back a step, into the circle of her waiting spearmen. "Be cold, Your Excellence."

"I am," Baru said. A great wall within her shifted a little, and began to crack. What came through it was the urge to laugh. "I am."

She stood there by the door as Erebog's retinue left, waiting for Tain Hu. Unuxekome came out of the longhouse, flushed and breathing heavily, and shook his head at her. "I miss sailing." He went off into the dark without escort.

Baru thought about going after him; she missed sailing, too. But it would be unsafe in too many ways.

A ND then it was the vital day.
   They sat for their council in the Hill House, on the little rise at Haraerod's center where long ago a mutinous Maia warlord had planted her banner and, liking the way it moved in the breeze, said *come, rest and sing; I will make a safe place for joy.* In a council room of redwood and marble the Haraerod town guard prepared eleven high-backed chairs beneath eleven standards. A comet for Vultjag, a stony peak for Lyxaxu, a mill for Oathsfire, a sail for Unuxekome, a man cast of clay for Erebog. There the rebel north; and then the Midlands, a steer's head for Ihuake, a swollen reservoir for Nayauru, a spearhead for Pinjagata, a gleaming crystal of salt for Autr, a rearing stallion, impaled, for Sahaule.

And an open hand for Baru, though the hand was Stakhi pale, not the color of her skin at all.

When Nayauru entered with her consorts and her retinue Baru stared, astounded by the instant of recognition, the repair of frayed memories and half-built connections. Idiot, she thought, idiot, idiot, why didn't you *remember*? But it didn't matter now—the recognition had come too late. Nayauru had come at Baru sidelong, sly, and found a way to map out her blind spots, to bait her with a chum of pride and vanity and observe the shape of her teeth when she bit. The Dam-builder had made her own designs out of the powers and principles Baru disdained, and thus escaped notice.

But now Baru had marked her as an equal. Now Baru could see Nayauru's own blindnesses in turn, her neglect of detail, her trust in ferocity and passion and the noble virtues over subtlety and the sly arrangement of common things like coin.

If she could be won—if she could just be won—ah, but that was a dangerous hope.

The Dam-builder met Baru's eyes. Her control was perfect: Baru obtained nothing from them. Over her shoulder Oathsfire pulled at his beard and looked uncomfortable.

Ihuake came last, a silent power who hushed them all with the stormcloud weight of her presence. She had years on Nayauru, and all the authority that came with them; she was rich in dress and gem and bracelet, in the strength of her retinue, in the hush that she trailed as everyone saw the fury in her, yoked up and ready to be set to work like a prize bull. Duke Pinjagata marched at her side, a living lance, his strangling hands loose and ready.

"So." Baru took the initiative. "Let us begin."

At once it all went awry. Unuxekome lifted a hand in caution. "No one else should speak until an ilykari has blessed our meeting."

Autr Brinesalt, sprawled and massive, traded glances with Sahaule Horsebane across their beloved Nayauru's seat. "We are not all rebels yet." He adjusted himself, contemptuous, ferociously strong. "Treatymont would permit no ilykari blessings."

"Treatymont would have no meeting here at all," Lyxaxu said. He had come into the council with a terrible focus, the aspect of the fox that he sometimes showed.

"Why not?" Sahaule opened his hands. "We've come to settle the dispute between Nayauru and Ihuake, the dispute that Vultjag's bandits"—his eyes flickered to Baru, to Tain Hu, dressed in leather and mail—"interfered in. This is a legal peace conference between the great powers of the Midlands Alliance. You are the intruders here."

"A technicality." Old Erebog waved the young duke's words away. She'd taken long night council with Xate Olake, but showed no sign of weariness. The Crone had stamina for matters of state. "They gave you freedom to meet us only so that you could demonstrate your loyalty by *refusing* to meet us. If you wanted to play at loyalty, you chose unwisely."

Nayauru, gowned in white, framed between her two mighty consorts, made a soft sound of mirth. "Wisdom in choice? This from the Duchess of Clay, whose wisdom left her only the choice between starvation or rebellion? You sold your allegiance to Lyxaxu for wheat and citrus."

"Ah." Erebog reclined, weighing the point in one gloved palm. Baru fought a chill at the cold empty disregard in her eyes—a skull's patience for the passions of the young. "My neighbor came to my aid, and so I rewarded his loyalty. You attacked your neighbor Ihuake to curry favor with a foreign throne. How should *you* be rewarded, hm?"

This had to be controlled.

Baru spoke into the briefest gap before Nayauru's retort. "The Masquerade thrives on information." Control the space. Use height and voice and strength of limb to pull at their regard. If she seemed foreign all the better—she would hook them and draw them up out of the sea of their own politics. "You all knew this. You came to this council knowing that Treatymont would hear of it. You came knowing that you committed an act of open sedition." She looked to Ihuake, to Nayauru, then to their clients. "You knew that this council would meet to answer one question: will the dukes of the Midlands join us in revolt?"

Lyxaxu caught her eye. Shook his head fractionally. She knew she'd erred even before Ihuake spoke, her voice like distant hoofbeat: "I came for another question." She looked to Nayauru with the distance and menace of a thunderhead. "A question for my ally, my sister-by-oath. For the woman who has shown us all how greatly she hopes to be queen."

Silence in the hall as Ihuake breathed out, in, spoke again: "Why did you betray me?"

Ah, well. So much for control. Baru let the dukes go.

Ihuake excoriated Nayauru for her betrayal—why had she attacked? Ah, it was purely self-defense, of course; Nayauru's landlords, terrified of the Fairer Hand's hold on the peasantry and sickened by the crimes of the interloping Coyote, had demanded retaliation against Ihuake. Unuxekome called *that* a lie—everyone knew Nayauru's great game. Autr and Sahaule rose up in rage at Unuxekome; Nayauru reined them in, to seem gracious, but still the rebel North accused her of secret collaboration with the Masquerade. How could she have betrayed Aurdwynn's ancient need for freedom? Was she so desperate for a throne?

On and on and on.

Baru listened with half her mind, searching through her points of leverage. They needed the damn Midlands to beat Cattlson. What gave the Midlands its livelihood? Craftsmen. Cattle, soldiers, and clean water. Trade—trade both ways: raw materials from North to coast, food and imports from coast to North.

Forget the bonds of blood and honor. Those were Nayauru's tools. Chase the structures:

Whether the Midlands fell in with the revolt or the Masquerade, they would suffer the heaviest price. They would pay on the battlefield and in the market. And for all their power, Nayauru and Ihuake needed to keep their landlords and merchants content. Rule of Aurdwynn entire had to be secondary to strong rule of their own land.

Like Tain Hu before her futures contracts, they were being asked to assume too much risk. Instability cut them more deeply than the forested North. So they looked to the power with the greatest stability— the Masquerade, its center of strength distant and protected. They would not be drawn away from that stanchion. The rebellion would fail.

So if Baru could not offer them stability—ah.

She surfaced from the trance in the midst of an argument about marriages—someone had called Nayauru *licentious,* an Aphalone word, a Falcrest word. No matter. She had the gage of it now. She took control.

"What you risk," Baru said into the clamor, speaking as if she were the only voice, "is an Aurdwynn without dukes."

One more moment of clamor and then silence fell. Lyxaxu smiled a fox-tooth smile, understanding, while the others looked at her in bafflement.

"Explain yourself," Ihuake said.

"The people want to be free." She held out one hand, palm open, turned up. "I have given the serfs and the landlords the thought of life without you. If you stand against them, they will rise up and they will destroy you. You could turn to the Masquerade for safety, as they have always wanted." She stood, so that she could move her voice lower. "Cattlson told me that they needed the dukes afraid of the people, and the people afraid of the Masquerade. But now you are afraid of me, and the people are tired of fear."

She extended her hand, offering them the invisible weight balanced on it, the fulcrum of history. *Baru Fisher, beloved of Devena.* "Falcrest came to power by overthrowing its own aristocracy. They wrote the *Handbook of Manumission* in the blood of dukes and kings. You sit here thinking that perhaps Treatymont and Falcrest can offer you safe power, but they will discard you like leavings when your time is finished. They want to tear down the duchies and polish Aurdwynn flat like the mirror of a Stakhi telescope. Turn to me instead. Turn to the people you have ruled. Only we can secure your future."

A hush. An instant for Baru to feel a little satisfaction.

And then Nayauru Dam-builder spoke, Nayauru whose words broke the silence like snakebite.

"You offered my people nothing but rapine and savagery." She stood to match Baru, dark and intent, her youth ferocious, like an obsidian knife, a Taranoki blade. "I went to war with Ihuake my neighbor, my ally, to save my people from the grind of Masquerade march. It was an honest war, fought by spear and stonework, by the sworn armsman and the levy. And you, Baru Fisher, daughter of a foreign land—how did you answer? You set your Coyote on my forests and villages. On families and children who never chose to fight."

She spat on the floorboards. "What your soldiers did at Imadyff cannot be argued away. I heard of men disemboweled and mothers burnt. No words in any tongue can disguise that."

"War has never spared the innocent," Lyxaxu said softly.

"No." Nayauru's lips curled in disgust. "But neither has it pretended to love them. I will never give my people to Baru Fisher, who conjures power out of lies."

THE first day of council disintegrated in abject failure.

Tain Hu tried to catch Baru on the way out. "See to the Coyote," Baru commanded, and shrugged her off. Frustration and humiliation moved her—and desperation, too, the premonition of the test ahead driving her to solitary action. She had promised the Midlands. She would *have* the Midlands—by her wit and her will she would deliver it, without Nayauru's pacts of marriage or noble covenants, without even Tain Hu's counsel.

If she couldn't manage that, what hope was there?

Baru marched on Duchess Ihuake's camp, her stubbly red-eyed Sentiamut guards shifting uncomfortably between polished plumed ranks of the Cattle Duchess's spearmen. Duke Pinjagata stood with the guards, inspecting their spears; when he saw Baru he raised a hand in salute. "Evening."

"Your Grace."

"Your Coyotes fought a good campaign. Spared me some ugly work. I'm grateful." He plucked a splinter of ash from a spearshaft and glared at it. "I hear you're marching with Stakhieczi jagata. Gave me my noble name. Curious to see their kit."

Baru nodded at the doors of the duchess Ihuake's guesthouse. "And is she grateful, too?"

Pinjagata turned to consider her for a few silent moments. "Devena guide you," he said.

Alone and unarmed, Baru went into the duchess's longhouse.

Of all the Midlands powers, surely Ihuake had the strongest reason to cast for the rebellion. Nayauru had attacked her unprovoked, unwarned—the Masquerade had supported Nayauru in that war. Honor would turn her to the rebellion, or wrath, or greed. She had to come over. Her ranks of cavalry and Pinjagata's spearmen could turn the war.

She *had* to.

Duchess Ihuake waited in her audience hall, seated at the center of a marble tilework, a mandala in white and red, a whirlpool in stone.

"Kneel," the duchess commanded.

Baru, choking on pride, on too many days in the woods, hesitated. But her hesitation bought her nothing.

Ihuake, gorgeously fat, skin the color of fallow earth, golden bracelets chased with patterns of steer and horse, all the picture of imperial Tu Maia wealth and beauty, waited with a gracious smile. How powerless Baru must look: peasant-thin, muscled like a laborer, without title or children, without any authority at all.

Baru knelt and bowed her head.

Ihuake crossed her arms. "You've built a rebellion out of shadows." She had a rich voice, a ruler's voice. "Tricks of ink and paper wealth. Phantom armies of unarmored woodsmen. The promise of a marriageable hand without sated lovers or proof of fertility. I listened to you in that council, prophesying an end to dukes, and I thought: perhaps she has only bluster."

Baru opened her mouth and the duchess, frowning, raised a hand. A guard clapped his spear against the stone floor.

She was a foreign-born commoner in a duke's court. She hadn't been given leave to speak.

"Duchess Nayauru betrayed me, and I want her skinned for it." The Cattle Duchess's treasury chimed softly as she moved. "But I understand her reasons. She wants my herds, my grazing land—just as I want her dams and mills. She wants her children to be my grandchildren, and my name bent at the foot of her throne. She thought she had a chance to claim all this, and to earn favor in Treatymont's eyes. Rebellions are opportunities. What opportunities can you present me, Baru Fisher?"

She opened a hand in permission.

Baru spoke without anger, without pleading, with desperate control. "You gave the Army of the Coyote freedom to roam your land. You gave us men and supplies. In return, we defeated Nayauru when she attacked you. Your investment was rewarded."

Ihuake waited a moment, as if Baru's thought were incomplete. When Baru said no more, she spoke:

"But my debt to you is only a shadow. It exists only as a belief. Perhaps I choose to disbelieve it: now I could give you to Treatymont, and in reward, they would annihilate Nayauru and grant me her land. Or I could listen to her bleating, accept her reparations, and join her in hunting your Coyote down." Ihuake eyed Baru like a gangly foal, the disappointing issue of a prize stud. "I came to this council to hear the rebellion's offer. But you cannot outbid the Masquerade with shadows, O Fairer Hand. We remember what happened to the last southern duke who declared for you: Radaszic's people bow to the stag banner now. We remember the Fools' Rebellion, and the fate of those who leapt too soon. If you want me to risk war against Treatymont, you must offer me *substance*."

The Traitor's Qualm.

Baru set her jaw and met the duchess's eyes. She considered and discarded one last plea: *is a free Aurdwynn worth nothing to you?*

Aurdwynn had not been kind to dukes who spent blood for ideas. Aurdwynn had been kind to those who spent blood for power.

Aurdwynn and the world. Taranoke, after all, did not rule Falcrest.

"I hear your question," she said. "Look to my answer soon."

24

THAT night, Baru called Xate Olake to her tent for counsel. The Phantom Duke came in while she ate, found her picking apart a roasted chicken bare-handed, licking at the salt.

"Sit," she commanded.

Olake settled himself, groaning, across from her. "Winter has ruined your Incrastic manners." He stripped his gloves and scanned the tent with practiced caution. "Or perhaps it was Tain Hu that made you feral."

"Duchess Vultjag's decorum needs no description." That made him smile. She cracked a thigh bone. "I wonder if my winter tried me as deeply as yours."

"The scurvied wilderness or the Treatymont abattoir? Hard to know." He closed his eyes and wound his cloak tighter. "I had an ear on every wall and an eye in every lamp. And I watched it all undone." Here, like strangled punctuation, the sound of his hissing laugh. "You should have seen the streets this spring. Blood in the meltwater."

Baru set the two broken pieces of bone down and licked marrow from her teeth. "Did you order the death of Muire Lo?"

Xate Olake opened his eyes a little. In the dark his blue-slit gaze colored like a bruise. "The Masquerade battle plan I brought. Only Yawa and I can read the code it's written in. Remember that."

"Is that a yes?"

"It's a reminder, child. I've played games of blood for a long, long time. I know how to keep myself valuable."

She stripped the meat from a wing. "If you and your sister killed Muire Lo, then you want me to believe that it was necessary."

Xate Olake gave a weary sigh. "Forget the dead."

"I will keep my own accounts."

"I said *forget him*!" Olake's roar made her start, and she snapped the wing between her fists. "I killed him, or I didn't, and it was necessary, or it wasn't. The boy's life doesn't matter now. If you cannot win the

Midlands, Cattlson's attack on the River Inirein will succeed, and his troops will have a highway into the heart of rebel territory. That harbor at Welthony where you drowned so many marines? It will be flooded by thousands more. Marching up on us like angry revenants. Aurdwynn hangs in the balance."

"The Inirein. Interesting." She sat in thought for a moment, moving pieces across her mental map. "That's his plan? He'll put all his strength east, to take the river?"

"He plans to use the river to move troops north into our heartlands. He's pinned his whole strategy on it. If we can meet him on the flood-plain at Sieroch, just short of the river—" The lines around his eyes crinkled, like writing translating itself. "One decisive battle will give us the war."

"If we have the spearmen and the horse to win."

"If we have a united Midlands behind us."

Baru set aside the chicken carcass and raised herself to a crouch, balanced on her toes and fingertips. "Convenient," she said. "I've been going over the books. We've spent ourselves to death. Unless we resort to wholesale pillage, there's not enough left in our treasuries to campaign through another winter. Not even enough to last until autumn, if we have to besiege the coastal forts. Or Treatymont itself."

The old man held her in a wary regard. "We won't need another winter if we can defeat Cattlson in the open field."

"Or someone knows that our only hope is a single decisive battle, and they sent you here with a false battle plan to draw us out."

Xate Olake's wry gaze reminded Baru of the years he'd spent in Treatymont, bricking the foundations of rebellion, playing long games. "What Falcresti chemistry or coercion could do that? They would have to pluck my guts out my eyes before they could break me. When I betray rebellions, child, I do it only by my own will."

"And your sister? The one who fed you Cattlson's plan?" Baru did not hide the menace in her smile. "Perhaps it is *her* will."

The Duke of Lachta hesitated, and Baru thought: Ah—even you doubt her. Even you believe that no one can lie so ably, so completely, about her true loyalties.

But Baru knew it was possible.

"We have no choice," Xate Olake said. "Either we unite the Midlands and march to meet Cattlson, or we wait out the summer and run our treasury dry."

Baru took up her writing lantern, the sturdy little oil-burner she'd trusted all winter, and lifted it between them. The light put shadows in every crag and fold of the duke Lachta's face. He looked older than the world.

"Duchess Nayauru will never join a rebellion I lead," she said. "She cannot forgive the Coyote. She will not abandon her dream of a reborn Tu Maia empire."

Lachta held up a hand against the glare of the lamp. It made a fingered shadow on his face, like a raven wing. "If she goes with Cattlson, so will Autr and Sahaule. They will counterbalance Ihuake and Pinjagata and we will never win a battle."

Baru looked at the canny old man in her tent and thought, a little ruefully, that he was too old and too clever for her, that it would be the height of arrogance to think she could surprise him, impress him.

But arrogance or no, she spoke.

"We can solve all our problems in one stroke. We're running out of money to sustain a campaign. We cannot allow Nayauru and her consorts to go over to Treatymont. And Ihuake will not join us unless I can demonstrate my strength. So—"

Baru wiped grease and marrow on the hips of her trousers. "Tomorrow night we murder Nayauru, Autr, and Sahaule in their camps, kill everyone who marched with them, and order their duchies pillaged for funds. Ihuake will receive Nayauru's richest lands as a gift. Duchess Erebog will take the rest."

So easy, so decisive, spoken that way.

So much blood in so few words.

Xate Olake's lips curled. It was not disgust. "I was afraid," he said, "that you would insist on finding a subtler way."

Baru selected another marrow-rich bone and felt for the breakpoint. "Did you really give me a slow poison last summer?"

"Child," Xate Olake said, with a kind of wary fondness, "I thought you would bring yourself to ruin without my help."

SHE called for Tain Hu, then stopped the messenger before he could take three steps. It would be unsafe to see her now, unsafe to look her in the eye and command her, or to wait in silence for her hunting look, her golden eyes searching for a path in. It would be unsafe.

"Bring me an ilykari instead," she commanded. "Someone trusted."

The priestess who came must have been one of Unuxekome's divers— she had the broad-shouldered, long-legged look of a deep swimmer. It could have been a coincidence that she had Baru's Maia skin, or some ill-thought attempt to make her comfortable. She looked a little like Nayauru, and much more like Cousin Lao.

"Rest," Baru ordered. She'd strung up the oil lantern and it cast flickering shadows like a sickly sun.

The woman sat in silence. Baru watched her arrange herself, tracing the geometry of muscle and limb with uneasy fascination. She was strong, tall; she had power in the breath that filled her chest, in the line of her thighs. Through labor she had made herself able. A small ability, in the scheme of the world—only the power to dive deep, climb high, to win laughing contests of strength and draw eyes that admired that strength. Not a power that would bankrupt dukes or change the names of islands. But power enough to rule a tent, to surprise Baru with violence or other sudden acts.

Baru wished she'd cleaned out the ruins of the chicken.

The priestess waited in contemplative peace. A devotee of Wydd, then. "What do you do?"

The priestess frowned for a moment as she parsed Baru's awkward Iolynic. Her eyes were strange and round, Stakhi-shaped. "I am a pearl diver and a midwife."

"You've come a long way for war. You must be a mother, a sister, a daughter. How do you know your family is safe?"

"The same way as all the other fighters. My great-family shares its house. There are a hundred hands among them. A few young men and women can be spared in time of need."

For all her whirling disquiet, Baru could not help but note: Cairdine Farrier would be fascinated. The Imperial Republic thought of families as a man and a woman, thought of the mother and father as fixed necessities. But here, as on Taranoke, they had always practiced other ways— useful ways, methods that liberated strong young hands for labor and war—

Not so fascinated. He would only be curious how to repair it.

The thought curled back around into the heart of her unease. Suddenly she wanted to weep: she could not escape it. "I have committed a terrible crime," she said, voice firm, controlled, machined to a polish. "So terrible that I feel I can do anything, commit any sin, betray any trust, because no matter what ruin I make of myself, it cannot be worse than what I have already done."

"Speak," the ilykari murmured.

Baru tried, and it all caught in her lungs, a tumor, an avalanche, a drifting Oriati mine. The *size* of it, the depth of the roots, the test she faced, the doom she had brought down on herself.

"I cannot," she said. "I cannot speak."

"What do *you* do?" the priestess asked. Perhaps this was some method of Wydd, turning her own questions back on her to reveal her secrets.

"I try to save my home," Baru rasped. "Everything I do. For Taranoke."

"You've come a long way to do it," the priestess said, and left the rest of the mirrored question unspoken, the *mother* and *sister* and *daughter*, the *how do you know your family is safe*?

"Too far," Baru choked, unable to weep, unable to want to, to make herself believe it could ever be safe or right. "I've come too far."

A T daybreak she went to Tain Hu's tent to order the killings.

She found the duchess Vultjag engaged in a curious ritual with Ake Sentiamut. They knelt across from each other on the ground cloth, a wooden game board between them. Baru had studiously avoided learning the game of rule—learning would surely involve losing a number of games, which would make Tain Hu insufferable—but she knew the principle: pawns claimed land, nobles took power from pawns to fight other nobles. But here Tain Hu's nobles seemed fed by something else. She read from a little leather-bound book, her lips making awkward hesitant shapes, and depending on her performance at this mysterious task, Ake smiled, or laughed, or shook her head and killed a few of Tain Hu's pawns. It must be a learning game, then—a way to keep Tain Hu's attention, penalizing or rewarding her standing in the game according to her performance in the book.

How curious they were together: Tain Hu a nighthawk, a panther, and Ake a pale white-gold fawn wrapped up in bearskin. And yet they did not act unequal.

Baru watched them in silence for a moment (the guards had not an-nounced her: in camp Coyote-men knew that crying out the Fairer Hand's presence would only mark her for assassins). Tain Hu sat with her strength coiled, her eyes sharp with concentration, and at times she spooled her unbraided hair around one finger in thought. Baru took a kind of delight in this: in the field Vultjag would never have per-mitted that gesture to slip. And so strange, too, the way she spoke to Ake, each of them interrupting the other, their gestures lively and unconsidered, their laughter free. When Tain Hu looked away, jaw set, troubled by something she had said or some problem that occupied her mind, Ake reached out and clasped her wrist with easy camaraderie—and it meant nothing more that Baru could see, asked nothing in return, disguised no secret missive or hidden maneuver.

It would be nice to stand here a while longer, and watch this world she had never been part of. But dangerous, too—

"Vultjag," Baru said. "A word."

Tain Hu startled a little, and Ake hid a laugh at that. They stood to-gether, bowing their heads, and Tain Hu dismissed her ranger-knight with a clap on her shoulder and a murmured word in Stakhi. Baru caught the secret handoff they made through the swirl of broadcloth and bearskin.

"Come," she said, more lightly than she actually felt, "don't be bash-ful. Show me."

Ake looked to Tain Hu. Vultjag arched a brow. "The Fairer Hand commands it."

So Ake gave Baru the book as she stepped out of the tent. Baru turned it over and read the title, printed in neat blocks of Iolynic: *A Primer in Aphalone, the Imperial Trade Tongue; Made Available to the People of Aurdwynn For Their Ease.*

It was like holding a centipede. She wanted to hurl it away.

Tain Hu watched her with a disinterested half smile that might, last year, have hidden from Baru her profound self-consciousness. "I'm learning to read it. So I can spy on your letters," she explained, lips half-parted, eyes sly: all her countermeasures set. "And those books you read, too. Learn what madness drives you, hm?"

Baru acted, so that she wouldn't have to think: she stepped into the tent, into Tain Hu's space, and with her own fierce eyes and confident stride seized a kind of control, in that she startled Tain Hu and made her freeze a moment.

Baru, close now, offered the book. "You said there was nothing worth taking from the enemy."

"Perhaps an item or two of note." Tain Hu clasped the book but did not take it, and for a moment they were joined by it, their fingertips not quite in contact but still mutually aware. "I have some regard for a few products of the Masquerade system. They can be useful. Or delightful."

She tucked a lock of wild hair behind her ear. It slipped loose at once.

Her damned eyes, so close, so cutting; her awful hateful unforgettable smile—and Baru already in a panic, tossed by the book, by the things about to happen. Desperate to avoid an error she terribly wanted to make, Baru seized on a blunt instrument, sniffed, said: "A few useful products, yes. They did wonders for dental hygiene."

Tain Hu laughed. "Spoiled ass. All those latrines dug, and you still complain about morning breath?" She stepped away and went to her field kit, to find a pellet of anise to chew. "How can I serve? Do you have an answer for Nayauru?"

"Why aren't you with her?"

"Hm?"

"She's proud, capable, and ambitious. Young and lovely, too. All cause for your interest."

"Undeniably true." Tain Hu tossed a pellet of anise seeds wrapped in mint. Baru caught it, fumbled, and caught it again. "Her tastes don't run to that kind of alliance, though. As I'm sure you've seen."

"That's not the sort I meant." It was easy to pretend to be cross. "Why do you all do that? Every time anyone mentions Nayauru I hear these snide asides about her love of men. She engineers majestic dams and fine roads, her troops are formidable, her ambitions plain and her alliances firm. Are you all so menaced by her that you feel the need to reduce her to a—a docklands pimp sampling from her boys?"

Tain Hu chewed for a few moments, narrow-eyed. "You respect her."

"I do. I do." Baru let herself sigh. "She's cunning. She might outplay me again."

"So how do you plan to—"

"Without any subtlety."

Tain Hu stopped chewing.

"I'm having her killed," Baru said, holding her field-general's stare. "Her, Autr, and Sahaule. Murdered in their camps tonight."

After a moment's unblinking regard, Tain Hu came forward into the center of the tent and knelt, arms braced against the earth, gold-black eyes fixed on Baru's with a ferocious loyalty that concealed nothing. Baru's heart trembled, because she saw the truth there, and the plea, too—Tain Hu's honor, her regard for Nayauru as a fellow duchess and a worthy foe, and for herself as a noblewoman who did not need midnight knives.

"My lord," Vultjag said. "As you command."

"No," Baru said, and then, more roughly, her throat choked as if by drink and smoke, "no, Vultjag, not you. I will not ask you to do it. I have other weapons to employ."

Tain Hu would not avert her eyes, would not blink, and although the danger now was different than the menace of half-open lips and panther strength, it was not less awful. "You are the Fairer Hand," she said, "and I am your field-general, oathbound to earn you victory at any price. I will not shrink from that oath." And then, her cold breaking, her voice raw and rampant: "I rule a small land, poor in wealth and arms; I have no husband and no heirs, no great alliance and no well-made dams, and thus few strengths to offer my lord beyond my cunning and my loyalty. Do not deny me the exercise of those as well."

She would not look away.

Baru, falling toward disaster, chose a lesser kind of weakness over a greater one. She took Tain Hu by the forearm, a warrior's clasp, and drew her up eye to eye. "You are my sworn instrument, my best weapon," she hissed, with all the furious strength she could manage. It was a lie, in that it concealed the truth; but it was also true. "Loyalty runs two ways, Your Grace. I would not waste my finest sword on a task better fit for poison."

Tain Hu's jaw moved in a kind of scowl, drawing up her ferocity over whatever else she felt. "My lord," she said, and was silent for a little while.

In the strength of her grip Baru felt all the gratitude Tain Hu couldn't voice.

Baru could have let the silence go on forever. But after a moment Tain Hu spoke again: "Not Xate Olake. He was the finest of spymasters in Treatymont, but his network is compromised and he needs rest. Not Oathsfire—he has no talent for subtlety. Lyxaxu might arrange it, but he . . ."

"Philosophy might impede him."

"Yes. An idealist. Erebog terrifies me—so I think the best choice must be Unuxekome."

"His ilykari?"

"Yes." Tain Hu dared a little smile. "They are accustomed to moving in secret. Certainly they have kept my confidences before—and perhaps yours, too; is it true you called Ulyu Xe to your tent for company?"

"The diver? I didn't ask her name."

Tain Hu punched her in the shoulder. "You devil."

"No!" Baru floundered. "I don't mean—I called her for counsel, not—"

"Keep your secrets, my lord." Tain Hu's smile passed. "Unuxekome is the best choice. But be very careful."

On the way out of the tent, Baru paused and looked back. "I know you could do it," she said, out of some terrible, unwise loyalty. "I do not doubt your ability, Your Grace."

The duchess bowed low, her armor sealed up again, her face wry. "Trust me to know when the best thing I can do for my lord is nothing."

THE Sea Groom's guardsmen opened the way for her, murmuring in Iolynic and Urun: *justice, justice, the fairer hand.* She found him alone at his breakfast, bundled against the morning chill. "I need to ask something of you."

He looked up from his maps and papers, smiling out of a troubled frown. "Anything," he said, not insincerely. "It's been too long since one of your plans nearly killed me. What can I do?"

She explained what Xate Olake had discovered, why Nayauru and her consorts would be their undoing, and what she'd decided to do about it. Unuxekome listened, nodding occasionally, pursing his lips once. "You will be told that this is not the Aurdwynni way," he said, once she'd finished. "That it violates ancient codes of noble conduct. Well, I lived the Fools' Rebellion, and I saw the worth of noble conduct in times of civil war. All the mortar in Aurdwynn reeks of blood."

How differently he reacted than Tain Hu. "You can arrange it, then?"

"I can, and I will. And if you'll permit it, I'll ask for something in return."

She grinned, not displeased by his forwardness. "Try me."

"I'll arrange the killing." Unuxekome put his bread and wine aside and leaned forward, wrists crossed in his lap. "And when it's done, I want you to come south with me, to Welthony."

Ah.

She'd expected this, in a sort of distant, intellectual way, though perhaps from Oathsfire. Unuxekome had asked her why she wanted to rebel, had said: *my maps say Taranoke.* He had always been kind and respectful and patient. But he was still a duke, with a mind for power.

Maybe he had found a story that ended with something he wanted more than a ship on wild sea.

"Wait, wait. Let me make my case." He held up his hands. The rope burns around his wrists had faded into a bracelet of scars. "Of course it's a selfish request. We're all thinking of the endgame, of who will be king. But your talents lie in administration, and you'll govern better with access to my ships. A husband and children will legitimize you." His eyelids flickered, lips quirked, a rogue's expression, a who-me? play at innocence. "I think it's the rational decision, Your Excellency. But I'm no accountant."

What secret had he given the ilykari priestess in the temple of oil and light? What truth could destroy him?

Why had her thoughts leapt right there? He was a duke. This was a matter of politics. Not an attack. Not from his perspective, at least.

Unuxekome watched her with calm confident eyes. She wanted to refuse outright, driven by that same instinctive sense, old as her friendship with Aminata (oh, Aminata—would she have heard, by now, of the traitor Baru Cormorant?) that her body would not be a political instrument.

Driven, also—and how secondary she had allowed this to become!—by the knowledge that this was not something she wanted. Not someone she wanted.

But she *needed* Unuxekome.

Until this conversation, she'd thought of him more as friend than an instrument. Dangerous. Stupid. Foolish—the test was so close. But if she rejected him, if she seemed intent on giving her hand to someone else, how would he react? Oathsfire had been Vultjag's rival for years after just such a rejection . . . and Baru could afford no mistakes, no errant pieces, no matter how gallant and good.

She would have to be more and more ruthless as the end approached.

Baru smiled, eyes a little hooded, voice a little low. "You'll understand, I hope, if I hear the other offers. Take some time to consider."

"I'd expect nothing less."

She should make a joke. Laugh throatily. Lift her chin or hold his gaze, to say: *keep your hopes high.*

"I want them all dead," she said. "I want it done tonight."

25

NAYAURU ruled the second day of council.

Baru made no effort to defeat her; perhaps she couldn't have, even if she'd summoned all her faculties. With Autr and Sahaule guarding her rhetorical flanks, the Dambuilder made a powerful and articulate case that the Masquerade could not be defeated, that Treatymont's patient silence had to be read as mercy—a chance for the rebel dukes to repent and commit to the one course that would earn them clemency.

That course, naturally, was turning Baru Fisher over to Xate Yawa and Cattlson.

Even knowing what was to come, Baru could not resist one last plea. "Why do you hold to your loyalty when they see your couplings as anathema?" She marked Autr and Sahaule with a gesture, but her eyes were all for Nayauru, for the young woman who could—by appearance, or ambition, or will—have been her kin. "Incrasticism would dictate the fathers of your children and the future of your line. Why hold to this loyalty?"

"Because the Masquerade will remain whether I am loyal or not." Her anger at the Army of the Coyote seemed genuine, fierce, and it colored every word she spoke. "I have other ways to fight. Methods with a chance of success. No one in the world has any hope of tearing Falcrest down from outside its walls. Even if we win, even if we drive them into the sea, they will return with honey and with wrath. We would be stronger within them, learning how to make our protests heard."

Nayauru's resemblance to mother Pinion went no deeper than her choice of partners, two men who were nothing like Salm and Solit, nothing at all. This was a terrible thought, and more terrible still was the defense Baru found herself deploying—the proof of strict limited inheritance, *one mother, one father,* and it made her ill to take comfort from it, but she could not stop. . . .

She lapsed back into silence and watched Nayauru, thinking: you are proud and fierce, and noble, and that will be the end of you. I have found your blindness, as you found mine, and it is the same, it is the power of blood.

You are noble and I am not. I am unbound by noble law. We respect each other, now, and so you will not believe I am capable of this.

But I am.

Outside, in Haraerod, in the camps and longhouses, the ilykari passed the word, to the siege engineers, the longbowmen, the riders. On out into the forest, where the waiting Coyote roused itself and began to circle.

Slaughter them tonight.

The council broke.

Baru left the chamber with singing nerves and a dry throat. Guards waited with horses for Baru and Tain Hu. She rode through Haraerod's pitted streets, clumsy and unsure on horseback, heading for her camp.

Twice Tain Hu signaled: first that they should break from the road and enter the forest, and second that they should summon more guards, perhaps Dziransi's jagata with their shining plate and long reach. Each time Baru shook her head. Nothing could be permitted to seem out of the ordinary.

She hadn't even made eye contact with Unuxekome during the council. The time and shape of the massacre was up to him.

Ake Sentiamut came out of the Coyote camp to meet them. "Riders came for you. The Duchess Nayauru requests an urgent audience. They're waiting to convey your response."

Baru thought, in Aminata's voice: *oh fuck.* "Of course. Inform them that I'll meet with the duchess back at the Hill House."

"You can't go." Tain Hu seized her shoulder, gloves ringing on mail. "Where is all your calculation? Think of the risk."

"She's probing for a trap herself." Baru looked down the valley, across the spangle of Haraerod proper, to the distant firelights of Nayauru's camp. Tain Hu's touch was a trouble and a comfort all at once. "If I refuse, she'll know what's coming."

"Then lie. Send word you're on your way, and make for the woods."

"She did not come so far through foolishness. No, I imagine we're being watched." She took a breath against the pounding of her heart. In the west, the sun had just begun to set. "But you're right—this is dangerous ground. Find Xate Olake. Ask his advice."

Tain Hu returned at a hasty gallop, reining her white charger to a noisy stop. "He knows a man who he says can see any treachery. A Stakhi woodsman who saved his life. He's sent the man ahead to the council house as a sentinel."

"Good." Baru coaxed her mare back toward the Haraerod road. "Let's go."

"Keep the camp quiet," she called to Ake. "The usual vigilance. I expect no alarm tonight."

TOWNSPEOPLE with scurvy-red eyes and wary faces, bent over the last work of the day, watched Baru, Tain Hu, and their guards come back in to council. In the dying rustle of near-dark their hoofbeats seemed profane, disruptive.

Somewhere out there, Unuxekome's plan loped toward the smell of blood.

They came to the cobbled square, the council house, its windows full of lamplight. Tain Hu chose two of her riders. "Go ahead. Look for treachery."

Baru, itching and uncomfortable on her cantankerous mount, imagining all the ways Unuxekome could fail, chewed a bloody flap off the inside her cheek.

"Easy," Tain Hu murmured. "The spear is cast. Let it fly." Baru nodded slowly, counting her breaths, and spared Tain Hu a grateful glance. The duchess touched her shoulder in reassurance.

The report came—nothing amiss. Nayauru and her honor guard waited inside the house. There was no sign of Xate Olake's man.

"Let me go in your place," Tain Hu said. "Let me spring the trap."

"You?" Baru stuck her jaw out, scowling a serious Vultjag scowl, and rolled her shoulders in mockery. "Who'd ever mistake you for me?"

Tain Hu's grin passed in a blink. "Be serious. She'll take your life."

"She's marked me as an equal. She won't resort to treachery."

"You don't know that." Vultjag's voice dropped. "I vowed to die for you—don't make a liar of me."

Baru inhaled deeply, remembering dinner on the River House's balcony in Welthony, waiting for the harbor to begin exploding. She had done this before, and survived. "We go together. Ride with me."

They crossed the square in the rising dark. Great black clouds moved to the west, shadowing the sunset.

Movement flickered in the Hill House. Dark shapes occluded the lamplight—a sudden agitation of shadow, an eruption of violent incomprehensible angles. As if a caldera god had come up out of the earth armed with ash and obsidian. Baru froze, expecting bowmen in the windows, from the rooftops, or the detonation of Oriati explosives buried beneath the square, or quicklime to blind and burn—

The doors of the longhouse opened. Duchess Nayauru stood in a wedge of lamplight, her billowing dress soaked in luminance.

When, Unuxekome? *When?*

The Dam-builder stepped forward into the square. Light fell across her face, her proud Maia nose, her oiled hair, across the bubbles of white froth that sputtered and popped on her lips and beneath her nose.

Whatever she meant to say, fury or hate or regret, came out as a gurgle. Her last breath left wet and desperate.

She fell facedown onto the cobblestones. The crunch of bone carried.

"What?" Tain Hu murmured, as the Vultjag guards cried out to each other. "*What?*"

Through the open doors Baru saw the council chamber, the circled chairs and the eleven glorious banners. Full of corpses in Nayauru's colors. They had died in agony, clawing at each other, trying to get to the doors.

Looking at the fallen woman, at the noble dream dead on the paving stones, she felt not the littlest triumph.

Tain Hu hissed in warning.

Out of the massacre walked a man, a wet rag wrapped around his face, his hair long and brilliant red. (Could it be—!? No, no, not here, not him—) He wore filthy woodsman's garb and walked with a hunched, painful gait, folded up around his chest.

"Xate Olake's woodsman," Baru guessed, raising a hand to hold back the guards.

Tain Hu's voice, tight with alarm: "What happened here?"

The agony of the dead said they'd been killed by gas, the kind of war-poison whispered of in stories about Falcrest's Metademe. But how would a Stakhi woodsman arm himself with a weapon so—

A Stakhi man? *Could* it be?

No. Surely not.

The man loped away from the council house with eerie smooth steps. Baru shivered in some kind of corporeal recognition. It was not who she'd thought, not at all.

But—

He unwrapped the rag from his face (it came away sticky, rank with chemicals) and took a slow breath. Lifted pale features, skin reddened by a terrible acid burn, toward the fading sun.

Tiny precise muscles moved in his neck.

He looked to Baru.

"The Fairer Hand," he said in Stakhi, and then, in heavily accented Aphalone, a perfect counterfeit: "The work is done. Tell Xate Olake I did not fail him."

He coughed wetly and touched his chest, where the crossbow bolt had wounded him and sent him into the river.

"Who is this?" Tain Hu asked. It had grown dark enough to see the fires that ringed Haraerod behind her, towers of dirty light to the west and southwest, where Nayauru and her allies had camped.

Baru stared in paralyzed silence at the Clarified remora, at Purity Cartone.

THE ilykari killed Nayauru's allies with their own horses. Disguised as maidservants and laborers from Haraerod, the ilykari passed unchallenged through the Nayauru bloc's camp and the forests beyond. A phantom army buried in the social context, marking sentries, passing messages in the careful steganography of the persecuted.

At their direction Oathsfire's siege engineers moved into the woods to the southwest and the town to the northeast. Began to set firebreaks with quicklime, naphtha, and oils.

Smoke would start the bloodbath. Poison would seal it.

Nayauru's forces had brought warhorses: a show of strength, and a weapon of deterrence, mighty in battle. They needed to be fed.

While the dukes sat in council, the ilykari poisoned the warhorses' feed.

Just before sundown, the Sea Groom signaled and the word went out. Engineers set torch to oil.

When the fires began, when the wet forest smoke and furious heat of the burning Haraerod outskirts rolled down on Nayauru's camp, the sick frightened warhorses broke discipline and bolted, first in clusters, then a stampede, trampling and whinnying, shitting in diarrhetic clots. Chaos erupted, a roaring stinking mess of collapsing tents.

Autr Brinesalt heard the uproar and knew why his gut had been knotted in dread all day. Sahaule Horsebane heard the alarm and, before any other thought, wished that he had taken a moment more to hold Nayauru and whisper his love.

From the forests, from the Haraerod rooftops, Duke Oathsfire's ten companies of elite longbowmen opened fire.

Nayauru's dukes had not been complacent. Duke Autr's own engineers and scouts, able and alert, had spent two days proofing their camp against fire. Sahaule boasted men of extraordinary discipline. But their sentries had been deployed too widely, hunting for the Coyote in the woods. Their best spies had gone to the rebel camps or into Ihuake's court to listen for treachery, and so missed the ilykari entirely.

Nayauru had counseled her consorts and advisors to expect betrayal.

They had looked for the signs. Drilled the troops. Arranged their pickets. Against the cunning of the ilykari, who had sent Falcrest's riches to the bottom of Welthony harbor, their vigilance failed them.

Sahaule's loyalty cost him his life. He gathered his guard and rode for the Hill House, hoping to save Duchess Nayauru. Oathsfire's bowmen spotted his column and devastated it. Sahaule crawled out from under his dead horse and made it nearly half a mile on foot, staggering forward, cursing the name he bore and the vengeance it had earned him, before a certain vengeful Ihuake levy found him.

What happened between them was the end of a different story.

Mighty Duke Autr went out into the chaos to rally his camp. An ilykari slipped close to strike at him, met the Salt Duke's spymaster, and lost the duel of blade and poison. Autr used drums and trumpets to pass the word—*march northwest, rally on the Belt Road*.

He might have rallied a retreat. He might have calmed the chaos.

But Lyxaxu's howling Student-Berserkers entered his camp and began to rope themselves in the entrails of disemboweled men and horses. Somewhere in the whirlwind, Autr's spymaster bled to death from her knife wounds and a second ilykari, still shadowing the Salt Duke, avenged her mother.

Autr Brinesalt died calling out to his orphaned son.

Trapped between two fires, choking on smoke, leaderless and dismounted, the Western Midlands forces tried to flee on foot, and found themselves impaled on one last treason.

Haraerod's own guard phalanxes, citizen-soldiers bought by coin, by sidelong words from the duchess Ihuake, and most of all by the belief that they could fight for the only ruler who had helped them through poverty and winter, filled the gaps between the firebreaks. Nayauru's exhausted, asphyxiating, dismounted soldiers faced a wall of more than a thousand twelve-foot spears crying, *A fairer hand! A fairer hand!*

The survivors of the massacre tried to turn back.

But the panicked stampede of men and horses behind them, still acting on the order to march for the Belt Road, pressed them forward.

Oathsfire's bowmen, firing down into the crowd of targets, ran themselves out of arrows.

The phalanx did not run out of spears.

By morning a quarter of Haraerod had burnt to the ground. The Fairer Hand's men gave the townsfolk stern warning—the mountains of human and animal corpses heaped on the killing grounds would have to be burnt, and all drinking water boiled for weeks to come.

Those who had lost a family member in the cataclysm would be paid one gold coin per head, and three coins for a ruined home.

B ARU would not go near Purity Cartone until he'd been manacled and bound, his wrists and ankles tied to heavy stones, his clothes torn from him and searched for knives or darts or reagents that would mix into killing gas.

Tain Hu protested fiercely. "Why would you do this? This woodsman saved your life, as he saved Xate Olake before you. He killed for you. What has he done to deserve this?"

Baru stood in silence, afraid to move or think. Petrified by the Clarified, by the physical danger of his presence, by the greater menace of all the things he was a talisman of. Had he dyed his hair so brilliant red to carry a message? To say—*remember*—?

At last, after cold consideration, she spoke. "He is an instrument of Falcrest, a man bred and conditioned to serve as a spy and assassin. He could be here on Cattlson's orders."

"Why would Cattlson order the death of Nayauru? Why would Cattlson send this man to *save* Xate Olake?"

"Do you remember when you took me to see the riot? What you told me then?"

They have a clever technique. A favorite strategem of Xate Yawa, of the Masquerade, of the ruling power behind the Faceless Throne.

Tain Hu touched her lips with two splayed fingers. "A honeypot. You fear this man was sent to buy our trust, so he could betray us at a key moment."

"Just so." Just so, just so. But why Cartone, a man known to Baru, to Duke Unuxekome? Why not another Clarified entirely? Were they in such short supply?

One of the guardsmen beckoned. The prisoner was ready.

"Permit no visitors," Baru told Tain Hu. She nodded. Of late that simple gesture of respect made Baru uneasy with warmth.

Baru went down the steps into the yellow lamplit cellar where they had cast Purity Cartone.

The Clarified looked up at her, face red with acid burn, and began to cry.

"Command me," he begged. His face blinked from emotion to emotion in eerie flashes—childish grief, a lover's joy, thoughtful concern, a string of perfect counterfeits, like the semaphore flags of a burning ship: *help, help, help.* Through it all he wept clear silent tears. "Make use of me, Your Excellency. Give me use."

She looked at him and saw wreckage. Not a person in distress, but a broken machine.

Perhaps she chose to see this. It was easier than the alternative.

"Suspire," she said, hoping the command word still worked. "Tell me your mission here."

"I have no mission." He sat among his limp bindings, hollow. "The Jurispotence punished me for failing to stop you at Welthony. She castrated me, to end my line, and told me that I had been judged a failure. Clarified no more. Cast out." He rocked gently, an idle movement and yet still somehow wrong, wounded, all his smooth calibrated motions skewed and out of tune. "I could no longer find orders from the Jurispotence or the Governor."

Pity seized Baru. This man had been made to serve the Imperial Republic, designed and conditioned even before his birth. And what had they done to him? Acid wash, and worse—

They had cast him out, and in doing so, they had broken off all their hooks in him. They had given him to Baru.

Could Xate Yawa have done it by intent? Sent him to Baru as an instrument?

"You came to me for orders," she said. "I am the Imperial Accountant, the highest authority left in your reach. You used Xate Olake to find me."

"I escaped the Jurispotence once she renounced her authority over me. I sought you out." He made a perfect face of desperation, a blank skull trying to sign emotion with mastercraft masks. "You still serve the Imperial Republic, and I am still permitted to serve you. By transitivity I may still fulfill my purpose."

That old sick joy, her first and favorite drug. Control. "I do serve Falcrest. Fear not: you will serve me. Tell me why you killed the duchess Nayauru."

A simpleton's smile—relief, and pure pleasure. At last he could obey again. "Your spymaster ordered it."

Xate Olake overstepping his place. But it had been a wise and ruthless stroke, the class of gambit that had earned him and his sister a duchy and a Jurispotence. "Tell me everything you know about the Masquerade's strategy for the summer."

"Cattlson seeks one decisive battle at the Inirein. He hopes to secure his authority in Falcrest's eyes by restoring order to Aurdwynn before the next tax season. He has an abundance of food, but also of disease, and no money left to sustain his administration. Principal Factor Bel Latheman, to whom he trusted his finances, has been distracted from his duties by his new marriage to Heingyl Ri, who manipulates him against Cattlson."

Xate Olake's intelligence confirmed. Good. It would have to be verified again, in case Xate Yawa had arranged all this, but there were scouts for that. "What did Nayauru want? Was she there to kill me?"

"I don't know."

"Who ordered the death of Muire Lo?"

"I don't know." Tears filled Purity Cartone's open honest eyes. "I'm sorry."

Hush, she could say, hush, it's all right. But Cartone the mechanism wouldn't care. His only comfort was subservience. They had made him that way.

Instruments of the Masquerade deserved no compassion.

She stepped closer, to speak softly. "Tell me everything you know about Xate Yawa's true loyalties."

"The Jurispotence?" Purity Cartone recoiled in his bonds, stones shifting against the floorboards. He sat for a moment, gaping, as if astonished by something he'd discovered.

"She has no authority over you," Baru assured him, soft, coaxing. "I am Falcrest's truest servant in Aurdwynn."

"Xate Yawa serves the future of Aurdwynn. She cares only for her ability to control that future, to guarantee a distant peace." The Clarified sighed with inner release. "Through the Priestess in the Lamplight, she thinks she controls the very ilykari she persecutes. Spends them like coin to buy Cattlson's trust. But she is deceived. The priestess does not serve her. The paramount masters observe Xate Yawa through their agents, and consider her promising. She may be chosen for exaltation."

"What?" Forgetting caution, Baru stepped closer, kneeling. "Again! *Tell me that again!*"

"The paramount masters. The mind behind the Masquerade. A closed circle, each member balanced against another. Chosen by invitation and test to dictate the Imperial Republic's grand strategies of policy and heredity." Bliss in his voice. How *forbidden* this act of service must once have been—

"What agents among the ilykari?" Baru set her palms on the floorboards and leaned in to hiss. "Who? Who is the Priestess in the Lamplight? *Who among the ilykari serves Falcrest?*"

Purity Cartone smiled brilliantly, conditioned triggers clattering deep within him, drumming out rewards. "The priestess of Himu in Treatymont. The one whose temple hides above a lamp shop."

The secret-keeper. The ilykari who had written in old Iolynic all the things that could destroy the rebels.

The woman to whom Baru had confessed her second-gravest sin.

The woman who had recorded it for all eternity on palimpsest.

"Purity Cartone." Her voice a serpent's hiss: later she would remember it with a thrill of unease and triumph. "I have a task for you."

TAIN Hu and Xate Olake stood with Baru and watched the Stakhi woodsman ride south, his roan palfrey sure-footed, his pace swift.

"Shame," Xate Olake said. "I rather liked him. An honest fellow, I thought." He wrinkled his brow at Tain Hu. "A *Clarified,* you say? I suppose it could be so. He said Xate Yawa had sent him. . . ."

"I found a use for him," Baru said. "A useful task, at a safe distance."

Hoofbeats pounded behind them—Duke Unuxekome and his honor guard. The Sea Groom dismounted in an easy leap, athletic and sure. "I ride for Welthony, to rally the fleet and guard the Inirein's mouth." He opened his palm to Baru. "Will the Fairer Hand need my ships?"

Baru thought: I wish I could hear you call it *Taranoke* one more time. I wish you wouldn't take this the way you're going to.

"Your ships have the finest admiral they could ask," she said, smiling. "And your ilykari served me well. Look for my riders weekly, and be wary: when Cattlson marches, you will be his target."

What she did not say was the thing Unuxekome wanted to hear: *yes, I will need your ships—best I go to Welthony, with you. . . .*

Unuxekome's eyes tightened: one moment's disappointment, or hurt. He closed his palm. "May the battle go our way, then." A touch of aspersion, then, a break in his grace when he spoke the name: "Perhaps Oathsfire's longbowmen will carry the day."

"Your Grace," she said, the cold already taking her, the numb calculations that had carried her this far. "Wait."

He raised his brow in question. A handsome man, certainly, Baru thought; a fine figure, and not unintelligent. She could see no jealous fury in his eyes. No sudden curdle toward resentment.

But now, from Purity Cartone's intelligence, she knew that the ilykari could not be trusted. Unuxekome, above all others, was entangled with the ilykari. He had used his diver-priestesses again and again.

The need to be ruthless would only grow, a rising peak, a steepening precipice tipping toward final cataclysm. She had to *harden* herself. Remove all weakness.

Yes. It had to be done.

Unuxekome had always wanted to be a hero.

"I would be *most* impressed," she said, coyness in her voice, a suggestion of intimacy that drew Tain Hu's frown, drew from Unuxekome a brief exhalation, "to see the Masquerade's navy rebuked from our shores."

26

On a warm wet morning soon after the slaughter, Baru invited the duchesses Ihuake and Erebog to march up the flanks of Mount Kijune and survey the division of their prize.

In one way this was a kind of escape—she'd breathed enough of Haraerod's corpse smoke. But she, too, wanted to see the prize divided, the yield of her work, the proof of her most appalling and necessary methods. It would give her confidence for the endgame.

She sent Tain Hu to whip the Coyote into its next march, and brought the Stakhi brave man Dziransi as her bodyguard instead. This, too, was a kind of escape. It turned out he couldn't ride. No matter: it gave her an excuse to walk too, sweating, head down, counting and factoring the slow rhythm of her heart.

When the sun burnt away the mist, they looked out to the west from the broken turrets of an ancient Stakhi redoubt and saw the blue-cream reservoirs and new-tilled fields of the Duchy Nayauru sprawled vast and fertile and already aflame. From such a great distance the movement of soldiers was invisible. But the smoke was its own banner.

Erebog tsk'd and beckoned an armsman for a parasol to keep off the sun. "Are those your cavalry? Already so far?"

"My horse. And the Coyote-men." Ihuake glanced back at Baru. "I told them to burn anything that resisted."

"Aren't you worried for the safety of your new fields?"

When Ihuake turned her left wrist just so, it rang a bracelet of jade against a band of platinum like a distant bell. "The dead will be good fertilizer."

Erebog, shadowed, glanced back to Baru too, and her face was wry— maybe offering shared mirth at Ihuake's theater, or shared joy at this great feat of treachery. Duchy Sahaule and Duchy Autr were hers now. Her children would inherit more than a bitter clay-pit.

Baru smiled back, as if to say: see? I can be so very cold.

Erebog touched the flank of Ihuake's horse. "Didn't you bring any shade? Would you like a spare parasol?"

"You sound like a grandmother."

"I am."

"Like a grandmother with a lot of stupid, poor children."

Baru had to bite her fist to keep from laughing. The Cattle Duchess would not stoop to mere parasols—her men were already assembling a command tent. Erebog, untroubled, plowed on: "Perhaps it is so; perhaps some of them would benefit from wealthy, well-read spouses?"

Dziransi murmured to Baru, his Iolynic jagged, "Fairer Hand. Speak now?"

The Stakhieczi fighter wore the breastplate of his armor, a steel ingenuity that no one in Aurdwynn could have made. Baru wanted to peel it off him like a crab shell and take it for study. But the man had worth, too: steady discipline, a sober jaw, a reserve Baru admired, even if it was enforced by language barriers.

And above all else, he represented a hidden power.

"Come." She took him by the shoulder and guided him away from the duchesses, to the crumbling wall. "What is it?"

He looked west with strange green eyes, like barite fire. "Very beautiful. Very flat. Rich land. I do not know land like this. Mansion Hussacht— carved from mountains." He drew a pattern in the air, like steps. "Waterfall engines. Terrace farms."

She ventured a few words of Stakhi. "Your people—come south? Trade. Marry. Warmer land."

Dziransi stared at her for a moment, his jaw quaking with desperately repressed mirth. Baru, embarrassed, went back to Iolynic. "That's what you want, isn't it?"

"Soon I will tell you what we want." He settled his weight on the haft of his long spear. "Soon I will be ready to ask. In the right place, under good stone. Tell me now: what will happen to—" He reached west, toward the rich burning colors of Nayauru. "Flat land?"

Baru tested the strength of the ancient stone and leaned up on it. "Ihuake's siege engineers will go to Dawnlight Naiu and threaten to open the dams. Facing the ruin of all their holdings, Nayauru's landlords will revolt against her loyal lords and sue for peace. One of Nayauru's surviving children will be married to one of Ihuake's, and then Ihuake will rule the Midlands. Erebog will get Nayauru's clients."

"Erebog." The Stakhi word came easily to his tongue, like brick-work. "Erebog asks me dangerous questions. In Stakhi, Mansion-tongue Stakhi, not Aurdwynn accent—she asks about man she loved. Clan lord she loved."

"What did you tell her?"

Dziransi touched the masonry with one gauntleted hand. When he found a loose stone he frowned at it. "I tell nothing. Silence is stronger. But I know he fell. Mansion Uczenith lord—he fell."

Precious insight. Baru grasped for more. "He overstepped?"

"He wanted to bind his mansion to Erebog. Get flat land to make himself a king. But he was not necessary. We only accept necessary kings." Dziransi rapped at the loose stone and it tumbled out of the wall. "Now the Mask comes at us. Now we make Necessary King. He looks for advantage, as Uczenith did. But he is greater. You understand? His hand is broader. He—" Dziransi gripped at the air. "Constellation man. Wide eyes. Long arms. He makes himself strong. Flat land is very strong."

"The Necessary King sent you south," Baru said, but got the chance to ask no more: Ihuake and Erebog, dismounted now, came sweeping over. Erebog snapped something in Stakhi and Dziransi's face closed up in stern indifference.

Ihuake drew a naked platinum circlet from her left arm. "Your hand." When Baru offered her right hand, Ihuake slid the circlet over her wrist, up her arm until it cut into Baru's strength.

"For what you did to Nayauru," Ihuake said, hand still on Baru's arm. "It was a venal act, an ignoble thing. But it got me what I want, and that I value above all else." She turned the circlet and it slipped on the sweat of Baru's arm. "You think you'll be my queen now?"

Baru remembered kneeling to Ihuake, common-born and desperate. "I think I'm going to win another war for you," she said, chin high.

"You couldn't win a pissing contest without my cavalry." Ihuake looked over Dziransi with cold assessing eyes. "But you've gathered a curious strength, coyote woman. Himu breathes through you. If you get your throne, remember this—I was hungry. I used you to kill Nayauru and take everything I wanted. I am fed now. Keep me sated, lest I grow hungry again."

Erebog rolled her eyes. "Listen to yourself. You sound like a milk cow, lowing for blood and land. At least Nayauru had a vision."

"I want exactly what Nayauru wanted." Ihuake's voice rolled over the Crone like the breaking of a dam. "I want to make a new empire for my people. I want to reclaim my blood and history from the interloper out of Falcrest. I differ from Nayauru in one great respect: she is dead, I am ascendant, and my children are going to fuck her name out of every song and book of noble lineage. And yours too, Erebog, yours too—which is the *best* you can hope for, you poor wretch."

Erebog laughed at her, and might have said something cold and distant and very old. But Baru held up a hand to silence whatever might have come next. "I value one thing more than your cavalry, Ihuake," she said, "and it is the same thing that permits me to trust you. You're very honest."

IHUAKE'S cavalry and Erebog's phalanxes stampeded over Nayauru's land. Nayauru's landlords, desperate to restore calm and protect their claims, murdered Nayauru's loyal vassals, named one of their deceased ruler's infant sons duke, and sued for peace. Ihuake promised her daughter to the child. So it was done.

She had her prize: Nayauru's land and treasury. She declared for the rebellion.

Erebog committed her scurvied, hungry soldiers to the occupation of Nayauru's land. Too depleted by winter to join the battle to come, they would serve as a garrison against the leaderless and furious duchies Autr and Sahaule. A summer of raids and pillage against Nayauru's former clients would, Erebog felt, restore her troops and her own treasury to fighting shape.

The rebels gathered their strength for the final battle.

Southeast toward the Inirein—the great artery that connected Welthony to the rebel North. Southeast went the ranked and serried phalanxes of Duke Pinjagata, and the torrent of horse and livestock from Ihuake's pens, and all the wages and supplies stockpiled by Oathsfire.

On the Sieroch floodplain, where the road from Treatymont came east to the river, they would meet Treatymont's awakened wrath.

The Fairer Hand and her field-general returned to the forests of the North to rally the fighters they'd fed and armed over the winter. They were met with rapture, a clamor of joyful disorder—ilykari and mothers, sodomite-husbands and merchants, all crying out to the avatar of their new liberty. Reaching for a future free of the Incrastic disciplines that would bind their bodies and labors to Falcrest's design.

Tain Hu and Baru Fisher rode side by side through days of hawk call and redwood.

A forest of spears walked with them to the Inirein. Phalanx after phalanx. Boarding Oathsfire's barges for the rush downstream to the great camps at the Sieroch floodplains.

At the end of their passage, the duchess and the fallen Imperial Accountant returned to Vultjag and saw the valley speckled by the shadows of circling raptors, small hunting signs on the redwood canopy. In the north, the waterfall crashed through the sluiceways of the limestone keep. They sat in their saddles at the fellgate crest, the duchess Vultjag taller and more relaxed than Baru, who still had trouble making friends with horses.

Tain Hu drew breath. "If we win against Cattlson. If they give you a throne—"

"Not now," Baru said, afraid to let her terrible weariness show, her wrenching sickness at the thought of tests to come. "Speak of something other than battle and thrones."

In the valley before them a hawk stooped on some invisible prey. "You sound heartsick," Tain Hu said.

Baru shifted in the solid-treed saddle and, unable to find relief, stood in her stirrups. She gazed out over the valley, the river, the little constellations of house and quarry and mill. "The people in Duchy Nayauru." The people she'd bartered to Ihuake like cattle. "Are they much like yours?"

"I don't know. I've never gone west. The Maia blood is strong there, though, as it is in me."

Baru smiled sidelong at her. "I thought you knew everything about Aurdwynn."

The duchess looked hurt. "The land is vast. There are as many villages in each vale as stars in the sky."

"You're off by . . ." Baru squinted. "Several orders of magnitude."

Tain Hu shook her head ruefully. "Xate Yawa should ban the marriage of accountants and poetry."

A murmur of activity behind them. Two men came forward from the retinue—first Dziransi, and then Xate Olake. Dziransi, somber and grave, cast down his eyes and spoke in Stakhi.

"He wants to sit in council," Xate Olake translated. His voice thickened with urgency. "He says he has seen enough, and now hopes to act. I know what he wants, and I know what it could mean for Aurdwynn. *Listen* to him."

"No relief for the Fairer Hand," Tain Hu muttered. "Remember my warnings about him and his nation." She turned to the spymaster. "We will go to my keep, then, and speak in safety."

Baru spurred her mount downslope, seeing, for a moment, only a chasm before her, an avalanche of consequences drawing her down to the end.

She'd known all along that this moment would come. She hadn't expected it to rise up and swallow her. Hadn't expected the mistake she'd made.

TAKE the throne," Tain Hu said.

They stood on the dais in the waterfall keep's audience chamber, the long rafters red in torchlight, the air thick with pine. The muddy boot-tracks of a thousand petitioners, left unwashed, traced the way from the door to the duchess Vultjag's seat.

"It's yours," Baru insisted. "You're the duchess."

"I'm your field-general, sworn to serve. I can't sit above you."

"I don't have any formal standing. I'm a commoner."

Baru expected a retort, some levity of ducal protocol. Instead Tain Hu looked into the distance. "You should be seated when he asks you," she said. "It's tradition."

"Sit. I'll stand by your side. I'll be higher than you, and you can keep your rightful station."

"The Fairer Hand indeed." Tain Hu sat in a rattle of mail on stone. "Are you ready?"

The stiffness in her voice asked some other question, and Baru looked to her, hurt and troubled, hoping to help. But now Dziransi came through the door, armored and stern. Xate Olake walked beside him, washed and plainly dressed.

The armored brave man, emissary of a power beyond the Wintercrests that the Masquerade was not even sure still existed, drew to a halt at the base of the dais. He spoke in a low, respectful crackle of consonants, the Mansion-accented Stakhi of his home. His cadence sounded like oath and solemn ritual.

"My people were the father of Aurdwynn," Xate Olake translated, "and yours the mother. We fought the Maia for this land until beetles ate their empire and the cold broke ours. Aurdwynn remained as we dwindled into the north, clinging to our mansions beneath the peaks, fighting for brine and citrus and arable land. The Great Assembly shattered, and we fell into civil war.

"Now the Stakhieczi rise in fear of a new power on the Ashen Sea, an empire of coin and lies. The Masquerade would see its laws written in all flesh. Already it has stolen our fairest prince, plucked from the deck of his ship. From among the brothers of the lost we have crowned a Necessary King. He has carved stone and beaten steel into shapes of war. He has dispatched his chosen jagata to scout the lay of the world."

Dziransi paused. Xate Olake bounced his beetled gray eyebrows in almost comical excitement. At Baru's side, Tain Hu exhaled a long, astonished breath.

Dziransi spoke again. Xate Olake followed:

"The Necessary King, a man of Mansion Hussacht, a brother to me, sent me south to chase rumors of rebellion. He sought allies. I found him something more."

Xate Olake grinned explosively and rocked on his heels. With a gleeful rise he finished, a moment behind Dziransi:

"I found a worthy queen. Together—" He swallowed an exhilarated laugh. "Together Aurdwynn and the Stakhieczi Necessity can turn back the Masquerade."

Dziransi knelt and waited in silence.

Everyone thought she would be queen. It had been an implicit truth of the insurrection, a condition everyone else had agreed on behind her back, somewhere before the beginning.

She looked to Tain Hu, tense and rigid on her throne, a green-brown arrow fletched with raven hair. The duchess looked back, and twitched her chin toward Dziransi, as if to say: *he's asking* you, *not me.*

I don't want a king, Baru thought, and then, against the iron cells of her self-restraint, through the bars and gears and endless flagellation of her careful denial, although thinking it felt like sliding a long splinter up beneath her thumbnail—

I know what I want.

Tain Hu's eyes, empty as a storm night.

Baru spoke with care, with smooth assurance, with the stolen inflection of a noble lord. "Many men would be my king. Many men would buy my hand with gifts. I have been offered fleets of swift ships and columns of fine bowmen. Now I am offered a nation. But I cannot see this nation. I cannot look over the mountains and touch its stonework. I cannot know the character of its king."

Dziransi spoke to the floor. Xate Olake stared at her with mingled horror and respect as he translated. "In matters of state, we must always be careful engineers. We must build a truss of gift and obligation. The Necessary King is prepared to demonstrate his strength, and the victories it might win for you. Two thousand Mansion Hussacht jagata wait by the headwaters of the Inirein. At your request, they will come south to Sieroch and join the battle. This gift the Necessary King offers without condition, save that you know him to be generous and his men brave."

To see Cattlson's face, on the field at Sieroch, when two thousand Stakhieczi warriors lifted banners against him—to hear the tumult in Falcrest when they saw the ghost empire in the north corporeal and furious—

"You cannot refuse," Tain Hu murmured. "You cannot refuse a man who offers victory with one hand and sets ten phalanxes at the head of the Inirein with the other."

Xate Olake's eyes begged her to be sane.

What could she say? A gift this large was no different from coercion. How could it be refused?

And it would work to her advantage to draw out this hidden power.

"I accept," Baru said, and through Tain Hu's sharp absence of breath, her abrupt utter silence, the rest: "I accept the gift. Tell the Necessary King that I will meet him after our victory, and judge whether I accept him as a man."

TWO weeks passed in a blur of ink and starlight. Baru wrote letters until her wrists cramped, dictating monetary policy to Oathsfire, penning sermons for the restless levies at Sieroch, responding to Lyxaxu's newly resumed philosophical inquiries about Masquerade policy. He wrote this:

How can you, a rationalist, believe in our chances of victory strongly enough to rebel? Do you not fear their gradual return? Do you see any hope for us in five decades, in a century?

She wrote:

Duke High Stone, above all else I promise this: I have planned for the long term.

How long ago she'd stood on the balcony with him and heard him say: *Revolution is a filthy business, and prices must be paid. But I am not your coin. . . .*

The trouble with philosophy, Lyxaxu had said, was that it so often failed to survive a test.

She saw little of Duchess Vultjag. Tain Hu had been gone too long, and needed to set her house in order—but that was an excuse, wasn't it? They'd walked side by side through the winter, Fairer Hand and field-general, equals and comrades. They'd spoken as friends. Sometimes as—well.

But now the Stakhiezci bargain raised itself to say: one of you will rule, and one will serve.

Tain Hu was avoiding her.

In her absence, Baru found herself taking counsel with Xate Olake, beer-soaked but no less crafty for it. A deeper drunkenness had taken him, the exhilaration of an old man who had planned to die before he saw his dreams made real, and then, one morning, found those resignations undone.

"I wish Yawa could see you now," he said. They'd gone to raid Vultjag's larder for interesting cheeses. "She's caged herself in cruelty. Taught herself to believe in a world where nothing goes right except by the harshest exercise of power. She thought you were just a girl, you know, too young to lead. She forgot—" He belched. "Mathematicians do their best work young, eh? A Falcresti told me that."

"What will Xate Yawa do when we besiege Treatymont?" Baru found herself drawn along by the old man's optimism. "The mobs will tear her apart."

"I'll save her, of course." Xate Olake's eyes gleamed over his tankard. "She's saved me often enough, in all the years when I played Phantom Duke. Devena knows these things come back around."

THEY waited for word from Unuxekome: *Cattlson is marching on the Inirein.*

But it did not come.

One sun-drenched day Baru set out to visit the place where Muire Lo had been cremated and, at the keep's gate, found Tain Hu waiting in place of her guards, hair bound up, blade at her side. She had gotten too sharp to remember, somehow: every time Baru saw her she felt a little start, a shock of surprise at the grace of her motion, the fierce impatience knit up in her brow, the dawn color in her dark, dark eyes.

"Duchess." Baru nodded to the absence of armsmen. "Will we be safe?"

Tain Hu looked at her with sarcastic skepticism. "You walked these woods with me when I had every reason to kill you."

The absurd memory made Baru chuckle—audits and archery, when her greatest concern was *stopping* Tain Hu's uprising. "I wasn't afraid of you."

"Perhaps you should've been. Perhaps you still should be."

"Oh? What new danger would I have to fear?"

Where the Tain Hu of winter past would have smiled, would have risen to the bait and done something almost but not quite utterly improper, the duchess Vultjag lowered her eyes in deference.

"Would you have your field-general's company?"

Say the wise thing, Baru. Say no. Be hard.

"Of course," Baru said, and smiled a stupid honest smile, one calculated to win no advantage at all.

They walked the forest path through geometries of sieved and scintillescent light. A bird called above, and Baru, remembering old habit, thinking of Taranoke, made a note in her census: *one hawk*.

"There's something here." Tain Hu took Baru's gloved hand (alarm, stomach-turning giddy *alarm*—but Baru would not resist) and drew her off the path. "A sacred place. Built long before the touch of any empire—even before my ancestors."

"How did your Maia foremothers get a noble line with a Stakhi name?"

"Very proactively." She parted the brush. "There's a henge ahead."

A relic of the old Belthyc people, who had birthed the ilykari, who had made words like *Imadyff*—and there, like everything, this wrapped back around to horror: ice in her gut at the thought of that hamlet, at what she had allowed to happen there, at the slaughter it had driven.

To hide from the memory, Baru tried to pull away, just so Tain Hu would firm her grip, just so she could feel the strength in that guiding hand.

Thorns pricked her calf. Baru ripped them away, cursing softly in childhood Urunoki, grateful for her gloves. The duchess laughed a little, delighted, perhaps, by the way Urunoki sounded like a drunkard's Aurdwynni Urun; or by something else.

They came to a clearing, a well of light, a ring of broken, moss-encrusted stones. Tain Hu moved with hushed awe. "Can you feel her?"

"Which Virtue?" She was so like a mountain cat.

"Wydd. Her stone endures best."

Wydd: passivity, obedience. Strength in endurance. Death, erosion, and time. "I'd rather have found Himu," she said, showing off.

"Dangerous to call on her in springtime. Genius and birth are twins of hemorrhage and cancer." Tain Hu's breath caught. "Look here. The moss has been fed."

Beneath her hand the moss had grown thick and green in the shape of some ragged unmistakable sign—a lichen rune printed on the stone. The duchess looked around the clearing in sudden alarm. "This is a Belthyc art," she said. "They were here."

"Pureblood Belthyci?" Baru cocked her head. "I thought they'd all been—"

All been what? Civilized? Tamed? Turned into servers in fashionable Treatymont longhouses?

"A few of their tribes persist here in the North, deep in the woods. Irritations at best. Savages when their whims move them." Tain Hu touched her sword. "My rangers have been lax to let them so near."

Baru spoke with unchecked anger. "In a few generations the Falcresti on Taranoke will say that about the pureblood remnants of my people, and send their own rangers to drive them up the mountain."

"Hardly the same. The Belthyci live on in our mingled bloodlines.

These woodland tribes are just a fragile remnant. Their season is gone." She brushed the moss from the fallen stone. "There. Fair warning to them."

Fair warning. Maybe some soldier at Jupora had given fair warning to father Salm. "When you speak of bloodlines and fragile remnants, you sound like Cattlson."

Tain Hu stiffened. Her eyes were sharp enough to cut. "Who are you to invoke Cattlson's name?" A little sneer on her lips. "*I* haven't been making games of marriage."

The ruin inside Baru, the yawning precipice, had filled her up with scars. She swallowed the jibe, let it strike that barren tissue, felt it only as a distant prick. "No game I ever chose to play," she said. "I would not be courted by these men—not Oathsfire nor Unuxekome, not the lords of the Wintercrests, not any other. But I made the right choice for Aurdwynn. I must think of my people."

"Your people?" Acid in Tain Hu's voice. "*Yours?*"

Baru turned away, pretending indifference to Tain Hu's anger. Just scars, in her gut, in her throat. Just numbness.

"I couldn't refuse." She stared out into receding geometries of light and shadow, redwood trunks and reddening sunlight. "You told me yourself. *You cannot refuse this man*—you said that. What else would you have had me do?"

"Find a means of alliance that doesn't make a prize out of your womb." Tain Hu lashed out at something, a sound of sudden breath and motion. Stone rattled against stone. "I refused Oathsfire all those years ago, and I still have my duchy. I still have my power. Perhaps my people suffered for it—"

Baru might have thrown her own words back at her: *I rule a small land, poor in wealth and arms; I have no husband and no heirs, no great alliance and no well-made dams, and thus few strengths to offer my lord....* Might have said: what do you think to offer me, Tain Hu, if your own counsel has brought you here?

It would be a good move. It would set her in her place. But Baru would not say it.

Tain Hu's voice a growl, her anger smoke, disguising her movements. "Pay some other price. You do not need to spend yourself as coin."

"Your Grace," Baru said, eyes pressed shut. "I am not promised yet."

A terrible unwise unwanted thing trembled alive inside her, a thing she had known for a long time, a thing she could not yet acknowledge nor admit. A vast mistake. The second worst thing she had ever allowed.

Perhaps, on review, the worst.

Tain Hu's hobnailed boots made soft spark-sounds on the fallen henge stones, gentle scrapes on the moss. Her voice came like low smoke, blown in from a fire too close: "Something burdens you. I saw it in the winter. Now I see it again."

"Duchess." Plea in her voice. A protest of crows in the near distance.

"Are you weary of the war? Does the pillage sicken you? You would rule the wolf land, Baru Fisher. Every winter we freeze our stillborn in the ice because the ground will not yield a grave. Have you had too much of blood and corpse-flesh? Is it that?"

"Your Grace. *Please.*"

Tain Hu's boots came two steps closer. Baru wished she could close her ears just as she shut her eyes. "What great secret rots in there, child of Taranoke? What awful truth would you conceal? You have betrayed so much already. What other crime do you fear?"

A hand on her shoulder. Deerskin glove, smooth through broadcloth and leather and linen and her own flesh.

If you close your hand with all your strength, Baru thought, I will crumble into ash. Nothing will remain.

What have I done?

What have I done?

She stood in utter stillness, unable to advance, unwilling to withdraw, the charge of Tain Hu's touch galvanic, annihilating.

Everything she most wanted in this instant would destroy everything she had most wanted for all the rest of her life.

Your Grace, she began to say. Tain Hu. I—

Contact broke. Tain Hu released a ragged breath and drew away. "It will grow dark."

"I'd hoped to see the stars."

"There are safer places under the same sky." Duchess Vultjag spoke with a terrible, unwanted deference. "You were right about the Belthyci, Your Excellence. I misspoke. They deserve my respect."

"Hu," Baru began, grappling with chains of implication and consequence, trying to set the incendiary impossible words one after another without detonating the whole thing, trying to find a way out, a way to stop, a way to go on. A bridge across the bottomless, red-haired chasm.

There had to be some way—

But a long low boom sounded in the distance, a terrible exhalation: the waterfall keep's great horn, blown in signal. The word had come.

Tain Hu looked at her with quiet, loyal, agonizing resolve. "It's time."

The Masquerade's patient quiet had ended. Cattlson marched to war.

BARU gave one last order before they left Vultjag. "You'll remain here," she told Ake Sentiamut, and then, against the hurt in the woman's eyes: "We need a strong hand in Vultjag. I know you have the duchess's trust."

Ake bowed to Baru, and to Tain Hu. "Your Excellence. Your Grace."

If there were other things she wanted to say, her loyalty did not permit them.

27

TAIN Hu led her rangers and phalanxes downriver along the roaring Vultsniada, the men on the banks pacing the barges through warm idyll days and wolf-howl nights, until at last the river passed between high white cliffs feathered in terns and joined the great Inirein in the south of Duchy Oathsfire.

The Mill Duke's waterwheel banners flew in greeting. On the far bank marched his bowmen, cohort after cohort. When they saw the banners of Duchy Vultjag they gave no response, but the coin-and-comet sigil of the Fairer Hand drew a resounding cheer.

"He bought the yew for all those bows from Duke Lyxaxu." Tain Hu surveyed the columns of bowmen with hard eyes. "Always brothers, those two."

They stood together at the prow of a river barge, and behind Tain Hu the snowcapped Wintercrests bit the clear spring sky.

"You sound bitter," Baru said. They'd talked about this once before, in winter, and Tain Hu had said: *He wanted me. He wanted my land and he wanted his heirs. He was gracious, generous, chivalrous—he couldn't understand why I refused. It poisoned him. His courtship was perfect, so he understood that the imperfection, then, had to be with me. And Lyxaxu, of course, Lyxaxu with all his wisdom and philosophy— Lyxaxu still stands with his brother.*

Baru had asked what she should take from this. Tain Hu had said, with cold venom:

That we are not free. Not even when we march beside them, nor even when we lead them. Freedom granted by your rulers is just a chain with a little slack.

Now she said: "Bitter no more. Aurdwynn must set its past grievances aside, Your Excellence." And Duchess Vultjag bowed her head in respect to her sworn lord.

She had grown so distant. Something Baru had done in the forest, or failed to do, had spoken to Vultjag—said something final.

From the road beside the river came the sound of horns. Baru shielded her eyes and looked for the dust of Oathsfire's guard.

"Your Excellence!" Xate Olake clapped her shoulder, Dziransi a respectful two paces behind him. "I have news. From the headwaters, from Ihuake's capital, and from Welthony."

Something had happened to the old man along the river, some poison drawn out of him by the clear meltwater, by the thousand marching banners. Baru could see in his teeth and brow the sense of an approaching end.

"Your Grace," she said, unable to repress a smile. "Remarkable how you remain the spymaster of Lachta, even deprived of Lachta."

Time for one last look across the board. One last chance to ensure all the pieces had been set in their places.

So much depended on everything happening at just the right time, the right place.

"Flattering old men might have gotten you this far, but Cattlson's arrayed a force you won't be able to trick your way around." Xate Olake smoothed a letter between his forefingers. "Duke Unuxekome says that Cattlson marches on the Inirein with five thousand Falcresti regulars and a thousand engineers. He's skirting the north edge of the coastal marshes to make best time. His route will take him across the Sieroch floodplain, just as he planned."

"So few?" She had accounted the troops camped at Sieroch again and again, estimating rebel losses to disease, starvation, desertion. "We'll outnumber him four to one."

Tain Hu exhaled between her teeth. "Count again. Those are only Cattlson's regulars."

Duke Heingyl. Of course. Baru waved to Olake—*proceed*.

"The Stag Hunter brings his full strength. Ten thousand drawn from Duchy Heingyl and his conquests in Duchy Radaszic." Xate Olake rubbed the roots of his beard. "And four thousand cavalry, including the Stag Hunter's elite."

Twenty thousand men. An enormous force. And on the open floodplains at Sieroch, his cavalry would be free to maneuver. They had chosen their ground well.

Baru made a quick computation of supplies and consumption. "They cannot feed so many for long. He means to strike directly at our army. End the war in one battle."

"Wisely so," Tain Hu said. "So many of our levies are scurvied and starved. Cattlson wintered with his granaries full. Fighter to fighter, his phalanxes will have the edge."

Olake pointed across the river. "Then we don't count on the phalanx line. We win with archers. With cavalry."

Could they split the army? Let Cattlson waste his fury against a decoy while they outran him, took Treatymont, waited for him to starve? No, that would be madness—Baru didn't know how to fight that way, couldn't pretend to be a general. Nor could the vast force camped out at Sieroch possibly manage it. The individual duchies' soldiers had their own doctrines, loyalties, language . . . impossible to divide them and retain any coordination.

They would have no choice but to meet Cattlson in their full strength, and bet everything on one battle. They would outnumber him by a small margin.

Uncomfortably small, by an accountant's standards.

She had to defeat Cattlson. Of this she had not the littlest doubt—she had to bring the war to a swift, focused conclusion, an indisputable rebel triumph.

Everyone was waiting for her to speak.

"What of the marines?" Baru asked. "The reinforcements from Falcrest?" More than any other force at arms, the rebels had to fear them. Masquerade regulars were, by intent, a variegated and underequipped bunch, meant to menace the occupied and offer no threat to the Parliament they might rebel against.

But the marines, Falcrest's favorite and most loyal spear . . .

When the end of the rebellion came, the marines would write it. Of this, too, she had not the littlest doubt.

"Word from Xate Yawa says their marines will land in Treatymont and garrison it while Cattlson marches. A waste of their best, if you ask me, but I am no field-general."

Tain Hu looked downriver, thinking, perhaps, of Unuxekome, who had always seemed friendly with her in council. "If they changed course, they could still land at Welthony."

Welthony would give them the Inirein's mouth, and a way to strike north. Too late to matter at Sieroch, though. Baru saw the politics—Cattlson wanted to demonstrate victory without Falcrest's support. He'd built his reputation on his rapport with the dukes, and so he would go to war like a duke.

Like Baru, he wanted to prove that he knew how to master Aurdwynn.

Baru gestured again—on to the next concern. "The next letter? From Ihuake's capital? Tell me our western flank is secure."

Olake coughed. "There have been revolts in Duchy Nayauru. I am assured they will be suppressed." (Of course they will, Baru thought, with black amusement. We are in the business of crushing revolt now.) "Some strange force has emptied the woods of forage and filled it with enemy bowmen. Erebog's troops have encountered enormous difficulty; the Crone regrets that she will be unable to spare forces to join us at Sieroch."

The Masquerade's winter policy at work again. Could Erebog be party to some secret arrangement—a web arranged in the high north . . . ? Perhaps Lyxaxu would know. Perhaps Lyxaxu would be party, too, though surely he would not split from Oathsfire—

Her mind felt like it might spin apart.

Tain Hu hissed between her teeth again, seeing some other difficulty. "If Erebog can't hold her new clients, then we should expect cavalry from Autr and Sahaule to join Cattlson at Sieroch. Perhaps another two thousand. The Horsebane and the Brine Duke had many sworn riders, and they'll want revenge for what we did at Haraerod."

Damn. *Damn.* Erebog should have—but there was nothing to be done about Erebog now.

"Your Excellence. Erebog has fallen victim to jagisczion." Tain Hu spoke with urgency and forthright focus—but still those downcast eyes, that eerie deference, as if she was rehearsing a part she would play for a long long time. "Cattlson and Heingyl deployed their woodsmen to bog her infantry down in forest war, liberating the cavalry of Autr and Sahaule to swing east. This tells us how they plan to win at Sieroch."

We are not the only players on the board, Baru thought. We are not the only cunning thinkers with a map and a will to triumph. We must be wary.

So very close to victory.

She pointed to Dziransi. "He, at least, must bear good news. Is the Necessary King's gift on its way? Have the jagata sailed?"

Xate Olake translated the question over and the answer back. "The tail of Duke Oathsfire's column has already sighted them. They will join us at Sieroch."

"We are fools," Baru murmured, "to go into this battle without the certainty that we have already won it. We are all fools."

All the careful manipulation of coin and grain and cattle and marriage, all the delicate alignment of vectors. And it would all be reckoned here, in two masses riding lathered horse and casting their spears, killing potentialities as they killed each other: *It will be this way, not that way! This way and no other!*

"Eat your onions," Xate Olake said. "We'll need the luck."

"Nothing can be left to luck," Baru said, and felt their eyes on her as she turned away.

S HE could feel everything racing toward Sieroch. Felt it in her ears, like the pressure of diving too deep in the clear water off Halae's Reef.

Baru went ashore to pay her respects to Duke Oathsfire. They rode the riverbank between ranks of laughing bowmen and the barge-clotted river, speckled, now, by the fall of a gentle spring rain.

"I was cruel to her," Oathsfire said. Baru followed his gaze and saw Tain Hu, at the prow of her riverboat, calling orders across the water. "When we were young. And when I left my wife. Cruel to her, both times, in my clumsiness."

"She speaks of you with respect," Baru lied.

"Does she?"

"Your Grace," Baru said, looking down on the compact duke, his beard and brawn, the richness of his tabard and cloak and boots. "Aurdwynn must forget its past now, and look to its future."

"I said something like that to Lyxaxu once. He told me—" Taken by some particular mood, Oathsfire opened one bare palm to the rain. "Every moment is an edict spoken by its past. The past is the real tyranny."

"I regret, then, that we cannot aim your bowmen at anything but our future." She struggled briefly with her borrowed rouncey horse, and only made it more cantankerous.

"It is enough." He looked to her with a strange wide-eyed frankness, a child's regard. She did not expect it from the man who had spent so long bickering with Unuxekome and playing for her hand. "I am glad to be part of this fight. Glad to do something I know is right. I think I always needed this more than coin or family."

But family was on his mind. "Your Grace, will you be able to fight alongside Tain Hu?"

"Am I a petty man, you're asking?"

She looked at him in surprise, struck by his awareness. "You *have* been speaking to Lyxaxu, haven't you."

He laughed. "We had all winter to continue our dialogs. And yes, yes, I think I was a petty man. I envied Lyxaxu, you know, even though he was my friend. His looks, his love, his—his *certainty*. I coveted them. I made myself rich off the river trade just so I would have something he lacked."

"You will not die at Sieroch," Baru said, because although she could not know that, she felt some new fatalism in Oathsfire's words. "You need make no confession to me."

"But I must. A good man never goes to battle dirty." He stroked his horse's neck, smiling gently. "I took such vindictive pleasure when you sent Unuxekome away, you know. The Sea Groom and his salt and his smiles—I hated him, hated the way you pinned your plans on him, the way you spoke to him, the respect you gave him. When he left, I was sure all my bowmen and barges would give me a suit." He flinched as the distant mountains strobed with lightning, and then laughed at himself. "I wanted to be king. Or, maybe—to be the kind of man who you would want as king."

Baru pitied him, in spite of herself, in spite of the little anger down there: *All of you jousting for me like a prize. You could have spoken, and had your answer.* "You know about the Necessary King, then. The offer he made to Aurdwynn."

"I have my spies in Vultjag's court." The wide child eyes had gone, replaced by a kind of stillness, an inner peace. "You face a terrible choice, Your Excellence."

"What is it?"

"You will need a king. If you are to rule, you will need children to avert civil war. And the more you have, the stronger your position will be, the firmer our confidence in your dynasty." He avoided her eyes, looking instead to the marching longbowmen. Beneath his beard he flushed a little. "Among the Maia you would seek many fathers. Among the Stakhi, only one. I have heard it whispered that on your home the men are sodomites and the women must dress as boys and go among them. Whatever creed you follow, Baru Fisher—and I will not pretend that I do not favor the Stakhi ways, that I did not meet some of the Masquerade's edicts with gladness—soon you will need to choose a general for the army at Sieroch."

"And it will be a sign of my favor."

Now he spoke with obvious care, his stillness troubled. He wanted to be selfless, but he was still a duke, and he had pride. "If you pass through victory at Sieroch without the appearance of a lover, real or intended, many will give credit to the whispers directed toward your association with Tain Hu. That you are sterile, a gelding. Or a tribadist, drawn only to fruitless congress, a threat to your own dynasty. Or a creature made in Falcrest, bred in the Metademe to pass among men and women, but separate from them. Like the Oriati and their lamen."

He made the recitation seem obscene, and Baru did not hide the cold in her voice. "Or they will know that I have given my word to a distant man, and that I will keep it."

"Is that true?" he asked softly. "Please, tell me. I thought you had yet to judge him. I thought perhaps I—still had a chance to speak my case. It is not only ambition."

"You fool." She spoke rashly, unwisely, but with honesty. She had never wanted to care about these politics of courtship, the intrigue of who would own her and what everyone would think about it. "You cannot care for me. We've hardly met."

"I spent the winter listening to my people cry your name." He stroked his charger's mane between thumb and forefinger. "A good duke looks to his people's loves. I have, of late, wanted to be a better duke. So. Perhaps I studied too well."

The noblemen of Aurdwynn had clearly been raised on some profound lie about courtship. In no mood for more lies, she lashed out, spoke with care only for her own thoughts.

"You court an illusion. A mask. You could have been my comrade. You will never be my lover."

She struck his pride. She saw it in the way his eyes hardened. "My man in Vultjag says you walk into the forest with the duchess. I know her appetites. Please, Your Excellence, look to the future of Aurdwynn." He still spoke with an earnest open need, but now it filled her with wrath. "*You must have children.* Don't squander our victory on the Maia perversions of your youth. Don't break the alliance over rumor of your ill-chosen bedmates."

She seized his horse by the bridle, gloves tangled in the leather tack. "Duke Oathsfire," she hissed, furious, affronted. "Will you fight at Sieroch? Will you lead your fighters, and in turn be led by those I set above you?"

"Yes." He lowered his eyes, in shame, or in resentment. "You are the Fairer Hand. The hope of Aurdwynn."

"Good. Then see to your responsibilities, as I will see to mine."

She rode ahead, up a gentle rise, and at the crest found herself looking down across the floodplains, irrigation channels shining, the fat river lapping at the levees, stained by the effluent of the army—the enormous camp gathered there, a colony of tent and horse and cattle and banner planted in fertile earth. A painting in steel and horseflesh and sweat.

The rebellion in Aurdwynn, gathered at Sieroch, waiting for its queen, and for the name of her chosen general.

WHEN the Stakhieczi jagata came to Sieroch, the army was complete. The sight of them raised awe and fear among the Aurdwynni: ghost-pale brave men, leading their cadres of armorer-boys aspiring to one day wear the plate themselves, and grim-faced gray-haired women with ash flatbows, whose eyes snapped like heat lightning.

The army was complete. So easy to think that. Very swiftly Baru learned the truth was much harder. Duke Lyxaxu had command of the camp and he brought her into his tent with curt alarm: "Plague and chaos. I keep this walking cataclysm bound together only by the most desperate exercise of my learning. We must fight, or they will eat each other like dogs."

Baru scanned the ledgers. "You kept fine records." In truth they were better than fine—Lyxaxu had managed a miracle.

"I don't need flattery." The fox in his eyes snapped at her. "Look at the numbers."

The army swallowed bread, beer, and coin at an unsustainable rate.

Old resentments bred internal violence and that violence bred new resentments in turn. They were killing each other in brawls, coughing up their lungs, choking up the Inirein with their bloody shit and the sky with the ash of their corpses.

An army in camp was a *terrible* thing.

But Lyxaxu had done the necessary work, dividing the camp into wings, assigning commanders, messengers, procurement officers, treasurers, constables, herbalists, translators, wheelwrights and hunting-wardens and every other kind of specialist. He had bricked together the skeleton of an army out of the bickering and the floodplain silt.

"They are enough." Baru set down the papers. "Lyxaxu. You did well."

Aurdwynn had its legion, twenty-five thousand strong. Tain Hu, at last, had her wish—yes, that was good, they could use Tain Hu's name: an Army of the Wolf. Lyxaxu had even arranged for training. It could deploy in a line, send out its squadrons of cavalry, pass simple orders, advance and assault. Probably not make an orderly retreat, that most difficult of maneuvers—but if it came to that they had already lost.

"I could have managed no more," Baru told him, profoundly grateful. "What can I offer in gratitude?"

"I miss my wife and children. I want only a safe future for them, and for my people." She expected him to remind her of their bargain, but he only snapped his fingers and sent two of his guardsmen for beer. "Duke Oathsfire hoped to speak with you."

"And he has."

"Ah." Lyxaxu considered her with level, undemanding eyes. "I see you were unmoved?"

"I will not marry him." She spoke to the fox-sign hidden behind all his etiquette. "I know it was your design. I know you supported him. But he does not bring me advantage."

"So be it."

She held his gaze and wondered. He had such lively eyes, but something had come into them: a weariness, or a shield. "You have some concern?"

"No." He shook his head. "Oathsfire has tempered his pride. He will accept it. It is only that—well." When he straightened it was like a willow unbending: she had forgotten his height. "I have a question to ask you, about your future. But allow me to raise it in my own time."

"Of course." She went to the plotting table at the center of his tent. "How long do we have before the battle?"

"Unless he sends his cavalry forward, Cattlson will be upon us in three days." Lyxaxu tapped the parchment, tracing the calligraphy of some masterful ilykari scribe. "Coyote scouts hold the woods and roads. We will see the Masquerade's approach in time to respond."

Her Coyotes. Men she had known and led. All of this went forward as designed, as their converging schemes had dictated. She had expected this battle would come, with all its fearful cost—but she had not expected she would care so deeply for Coyote-men.

She frowned down at the map, hunting the weighted banners and pinned lines of yarn that marked the motion of troops. "Look at Cattlson's march. The deployment of his scouts and skirmishers. His southern flank is naked."

"Yes. Nothing guards his force from a naval landing, or an attack from Welthony."

"Do they not fear Duke Unuxekome?"

"I sent word to him this morning." Lyxaxu studied the map with troubled eyes. "I fear what we may learn."

WORD came with the next sunrise. Duke Unuxekome the Sea Groom, friend to pirates, implacable enemy of the Empire of Masks, supplicant for the throne of Aurdwynn, beggar of stories, had gone to war.

While Baru rode with Oathsfire alongside the Inirein, the combined ships of Duchy Unuxekome and the pirate Syndicate Eyota struck at Province Admiral Ormsment's Fifth Fleet. It made for a terrific story, the germ of a legend: the greatest naval battle since the Armada War.

Unuxekome led forty-three ships, lateen-sailed dromon war-galleys armed with rams, mines, siphon-fire, even the latest Oriati torpedoes, in an attack on Treatymont's Horn Harbor. His target was the Masquerade marine flotilla. He meant to pin the defenders against their arriving marine transports, burn them all, mine the harbor, and set a blockade.

(Baru had told him: *I would be greatly impressed to see the Masquerade's navy rebuked from our shores*—and she had known, she had *known* what he would do.)

Any good story about a swashbuckling sea duke needed a worthy foe.

Admiral Ormsment, Baru's dinner companion the autumn past, ascended now to command of the Imperial Navy in Aurdwynn, turned out to stop him with seven frigates—*Scylpetaire, Juristane, Commsweal, Welterjoy, Stormbreed, Dominaire,* and her flag *Sulane.* Behind the frigates she held her great torchships *Egalitaria* and *Kingsbane.* Her nine stood against the rebel fleet, transports strung vulnerable at their back. *Kingsbane* still suffered from the rudder damage done in autumn by the ilykari diver attack.

Unuxekome circled west to gain the weather gage. The stories reported his calm commands, beaten from ship to ship by the drums: *Marines to the rails. Ready oars. Prepare to sand all fires. Form line abreast.*

Charge.

The rebel fleet swept down on Ormsment, wind at their backs.

Nine against forty-three and Ormsment could manage her figures: her frigates broke and ran, south and east, out to sea. The two huge torchships rowed north for harbor in desperate asynchronous strokes. If they could not save the transports, these maneuvers said, then they would flee and fight another day. And they couldn't save the transports: great clumsy ships full of marines, naked now, ready to die.

This was the story Ormsment told Unuxekome.

Reports of drumbeats from Unuxekome's *Devenynyr* suggested he might have seen the trap. But the momentum of his hungry forty-three could not be broken. The Syndicate Eyota ships stooped on the line of transports.

In the pirates' story they were a prize.

In Ormsment's battle plan they were a wall.

There were no marines aboard. Instead the transports carried torpedoes in wooden racks. The twin-tailed copper eggs were inaccurate, unreliable, their rockets prone to drowning as they skimmed along the surface of the water. But the transport crews, drilled and disciplined, could fire a salvo of ten every other minute.

Smoke and spray tracked the torpedoes across the waves.

Syndicate Eyota's sailors were seasoned, the captains alert. Cries of *torpedo, torpedo!* went up. They broke off to the south and east, away from the Horn Harbor, leaving their lead ships holed and foundering.

And found Ormsment's frigates crashing back down on them across the wave tops, ranging rockets shining.

To the north, *Kingsbane* and *Egalitaria* opened their sails and hooked west, then south, behind Unuxekome's fleet. Ormsment's desperate retreat had only been a way to scatter her ships—position them to box Unuxekome's force. Now the trap was complete. The torchships were the western wall, the frigates the southern, the torpedo-rigged transports the eastern. To the north was the Horn Harbor and the shore.

Syndicate Eyota's privateers ran aground or burned. The Falcresti warships danced their gruesome steps, closing to barrage with incendiaries, pulling back out of range. The Oriati had a three-to-one numerical edge, strengthened when fresh-minted *Dominaire* caught her own sails aflame and had to withdraw. They fought like wolverines. It didn't matter. Ormsment had Masquerade seacraft, Masquerade hulls, Navy crews, and the Burn.

Most of the Syndicate Eyota sailors had lost ancestors to the Armada War. Now their children would know the same grief.

Unuxekome led his ships in a charge back up the weather gage, a glorious hell-bent attack on the torchships. Those of his ships that came through the rockets and the hwacha barrages, those crews who poured enough sand on the fires, those captains who kept order through the poison smoke and the impossible shrieks of men drowning *and* burning alive at the same time, met the bane of Oriati Mbo, the dread arbiter of the Armada War—the Burn siphons of torchship *Egalitaria*.

In Treatymont, the crowds gathered harborside caught a wind full of incinerated screams.

Torchship *Kingsbane's* replacement rudder failed in a turn. She drifted out of her formation, siphons far off target. Somehow *Devenynyr* got abreast of her, burning furiously, and the last sign anyone saw of Duke Unuxekome alive was his banner raised to signal boarding. Masquerade marines waited on the rail to greet him, firelight reflected on their speartips, on their white steel masks.

On *Egalitaria* they waited breathless for the fire to spread to *Kingsbane*, for the Burn stores to go and turn the whole torchship into a crematorium. But naval discipline and naval damage control fed by bunkers of piss-soaked sand quenched the blaze.

Devenynyr was still burning, white and sputtering, when she slipped under. So went the ending of the story of Duke Unuxekome.

Ormsment's story went on a little longer—through the empty trans-ports and the marines who should have filled them.

The real marine transports landed at Welthony that evening, barely two days' march from Sieroch. They knew how to pass the minefield into the harbor—as if an agent among the ilykari divers had marked a safe passage.

Falcrest's white-masked elite came ashore.

28

THE last council. Pinjagata and Ihuake. Lyxaxu and Oathsfire. Dziransi. Xate Olake. Vultjag.

The Fairer Hand.

The others spoke of the new disaster, but she sat in a cav-
ernous silence. Tabulating her victims. Duke Unuxekome. Muire Lo. The
Duchess Nayauru, the dukes Sahaule and Autr. The citizens of the village Imadyff, of Haraerod, of Duchy Nayauru, all of whom had loved her
as the Fairer Hand, all of whom she had fed to the war. The man her
guards had accidentally killed—who was he? Ola . . . something? Ola
Haerodren? He had put it down in the well, whatever that meant. Now no
one would ever know. Baru had snatched up his story and put an end to it.

All of them grist in the gears of her machine. The machine she had
built, or become.

And father Salm. Taken by nameless Imperial soldiers for the crime
of sodomy. Perhaps they had killed him in the prescribed way. Perhaps
he had been brought to a hidden place for *treatment*.

Ground under the gears of another machine: the empire in Cairdine
Farrier's eyes.

An empire she had to change. Whatever machinery it took.

Sousward.

*You are a word, Baru Cormorant, a mark, and the mark says: you,
Aurdwynn, you are ours.*

They changed the name to Sousward.

The dread in her stomach felt like falling. She thought of Taranoke,
of the caldera, of the fire sleeping down there. The precipice.

Everything would go forward as it must.

"We march at first light," she said. "West across the Sieroch plain."

They'd been arguing over how to blunt the marine attack from Welthony, how to save their southern flank. Tain Hu understood first. "We
attack?"

"We meet Cattlson in the field before the marines can link up with him. We overwhelm him completely." She looked to weathered wary Duke Pinjagata, famous for the discipline of his fighters. "Only shock can save us."

"You aren't listening," Lyxaxu snapped. His anger startled her— Lyxaxu, of all of them, in panic? "They *knew* Unuxekome would attack. They were *prepared*. Someone betrayed him to the Masquerade. Someone let the marines through the Welthony minefield, so they could land on our southern flank. There is a spy, or a network of spies, among us."

"I know who it was. I've already taken steps." And that was true. Somewhere out there Purity Cartone smiled in happy obedience, hunting his assigned quarry, maybe already thinking back on the kill. Unuxekome's fleet movements had been compromised by his own ilykari, but Baru had identified the spy back in Haraerod and dispatched her own.

Nothing could be left to chance.

Baru raked the gathered dukes with all her cold. "Our only hope is to defeat Cattlson and Heingyl on the Sieroch plain, then wheel and meet the marines coming up the Inirein. They may be Falcrest's finest. But they have no cavalry. Do you understand? If we defeat Cattlson tomorrow, we will have time to rest the army before the marines arrive."

"She's never led us wrong." Oathsfire considered the lamp at the center of the circle. He spoke with a new strength, grown in spring—a force of conviction or belief that told Baru, somehow, that he no longer had his own status first in mind. "Not in my estimation. Not yet."

Ihuake eyed Baru in quiet consideration, her nobility drawn about her like an iron cloak. "Never led you wrong? Has she ever led you in battle? Even once?"

"I slaughtered three dukes for you." Baru showed the Cattle Duchess her canines. "I gave you all your hungry dreams in one night."

"Bluster," Xate Olake murmured. "Careful."

"I am done with care." Baru rose. "I will go across the Sieroch alone if I must, and face them with only the dawn at my back. But I will go."

"I will go with you." Tain Hu stood, her smile wry, hungry, and almost—almost—met Baru's eyes. "Cattlson will remember the last time we two challenged him."

"Tomorrow on the Sieroch." Oathsfire looked to Lyxaxu. "Rare is the man who chooses where to die, my friend."

"Terrible choices," Lyxaxu breathed. Where was the fox in him? Where was his own conviction? "Every way we turn."

Pinjagata spoke at last, leather-tongued, flinty. "We march at dawn. Set a quick pace all day. Strike with fading light, worn horses, exhausted men. So be it. But who will command our newborn Wolf? The camp wants to know. Who is our general?"

The circle looked to Baru.

"I will give the phalanx line to Pinjagata. The bowmen to Oathsfire. Dziransi, you will lead your phalanxes as reserves for Pinjagata—Xate Olake, tonight you must be sure his jagata fighters understand our drumbeats. The Coyote-men can choose one of their own to command the scouts and skirmishers."

"But the van." Ihuake's voice like plains thunder, like the hoofbeat of her herds. "The other places are secondary. Everything depends on the action of our horse. Who will lead the cavalry? Who will call the charge that breaks their line?"

"I have only one field-general," Baru said.

From her place in the circle Tain Hu raised her eyes and her face shone gold in the lamplight.

"No. She has no ducal cavalry of her own." Ihuake crossed her arms. "No feel for the momentum of it. I could offer better. My son Ihuake Ro."

All this was true. But Baru had weighed the factors, and decided.

"Tain Hu has what matters," she said, her heart rejoicing, her throat full of glass. "My trust."

WHEN she was alone again Baru snuffed out all the candles and thus hidden from herself she tried to let herself weep in fear. Still it would not come. She had built the dams too strong, polished the gears too perfectly.

Bargained too well.

She sat in the dark and fell through the hollow of herself for a time. But helplessness came uneasily to her. After a while she rose and went out to walk the edge of camp, through huddled fires and the smell of roast and sickness.

Stone-curlews wailed to each other across the dark. Another sort of bird whispered past above. Nightjar, Baru tallied, or nighthawk. She couldn't tell. Her census had slipped.

She found herself walking uphill, seeking the highest stone promontories to the north. It might have been some Taranoki islander factor, something in the blood. Or she might have known where she would find Tain Hu, sitting cross-legged, looking out over the galaxy of campfires on the Sieroch below.

"Your Excellence." Tain Hu bowed her head.

"Vultjag." Baru wet her lips.

"I am honored by your trust. I will not fail you tomorrow."

More than anything else in the universe, more than the power to dictate law at Taranoke, more than the knowledge of the count of stars in the sky, Baru wanted in that moment to speak the truth.

But she had no tongue for it. She had burnt all her truth away. Alloyed it into the machine.

Her voice came husky, choked. "I don't deserve this. I haven't earned it."

"The honorifics? The deference? The army and all its followers camped before you?" Tain Hu rose to a crouch, to her feet, in a single powerful uncoiling. A mantle of starlight glinted on her broad mailed shoulders. A disquiet gleamed in her eyes. "What would you have me call you, then? My friend? My sister? You are my queen, or you are not. I swore an oath. When you doubt yourself, you doubt me. Do you doubt me?"

"There's something I should tell you," Baru said. It came out a rattle, a hiss, not like a lie would have, no; not smooth, not calm, not confident. Lies on her tongue, grown into the flesh of it, oiled in her blood. Allergic to the truth. "There's something I have to say."

She came so close, and so far. Like the paradox of the man walking halfway down the Arwybon Way, and halfway again, always so close, always a compound infinity from his destination.

But Tain Hu took her by the jaw, the heel of her gloved hand cupping Baru's chin, leather-bound fingers across her lips, gentle around the flare of her nose. Measuring her, just as Baru had measured Tain Hu in Cattlson's ballroom, judging the cut of her cheekbones, her nose, her chin, the markers of heredity, of blood.

Closing her mouth, so that she could speak nothing, not the lies, not the truth.

Baru shut her eyes against the force of her own response.

"Tell me tomorrow," Tain Hu said. "After the battle. Only then."

* * *

A T dawn the drums began to beat.

The Army of the Wolf marched west across fertile Sieroch ground and their passage raised no dust. Late in the day they came to the killing ground.

This was the shape of the battlefield, the crucial shape:

South was an impassable marsh. North, past the Henge Hill where Baru would establish her command camp, were the plains that stretched up to Duchy Pinjagata, greening in the spring. Cavalry land. The phalanx line would fight between the marsh and the hill, but the horse would swing north, out onto the plain of low flowers.

And before them—

Before them the land dropped a little into a shallow bowl divided by the Sieroch Road. Like an arena. Past that little bowl rose the forest, gnarled, ancient, untouched by logging.

Baru had been terrible at geography, once. But she could learn.

At the edge of the forest, where the road came out, the enemy's banners moved in swift disciplined lines. The stag of Duke Heingyl on the wings and, at the center, a mask ringed in clasped hands.

Cattlson had come.

Baru watched from the Henge Hill, where she stood with Xate Olake. The spyglass he had gifted her was battered, but she hadn't seen better optics since her last time aboard *Mannerslate*. "Stakhieczi, of course," Xate Olake explained. "Even Falcrest copies them."

She watched Cattlson's army array itself for battle.

"They're hurrying into formation. Good." She lowered the glass. During the march she'd made a feverish review of her books on war. "I was afraid they might just withdraw."

"They'll fight." Olake snatched a fly out of the air. "No reason not to."

"You're so certain."

"Cattlson's a stubby little prick of a man, but he's not inept. They know we set a grueling pace to make it here. They know that half our troops are already dying of starvation. And they're afraid we'll set the woods alight around them if they retreat." The Duke of Lachta wore a fall of borrowed mail, carried only a crossbow and a short knife—to cut his beard off, he'd said, in case it looked like he'd be captured.

"Wise of them," she said. "The Coyote's always looking to burn."

A patch of color caught her eye. She checked the spyglass again, and found a great banner stretched between two poles: a white mask, antlered, ringed in multicolored hands. Beneath the banner cantered cavalrymen in masked helms, their horses armored head and flank.

"Cattlson's here." She gave Xate Olake a wry smile. "He spent the winter and half his treasury on a new standard."

"Vain prick. Can you sight him?"

"No. His guard, though."

On the low ground to her left, in the space between the Henge Hill and the marsh, the Wolf's first-rank phalanxes settled into a line of battle. Bowmen and reserve phalanxes made a checkerboard behind them. The Mansion Hussacht jagata waited among them, ready to be thrown into the fiercest fighting. Elite reserves committed at the right moment could save a battle—or win it.

And to the right—

To the right, out on the flowered grassland, squadrons of Wolf cavalry milled and grazed. Tain Hu had raced them into position, taxing horses already on the verge. Now her signalmen flagged for rest. Too late for some: Baru's spyglass found dead horses and dismounted men, some walking back toward the line, some grieving by their dead steeds or hesitating to offer mercies to the loyal dying.

The horses, too, had reserves. Duchess Ihuake, still stewing, rode with them. During the march she had complained about Tain Hu stealing troops she had no need for, giving orders that made no sense. Baru had no time to attend to her pride. Ihuake and the reserve cavalry would stew in the east.

The cavalry battle would happen on the north flank, the right flank. At the center, the phalanxes would meet. The left flank didn't exist: it was a swamp for cranes and krakenflies.

If both centers held, then, Tain Hu's horse would determine everything.

"You know anything about battles?" Xate Olake murmured in her ear. Wisely: not a question for the drummers and the bannermen behind them to overhear. "Not war. Battles?"

"All that I've read." Set-piece battles between armies in the field, what the *Handbook of Field Literacy* called "meeting engagements," were rare beyond description. And here they faced one, driven by politics, by logistics: Cattlson wanted to win to please his masters, and Baru needed one clean victory to seal up the rebellion's future.

The *Handbook* also said that the first side to strike usually lost—their infantry line disorganized by the advance, flank opened to the devastation of a cavalry charge.

But Baru could not count on battle to be as predictable as economics.

A great voice rose from the enemy center, five thousand in ragged harmony, echoing the words of their officers echoing the words of Governor Cattlson. *"BARU FISHER. SURRENDER AND THE JURIS-POTENCE WILL BE FAIR. SHOW MERCY TO THE SONS OF AURD-WYNN."*

Above and behind Baru, the coin-and-comet banner she had chosen snapped and cracked in the wind. Taunting Cattlson. Marking her.

"I wouldn't worry. Suspect we'll win." Xate Olake squinted into the afternoon sun. "A good part of the men on the line over there are Radaszic levies. Heingyl murdered their duke and took them from their families right before planting season. We just need to give them a little push. They'll break."

"You believe that? Even with the fear of Xate Yawa in them, their families under Heingyl's rule, and their bellies full of Cattlson's grain?"

"Certainly I do." He spat into the hilltop grass. "Spymasters never lie."

White light glinted from a distant block of faces. Masquerade regulars, anchoring the enemy center. Drumbeats thundered across the field.

A rider on a half-dead horse struggled up the hill. "Coyote-men in the forests send word the Mask's drawing up some heavy equipment."

"Hwachas, I suspect." How puzzling to still feel that little twitch of fascination, even in the face of death. She'd *read* about hwachas. "Pass the word to all the men: expect arrows, fire, much smoke. Hold firm."

"There's the Coyote," Xate muttered.

White smoke rose from the woods behind Cattlson's position, Coyote-men lighting fires, dumping linseed oil over wet wood. The spring wind off the sea carried the plumes northeast, into the back of the Masquerade lines.

They'd thought the smoke would cause confusion and fear. Now Baru's own fear spoke: *we are only giving them a cloak to hide their movements*—

The armies stared each other down over shield-rims, each side a great line of fighters, less than half a mile apart.

"Oathsfire's bowmen should be firing." She raised her hand to call a rider. "What's he waiting for?"

"Wait." Xate Olake plucked strands from his beard. "Wait. Trust your commanders. He knows the range."

She lowered her hand. Listened.

Patterns of drumbeat and silence, all across the field. Baru fell into trance, into the analytic cold. Saw the formations, the phalanx line and the cavalry wing, with an engineer's eye. Imagined the brace of loyalty and ferocity and discipline that held the soldiers in their places even in the face of barbed spears. Understood what the books and the generals always repeated: that armies did not kill each other, they *broke* each other, that the day would be won when one army believed it could not survive.

A matter of deception, of conviction, of lies made true through performance. Like everything else.

Through her spyglass, lines of empty steel masks stared back. Blue-gray regulars, Falcresti and Oriati, Aurdwynni and maybe even Taranoki. Shoulder to shoulder in service of a faceless Emperor on a distant throne. Led by a man who wanted to have a good tax season and please a distant Parliament. And around them, filling out each end of the line, the combined phalanxes of Heingyl and Radaszic, fighting for that same distant mask, that same alien Parliament, out of fear and hope and plainspoken duty. Fighting, even, for love of their lord.

"This is not their home," she said.

Xate Olake grunted. "It isn't yours, either."

"No." She smiled through her fear. "But I have had some years to convince you otherwise."

Steady drumbeats down the Army of the Wolf line. *Hold. Hold. Hold.* The first-rank phalanxes waited, spears raised in a terrible forest, for orders to march, or for a charge to set themselves against.

"Look!" Xate Olake hissed. A cry went up from the bannermen and drummers on the Henge Hill, echoed all down the line.

A red rocket arced up from the center of the enemy line. Erupted in a starburst, a heart-tripping *thump.*

The masked ranks parted. Like ghost roads opening.

Stag banners moved in the smoke.

"What is it?" Xate Olake muttered. "What's he have for us . . . ?"

Columns of chestnut horses and plate-armored riders cantered forward between the Masquerade infantry. Baru, dry-mouthed, found Duke Heingyl's guard among them, their mounts shielded by crinières and spiked champrons. And there he was—the Stag Hunter himself, offering words of courage to his young retainers from his black charger.

"They put their cavalry at the center." She frowned and tried to remember if that had been in the *Manual.* "Have you ever heard of a general putting his cavalry in among his infantry? What does he intend? A charge into our phalanx?"

"I hope so." Xate Olake wound another white strand of beard around his fist and tugged. He made a small grunt of pain. "I hope he charges right across that little valley and up the hill into us, the stubborn honor-bound prick. Unless they disrupt Pinjagata's line with all those longbowmen they neglected to bring, they'll murder themselves on his spears. Then Tain Hu can meander in from our right and sweep up the infantry at her pleasure."

All those longbowmen they'd neglected to bring—

Oh.

"Drummers," Baru called, breath coming hard. "Signal down the line: brace shields for volley."

She bit her cheek, tasted blood.

And as if in answer, out across the field, Cattlson's hwachas began to fire.

FALCREST'S hwachas fired two hundred steel-tipped rocket-propelled arrows in one burning instant. The first solitary shots found the range and wind. Siege engineers tracked the sputtering flares, adjusted their aim, and opened the battle at Sieroch.

In the first second they fired more than six thousand arrows.

The valley glowed with the sparks of their ascent. Darkened beneath the shadow of their flight. Madness seized a few Wolf fighters, a hypnosis of terror and firelight. They watched the arrowfall in rapture.

The drums beat: *shields, shields.*

Duke Pinjagata, who fought on the line without guard or banner, set his shield into the upraised wall and nodded to his huddled neighbors. "Don't piss on me," he said.

The hwachas killed the poor.

The soldiers of rich or war-seasoned duchies, Oathsfire with all his coin and Pinjagata with all his veterans, had shields of quality. But impoverished Lyxaxu and Vultjag levies found Masquerade steel punching through shield-rims and centers, feathering their arms and hands and thighs, toppling screaming men and women and leaving their neighbors exposed, naked, dead. Ihuake's best craft went to her cavalry—her levies, treated like chaff by her battle doctrine, suffered worst of all.

(Baru saw the patterns of death and understood their reason without the need for thought. This was her gift, her savantry.)

Fire and tumult bloodied the Wolf. Cattlson gave no quarter. The second unit of hwachas fired while the first reloaded.

And in the air behind the rising salvo, another red signal rocket cracked.

Duke Heingyl's cavalry cantered forward. Gathered their lines, made their spacings firm, lowered their lances.

Blew their horns.

"Well, I'll be fucked," Pinjagata told his neighbors, huddled under their upraised shields. "I think he's charging."

And so Heingyl's cavalry charged. Accelerating downslope beneath the firefall, rising from trot to canter to full gallop, hurling themselves into the huddled, wounded tortoises of the Wolf phalanx. Even a warhorse could only gallop a little ways. But that little way was far enough.

"Hold," Pinjagata growled, trusting his fighters to pass the word, trusting them to fear it more than they feared the arrow or the onrushing horse. "Hold or you're dead. You and everyone you love."

The hwachas would let up before the cavalry struck. There would be a few moments to raise spears, to brace against the rush.

The line just had to hold.

I wish, Baru thought, that we had had time to plant stakes.

Xate Olake ripped out a patch of his sweat-soaked beard. "Stakes," he said. "Where are our stakes?"

Heingyl's charge streamed down the enemy slope, hit the valley floor, and began to climb, pounding toward the junction where the phalanx line met the Henge Hill. Where Ihuake's levies with their rotten shields struggled to re-form.

Four thousand horsemen cast like a killing spear against an untested phalanx in complete disarray.

The hwachas did not cease fire. The next barrage fell into the reserves instead. Drums pounded among the Stakhieczi jagata, a rallying tone. Longbowmen hid beneath wicker screens.

Oathsfire, Baru thought. Oathsfire, you idiot, you bearded ass, start shooting—

"Oathsfire," Xate Olake grunted, "you stupid *fuck*—"

A call from down among the screams: *loose!*

And at last Oathsfire's longbowmen began to fire. Arching salvos over the line. Direct shots down from the Henge Hill, raking Heingyl's charge.

Ah, Baru thought. He didn't want the hwachas to know where he'd deployed. Not so stupid—

"Ihuake's moving!" one of Baru's staff called.

Behind them, to the east, steer-headed banners rose. Ihuake's cavalry reserve charging forward. "Too late to matter now," Baru said. It would come down to the clash of horse and spearman.

Or—

What was this?

Heingyl's cavalry hooked sharp north, abandoning the charge. Longbow fire from the Henge Hill swept their flanks. Chargers tumbled, reared, screamed. Armored riders fell.

The horn of Heingyl's guards sounded again and again, calling to his company. The mass of armored horse moved north, an endless run of cavalry, snorting and frothing, pounding the earth. Racing parallel to the Wolf line. Not a charge but a—what?

They could've broken through. They could have pierced the line, opened a hole for the infantry behind them. So why—Baru's mind raced— *why break north*—

Because one breakthrough in the center, thick with reserves, would not decide the battle. Disaster at the flanks, among the Wolf cavalry, would.

"Signal Tain Hu." She spun, roaring to the bannermen and drummers gathered on the hilltop. "Raise flags to Tain Hu! They're coming for her!"

After the battle, Tain Hu had said. *Only then.*

So many things meant to happen afterward.

On the flower plain, the duchess Vultjag's cavalry moved west, banners streaming. Just a cautious probe, checking for traps before she charged the Masquerade flank.

She hadn't seen the mass of Heingyl's horse. Hadn't noticed the armored pincer that would cut her own retreat.

"Get her back!" Baru shouted to the signalers. "Draw her back!"

Across the valley, another rocket thumped its signal. The Masquerade phalanx began to advance.

Baru wheeled back to the bannermen and drummers to demand another signal, calling Oathsfire to shift his salvos—and something caught her eye. A group of Wolf bowmen and a handful of riders, climbing onto the Henge Hill. They carried no banner. Their simple gear made them Lyxaxu's, but he should have been deployed on the far left, holding the swamp flank with his Student-Berserkers.

Why had these bowmen come? And—there, on horseback, Duke High Stone himself. Lyxaxu, tall as the Wintercrests, the fox aspect burning in his eyes.

Gesturing to his bowmen: *ready fire.*

"Duke Lachta." Baru took the old spy's arm, putting all her iron into her voice. "We have a complication."

Lyxaxu's bowmen fired into Baru's drummers, into the bannermen. They fell and screamed and the bowmen rushed forward to cut their throats.

I shook your hand, Baru thought, against all reason and practicality. I shook your hand! I *promised* you!

The Duke Lyxaxu and his riders came for her.

29

BEHOLD Sieroch:

The Wolf phalanx. Spearmen out of five duchies and two nations guarded by their neighbors' shields. Wreathed in smoke. Wading through beloved dead. Banners burnt away by hwacha-shot. Rising, now, under the only colors left to them, the only fire still their friend.

Evening light on twenty thousand spears.

They stood their ground, blood pounding, terrified and exhilarated and urine-soaked and drug-crazed each to their own degrees, stirred by the drums, by Pinjagata's relayed words, by the longbowmen still firing over their heads even as hwacha fire closed in return.

Hold. Hold.

Waiting for the enemy, for their ten thousand collaborator-countrymen arrayed on the flanks, for the blank-eyed center of five thousand Masks with hooked pikes, heavy shields, instruments of breath and fire.

North, Heingyl's four thousand heavy cavalry raced in behind Tain Hu's five. Her formation responded clumsily, erratic, wavering between a westward advance and eastward retreat. The horses moved as if over-burdened. The men milled as if cut loose from all command, as if Tain Hu gave them no guidance.

On the Henge Hill, the Fairer Hand's banner toppled among the broken stones.

SO this was it—done in by her own idiot trust. She had known Lyxaxu for a clever man. But he had seemed so idealistic. . . .

So close to the end. Swallowed up before the precipice could take her.

"Lyxaxu," she shouted into the clatter of the oncoming horses. "Lyxaxu! What price did Cattlson offer?"

Xate Olake stepped between the riders and Baru, an old man in loose chain, flush with anger. "Boy," he growled. "What have you done?"

The wedge of horse, fourteen strong, drew up before them. Pale Stakhi-blooded riders looked with wary readiness between her, Xate Olake, and their duke.

Lyxaxu spurred his horse forward. "Duke Lachta. Your Grace. I know what you've done for the cause. Stand aside, and let me save us all."

"How did they buy you?" Xate Olake spoke with calm, enunciated menace. "I know the things you love. Medicine for your wife? Free marriage for your daughters? Will they bring you to Falcrest and sit you in Parliament and *civilize* you?"

Duke Lyxaxu stared for a moment, and then began to laugh. "You mistake me," he said, and then, a moment after Baru, recognized the sound behind him, the rising roar of hoofbeats.

The banners of Duchy Ihuake broke the crest of the Henge Hill. The Duchess of Cattle's cavalry reserves, and the duchess herself.

Lyxaxu drew his sword, mouth narrowing, eyes intent. Spurred his charger toward Baru without mercy or hesitation.

And she drew in reply, Aminata's boarding saber whispering free of its sheath. The Naval System live in her muscles, in the angle of her arm, the coil of her stance.

The sword alone would not save her.

Lyxaxu's guard, uncertain, hesitated a moment, or turned toward the horsemen rising behind them, toward Duchess Ihuake's roaring profanity, *catamites, cum-drippings off a limp Falcresti cock, cowards all—*

But the duke Lyxaxu swept down on Baru, marten mantle wild in the wind.

"Shoot," she said.

Xate Olake's little crossbow snapped. The quarrel took his target beneath the jaw. Duke Lyxaxu, the scholar-lord of High Stone, husband and father, fell from his saddle without any final word or expression, without even a moment to know that he had died and to consider the ontology of it.

"I can't believe it." Xate Olake looked at the dead man and shook his head. "I thought he had principles."

"I can," Baru said.

Ihuake's reserve cavalry smashed into Lyxaxu's guard and tumbled them to the earth. The Duchess of Cattle, aloof, skirted the killing ground and trotted her mount toward Baru.

"Your banner fell," she said. "Thought I might climb the hill and piss on your corpse."

"You've rather botched the chance," Baru said, thinking, *I do not want to speak, I want to mourn this man, his widow, his orphans, the thoughts he did not share.*

"Well." Ihuake shaded her eyes and looked out over the battle. "I saw Lyxaxu's men coming, bannerless. Never trusted him—he thought too much. In any case, I suspect your creature Vultjag is about to get us all killed, in which case the chance to piss on your corpse will still come around."

Baru reached for her spyglass, eyes already going north. But she could not bear to look.

"Help me raise the banner again," she said.

Something near at hand. Still in her control.

THE two phalanxes closed shyly.

Once battle was joined, once they locked in full shield-press, there would be no easy disengagement or maneuver. The line would be drawn, its center and its flanks set. They would have to stab each other to death until someone broke and ran, or until cavalry swept down on the flank or rear and ended them.

And the cavalry battle had not yet been won.

Oathsfire's bowmen kept up a withering fire, prickling the enemy's northern flank, killing the poor conscripts drawn from subjugated Radaszic. The Masquerade hwachas fired their last salvos in reply, racks exhausted.

Behind Treatymont's line, Governor Cattlson's guard cantered under their vast banner. And on the north plain, among the yellow flowers, the jaws of his trap closed on Tain Hu.

Four thousand riders under Heingyl circled behind Tain Hu from the east. And, now, the other jaw, the hidden stroke at last revealed—two thousand cavalry drawn from Duchies Autr and Sahaule, screaming revenge for their murdered dukes, for the atrocity at Haraerod, broke cover from the edge of the forest. Closed in from the west to crush her.

A debt! they roared, mocking the accountant who was their enemy. *A blood debt!*

The Army of the Wolf had picked the wrong cavalry commander. Tain

Hu's five thousand horse faltered, wavered, circled. The bulk of her armored riders were Ihuake's, Midlands men with little love for the forest duchess, the brigand bitch of Vultjag. The grueling day march had left their horses tired and dehydrated, eager to bear a lighter load.

Disorganized, caught between six thousand heavy cavalry, unable to flee to one flank or the other, they stood no chance on horseback.

So Tain Hu signaled, and they gave up their horses.

"Trade horse!" Throat after throat picked up the command. Carried it from Tain Hu to the farthest wing. "Trade horse and form line!"

All the indecisive milling had been a disguise for a different sort of chaos. Positioning. Preparing. Now armored men with spears and longswords gave up their mounts. Traded them to new riders.

The Coyote-men hidden in the flowers and grass. Skirmishers and bowmen. Ready to ride.

The rangers had been sent ahead as scouts, and as an opportunity. Tain Hu had given the task to the men she trusted most: fighters from Vultjag, Sentiamuts and Alemyonuxes and the rest. *Conceal yourselves. Await the chance.*

Remember: a light horse rides more swiftly.

The heavy cavalrymen who gave up their horses formed a phalanx, spears up, aimed toward Heingyl's four thousand heavy horse. For this they were utterly prepared. Dismount to phalanx was a basic task, part of any horseman's drill.

Letting skirmishers steal their horses was not. But Tain Hu ordered it, and they obeyed.

Three thousand freshly invented light cavalry broke south on their new steeds, Tain Hu and her guard riding beneath the comet banner at their head, her white mount spurred to the edge of heart-burst, a comet of its own.

Behind her the two thousand remaining heavy horse she had given to Ihuake's son—a fearsome cavalry commander, blooded and eager—peeled away to the west and charged the men of Autr and Sahaule, calling: *a fairer hand!* For Ihuake Ro had seen Baru Fisher, and had his own hopes for a throne.

A thunder of hoof and impact rolled down the plain. The battle in the north was joined.

And a second thunder answered.

Beneath the Henge Hill, in the shadows of the forest, the two phalanx lines clashed—sprint to contact, a bone-shattering collision of shield walls. Grunting scraping scrum and press. Fighters stabbing, screaming, eyes shut against the rain of wood splinters, the hail of broken spears.

At the center, Pinjagata's spearmen met the Masquerade regulars, and the Duke of Phalanxes found himself pressed back. The Falcresti armor turned arrows. Their spears did not splinter. Their engineers hurled acid and gas and fire over the shield wall.

Their masks stared, white, remorseless, full of alien will.

Hold, Pinjagata called. *Hold*! But this time it was a plea.

THE Fairer Hand's banner rose again. Cheers answered it.

Beneath the Henge Hill the lines bent and mixed. On the Wolf right, Ihuake's hwacha-wracked levies, backed by fresh reinforcements, pressed the Radaszic arm of the enemy phalanx to a standstill. Here the spear thrusts were halfhearted, the gaps wide. No one in the scrum wanted to leap screaming onto a forest of spears.

On the far left, Lyxaxu's Student-Berserkers broke themselves against a disciplined Duchy Heingyl phalanx. Drug-mad, blind to pain, they threw themselves into the grinder. But they could not intimidate the twelve-foot spears, could not scream past the wall of shields. Terror came over the Lyxaxu phalanx behind them. The invincible berserkers hadn't broken the enemy, hadn't been carried past shield and spear in the fists of ykari Himu.

They died like mortal men.

The left wing of the rebel line shifted. Crumbled. Pushed back by Heingyl fighters chanting *honor the word!*

For an instant, breakthrough loomed.

Mansion Hussacht's jagata stepped into the gap, cadres ranked behind their shining brave men. Now Heingyl's men recoiled, faced with the armor of the Masons, the cry of a reborn North.

But the jagata had been committed too soon.

By shoring up the left, they abandoned the center, where Treatymont's masked regulars met Pinjagata's finest, found them not fine enough. Pushed toward total breakthrough on the wings of Imperial superiority.

Baru watched the center bend with her fists balled. If she lost—if Cattlson won—if the marines came and found a battlefield in ruin, crows picking at the rebel dead—

Your errors will be written on your blood and sex. You must be flawless.

"The north," Xate Olake said, in wonder, and Ihuake took up the call: "Look to the north!"

Northwest, two masses of cavalry circled in melee—Ihuake Ro set against Nayauru's avengers. Northeast, a line of three thousand spearmen knelt, weapons up, and met the charge of Heingyl's heavy horse, fencing them away from the main battle.

But some of the Stag Duke's cavalry had slipped the net. Heingyl had seen Tain Hu's gambit. Heingyl had gathered his guard and made chase.

They rode south, quarry strung out ahead in their thousands—a mass of horse, Tain Hu's white charger at the head, her most talented bowmen firing back at their armored pursuers even as they sprinted for the main line.

Yard by yard Heingyl's fresher horses closed on the Coyote-men. Yard by yard the Coyote-men swept down on the phalanx line, on the Masquerade's exposed flank.

Exhausted horses stumbled, slowed, fell behind, died on their feet as their hearts exploded. Heingyl's men overtook the stragglers and murdered them, accelerating now, closing for the kill. A lighter horse rode faster—but a fresh horse was faster still.

Baru heard herself cry out. Felt the sliver that stitched her heart. The analytic trance had abandoned her. Tain Hu's great gambit had come so very close to success. But Heingyl's band would overrun her like a scythe.

Duchess Ihuake, astride her horse at Baru's side, spat into the fallen hengestones. "I'll be damned," she said. "You dishonored me by leaving me in the reserves, Your Excellence. And yet now I confess you set me in the right place after all."

She lifted a hand in command. Her drummers took up the signal.

Ihuake's cavalry reserve came down off the Henge Hill in a flying wedge. Smashed into Heingyl's flank moments before he caught Tain Hu's main body. Broke his formation, drove them northwest by sheer shock, cast down their broken lances and set at Heingyl's men with sword and hammer.

The Stag Hunter killed four men and beheaded a horse, crying *honor the word!* and then at last one of Ihuake's fighters opened his black mount's gut with a long-lance, and he fell tangled in his banner beneath the hammers and the hooves. To the end he fought, honor-bound. But no one could have any doubt his last thought was for his daughter.

And Tain Hu had her opening, her wide flank. No cavalry screen to stop her.

She stood in her saddle, gesturing to her riders. *Forward. Forward. One last effort—*

Horses frothed and faltered and screamed beneath the desperate spur.

The Coyote-men swept in behind the Masquerade line. Raked it with bow-fire and javelin-casts, a whirlpool of three thousand horses, a stinging hive. Fighters in Cattlson's phalanx, bent to the labor of spear and shield, utterly focused on the breaking line ahead of them, found arrows and lances taking them in the back and the neck.

The Coyote-men scythed them down by the hundreds.

And Tain Hu, bent over her white charger, leading an echelon of her ranger-knights, charged Governor Cattlson's personal guard.

They saw her coming, and charged back.

Baru found her spyglass, cursing her trembling hands. Lifted it, breathless, heart seizing, trying to focus. Found the unarmored woodsmen, Tain Hu among them in leather and mail, a gull-white bolt galloping toward the cream of Treatymont with their fresh chargers and shining plate.

"Turn off." Xate Olake balled his fists. "Hu, you fool. Turn off."

The two companies bore down on each other.

And the Vultjag cavalry turned off. Wheeled away from Cattlson's charge at the final instant. Cast their spears. Fired their bows. Tain Hu flickered through the tunnel of the spyglass, steering her horse with her knees, taking aim. At her side a man in Sentiamut colors took a cavalry lance through the throat.

Governor Cattlson, mask enameled red, swept down on Tain Hu. The Duchess Vultjag dropped her bow and grabbed for her sword.

Smoke from the burning wood drifted up to cover her.

"No," Baru croaked.

"The wind will change—" Xate Olake was watching too.

The south end of the Masquerade line broke first. Duke Heingyl's levies, pressed by Mason spears and the sound of screams, fled before the Hussacht jagata.

Then the north end snapped, demoralized Radaszic soldiers crumbling, unwilling to die in a battle they had no stake in. Even as the center pressed forward, the wings of the enemy phalanx peeled away under pressure from the front and death from the back.

"We're winning," Xate Olake breathed. "We've *won*."

Baru kept her eye on the spyglass. Found a rift in the smoke.

Dead horses everywhere. Two shapes moving on foot. A red mask—a wolfskin cloak. Cattlson, sword at the ox guard, leaping forward to strike. Tain Hu bare-armed and whirling, slipping on blood and intestines, clawing for room.

The smoke closed again.

"Your Grace," Baru said, her voice papery. "We win when I am satisfied we've won."

Suggestions of action, between drifts of wet smoke—a spearcast, a mighty overhead blow, a brilliant flash of light as two blades threw sparks.

A kneeling execution.

She kept her eye bolted to the glass, as if she could make it a part of her.

A white charger burst from the smoke. Rider a cloaked figure, draped in white. Wolfskin, Baru realized. The cloak was wolfskin.

Cattlson. On Tain Hu's mount.

The rider raised eyes toward the spyglass. Lifted mailed fists.

Showed Baru the banner those fists trailed, the great mask and antlers, torn from its mounts, cut free. Not wolfskin at all.

Cattlson's standard, in Tain Hu's hands.

The fighters on the line saw it. Screamed in exultation, a thousand throats, ten thousand. *Vultjag! Vultjag!*

At Baru's side, Xate Olake choked: "I wish she had been my daughter instead." And he began to weep with joy.

THE army of Treatymont broke. Surviving cavalry disengaged from the flower-plains and pounded away southwest. The Masquerade regulars beat a bloody smoke-shrouded retreat. Panicked levies bolted alongside the fire-spooked deer, or surrendered, or burrowed into bear caves and gullies to hide and weep.

Give no pursuit, the order came. *Re-form. Make camp.*

The marines on the Inirein could be on them in a day. There were wounds to treat, shields to mend, dead to mourn. Traitorous Lyxaxu's men had to be disarmed and cast out.

But no discipline, no storm, no menace could keep the Wolf from celebrating its victory. Two decades groveling under the eyes of the Mask, breathing the acid fumes of Incrastic law, breeding to the dictates of the Jurispotence.

At an end.

Mansion Hussacht jagata laughed and drank with Ihuake riders, though laughter and beer were their only common tongues. Rival families out of Oathsfire and Vultjag reconciled decade-old grudges in tearful clinches. Invocations to the ykari and old illegal songs rang off the Henge Hill.

Wandering the ruin of the battlefield, a lonely pair of Pinjagata infantry, worried for their distant starving families, found the Masquerade's abandoned stores of signal fireworks. "I'll sell them," the first man told his friend, but she, frowning, replied that on any other night they could be mercantile—but tonight the fireworks would be free.

A great mass of Wolf fighters built a bonfire of wet wood, linseed oil, and masked corpses. Some protested that it would stink, but lo, there was corpse-lore to manage that, and it would be the stink of *victory*. Some even knew that the fluid of the spine and brain could be burned as sweet musky incense.

At sunset they lit the pyre, and as it drew in scattered companies it became the center of things, the axis around which their world, in brief defiance of astronomy and the dicta of Charitable Service schools, turned. Soldiers stood to tell their stories, to dance and drum, drafting the first layer of the Sieroch legend.

In a way, that legend was the real prize of the battle: a spark of defiance, a little gem of freedom reddened in winter and cut to shine on the Sieroch plain. Everyone here would carry the understanding home, that secret hard-won knowledge—that if they stood united together beneath a rebel queen they might defeat the Masquerade in all its fury.

By word and song they would tend that legend all across Aurdwynn, and it would grow strong, passed to friends and to their children. They would again remember: *Aurdwynn cannot be ruled.*

* * *

THE warleaders gathered on the Henge Hill at sundown. Duke Oaths-fire, bereft, looked on with hollow joyless eyes, and the others left an empty space beside him where his friend would have stood. "How?" he had asked, pleading. "*Why?* He was so wise. He had no reason. . . ."

But in spite of all his grief, in spite of Pinjagata's rasping lung-burnt coughs, they stood in circled council heady with the same joy that drummed the Sieroch around them. Cattlson and Heingyl were dead. Falcrest was very far away. Treatymont would fall. The common people of Aurdwynn rose in love of Baru Fisher and her gifts of coin and grain, her loping lean Coyote, her triumphant red-jawed Wolf.

Baru stood at the highest part of the circle, balanced on the tumbled stone of the ancient henge, sweat-soaked, exhausted, her boots worn, her gloves frayed. All eyes on her, but for Vultjag, looking out across the battle plain, her broadcloth cloak wrapped at shoulder and hip against the cold.

"The Fairer Hand will be acclaimed queen," Xate Olake said. His beard had suffered terribly in the battle and now he looked a little motley. "Can there be any question?"

"My landlords spend her coin," Ihuake said. She had given up her riding gear for ducal finery and rich rings, not out of any practical need, perhaps as a silent scream of joy. "I cannot deny the power of *that* claim. And I think she will rule well."

"Aye," Pinjagata rasped. "My people sing her name. She could give us peace." At that thought he smiled, and for a moment his breath seemed easier.

"Who then will be king? There must be a dynasty to unite Aurdwynn." Xate Olake opened his hands and turned to her. "I think it best to look beyond our borders. Will it be the Stakhi king? Or some Oriati man, whatever royalty they maintain?"

Ihuake lifted her chin, thinking, certainly, of her son. Pinjagata covered a long, dry cough. The question roused not a flicker of interest in Oathsfire's hollow, distant eyes.

Baru stood above them all on the toppled henge stone, like a premonition of a throne.

Who, then, will be king?

She could have lasted a little longer. Seen it through to the end, and saved herself. But today was for defeats, for triumphs, for great efforts to come to victory or ruin, and she did not have the strength.

Baru let the truth fall.

"I called on one sword," she said. "When offered the quiver, I always chose the same arrow. I put the harshest weight on a single back. And she has carried us here. She has raised us up. She is worth a legion to me."

She knelt on the fallen henge stone. Lowered her hand in offering.

Tain Hu, eyes afire in the twilight, reached up and took her wrist. Drew herself up onto the stone to stand at Baru's side. The wind caught her cloak and whipped it once, a soft utterance, before she drew it still—a sharp, sure motion, like a pull on the reins.

They stood together, Baru breathless, giddy, the hero of Sieroch a warmth against her side, a dry murmur in her ear:

"I had dared to hope."

Silence in the circle.

"What does this mean?" Oathsfire asked.

"It means," Xate Olake said, "that we know why she rebelled."

Pinjagata squinted. "I don't see the dynasty. Less I've made a mistake." His voice roughened with a kind of wry affection. "You never *did* tell me if you were a man. . . ."

"We should go," Oathsfire uttered, voice thick. "She has chosen. Leave them to their council."

Unspoken, there: *and leave us to ours.*

"She is our queen," Xate Olake insisted. "There are still ways for her to bear. This is no disaster."

"Quiet, Lachta," Ihuake said. There was a thickness in her voice, though it was not anger. It might be gladness, even, for she smiled. "Our questions will wait for tomorrow. For now, let them be."

The dukes turned away, leaving Dziransi standing, befuddled, until Pinjagata took his wrist and drew him off down the hill. He looked back at Baru in enormous confusion. Behind him she heard Ihuake laugh in unfettered delight.

Now they stood alone on the high hill and the sea wind cried between the ancient henge stones in the dying light.

"Imuira," Tain Hu whispered, an Urun word, a breath under the rising wind. Her voice trembled with things left long unsaid. *"Kuye lam."*

Those words Baru knew. They were the same in Urunoki, on her childhood home.

She touched Hu's shoulders, her high cheekbones, hesitant, conditioned, trembling against more than a decade of fear and repression and rigid self-control. Her skin felt transparent, burned raw. A sudden gust made her shiver.

Tain Hu's eyes were wide and close and utterly aware. She had been chewing anise and smyrnium. Baru could smell it, clean, sharp.

Fuck them, Baru thought. Fuck them. They can all burn. I will destroy myself if I choose.

On this one day I will not deny what I am.

"Forgive me," she said. "I've never done this before."

"Such an ascetic." Tain Hu chuckled warmly, and in that warmth Baru heard the life she had never had, would never reach. "Fear not. I am practiced."

"So many conquests," Baru said, trying to tease. But Tain Hu did not let her finish the sentence.

30

SHE stood on the peak of Taranoke with mother Pinion at her side. The island of her childhood—plots of sugarcane and black coffee, black beaches. Sea the color of deep sky lapping at the coral. The smell of iron salt and cooked pineapple. Endless stars.

Taranoke had its own politics, its own trade, its diseases and dismays. But to a child it had seemed perfect and solitary and whole.

Empire came on tempest wind.

The harbor choked with red sails. The forests fell and rose again, incarnated in tarred hull, incarcerated in main and mizzenmast. Plague swept the mountain and the plains and they tumbled the mingled dead into the caldera. Children slept in tufa schools, learning to love and marry by a foreign creed, laboring in the shipyards, *socialized federati, class one, no distinctions.*

The masks killed husbands with fire-stoked iron, and the screams were a reminder: *the old ways were not hygienic.*

"How grateful we must be," her mother said, that childhood voice, that vein of utter unquestioned truth. "To have soap and sanitation. To watch our children survive and grow and learn all the names of sin. How fulfilling our lives must be, now that we labor for a greater purpose. Did you know that we died of tooth abscess, child? It was very nearly the foremost cause of death. How grateful we must be for dentists."

Baru watched it all and with an accountant's mind made a table of the credits and the debits, a double-entry ledger, *hot iron for the sodomites* against *soap* and *dentists* and *a greater purpose.*

Pinion took off her smiling mother-mask and revealed herself as Cairdine Farrier, the jovial merchant, the portent with an engine in his eyes. "You had a question for me," he said, as in the distance the waves began to freeze, became steel and porcelain, a web, a road, a sluiceway that ran with blood and molten gold. From Taranoke east to the heart of things. "About the nature and exercise of power."

Cause and effect. Credit and debit. The world bound together, one system, one constellation. But she could not see the shape of it. She did not have the master book: second cousin Lao carried it away from her on a road of gloved hands.

"We have all the answers in Falcrest," Cairdine Farrier assured her. "Everything has been cataloged and assigned its rightful place."

"Even the rebellions," Baru said. "Even the rebels."

He lifted to his face a white porcelain mask blank of all expression and she knew his name was Itinerant. "We will extend our control," he said. "When the work is complete, when our hegemony is total, no one and nothing will act without our consent. *By volition* will be a synonym for *by decree*. The law of the Empire will live within every soul and cell. There will be no more pain or waste. Only harmony."

"What if Aurdwynn broke free?" She wanted to taunt him but she was full of gears and she could only offer it as a premise, an orphaned shard of logic, a rhetorical device deployed to enable a crushing rejoinder. "What if they could not be ruled?"

The mask looked on her with empty idiot eyes and drool puddled beneath its chin. The Emperor on the Faceless Throne.

"They have only the strength of rebels," he said, and his voice was a chorus. "Only conviction and ferocity and animal outrage. We have all the might of empire, virtues of coin and persistence and size, sinews of record and law and conscription and industry. Our strengths are of a higher order. We will return. We will buy them out and breed them down and lure them with joy and Aurdwynn, too, will wear the mask."

Fire smoldered in the Taranoke caldera as its people married flat-nosed foreigners or marched down to the ships to labor and fight abroad.

The mask said: "We always win in the end. We own the future."

"I knew this," Baru whispered.

Red rowan-fruit hair curled out from behind the porcelain. "You knew it from the start. In the long run, Aurdwynn *would* be ruled."

Ashy smoke made her hoarse, made the words falter in a burning throat. "And what pointless waste, those cycles of revolt and reconquest. What blood and labor would be squandered in decades to come. How much more merciful to find a shorter way. A sooner peace."

"A higher purpose," the mask said, in one voice now, a mocking harborside voice, the voice of the man called Apparitor. "So you became a special instrument, for an exalted design."

I will know the secrets of power, she told herself, clinging to that pillar. Knowledge is control. I will turn that power to my own use and I will save my home.

It has all been for Taranoke.

She found that in the dream, at last, she could weep.

W ARMTH.

She tried not to take it apart.

Warmth around her. The tent. The furs.

Stop, she thought. Go back. Sleep. Don't think.

Warmth in the circle of her arms. Pressed beneath her chin. Warmth in her heart.

"Mm," Tain Hu said. "Hello. Your *Excellence*." The contented slits of her eyes closed again. The weight of her body had made Baru's left arm numb. She turned a little, so that they would fit together more perfectly, and pressed her nose and lips into the join of Baru's neck and jaw. Her breath went out in a long sigh.

For one more moment: bliss.

And the engines woke, the scalpels and the geared schemes, peeling the *now* apart into what had been and what would come, a vivisectionist drawing out organs of consequence, smooth dripping links of *plan* and *outcome* and *risk* and *catastrophe*.

The accountant waking inside the woman.

Remembering her test.

Baru Fisher set her chin on the smooth cap of her lover's head and howled in silent grief.

There was no way out. The conditions had been set, the mechanisms primed, in distant cities, on docksides, in plotting-rooms, a covenant written in ink, in coin, in blood. This was the endgame.

There was no way out.

H OW long had she—?

There was power in Tain Hu. In her axe-carrying armor-bearing brawn, in her voice of edict and defiance. Even, by the rules of aristocracy, power in her blood.

What else would Baru ever desire? (And she had desired, base forbidden carnal want, in the ballroom, in the forest, from the very first glimpse.) What more could Baru find in her but that strength, that power?

Much more, it seemed. There was so much more to Tain Hu. So much left to be discovered. An inner sky, constellations barely hinted at, waiting to be mapped.

Tain Hu slept in open-lipped repose, her beauty not the permitted beauty, not the mother-fat of Urun carving or the purebred architectures of Falcresti art. A woman and a fighter and a lord, a nation alone.

So much more to know. The accounting could go on forever.

But time had run out.

*H*OW *to draw out the disloyal, we wondered?* She dressed in linen and long tabard and trousers, buckled on Aminata's boarding saber, and went out into the morning cold. The guard around Duchess Vultjag's tent had been posted wide. All familiar faces, Tain Hu's favorite armsmen from home. Discreetly inattentive.

Baru went through them, face averted, and up the slope to the place where the porters had brought her baggage. Found the ceremonial purse. Chained it to her side.

We have a favorite method.

She walked through the morning fires and the half-naked fighters hunting themselves for ticks, the smell of curries and coffee, the intersecting songs of Iolynic and Urun and two kinds of Stakhi. The men and women she had brought to Sieroch, in her own name.

She had *made* the Wolf—knowing all the while how it would end—

"Xate Olake," she called.

The old spymaster rose from his fireside, propped on the shoulder of an herbalist. "Your Excellence?"

"I have a task for you. A hard thing."

Was that sorrow in his bright jungle-crow eyes? Did he think he understood?

What she tried to tell herself was: *when this is finished, I will remake the world so that no woman will ever have to do this again.*

But in her heart she felt the pain like a swallowed razor, like glass dust in her cup.

"Go to the camp of the Vultjag fighters," she said. "Bring horses and a few men you trust—Dziransi and some of his jagata. Tell the duchess Vultjag that I have stripped her of her station. Tell her that today I cast her out."

Xate Olake waited, drawn and weary, ready to execute the orders of the queen he had helped to make.

"Take her north under guard. Tell her to ride onward until the Wintercrests swallow her. Tell her that if she ever returns to Aurdwynn, she will face death."

"There must be a dynasty," Xate Olake said, with a terrible understanding, a sympathy utterly misplaced. He had spent so long moving the pieces, striking down any threat. He thought he understood. "Even at such great cost."

We will give you what you most desire. What you have craved since childhoood.

And as Baru walked away, Xate Olake said one more thing, a perfect, unintended blow: "I'm sorry she made this necessary."

A ND that was that. The time was now, the terms exact, the bargain perfectly clear. She'd faced it, accepted it. She'd said: *I understand what you want me to do.*

Even now the rest of the clockwork would be striking the hour: *now now now.*

No reason to hesitate.

Baru put her face against her horse's flank and bristled her face, her eyes, with the hair and the stink, trying to weep again, to break open and run into the grass like pus. Nothing would come. Her heart had clotted.

I have committed a terrible crime. So terrible that I feel I can do anything, commit any sin, betray any trust, because no matter what ruin I make of myself, it cannot be worse than what I have already done.

And here it was. The crime had been committed long ago. This was only the reckoning.

She had said to the pearl-diver priestess: *it has all been for Taranoke.*

Baru saddled her rouncey and rode it east under no banner, out through the camp, unrecognized, unlooked-for, the drums of the morning call-to-march drawing groggy protests around her. She wore woodsman's gear, to hide from attention, and a helm, to hide her face. The bargain had never set an exact place or time—only conditions for the ending, a qualm broken, a victory won. And then a plan for extraction: *get clear, and trust us to be ready. . . .*

Without any outward sign or motion, in the wreckage of herself, she donned her armor, made it firm around her heart. Raised her mask: a cold discipline, a steel beneath her skin.

Grow comfortable, she told herself. It will never come off.

Baru, you fool. You arrogant, callous monster. You should have stopped this. Somehow.

On the eastern edge of camp a Stakhi man with long red hair waited on horseback, a grief-knotted neckerchief bright above his coat. The man who had come to her harborside and said:

Do you know the Hierarchic Qualm?

"It is time," he said. "Now, at the moment of victory, when we can be sure that even the most cautious traitors are unmasked." He grinned, a thrill of danger or victory or bloodlust. "You did well, bringing them to Sieroch, arranging a tidy victory. You did well."

"Stop!" Baru screamed at him. "Undo it! I *changed my mind*!" And in her fury she rode on him, beheaded him, trampled his corpse; turned back into camp and raised—

She did none of that. It would save nothing. The alarm might, in the short run. But the short run hardly mattered.

Her silent regard must have troubled him, for after a moment, the man named Apparitor looked away. The ghost that crossed his face might have been sympathy. "Come," he said. "I arranged the rest of it. The jaws are closing. We should be well clear."

Baru began to twist in her saddle, to look behind her, but Apparitor's hiss seized her and made her still. "No! Don't look back." His eyes were not as hard as his voice. "There is nothing behind you. You understand? Everything lies ahead now."

Together they rode east, through the sentries. Out across the Sieroch and toward the great roaring Inirein, the Bleed of Light, where the Wolf would march to meet the marines they expected, the marines who would never come.

For a while they passed in silence except for morning birdsong and the sound of water against rich earth. Baru closed her eyes, wiped away the world, and filled it with the memory of beautiful crimes.

The accountant in her said: *you made a good bargain.* And that had been true, for the woman at the dockside, the frustrated technocrat enraged at *Sousward,* desperate to find another way to Falcrest.

But that woman had not understood.

Someone shouted. A great thunder of hooves closed on them from the north—a file of armored horse, waiting in ambush behind a copse of incense cedar. Apparitor looked at her in incredulous amusement. "Sloppy," he said. "Very sloppy."

It's Oathsfire, she thought. He sat through the whole night, drowned in grief, gnawing on his friend's treachery, and when the sun rose he understood why Lyxaxu, most thoughtful and farseeing of all of us, would turn on me.

Maybe he read Lyxaxu's letters. Maybe he found some draft of that question: *Do you not fear their gradual return? Do you see any hope for us in five decades, in a century?* Maybe he'd understood why Lyxaxu had asked. Maybe he'd realized what her answer had to be, cold cunning Baru Fisher the accountant.

Maybe he wasn't sure he believed it. But he came out here to wait. And now, at last, he sees the monster he wanted to make his queen.

He'll kill me, she thought. And she felt joy.

Apparitor drew a device from his saddlebags and raised it above his head. A green-smoke rocket arched up into the dawn. "Ride," he said, bending over his horse's neck. "Ride hard."

She followed him, an empty mechanism. How had she done it? Until this morning came, she had somehow made herself believe that this morning would never come. She had known but she hadn't known. How could anyone do that? How could you know something *for a fact* and ignore it? Antithetical to all rational thought.

Oathsfire's men gave chase. She heard the Duke of Mills himself, screaming to her, and then the first bowshots hissing past.

Maybe, she thought, this has nothing to do with Lyxaxu or grief or understanding. Maybe they all agreed to kill me and Tain Hu and find their own queen. Ihuake, perhaps, married to Oathsfire. Better than two tribadists.

The whole world a dim play around her. Less real than the memory of Tain Hu.

New shapes in play ahead, though. Horsemen in red tabards and steel masks, bearing heavy crossbows. Masquerade marines—Apparitor's marines. Rushing their way.

"Ride," Apparitor shouted, his hair astream. "Think of what's waiting for you! Think of your reward!" He spurred his horse ahead.

But she hesitated. She did not race for safety.

Think of what's waiting for you.

Think of the Coyote-men, the Wolf, gray-bearded Xate Olake, the loyal guards, the ilykari divers, Tain Hu, Tain Hu, Tain Hu—

Why did it have to be this way? What had she ever done to bind herself to this outcome? She could have stayed in the camp and ordered a swift march north. She could have fractured her Wolf into its ducal pieces and sent them home, or run away with Tain Hu, fled into the Wintercrests. She could have found some way to betray her own betrayal. She was the key, after all, not the exhausted Wolf or the gathered rebel dukes; ultimately *she* was the vital weapon.

But then, of course, nobody would ever save Taranoke—

An arrow caught her exhausted rouncey in the rump. It screamed and fell, dragging its hind legs for a moment, toppling. She slammed to the earth, shouting, her head smashing around inside the loose-strapped helm.

A clean spring sky above. A gorgeous dawn.

If she wanted to die, she did not want it enough. Her body sprang to its feet, checking her sword, taking a few dizzy, spinning steps.

She looked up to see Duke Oathsfire roaring down on her, sword bare, wild hate and grief in his eyes.

A crossbow quarrel glanced off his horse's champron. She had a moment to see him blink in surprise. The second punched through his chest. He slumped across the reins, blood bubbling at his lips, and then fell.

You will not die at Sieroch. Another lie she'd told. Small, in the counting of such things.

Good-bye, Baru thought, good-bye, and turned to look for the shooter, the marines riding down to her rescue. Saw Apparitor, hand outstretched, the man who had offered her exaltation at this terrible cost.

His eyes fixed on something behind her, where her helmet chopped off her peripheral vision. He opened his mouth to call warning.

Oathsfire's guardsman rode down on her and his maul smashed the side of her helmet and closed her whole world like a door.

T HE Apparitor had arranged his instruments perfectly.

Duchess Ihuake drank her morning soup, drank the tetrodotoxin the Clarified had used as seasoning, the foreign poison against which she had built no tolerance. Her compliments went to the cook—*the new spice has left my lips numb*—and then in morning council she slurred and fell and passed into paralysis and died. So passed the Cattle Duchess, who dreamt of a new hearthland where her people could be free.

Her spymaster went roaring among the cooks. "Who did this?" he cried. "Whose hand killed our duchess?"

"The hand that moves us all," a chef's assistant said, and hurled a pan of boiling oil into the spymaster's face.

Pinjagata, the Duke of Phalanxes, reviewed his troops before the march, and though he labored to breathe through his battle-burnt lungs, they stood in their ranks and took pride in his nods. A pale smiling man in the first row dropped his spear and stepped out to knife him up under the chin. "Baru Cormorant keeps her own accounts," he said.

The spearman duke died on his feet. He never saw his country at peace.

Chaos in the Wolf camp as the warhorses fell paralyzed.

Blood and smoke in the streets of Treatymont, as Admiral Ormsment's soldiers stormed into rebel safe houses, poured acid into secret rooms.

In distant Erebog, where the Crone climbed her tower's steps, weary and heartsick from her war against Autr and Sahaule, dreading the news from Sieroch, burdened by the memory of love gone cold and silent, a workman spilled stinking caustic oil all across her. She rushed to wash and at the first touch of water the oil caught spectacular fire, unquench-able, a furious sparking blaze, a killing flame. So passed winter-eyed Erebog, the only lord of Aurdwynn ever bold enough to reach north.

The Clarified meant for the duchess Vultjag could not find her target. *Exiled,* the duchess's grim armsmen said. *Gone north with Xate Olake. By order of the Fairer Hand.*

Panic erupted in the Wolf camp. Word spread of a terrible plot— Oathsfire and Vultjag, secretly promised to each other, would overthrow Baru Fisher and rule Aurdwynn together. No! The Stakhieczi under the

Necessary King were already marching down the Inirein, intent on completing their centuries-old conquest.

The Wolf looked to its master. Messengers scrambled. Deputies and lieutenants shouted, red-faced.

But Baru Fisher could not be found.

The decapitation was complete. The rest of the design was the harvest—a great many seeds to be scattered to the wind. The real prize, after all, was the legend of Sieroch, the secret knowledge revealed here. The knowledge of how the Masquerade might be defied, and to what result.

A red rocket went up from the peak of the Henge Hill. The Clarified concealed there raised spyglasses to watch the result.

From the mists of the swamplands to the south, their flat-bottomed pole barges abandoned miles behind, their pupils still wide with the mason leaf that had let them navigate the night, the first marines rose from ambush cover and began to march.

They chanted as they closed, as the sentries scrambled to raise the alarm or stood in paralyzed horror, a booming chorus, practiced on the ships, on the barges, rehearsed without understanding—for who among Falcrest's marines spoke Iolynic?

SHE WAS OURS.

FROM THE BEGINNING. FROM THE FIRST DAY YOU SPOKE HER NAME.

FLEE TO YOUR FAMILIES. RUN TO YOUR HOMES. CARRY THE WORD: WE LOOKED OUT FROM BEHIND THE MASK OF HER. WE WILLED THE REBELLION'S BEGINNING. AND NOW WE WILL ITS END.

BARU CORMORANT IS AN AGENT OF THE THRONE.

SHE came back to consciousness in the stifling cabin of a navy warship, somehow convinced that she was asleep on a cushion of nothingness. Apparitor looked up from his chair, setting down a pen, closing a book in his lap. She caught a brief flash of a drawing: a man, slender, frowning, beautiful, his neck burnt. Unfinished.

Memory struck like a maul. *The past is the real tyranny.*

She had kindled the rebellion knowing she would snuff it. She'd promised herself her heart would not be drawn in.

But she had not made herself a fine enough machine.

"You can weep, if you need to," Apparitor said. "I wept when I earned my own exaltation. I wept for what I had betrayed."

She lifted herself on her hands, head swimming, staring down at the sheets tented over her breast and toes—and as Apparitor passed off to her right, he vanished. Not hidden from sight but *gone*.

Apparitor and his book and his chair and the whole right side of the cabin. Utterly absent.

By astonished reflex she looked to where he had been. The moment he crossed over to the left side of her face he came back, a discontinuous arrival, an apparition.

"No weeping? I see. Practiced at detachment, I suppose. The army gathered at Sieroch scattered, as we intended. Your work is done. Now others begin their tasks." He held up his pen, frowning, making a mark in the air. "We suffered a troubling loss in those final days, you know. An agent among the ilykari priesthood, vital to our project in Aurdwynn. She was a master-of-secrets for the entire rebellion. I suspect Xate of sniffing her out and killing her. Did you find any hint that—what are you *doing*?"

Baru moved her nose left and right while he watched with furrowed brow. Left, right, left—and each time she crossed to the right side of her nose, he blinked out of existence.

"Bring me your doctors," she croaked.

THEY have a clever technique. A favorite stratagem of Xate Yawa, of the Masquerade, of the ruling power behind the Faceless Throne. The honeypot. Suspect sedition and unhygienic thought? Give it a warm place to gather. Let the word go out. See who scurries out to take the bait. See who offers them support, who launders their money, who hides their secrets.

But a favorite becomes predictable. New techniques must be developed. The science of rule must be extended.

Why wait for an inevitable rebellion? Why accept the risk of betrayal at a key strategic moment? Aurdwynn cannot be ruled. All its dukes and faiths and bloodlines present a terrible puzzle. A sick system, unprofitable, unwilling to change to meet the demands of Incrastic development.

If you want to avoid a great fire, burn the deadwood. You only need a suitable spark.

A spark who understands that a quick and failed revolution now would be more humane than a bloodbath in ten years. Someone who looks to a more distant horizon. Craves a higher power, even at terrible, unanticipated price.

And next time Aurdwynn sees that spark, next time it raises its hands toward the heat, it will remember: *last time, we were burned.*

In Falcrest, in the Metademe, they condition prisoners just so: permit escape. Offer a rescuer, a collaborator. Slip a key in with the food. Let them come close to freedom, let them feel real triumph—*they would not let me this far!* This is the crux: give them the taste of victory, the certainty that *this* cannot be part of the game.

And then snatch it away. The collaborator betrays them. The key will not open the outermost door.

With enough repetition, most prisoners learn to ignore a key, an open door, a whisper to run. Led out onto the street, they will wait to be returned to their cells.

After a time, they begin to teach new prisoners the same.

VICTORY

BARU Cormorant's wound swallows half her world.

The surgeon aboard *Sulane* cannot explain it. The frigate carries her east with the trade wind to another red-sailed ship, *Helbride*. Apparitor puts her aboard with a terse farewell: "I have more work in Aurdwynn. Frayed ends that need binding. When I am done I will return with your last test. See to your condition."

It's grief, Baru thinks. It's treachery. She cannot escape the logic of it. She's put all her memories of Aurdwynn, all the things she cannot bear, into that side of the world. And she closed it off.

But why, then, can she still remember? Why does she stand at the rail, watch half the birds circle half the sky, feel like half a person? Why does she reach out in the night for the company of an absent woman?

Too far, she told the priestess in Haraerod. *I've come too far.*

She accepted the bargain without understanding the price. A terrible mistake, for an accountant.

The crew of *Helbride* venerates her. They aren't Navy. *Your Excellence,* they call her, the same old honorific but with a certain hush, an awed inflection.

They bring her to a secret place. A castle on the shore of a slate-sky land where seabirds call and the waves crash on the rocks. For the use of the Throne's agents, they say, the *Throne,* the hidden council. They call this place the Elided Keep.

For the duration of her stay, she is its lord and master. The stewards and servants tell her that they shipped her personal effects from Aurdwynn, although they could not find anything dear to her, so instead they brought banners and signs and trophies.

Good, she says. Put the ducal heraldries up on the south wall of the throne room. (There are burnt torn banners from the battle at Sieroch, banners of Oathsfire, of Lyxaxu, of Pinjagata and Ihuake, of Vultjag. Banners of her own.) Put the blades and pikes up there, too.

And on the north wall she hangs the signs of her loyalty: sheepskin palimpsests, marbled cream paper, her chained purse. A pristine Imperial seal from the Governor's House in Treatymont, the one Cattlson designed, with the stag antlers.

The surgeons at the Elided Keep have a diagnosis.

You are not half-blind. The wound runs deeper than that. They touch the side of her head, where the maul struck her helm.

Your brain can no longer understand that half of the world. The left hemisphere of your vision is your entire universe.

She can stand in the center of the throne room, turn on her axis like the world making a new day, and change who she is. Ducal standards and rebel blades. Or coin and purse and mask and ink.

A traitor either way.

Are you hungry?

Her bed rest has taken some of the strength from her shoulders and arms. She is voracious. The doctors set a plate of veal before her and she eats it too quickly. "More," she says. "I am weak."

You have only eaten the left half of the plate. They turn it half a turn and somehow it is full again. *Do you see?*

She tries to draw a clock, as a test. *You have crowded all twelve hours between six and midnight,* they say.

She begins to laugh, a wild, sobbing, lunatic sound. What else can she do? It's just blind chance. Just a maul to the brain, a bruise on the mind. It doesn't mean anything at all.

But it's so elegant.

There are stocks of chemicals in the castle, whole armamentaria of poisons and drugs. Stalking the midnight halls, paced by the ghosts of her victims, by the absence in her bed, she contemplates an end, a suicide, but in the end settles for swallowing salt, vomiting until she feels purged.

She has come so close to everything she wanted when this all began.

But now she knows she will not stop there. What she said to Tain Hu—*If they want change, they must make themselves useful to Falcrest. Find a way up from within.* The woman who said that is dead, the woman who heard the answer:

Some things are not worth being within.

At least she saved Tain Hu.

A month passes in the salt and the stone.

A letter comes for her.

Your efforts in Aurdwynn achieved six decades of forecasted progress in a single year. The power of the ducal aristocracy has been shattered, Governor Cattlson's unpopular regime swept from power, and the people made ready to accept a single, charismatic, progressive ruler. You drew out a Stakhieczi agent and gathered critical information on their resurgent monarchy. With the threat of rebellion defused, we can complete our goal of restructuring Aurdwynn into a fortress and resource base against the Stakhieczi threat.

A great deal of curiosity centers on you. We have had a native-born Stakhieczi representative for some time. An Aurdwynni candidate of Imperial Maia blood may soon complete her own ascension. But these racial types are well understood by Incrastic science. You will be the first Souswardi to step behind the Throne, bringing the mingled heredity of the Tu Maia empire and the stubborn Oriati federations.

You have proven yourself a worthy asset. All that remains is to complete your ascension. We will send one final test.

> *Regards,*
> *Itinerant*
> *Hesychast*
> *Renascent*
> *Stargazer*
> *(absentia) Apparitor*

They do not miss the soldiers and the Governor they sacrificed. Those lives were a fair price: fire to burn away the deadwood, teeth to draw the poison out.

A fair price.

She feels well enough to dare the keep's battlements: not the seaward wall, but the stonework that looks over the estuary. The clouded sky is steel and lamplight. A boy concubine follows in attendance. By old habit she tabulates the birds in the river and the marsh, a census of grebes, petrels, frigate birds, wading jacana.

"Are you an educated man?" she asks the concubine. "You must be. The Throne does educate its spies, doesn't it?"

"Your Excellence?" His acting is impeccable, his dark Oriati skin flawless, his build an acrobat's. Whoever sent him made a calculating choice. Almost the right choice. Not nearly the right one.

How much older can she be than him? Three, four years? She feels ancient.

She turns to face him. The estuary and the birds sweep off to her right and she loses them, even the calls, even the sound of surf. "Do you know the Hierarchic Qualm?"

The battlement drops into the outer yard behind him. He takes a nervous step forward. "Of course I know the Qualm," he says. "'The sword kills, but it is the arm that moves the sword. Is the arm to blame for murder, then? No. The mind moves the arm. Is the mind to blame? No. The mind has sworn an oath, and only does its duty, as written by the Throne. So it is that a servant of the Throne is blameless.'"

She waves him off. "Good enough."

"Does the Qualm console you, my lady?" he asks.

She watches a jacana as it walks on leaves. "What grief would I need consoled?"

The concubine edges closer, wrapping himself in his arms as if suddenly conscious of the sea wind. "It is said that you raised all of Aurdwynn in rebellion, but that in truth you served our Throne."

She laughs into the wind, touched by the boy's pretended naiveté. "It would be a cunning stroke, wouldn't it? To gather all that discontent under the banner of a rebel bureaucrat. And then—and then—"

The boy looks at her with wide eyes, pretending anticipation, pretending that this is not a test. An invisible hand probing her wounds.

"And then, in one deliberately timed stroke, to snuff that fire out," she says. "To send a message: we had you from the start. Baru Fisher was ours. Your rebellion was ours. The next rebellion will be ours, and the next, and the next, even when you think victory is real, even when you spill blood you think is dear to us. The Throne controls all."

"A cunning stroke," the boy agrees, still speaking to the rampart stone. "But, my lady, it is said that all bindings are mutual. To betray them, to lead them knowing that you would betray them, must have wounded you—"

She takes him by the throat and smashes him up against the parapet. He is taller but slighter, and she has lived a year as Baru Fisher, armored and armed, daughter of a blacksmith and a huntress and a shield-bearer.

"What do you mean to suggest, little watcher?" she hisses. "That I came to love my comrades, gray-bearded Xate Olake and the duchess Tain Hu? That I wept when I delivered up their armies? That I weep still, and look to old philosophy for comfort?"

The boy paws at her wrist. She leans in to speak softly. "Do you claim there is treason in my heart?"

"No, my lady," he chokes. Now he lets his hands dangle helpless, though he must have been schooled to fight. "No. No. You were loyal all along, and never wavered. They meant nothing to you. I beg your forgiveness."

She drops him. "I am blameless," she says. "I was an instrument. I feel no remorse."

"My lady." The boy lifts his slender chin and bares his throat. "I have overstepped."

Baru takes his throat between gloved fingers. His eyes are very wide and very brown with little flecks of gold and she thinks of Tain Hu. He breathes in quick frightened little gasps, and licks his lips, and closes his eyes.

Baru looks at the concubine's parted lips, smells the anise he swallowed to freshen his breath, and sees the other test. She has never taken the boy to bed.

Clever, she thinks, to offer yourself as a test. I should kiss you, shouldn't I? You and your masters think you've found a hold on me. But I could break that hold if I just leaned a little closer. If I looked into Tain Hu's eyes and made use of you.

She leaves him sprawled against the parapet and turns to the estuary so that he falls on her right and vanishes from awareness. She knows he must still be there, but her wound swallows him.

Beyond the circling petrels, there is a red sail on the horizon.

Mutiny in her heart. Fire in the wreckage.

"Boy," she says, hoping that he has not fled. "Go rouse my retinue. I'll meet them in the cove."

* * *

BARU watches the sea plead with the stone as the red-sailed ship makes harbor. At intervals her chamberlain takes her by the arm and turns her to face the Elided Keep, to remind her it exists.

I am maimed, she thinks. I will fail this test. It will all have been for nothing.

And then, mutinously: if I pass, will it then have been for something?

Taranoke. Falcrest, then Taranoke—

The red-sailed ship puts down a boat. She beckons for a spyglass and examines its passengers. Oarsmen. Marines. A figure cloaked in black wool, bound wrists to ankles. And Apparitor, with his brilliant banner of hair.

So the ship came from Aurdwynn. She'd had half a thought (ha) that Aminata might be aboard.

The boat comes ashore. Apparitor wades from surf to stone, smiling warmly, right hand raised in greeting. "Baru Cormorant," he calls, over the high protests of the sea birds. "Your ordeal nears its end. The rebellion has collapsed. Lady Heingyl Ri's passionate love for Bel Latheman gave us a symbol of reconciliation, and with Lady Heingyl—the Stag Duchess, I should say—installed as Governor and Xate Yawa recalled to Falcrest, Aurdwynn is at peace. The banner of the Imperial Republic flies unchallenged."

She keeps her left side open to him as if readying to duel. "What word is there of gray-bearded Xate Olake, Duke of Lachta, master of my spies?" she asks, cool, cold, her eyes held still.

"Dead," says Apparitor. "Burned out of his hole. I tracked him into the Wintercrests myself. We natives know them better."

She remembers holding the boy concubine's throat between gloved fingers. Trembles with the memory of it, the want to grip until his lying throat gave. "Well done," she says, smoothing her trousers against her hips. "Xate Olake was not easily outwitted."

"Easily enough, as it happened," the Throne's man says. He tips a hand as if putting the memory of old rebels into the harbor. "We are all eager to complete your ascension, to deliver your reward."

"The gift of a province leaves you in my debt," Baru says, cocksure, confident, secretly ablaze with the desire to turn and put this man and all he has asked of her to her blind right.

"The deal stands, of course. You stoked and quelled the rebellion, and in exchange, we raise you to sit behind the Faceless Throne." He gestures to the beached boat, the wool-wrapped prisoner. "Just one test. To be sure you did not play your part too well."

She wants to look at the boat, to rule out her worst fears, but she cannot show weakness by breaking eye contact. She lifts her chin. "I have given no cause for doubt."

Apparitor laughs. "The Throne doubts all loyalties, Baru Cormorant. The Throne, above all, desires control, and it does not control you yet. Though there are whispers—"

He steps closer, and Baru feels her chamberlain and her whole retinue draw away as if acknowledging their real master.

"It is rumored that you took no lovers for all your time in Aurdwynn," the Throne's man whispers, grinning a sly secret grin. "It is rumored that you are the daughter of a blacksmith and a huntress and a shield-bearer, two of them sodomites. Some say that this is the way all children are born in your homeland: to a mother and many fathers."

"How barbaric," she says. "How fortunate that I was taken away, to be raised in a school and to know the names of sin."

The man named Apparitor takes one step closer, ducks his head cobra-quick as if to bite at her, and suddenly—is not the Throne's man anymore. He looks at her with a kind of fierce, desperate honesty, and she almost, almost, trusts it.

But she remembers her own honesty with Tain Hu. What it hid.

"Fortunate indeed," he says. "Control, Baru Cormorant, *control,* by any means the Throne can secure. Give them no rein! Sodomites get hot iron, but we do not envy tribadists the knife. Are you ready to live with the yoke of that threat?"

Empathy begs from the bottom of her brain but she gives it no audience. Clever, she thinks, to send this man as a living warning—*he is as you will be.* "Is that a confession?" she whispers through the left side of her mouth. "Do I control you now, by threat of iron?"

He laughs in her face. "Your test, my lady!" he cries, and beckons to the launch, where his soldiers lift yards of wool from the shackled ranger-knight of Vultjag, the brigand bitch, the duchess Tain Hu.

* * *

S HE was supposed to be safe. Off the board.

But of course she came back, to face death, to try to save her home. What else did she have?

Baru always forgets: there are other players.

S HE waits in the cellars beneath the Elided Keep for an audience with her general.

Her parents cursed her with a hungry, disquieted mind, a mind for accounting, for the census of birds, for treason. Now she turns that disquiet on the traits of her wound. How far does it reach? Will it worsen? Will there be a day when she stands in the surf, the sea to her left, the land to her right, and forgets that there is a world beyond the waves?

She has clung to Aminata's boarding saber through all this. Now she works it from ward to ward, high left to low right, the ox and the fool and the rest. When she crosses over to her right side, the sword steals itself away. She can still feel the hilt, the weight, the play. Her body still works, over there. But the blade is a ghost.

And if there really is no wound? If she has locked up in that blind hemisphere all the offal of her treachery, all the loves and cares she gathered?

She shakes her head. Cuts right to left, opening the gut of a phantom foe. The way Aminata taught her.

"Your Excellence." The concubine with the anise breath beckons from the inner door. "The prisoner is ready for you."

She gestures with the blade, signaling her impatience. "Clear the room. I'll speak to her alone."

Somewhere in the past hour, her retinue abandoned its pretended whisper and gossip. Their silence as they file out admits to discipline. Apparitor comes last. "You will not do it in private," he warns. "There will be no tender words, no secret mercies. You will not give her the privilege of death by your own hand. You will order her execution, your men will drown her in the surf, and her body will go to Falcrest—so that we may know she died in pain, and not by some arrangement." His eyes crack. Something in him feels for her. Perhaps he did this himself, once. "I'm sorry. But it must be this way."

"She is an enemy of the Throne," Baru says coolly. "Why would I grant mercy?"

The crack of feeling in him seals itself. "Your ruthlessness will carry you far," he says. But it does not sound like praise.

He goes out, the concubine who is his spy scuttling before him. The outer doors whisper shut on fish-oiled hinges.

Baru turns to the inner room, trailing her blade like the leash of a hunting dog.

TAIN Hu sits across a narrow oaken table, shackled to a high-backed fir chair. Her jailors have stripped her of her salted leathers and gowned her in silk and iron. Her gyrfalcon face—broken nose, bronze cheeks, brown eyes—is unmarked. But all the might has gone from her body, all the armor-bearing brawn. She has been starved.

Baru tries to speak, to strike first. But words abandon her. There is too much to say, or only one thing to say. And no way to say it.

In the silence, Tain Hu lifts her eyes. "Your Excellence," she says, and bows her head, as if she were still field-general, and Baru still the Fairer Hand.

Baru sets her blade down between them like a little wall, just below the wine her servants left, and sits in the other chair. She wants more than all else to smile, and to answer the last thing Tain Hu ever said to her, that smiling sleepy greeting: *hello.*

Hello yourself, imuira. Kuye lam. In an orgy of self-punishment, between swallows of salt, she looked up exactly what it meant, to be sure of her memory. It brought her as close to the edge as she has ever come.

But it would only be mockery.

How could you let this happen? she asks herself. How could you let it be, knowing who you were, what role you were to play? You could have turned away, and spared yourself.

But she did not. She never could have.

Tain Hu watches her with desert eyes. "Are you here to kill me?" she asks.

Death may be the greatest hope she has left. "No," Baru says. "That happens tomorrow. You will be drowned by the rising tide, so the Throne may say the moon and stars judged you. Falcrest loves to align itself with such laws."

"I see." Tain Hu nods as if this were a right and proper thing. "Will my death bring advantage to Baru Fisher, my sworn lord?"

Baru pours red wine with a steady hand, filling one cup, then the other. She wants to beg, to rage: stop it. Abjure me, repudiate me, call me false, curse my name. Give me anything but this loyal calm.

"It will bring me advantage," she says. "It is the last test of my loyalty to the Throne."

"Let me propose a toast, then," Tain Hu says, and there is no sarcasm in her eyes, no hint of anger to soften the blow. "To your unshakable loyalty."

Baru looks left, so that Tain Hu blinks away for a moment. Out of vision, but not out of memory, gone from sight but not from the vanguard at Sieroch, her charger galloping white in a run of chestnut. Bloody face lifted toward Baru's spyglass, mailed fists clutching Cattlson's banner in triumph.

Her accountant's mind makes note: turning away hides the woman but not the pain.

Perhaps Tain Hu has snatched up the blade on the table while she looked away. Perhaps death is coming down through her blindness, and she will never know it.

But a moment passes and no strike comes.

Baru turns back to the table, back to awareness of Tain Hu. Her field-general watches her in silence. Baru moves a glass of wine across the table, crosswise. "I wanted to explain," she says. "So you would know what you'll die for. I thought I owed you that."

Already she sounds like one of them. A Falcresti creature. A traitor to her own childhood.

Tain Hu takes up the glass in callused hands, straining her shackles' play. "You owe me nothing. I swore to die for you." She shrugs precisely. The wine in her glass barely moves. "So it will be."

I see your strategy, Tain Hu, Baru thinks. I see the order of battle. You go to your death with exquisite loyalty. I measure my treason against your faith and it eats me up, now and for the rest of my life. It is the most hurt you can manage.

It will work.

"There is no Emperor upon the Faceless Throne," she says. "Behind the mask and the figurehead is a committee, a closed council. Each member—"

"—holds a secret that could destroy another," Tain Hu says. "So the

Throne's members are bound to each other by fear. And you were offered a seat, at the price of a dangerous service, raising false rebellion in Aurdwynn so the Throne could weed out the disloyal. You believed the Masquerade would inevitably reconquer Aurdwynn, and you thought you could ease the cost in blood. I know."

"How?" she whispers. "How could you know?"

"Your red-haired handler thought it safe to explain these things to a dead woman. It was a long journey east." Again Tain Hu shrugs. Again her wine lies still, as if boasting of her precision in all things. "I wanted to understand the woman behind the mask I knew. I spoke with him at length."

Baru closes her eyes. She must have known what she was giving Apparitor in exchange, just as she knew what she was doing at Sieroch, at the Fuller's Road. Of course she knew. Of course she knew.

"And what did he ask in return? What was it safe for a dead woman to tell?"

Tain Hu's mouth does not move but her eyes tighten in a little smile.

"Tell me." Baru leans across the table, across the blade. "Tell me what secrets you gave the Throne. Or does your play at loyalty not extend so far?"

Tain Hu does not flinch. "What secrets could I know about Baru Fisher? What truth did you ever give me?" She laughs quietly. "You were wise. You trusted only yourself."

"There was one," Baru says, her voice terrible to her own ears, burdened with the memory of crimes more beautiful and dear than rebellion or treachery.

Tain Hu looks at her own hands. She sets her glass down on the table, motion by motion, as if in awe of the working of her joints. "There was that." She nods thoughtfully. "But I wondered: Should I mention it? Would he care to know a lie? How would knowing a lie serve the purposes of the Throne, which seeks to bind by truth?"

There was that. That one night, and everything it acknowledged.

"It was no lie," Baru whispers.

"I wondered that, in the long nights after Sieroch," Tain Hu whispers in return. "I wondered if you could be fool enough to fall that way, even knowing what you were meant to do. I wondered if all the things you whispered in the night could be real, instead of a clever act, a way to blind me. I did not think you a fool, Baru Fisher, but of course I did not think myself a fool either, and yet I was."

She leans forward, palms flat, the sandy ruin of her close-shorn hair still damp with seawater. Her nearness summons sedition in Baru's chest.

"So I told him," she says.

So the Throne has its secret. Tain Hu has her small revenge. Hot iron for the sodomite, and for tribadists, the knife. Not *now*, of course, not while she is loyal. But if Baru Cormorant ever turns, ever slips, ever becomes a threat—the knife.

"I have counsel for you, now that we've both struck our blows," Tain Hu says. She leans forward on arms still corded with the memory of strength, and Baru remembers her leaning across the map table at Vultjag, pointing to weakness, here, there. "As your general."

Look where your counsel has taken you, Baru thinks bitterly. Why should I listen?

But Tain Hu did not defeat herself.

"Speak," Baru says.

Tain Hu's broad shoulders tighten. "You should kill me. To defy the Throne and secure your power."

"Have you heard nothing?" Baru snaps. "Did their man confuse you? I prove my loyalty by killing you, Hu. It would be no defiance."

"You will fail," Tain Hu says. "They know it. They hope for you to fail."

In the lamplight the wine between them looks as clotted as old blood. "I need only give an order," Baru says, and then, with a taunting spite she does not feel: "I can give hard orders, Duchess."

"You need to watch it happen, unflinching, unmoved. And you cannot." Tain Hu looks into the empty distance, watching her own death. "You will see the tide rising and you will beg for them to spare me. They will agree. They will grant you your ascension, and they will keep me as a pet, knowing you will do anything to keep me from harm. *I* will be their hold on you."

A flicker like the ghost of a smile at the edge of her lips. "Better for you," she says, "if you had let me die at Sieroch. Better if you had never tried to save me."

Baru wants to protest but it chills like truth. It has been in her dreams these past months, as she wondered what her final test would be: spare her, spare her; I will do anything to spare her. "But they have the secret they need," she protests. "You gave it to them. They *have* a hold."

"They would prefer something more . . . concrete. They fear you, Baru Fisher. They fear your wit, your charisma, your power to raise the commoner. They fear the loyalty you command. Without a powerful secret to bind you—something more than hearsay, and a curious absence of lovers—they fear the strength you will have among them." Tain Hu closes her distant eyes. "He told me none of this. He told me he expected you to execute me without a second thought. But you taught me to listen to myself when I sensed a lie."

The little distance across the table maddens like a rotten tooth. Baru wants to reach out to her, across all the blood and treachery between them. Wants to reach back across the months to winter on the forage line. "Why would you tell me this?" she asks. "Why would you give me *anything*?"

"Because it was no lie," Tain Hu whispers, and turns away.

Baru sits, and stares, and tries to make something of the hollow in her chest.

Her mind gnaws at all of it: could it be that Tain Hu is desperate to live, and hopes to trick Baru into sparing her? No, she would have no care for her own life, not with Vultjag and Aurdwynn lost—but could she be working to sabotage Baru's ascension, manipulating her into showing disloyalty to the Throne? Could this all be the Throne's test, like the boy on the battlements, played out through a broken Tain Hu?

She sips at her wine, pretending calm, and grips the edge of a cold truth: she came down here to speak with Tain Hu because she hoped it would make it easier to watch her die. Hoped there would be hate, shouting, vows of undying revenge. An enemy woman for her to drown tomorrow.

If I beg, she could live, Baru thinks. I would still have the Throne. They would sit easier for it, knowing I could be kept tame. And with time, she might forgive me—

Tain Hu's shoulders begin to shake. Baru's stomach curls. This, of all things, she hoped not to see: the general of Aurdwynn's armies broken and cast low. Death would be better.

But Tain Hu does not cry. She chuckles, raspy, low. "The hope of Aurdwynn!" she calls, as if rallying an invisible shield-wall. "Justice from a fairer hand!" And then she laughs, trembling with her mirth, quaking in her shackles, her eyes locked on Baru. "The hope of Aurdwynn!"

It goes on and on, and after a moment Baru finds it too much to take. She turns her chair to the left, so that the duchess Tain Hu falls away into nothingness, and the howl of her laughter reaches Baru only as an echo.

The hope of Aurdwynn, she thinks. And understands Tain Hu's game. She is still fighting.

The blade is still on the table, in the empty place to her right. Baru finishes her wine in slow silence. She wonders if Tain Hu knows about her wound. Whether she laughs and rails even now, and takes Baru's answering silence for strength.

THE tide comes in just before dawn. Baru Cormorant shackles the prisoner herself. Whispers one Urun word in her ear, laden, an eel-bite, and then draws away to say, perhaps in mockery:

"Congratulations on your victory, Duchess Vultjag."

Tain Hu does not weep.

Baru commands her marines to take Tain Hu down onto the stone bluffs below the castle, where the waves are harshest.

Tain Hu walks the whole way, even burdened by her chains. The marines fasten her to the stone, threading her shackles through rusted brackets. The sea laps and murmurs below.

Baru Cormorant, lord in passing of the Elided Keep, ascendant member of the Imperial Republic's ruling committee, watches from a spit of rock above. Apparitor paces behind her, his hair wild in the salt breeze. "If the wind picks up, the waves may dash her against the rocks," he says. "It would be a terrible death."

Baru stands without a coat, untroubled by the cold. It is not so deep as winter in Vultjag. "So it would," she says. "But Tain Hu was strong once. If she clings to her own chains, she may last long enough to drown."

Apparitor takes her by the shoulder. "Perhaps there is another way. Perhaps the Throne would accept her as a hostage."

"Do not test me," Baru says, her eyes on the dawn horizon. She takes census of the birds there. Finds a hawk circling high, as if riding a thermal above a forest valley. "I have had enough of the Throne's little tests."

The water rises. Tain Hu, wet to the waist, seems to drowse, her chains slack. "Hypothermia," Apparitor whispers. "The water is cold, my lady. If we were to raise her now, perhaps we could save—"

"I do not want her saved," Baru Cormorant says.

"Did you not love her?" the Throne's man hisses in her ear. "She told me about the night after your victory at Sieroch. You could have that again."

"Is that what she invented? Curious." Baru gestures to the marines on the rocks below. "Wake her up!"

One of them smashes Tain Hu in the shoulder with the butt of his polearm. She cries out, arching, her eyes wild. Her chains slip between pale, trembling fingers.

"'You are a worth a legion to me, Tain Hu,'" the Throne's man whispers. "Do you remember that? She told me you said that."

"I said many things."

The water rises. A low wind whips up froth. Tain Hu shouts hoarsely into the spray, her chains wrapped taut around her fists, biceps straining.

Baru spares a glance for Apparitor. "When this little chore is through, I have business in Falcrest. We sent a message to Aurdwynn, a demonstration of our reach. Now is the time to buy their loyalty. Ease taxes, grant marriage licenses, take mercy on their little cults. Grant them a few freedoms more."

"Causes you are familiar with, Lady Cormorant." The Throne's man draws his cloak about him.

"Of course. I know why you want me. I understand these people in my bones, my blood." She stares coldly down at Tain Hu. "Through me, you expand your control."

I wish you could see me, Hu, she thinks. Unflinching. Unmoved. The hope of Aurdwynn, giving them no yoke over me.

Even betrayed, cornered, you planned the battle well. A savant's work.

"Ironic, isn't it?" she says. "She might have lived to see her people free."

Apparitor has to shout above the whipping wind. "Why are you doing this? She could still live!"

You could still bind me with her, Baru thinks. If I just begged. If I just admitted what she was to me. I could go to Falcrest and sit at your table and you would know: *we have our hooks in her.* As they have their hooks in you.

But I will not be bound as you are. I will walk among your council and you will tremble at what you have unleashed.

A rising breaker crashes against the rocks. Tain Hu cries out into the dawn, trembling with effort. A frigate bird calls like a drum overhead.

Baru Cormorant sets her legs in a duelist's stance, closing off the Throne's man on her dead right, opening her left side to the dying woman below. She cuts at the air with a blade she does not have.

She accepted Apparitor's deal at the harborside in Treatymont thinking that she could trade Aurdwynn for rule of Taranoke. Why not? What would be lost, what evil done? The Masquerade would crush any rebellion. In her hands, she could ensure it was swift, merciful. And with her hard-won power, she could save her home.

But that will not be enough now.

Good-bye, she thinks. Good-bye, *kuye lam*. I will write your name in the ruin of them. I will paint you across history in the color of their blood.

The tide comes in. The Throne's man watches her, waiting for her to lift her eyes and make a census of the birds.

LETTERS

To my peers of the committee,

I hope that Itinerant has completed his case for my value as a contributor. I understand that my youth and heredity may arouse skepticism, but I assure you that my savancy has now been tested by experience.

I have completed my initial review of Apparitor's documents. We clearly face important strategic challenges: a resurgent Stakhieczi monarchy, backlash from our ongoing efforts to destabilize the federated governments of Oriati Mbo, an increasingly apparent pattern of epidemic disease in the unconquered west, and, of course, the disturbing findings of our expeditions across the Mother of Storms. (We must confront the possibility that these eyewitness accounts are not hallucinations, and that natural law on the supercontinent somehow differs from our own.)

In light of these challenges, I am heartened by the success of our colleague Hesychast's programs in the Metademe. The Clarified performed admirably in Aurdwynn. With increased access to Stakhieczoid and Maia germ lines via our subject populations in Aurdwynn and Sousward, I believe significant strides may be made toward new, specialized breeds.

In spite of these achievements, I urge the committee to recall my patron's favorite lesson. There are many kinds of power. As we continue to drive the Imperial Republic toward our goal of total causal closure, it is imperative that we avoid dependence on any single strategic instrument. Total, integrated control, from the basic mechanisms of heredity up through the ideological and intellectual movements of our entire empire, must remain our goal.

I look forward to working with you.

Regards,
Agonist

Dearest Aminata,

It's been too long. My service in Aurdwynn is at an end. For reasons beyond the scope of this letter, I will be traveling to Falcrest under an assumed name.

I read of your promotion to Lieutenant Commander. My congratulations. Upon her return to Falcrest, I intend to recommend you to Province Admiral Ormsment. You may wonder why a technocrat thinks to recommend you to a flag officer, and, well—more cause to hear my story!

When I came to you on Taranoke with a problem of hands, you taught me about the Navy's internal politics, the cabals and lines of patronage that define the officer corps. With Parliament beating the war drums at the Oriati, it strikes me that some in the Navy may be discontented with the current regime in Falcrest. I wonder if we could discuss Admiralty politics again, and the mutability of government.

Who would have thought this childhood code would serve us so long?

Find me at the return address. We simply must catch up. I have a remarkable wound to show you.

Regards,
Your sword thief

SUSPIRE SUSPIRE SUSPIRE
CAENOGEN CAENOGEN CAENOGEN
PURITY CARTONE
YOUR EYES ONLY
    CONGRATULATIONS ON YOUR SUCCESSFUL EXECUTION OF MY LAST TASK. YOU REMAIN MY FINEST INSTRUMENT. PARTICULARLY PLEASED BY RECOVERY AND RETURN OF TARGET'S PALIMPSEST. TARGET'S INFORMATION COULD HAVE SERIOUSLY COMPROMISED MY PROJECT.
    DISREGARD ALL OTHER AUTHORITIES. DISREGARD ALL RECALL SIGNALS. YOU WILL RECEIVE YOUR ORDERS DIRECTLY FROM ME. I AM NOW ONE OF THE PARAMOUNT MASTERS [ACCEPT STATUS CHANGE: CAENOGEN]. MAKE

FURTHER CONTACT UNDER CONDITIONED IDENTITY NOR-
GRAF WITH ALL DUE SECURITY.
   YOUR NEW ORDERS ARE—
   PROCEED NORTH INTO WINTERCREST MOUNTAINS
   CONTACT STAKHIECZI AUTHORITY "NECESSARY KING"
   DELIVER ENCLOSED MESSAGE. INFORM KING I HAVE
LOCATED MISSING STAKHI PRINCE. RETURN WITH RE-
SPONSE.
   DESTROY THIS LETTER
   CAENOGEN CAENOGEN CAENOGEN
   SUSPIRE SUSPIRE SUSPIRE

To the Imperial Jurispotence of Aurdwynn, Her Excellence Xate Yawa:
   I know your game.
   I've been playing it, too. I suppose I've already won, if you can call it victory. You played your part flawlessly, of course—I should have seen it from the start. Aurdwynn hates you as profoundly as it loved me. Your recall will look like mercy.
   The one called Itinerant found me, when I was still a child. I wonder which one of them found you, and when. I wonder what final test they'll set for you when your exaltation comes.
   I'd like to have you killed for what you did to Lo. But I cannot deny the accounting: I've done much worse than murder a secretary on suspicion. I used to wonder if you were a monster. Now I know the answer.
   If you want power in this world, power enough to change it, it seems you have to be.
   I'm sorry I couldn't save your brother. It might have been a mercy. He knew I had betrayed him, but now he will never have to learn of you.
   Still. I tried.
   I'll see you in Falcrest.

Video chat w/ Seth Dickinson:

purposeful people jamming - hard to picture the people.

Where'd it come from?
- Was a short story 1st.
- Hom - neglect @ end of book; brain damage
- Evil Overlord List.
- Baru was worse!

Baru's alcoholism:
- miserable, can't connect, too much control

Operating principle = what are you willing to do, utilitarianism
(I didn't ~~question~~ get the question (answer exactly)

Baru, herself:
- Very internal, boring calculations
- He wanted someone who faced racism, sexism, & homophobia
+ fought oppression.

Ages:
- Tain Hu & Oathsfire are youngest

He used the Fool's Rebellion as an excuse not to ~~obtain~~ explain
the complicated family ties.

How do we judge Baru at the end?
- Tain Hu is redeeming force.
- She remains totally committed to her goal, but she's become
more aware of other people's humanity.

How much of gender & our idea of it is cultural? Baru might
seem to be maternal in her protection of her home, but her
structure is different.

God's War, female speculative fiction, ~~Juttt Atota~~
Julie Albany, Fr.
Hurley

She wasn't given an end game b/c it would give the
book away, & she hasn't quite figured it out.